THE CONVICT'S COURTSHIP

OUTLAW HEARTS
BOOK THREE

KYLEE WOODLEY

Copyright © 2026 by KyLee Woodley

All rights reserved. No portion of this book may be reproduced or transmitted in any form or by any means - photocopied, shared electronically, scanned, stored in a retrieval system, or other - without the express permission of the publisher. Exceptions will be made for brief quotations used in critical reviews or articles promoting this work.

The characters and events in this fictional work are the product of the author's imagination. Any resemblance to actual people, living or dead, is coincidental.

Unless otherwise indicated, all Scripture quotations are taken from the Holy Bible, King James Version.

Cover design by: Wild Heart Books

ISBN: 978-1-963212-38-9

For Mike, my father-in-law—
Your stories were wild, your roots ran deep, and your love for Nevada and Virginia City left a lasting impression. Though you're no longer here to read these pages, may they echo the grit, grace, and Western spirit you lived so fully.

CHAPTER 1

Virginia City, Nevada
November 25, 1875

She had really gotten herself into trouble this time.

Clara Alexander knelt on the mine shaft floor, her head in her hands, the heat engulfing her. Throat raw from shouting, she drew in a ragged breath. The geothermal springs heated the earth until the mines felt like a midsummer day—even with snow piled waist-high outside on Mount Davidson.

This was not how she'd envisioned her first, unofficial job for the *Territorial Enterprise*. Ironically, she'd entered the mine full of determination—wearing men's clothes, her hair tucked up in a cap. Yet now, with the ore sample tucked safely in her pocket and each echo ricocheting down the tunnel, she wished to be anywhere but the Peterson Mine.

Clara pushed herself off the floor to wander on, the rough dirt sides of the tunnel hot to the touch. "Is it something I've done, Lord? I mean, I know I'm not Your favorite child, and that's fine. You have other children to dote on, and I will try to avoid trouble."

Something whispered against her leg. Clara froze, then slowly lowered to her haunches, searching the dirt beneath her. She startled as the smooth end of a tail swept across her fingers. Oh, thank heavens, it was only a rat. Soft and warm and real. Some men claimed mystic creatures called Tommy Knockers haunted the mines, alternately bringing good luck or calamity with them.

A rumble sounded from the earthen bowels.

Clara held her breath as she felt the iron tracks running along the earthen floor. One way led to a shaft and up to freedom, the other farther into darkness and heat.

The growling grew louder, like thunder still far away but drawing nearer. What if it was an earthquake or rockslide? She'd heard of miners getting trapped by rockslides. She pushed herself up and swayed to one side, her head spinning. Then she rushed forward, using the wall as a guide. A sliver of wood scraped her fingertip when she dragged it across one of the beams supporting the ceiling.

Louder, faster it came, chasing her into the deep until the backs of her eyelids seemed to glow. She stopped and thrust out a hand in front of her. "Is someone there?"

The rumbles ceased.

A scent lingered on the air, dust and something else. Not smoke, but if there was light, there must be fire, right? She eased one eye open, but there was nothing save her own long shadow stretching in front of her. Turning, she squinted into brightness that shone past an ore car. A tall, muscular man holding a lantern stepped from behind it, the candle flame glowing upon his shirtless frame.

He was as sturdy as any miner she'd ever seen—and half naked. Likely cooler than her in her overalls and a layer of ladies' underthings. He wore a red bandana around his head, and as he ducked to peer at her, it nearly grazed the transverse beam. Some said the mines were haunted, but she didn't believe in ghosts. Did she?

"You're not a Tommy Knocker." She cocked her head. "Are you?"

"*Mademoiselle*, are you hurt?" His thick French accent curled around every word.

Mademoiselle? So he knew she was a woman. So much for her disguise. No matter. She was rescued. Knees trembling, Clara bolstered herself against the side of the tunnel and laughed. "You are real. Oh, God has not grown tired of me yet." Tears stung her eyes, and she covered her face for a moment, only to sway.

He gripped her arms with large hands, steadying her. His nearness carried a faint, earthy aroma—like clay freshly turned.

Clara tipped her chin up, panting from the heat. "Can you guide me to the shaft?"

He touched her forehead, frowning, and said something in French before switching to English. "You need water. Come." He tugged her around the ore car and down the tunnel.

Clara's view of their progression from that point was spotty, coming in flashes when she looked up from navigating the dark, dirty way. When they came upon the activity in the mine, men shouted and the cars rumbled on iron tracks. Her guide warned another miner of the car he'd left in the tunnel. Would they crash?

Clara swayed, barely holding onto consciousness. The heat was so great and her limbs so very heavy, it was all she could do to remain upright.

They were moving again, at a quick pace. He held her hand, his opposite one lifting the lantern ahead of them. She followed in his shadow, the light glowing past black curls at his neck as they wove past half-dressed miners with pickaxes and crowbars, all tapping away with methodical rhythm.

Clara held tight to her guide. He led her into a room where men gathered around a large barrel of ice water. Light reflected off its foggy, grimy surface, yet the water called to her. Wishing she could climb into the barrel, she accepted the cup handed to her and drank long gulps. It tasted awful, yet she dipped the cup in a second time.

All around her, the bare-chested, bright-eyed miners stared at her. "My goodness. I am surrounded by troglodytes."

More than a few of them scrunched their eyebrows, and several chuckles murmured from the crowd. One miner spoke, his blond mustache curled on either side of his nose. "Bringing your lady friend to work, Vulpe?"

Her rescuer—Mr. Vulpe—tensed and pulled her a little nearer. "I found the lady in one of the tunnels."

The blond man smiled, revealing block-like teeth. "My name is Mr. Dodge Peterson." He offered his hand.

Clara let the water cup fall. It clanked against the side of the barrel, hanging by a chain. It seemed her identity as a female was known, but after being lost, it mattered little. "My name is—"

"*Non.*" Mr. Vulpe shushed her, his dark eyes catching firelight. "Do not speak."

Mr. Dodge laughed and tipped his hat to her. "I would be honored to meet such a fine lady." He slid his gaze down her as though assessing the value of a piece of ore.

Clara's cotton chemise showed between the undone front of her shirt. She gasped and covered herself, only to have Mr. Vulpe urge her behind him with one hand as she hurried to work her buttons. No wonder the men recognized her as female. She'd also lost the miner's cap she'd donned upon descending into the mine.

"The woman must be returned to town." Mr. Vulpe spoke sternly.

Cheeks hotter by the moment, for the men in the underground room peered at her as though she'd stepped from a sporting house, Clara gripped Mr. Vulpe's arm, ready to tell him to take her to the surface.

As though knowing her intention, he turned. "Come, let us go."

"You leaving your shift before the bell rings, Vulpe?" Dodge Peterson again. Unlike the shirtless workers, this man wore long pants and a buttoned shirt. Though shorter than other men, he carried himself and spoke with the confidence of a leader. He must be the foreman of the shift. Sure enough, he stepped forward, his hands on his hips. "Get back to work. I'll see the lady out."

Mr. Vulpe stayed like a sentinel between them. Stone still, he stared at his challenger, his eyes dark as iron and square jaw firm as granite.

Mr. Dodge fumed, his shoulder heaving. "Snooty Frenchman. You're fired! I never wanted you here, anyway, and when my father hears what you've done, you'll be lucky to find a job in all of Nevada."

Rather than respond, Mr. Vulpe turned and led her away. Though he guided her with alarming possessiveness, the glare he leveled on the men they passed chased away her unease. Clara sensed safety with him. Not just because of his good size. While the gazes of other miners roved over her like exploring hands, Mr. Vulpe's never dropped below her neck.

"Here is the way up." He stopped before the wooden frame of a shaft to hang a lantern and ring a bell. A metal cable led up into a black hole, correlating with the resounding crank of grinding gears. Mr. Vulpe let go of her and started toward a room off to one side. "How did you get down here?"

She bit her bottom lip. How could she answer without sounding ridiculous? A female reporter would be hard enough for him to accept, and she was dressed in miner's attire.

"No answer? Perhaps you have a beau who works here. He thought it would be a good idea to show you the mine?"

"No." She raised her chin. "I came down alone."

"Unlikely. Why come down at all?"

"That does not concern you."

"It does, actually, since I am responsible for you now and just lost my job protecting you." Mr. Vulpe grabbed a bundle of clothes, including a hat that he promptly placed on his head. "What is your name?"

Oh, no. She would not tell him that and have her family shamed. "I don't think, under the circumstances, that I should answer that, but I am very sorry you lost your job. I just needed to find the lift. I can make my way to the surface from here."

"I will not leave your side until I know you are safe." He knelt, his thick shoulder muscles flexing when he rolled his pant legs down around chiseled calves. "The sooner you are home, the better."

Making little impression in the darkness, the dim light of the single lantern he'd hung on a wall clung to him when he narrowed his gaze on her.

"Have you considered, mademoiselle"—he strode toward her, so large and foreboding that she had to take a step back—"that running around among men of this breed will end in your ruin?"

Unable to hold his imposing gaze, she put a couple feet between them. "When I descended the shaft, no one knew I was female."

"Doubtful. The lifts are crowded when the shifts come down." He glanced up as the lift, a large wooden platform supported by a metal cage, trundled into view.

She crossed her arms. "I was careful."

He smirked. "*Ma foi*, I doubt that."

So he thought she was a liar. "As you said, the lift was

crowded. No one could see my face, and I tucked up my hair and wore a hat. No one knew I was a woman. As I prefer it."

"As you prefer?" The slightest quirk of his mouth turned his hard features nearly boyish. "A lie, I would wager, since you have been watching me as though you enjoyed the time we spent together." He slipped into a blue denim shirt, winking when he closed the front over his broad chest.

So he'd seen her interest in him. More curiosity than admiration—as she'd never seen a man shirtless before. Blushing, she turned her attention to the shaft. "A wager you'd lose."

He chuckled, low and husky, chasing a chill up her spine, and though she wished to further deny his confident claim, she kept her lips sealed. Father always said she was a terrible liar, so why further embarrass herself?

Soon they were riding up the shaft in the cage, the pulley above working to raise them. The only light came from different levels they flew past since the speed at which they ascended would snuff out any flame. Mr. Vulpe crossed his arms with a coat thrown over one and a leg cocked out while Clara clung to the side of the cage.

She fingered the ore sample into her pocket. No one had searched her as they typically did the miners, in case one tried to steal precious metals from the mine. She just had to make it home and begin her article. Hopefully, Theo had not yet alerted her father or the authorities. If he had, search parties would be formed, pulling men from their work to search for a woman lost in the mines. Then her article would be met with outrage and no editor would ever hire her.

∼

*B*eau led the lady out of the lift, which came up into the shambled building that passed for the Peterson Mine entrance just outside the small town of Gold Hill. This

7

was a new mine, lacking the advanced equipment of wealthier setups. As Beau and the lady stepped from the cage into the dimly lit shelter, the lift operator, Mr. Perkins, eyed her and raised his eyebrows. "Your shift over, Vulpe?"

"*Oui*. We're heading to town." Beau tried not to shiver when a freezing wind whistled through the cracks in the walls.

"Best hurry, then." He glanced down as though not noticing the lady in pants. "There's a north wind blowing in." The operator nodded toward the door, which hung on rickety hinges. "Come over here so I can pat you down."

Beau, used to ore checks, raised his arms as Perkins quickly patted his pockets. "What time is it?"

Perkins stepped back. "A quarter to eight."

He'd lost his job within the first hour of his shift. Approaching Mr. Peterson was an option, but Dodge's petty nature made that risky.

Beau sighed, and the lady, who had been peering around the shack as though expecting to see something significant, turned at the sound. She was well-spoken and polite, moving with a gentility not even men's britches could disguise. If he was the gambling type, he'd wager that she lived on Millionaire Row in Virginia City.

When she met his gaze with eyes the deep blue of twilight, his breath thinned as it had the first moment he'd seen her. Perhaps she was a phantom. He would find out once they neared the shops with brightly lit windows.

"It is getting late. We must be going. Here, take this." Beau offered the lady his fleece-lined jacket yet kept his knitted scarf. It would at least help to keep his neck warm.

She shook her head, blond curls fluttering around her face. "I will not take your protection from the cold."

Truly? A wealthy woman who did not believe she possessed special privileges. "My mass exceeds yours. The cold will bother me less. Besides, you have your modesty to consider."

She glanced down at her pants and snatched the coat from him, murmuring her thanks. As she slipped into the garment, the collar of her oversized shirt shifted, revealing a birthmark at the base of her neck. His breath caught, memories surfacing of a woman with the blackest hair and olive-toned skin. When he'd touched a curl at her neck, she had turned, laughing, and smacked away his hand. Behind her, the French countryside lay green and peaceful while dappled light from leafy trees above warmed her face.

His heart colder than the breeze sneaking inside, he cleared away the memory, holding tight to what was real—the stench of sulfur drifting from the water pumped up from the mine, his aching shoulders and back, his cold toes in his boots, and that hole in the right sock. He wasn't in France anymore. This was America. He wasn't a husband anymore. He was a widower.

"But what will protect you from the cold?" She peeked up from the collar of his coat, the rest of her face hidden in the deep folds, reminding him of her youth.

"Here, Vulpe, use mine," Mr. Perkins said, reaching for a spare hanging on the hook where many miners' jackets swayed.

"Merci." He accepted it. After all, it would be a two-mile trek to Virginia City—assuming she was indeed from the wealthier town.

When he pushed the rickety door open, the warm lights from the lanterns spilled out onto the snow, aided by the lights from the nearby settlement of Gold Hill, which shone through the trees up ahead. Darkness had fallen hours ago. How long had she been in the mine? He had to get her home before every man in the area was out searching for her.

Beau offered his arm. The lady peered at the steep hills rising around them, then at him. After a moment of hesitation, she accepted.

"Do you live in Gold Hill or Virginia City?" Beau angled his head toward town.

"Virginia City." She studied the ground where wagon tracks pressed into the snow.

He hadn't bothered to look at the fresh tracks at the beginning of his shift, but he'd bet the second, narrower set was from a buggy, not the large wagon that brought groups of men to work. Was the woman looking for the rig she'd come in?

He led her away from the entrance to the mine. "Did the person who brought you tell you when he was coming back for you?"

She raised her eyebrows. "I will not respond again since you believe nothing of what I've said thus far."

"Fine." Probably better just to get to town.

The mines of the Comstock Lode were scattered across peaks of the Virginia Range, yet the primary mass was on the eastern slope of Mount Davidson, within Virginia City limits. These mountains were his hideout. His sole focus was to work hard and save money. Keep his head low and stay out of trouble. Challenging his foreman and claiming responsibility for the woman in the mine was not laying low.

They walked through Gold Hill—a town of about eight thousand inhabitants situated in a draw. Houses with picket fences stood near enormous heaps of waste dirt, piled so high they cloaked the rooftops. Church steeples pointed like needles into the sky, including the tiled spire of St. Patrick's Catholic Church.

The road to Virginia City wound up a steep hillside. Beau tried not to think about his predicament. He'd lost his job and now had to escort a woman home and speak with her family.

"Could you slow down?" The woman beside him panted, cheeks flushed scarlet, likely because he'd all but dragged her uphill from the mine.

Not very gentlemanly, but he wasn't used to being around women. "You all right?"

"Yes, but please allow me to catch my breath." She pressed a hand to her side, glancing out at the desolate hills dotted with sagebrush and old tree stumps—remnants of the logging years. The faint light of evening fell across her pert nose, clear eyes, and soft lips. No miner's face, that.

"We cannot wait. Your family will be looking for you. I should have alerted the sheriff in Gold Hill to your trouble."

A breath bloomed in front of her face. "I would rather you did not. My family would be shamed if it was widely known that I dressed in this manner."

"Then we must continue on." He offered his arm this time, and she took it more easily, as though trusting him.

At last, they began the ascent up the Divide, the neighborhood between Gold Hill and Virginia City. The lady who had refused to tell him her name clung to him more securely, her lips slightly parted as she panted. He fixed his eyes ahead—best not to stare like a fool.

Virginia City was more elegant than Gold Hill. Grander churches, businesses, and homes sprawled down the flank of Mount Davidson. Clouds hid the peak and promised more snow. Below, the burned heart of the city lay under fresh layers of white—eleven blocks of blackened rubble, while newly built structures lined the principal streets that cut through the wreckage.

The fire that had ripped through the town two months earlier had taken much, but the place was on the mend, fueled by hope and the money mined from the very earth it stood on.

The thoroughfare branched into C Street—the business district—and B Street, where Millionaire Row—or what was left of it—stood. The avenues were bright with light from houses, busy shops, and tall churches—though none so high as the mine headframes that rose above them.

The lady's teeth chattered. Nose rosy red and hair so fair, she reminded him of a snow fairy—something out of a tale.

Beau pulled off his knit scarf and shoved it toward her.

She raised both hands, palms out, and shook her head. "I could not possibly take more from you, Mr. Vulpe. You should not even be here. I wish you would return to your work. I can make it on my own."

Rather than respond, he wrapped the scarf around her neck, and she quickly took over the process. When she was done, she met his gaze with a smile so sweet and youthful he could hardly breathe. What was wrong with him? Here he was about to freeze to death, and he'd lost his job, yet all he could think about was the lovely, odd lady before him.

He cleared his throat and kept his voice low. "Might you reconsider telling me your name?"

Her brows dipped, and her lips pressed together, then sprang upward in a lopsided smile. "You don't recognize me? My father is rather famous. Allow me to introduce myself." She leaned in and dropped her voice to a stage whisper. "Miss Nellie Grant, runaway debutante and mine explorer."

He frowned.

She inclined her head. "At your service."

A flicker of amusement stirred. Beau grinned despite himself. He'd read about the president's daughter, Nellie Grant —her White House weddings and travels abroad. This woman looked nothing like the real Nellie Grant, but he'd rather pretend than argue.

"Miss Nellie Grant?" he asked. "I thought you were married and living in Southampton, England."

She blinked, eyes momentarily wide, then beamed. "Ah, you've been reading the newspapers, I see. I must confess—it was all a hoax. My marriage, a clever cover for my true mission —coming west to make my fortune."

"Well, Mademoiselle Nellie..." He lowered his voice, speaking softly as if sharing a secret. "I am afraid you shall have a *triste* surprise. It is winter, you see, and a terrible time to travel. Most passes are closed, *non*? You will be stranded here until spring."

She let out a sigh and touched the back of her hand to her forehead, all mock dramatics. "Alas, I believe you are correct, Mr. Vulpe," she said with a faint smile that settled there like snow that doesn't quite melt.

He resisted a shiver and rubbed his hands together. "I am surprised to find you without your entourage."

She straightened, eyes sparkling. "I ran away, seeking adventure in the Wild West."

"What a coincidence. I am in a similar situation."

"Hmm." She gave her chin a saucy angle. "And how has your adventure been thus far?"

How, indeed? All he did was work and try not to worry about the prison he'd left behind in Utah. But such an answer would kill the fictional conversation he'd developed with this strange woman. So he hunched his shoulders against the wind and met her eyes. "Very well. I made friends with the Tommy Knockers."

Her face lit like lantern flame. "What a tall tale. Besides, Tommy Knockers are Cornish, not French."

"Maybe the Cornish miners smuggled them in."

She actually laughed. "Is that so? I suppose it is plausible. Tell me, must they battle the rats for the Cornish meat pies miners leave them for good luck?"

"No. The rats are their partners. Why, they sniff out the food and report back to the Tommy Knockers."

"Ah, and here I thought the rats were friends with the miners. Don't they warn them in the event of a cave-in?"

"Yes. When the Tommy Knockers are angry or hungry, they cause the ground to shake. The rats run for safety, and in doing so, warn the miners."

Her rosy cheeks bunched with a smile, round and youthful —not like Amalie's high cheekbones, so tanned and warm.

Why was he thinking of Amalie? He'd avoided thoughts of her for years, and mostly succeeded. Why did the memory of her waver near just now when he was with a lady who looked and conducted herself so differently?

She looked up the dim snowy street with lights on both sides. "I suppose we should be going."

He agreed and they started off again. Snow crunched beneath their feet. Were they heading toward the mansions still standing after the fire, or had the lady lost her home and been forced to dress as a man to find work?

"Miss Grant" slipped on the icy street and gripped his arm for an instant, warming him through. She quickly let go. After all, men did not walk arm in arm, and she still needed to conceal her identity. He let her take the lead, and sure enough, she headed for Millionaire Row.

"My name is Clara." The lady gave him an apologetic glance as they passed the first charred remains of a mansion.

"Clara Grant, I suppose?"

She giggled yet ducked into the shelter of his scarf when a painfully cold wind swept down the street. "Of course."

"Beau Vulpe." He gave her the name he'd begun using after leaving the penitentiary—his legal name in France but not America, and always one he'd been unworthy of. If only he had a better one to give.

She slipped again, and this time, he wove her arm through his and covered her hand as he would when walking with any proper lady. It was dark, so no one should see them. He avoided her gaze, but her touch—despite the fabrics between them—was like the familiar embrace of a friend.

The sooner he got her home, the better. This woman warmed in him feelings he'd not felt since before the war. Her beautiful figure, her quick wit... He best keep his distance. He wasn't staying in Virginia City, and if he had a choice, he'd leave the States altogether.

CHAPTER 2

Standing before the great oak door of Alexander Mansion on B Street, Clara held her hand ready to knock. The moon hid behind thick clouds, and snow now fell heavier than it had when Mr. Vulpe started walking her home. He stood beside her, shivering.

Yet still, she couldn't bring herself to alert the butler. Why was the front door locked before bedtime, anyway?

What would she tell Father? He'd launch into one of his lectures about propriety and the vulnerability of a lady alone in a mining town. How he'd send her off to live with a relative if she continued down this wayward path. Either Grandmother Alexander back in Maryland, or Cousin Aubrey in California, who had just had a baby and could probably use her help.

Neither option appealed.

He couldn't possibly understand the anxiety that boiled in her blood when she sat still too long. Mother had been content to labor over her needlework for hours. Father had likely never known a woman who wasn't happy loitering at home.

Maybe she should sneak in around the back.

A large hand rose beside hers and thundered upon the wood.

Clara turned to Mr. Vulpe, still hunched into the too-small coat loaned to him. "Why did you do that?"

His breath clouded in the air. He said nothing—just looked at her, his dark eyes unreadable.

The coat strained at his shoulders, unbuttoned across the front. He must be freezing. His own protection from the elements still hung around *her* shoulders, warding off the gentle snow.

How would Father react, seeing her in Mr. Vulpe's coat?

She worked the buttons quickly and thrust it toward him just as the door swung open. He caught it, never breaking eye contact.

Discarding the coat did little to shield her from impropriety —as she still wore a man's shirt and britches.

The Paiute butler, Mr. Hancock, stood with his hands clasped behind his back, his shiny black hair neatly combed and face as solemn as ever. "Miss Clara, I'm glad you're well." His gaze narrowed as it shifted to her companion. "And you've brought home a young man. Won't your father be amused?"

Clara's shoulders dropped.

Mr. Hancock had worked for her father since arriving in Virginia City, and they had developed a quiet camaraderie over the years. But sometimes, she wished he wouldn't be quite so blunt. Grandmother Alexander's household staff would *never* speak out of turn—but this was the West. And in truth, Mr. Hancock's candor reminded her not everyone had to live by societal norms—to fit the expected mold.

He stepped aside. "Your father is in the study. Hurry along now, both of you."

In the foyer, a long stairway wound upward. Clara walked past it, heading for the parlor where she could leave Mr. Vulpe while she went to change. Warmth and the scent of Thanksgiving dinner wrapped around her like a blanket.

A sharp yip rang out, followed by the rapid patter of paws on wood. A blur of white and black fur skidded down the staircase, ears flared like butterfly wings in mid-flight. Hugo, her mother's cherished Papillon, bounded toward Clara with the frantic joy of a creature far too small to contain such devotion. He plopped down at her feet, tail sweeping like a feathered fan, and wiggled with delight.

Clara dropped to her knees, ruffling the dog's silky scruff around his neck. "Hello, old fellow."

Hugo had been Mother's final indulgence—a gift to herself in the last year of her life, when the illness had begun to steal more than breath. She'd named him after Victor Hugo, her favorite French author, and doted on him.

"Clara?" Father's voice echoed from down the hallway, followed by his quick step muted on carpet over hardwood.

She and Mr. Vulpe paused, still at the bottom of the grand staircase. "Please, don't tell my father I was in the mine. He'll be furious. He may send me away from Virginia City, and I've only just come home." Her eyes stung. "Please. I'll make it worth your while."

A shadow crossed his face. Clearly, her offer displeased him in some way. Still, he opened his hand to her.

She blinked. "I don't have money on me now."

His scowl deepened, and he withdrew his hand, muttering something in French she could not make out despite her familiarity with the language.

Before Clara could question him, Father entered from the opposite side of the room, his clean-shaven face flushed, his eyes wide—and then he wrapped her in his arms. Clara inhaled peppermint and cologne. It returned her to her childhood. She closed her eyes and melted into the safety of his embrace.

He held her at arm's length, gaze full of relief—until he saw her britches, muddy boots, and the men's shirt. "Where have you been? Theo said you were talking about a mine this morning and..." His eyes narrowed on Mr. Vulpe. "Who is this?"

Clara opened her mouth, but her throat clamped tight.

Mr. Vulpe offered his hand. "I am Monsieur Beau Vulpe. I work for the Peterson Mine."

Father shook it. The grip looked unpleasantly firm. "John Alexander."

A flicker of coldness passed across Mr. Vulpe's face, and he pulled his hand back a little too quickly.

Father didn't seem to notice. He turned swiftly to the butler. "Mr. Hancock, go after Mr. Atticus—he was on his way to alert the sheriff that Clara was missing. If you catch him, we can avoid a scene."

The butler rushed out, not even grabbing a coat. The front door slammed behind him.

Father turned back, his posture hard. "How did you come to be in my daughter's company?"

Mr. Vulpe glanced at Clara, silently giving her the opportunity to speak.

"I went to Gold Hill with Theo on newspaper business. I went down to inspect the Peterson Mine and collect an ore sample, but I wandered too far away from the miners and dropped my candle." A chill ran down her spine. "It was so dark. I thought I would never make it out."

"Theo came back with the rig saying he found it out by Peterson's new claim. That he thought you'd gone into the mine. As usual, he is protecting himself." Father studied her, eyes sharp. "Haven't I told you? I don't want you around Theo Atticus."

"Yes, Father." It was a shame she needed Theo's help understanding ore content to finish her report.

Father's gaze cut to Mr. Vulpe, burning. "What is your accounting of these events?"

Mr. Vulpe answered calmly. "I started my shift at seven. Your daughter was in a newer tunnel—alone. She was overheated but otherwise well. I brought her up immediately. No one touched her."

Father exhaled, pinching the bridge of his nose. "Thank heaven for that." He paused—then red dripped from his nostrils.

"Oh no—Father, you're bleeding." Clara pulled out a handkerchief, but he was already pressing his own to stop it.

Tears stung her eyes. She'd made him this upset.

Father spoke around the cloth. "I cannot believe you would do something so outrageous for this reporter nonsense."

Nonsense. Her dream—nonsense. Because he didn't believe in her. Because he didn't *see* her.

She pressed her lips together tightly.

Footfalls clicked on the floor above, and Clara's already knotted stomach gave a twist.

"John, is that..." Clara's stepmother, Tessa, peered over the banister at the top of the landing, her sharp New York accent cutting the *r* sound from Clara's name when she said, "Clara?" She swept down the staircase, her green silk dress flaring as she descended with Clara's little half brother, Daniel, in tow. She eyed Clara's clothes, her mouth dropping open. "What on earth are you wearin'?"

Clara stiffened, her lips feeling frozen when she responded. "I had a bit of trouble. This man, Mr. Vulpe, helped me home."

Mr. Vulpe watched her closely. The judgment in his eyes had faded, replaced by something gentler. Clara resisted the urge to lean toward him. He felt like a tree in the storm.

"I'm sorry, Father. I *was* reckless, but I'll be wiser now."

Father breathed slowly, likely to stop the bleeding. "Very

well. I'm glad you learned your lesson. Please go upstairs and ready yourself for supper."

Cheeks burning for having been treated like a child in the presence of the most masculine man Clara had ever encountered, she turned to Mr. Beau Vulpe. "I owe you a debt. Thank you for your kindness."

"Non. You owe me nothing." He looked away, as though she wasn't worth his time.

Clara hurried up the stairs, lacing her fingers together behind her back in a futile attempt to shield her bottom from those below. She reached the landing and looked back.

Tessa frowned at her but turned away as Father addressed Mr. Vulpe.

"I would like to thank you properly. Might you join us for dinner tomorrow evening?"

"Thank you kindly, but I work the evening shift at the mine." He shook Father's hand and bowed to Tessa, who gave him a curt nod.

Had he just lied to Father? After all, he lost his job helping her.

When Mr. Vulpe stalked to the door, he paused and angled his head ever so slightly. Clara held her breath. But he simply opened the door and, after giving Father a quick nod, faded into the night.

She turned up the stairs, steps heavier, though the notion was silly. Mr. Vulpe was a stranger, and she shouldn't be so affected by a man, even one so handsome. Perhaps that was some of the appeal, though. Or rather, the distraction. Which she did not need.

The pouch of ore pressed against her leg, reminding her of why she'd gone underground in men's clothes—courting danger and scandal. She had an article to write. It was too late to turn it in to the managing editor, Mr. Goodwin, tonight—but she'd go first thing in the morning.

This was the beginning of her writing career. The article wasn't anything grand and would serve to publicize the mine so people would buy stocks, but once Mr. Goodwin saw her talent, she would prove she belonged.

⁓

Beau rushed down the Alexanders' porch steps, a cold chill riding up his back. Why had he thought Virginia City was a place he could hide out? Here he'd run into an Alexander. John had to be a relation to Jesse Alexander, whom Beau—in a dark and desperate moment of his life—had kidnapped and tried to ransom just that spring. He'd never taken another man's freedom, yet it had seemed so important at the time to bring Jesse to his boss. Could it be coincidence and the men were unrelated? John certainly looked like a relation, but Mademoiselle Clara, with her fair hair and petite features, did not.

He paused on the walk, the temptation to turn around like a nudge to the shoulder. If Clara had told him her last name, he would have parted ways with her on the porch. No, he would have waited at the end of the snow-covered street and charred remains of Millionaire Row until she entered the house. Instead, he'd allowed himself to be drawn in by her playful manner.

He'd had the inclination to accept the invitation to dinner, since refusing might draw more attention to him—but he could not become further entangled with this family. Could he remain in Gold Hill and avoid them? If not, Silver City was a few miles down the mountain. No other strike was as rich as the Comstock, and if he was going to leave America for good, he needed money.

He sighed, shaking his head as he headed back toward the Divide. Beau had determined while he was in prison to be a better man—transparent and honest—because once he started compromising the truth, he lost track of right and wrong. He rolled his shoulders against the slimy feeling.

Lord, help me be better. A complicated prayer, since he was on the run and using an alias. He could not return to a place he was supposed to atone for his sins, to repay his debt to society, only to be forced into illegal work on pain of death. No, running truly was his only option, but the question that plagued him throughout his life returned like the ache of a broken bone in winter—would he ever belong and find peace?

CHAPTER 3

Clara pushed open the oak door of the Virginia City Reading Room, the scent of lamp oil and paper welcoming her like an old friend. Her boots echoed on the worn floor, muffled by a faded rug that stretched beneath the central table. The reading room bore the marks of both ambition and wear. Shelves sagged with well-thumbed books—Bibles, almanacs, novels. A roll-top desk near the window held blotting paper and a half-used inkwell. Oil lamps hung from iron hooks overhead, their glass chimneys smudged with soot.

She paused just inside, fingers tightening around the folded article tucked beneath her cape. No sign of Theo. She'd met him years ago when he worked for her father as a servant. At the time, he told her stories of a more glamorous life back East. He claimed to be educated, something she'd not believed until she returned to Virginia City to learn he was a reporter for one of the local papers.

She made her way to a pair of mismatched armchairs flanking the fireplace. Before she could sit, a whisper of wind accompanied a cold draft from the front door, and in stepped Theo. He moved with the easy confidence of a man accustomed to slipping between saloons and city halls, gathering stories like coins in a purse. The thin, neatly trimmed black mustache above his upper lip framed a smile that once made Clara's heart flutter.

He approached and grasped her hand in a firm hold, his Yankee accent distinct when he said, "Clara. Thank heaven you are well."

Rather than bear an emotional scene, Clara thrust the article into his hand. "Here it is—the Peterson Mine report. A rough draft, at least. I included the things we spoke of yesterday. You must add details on the ore. I sent it with our butler last night. Did you receive it?"

"Yes." He took the paper.

"And did you have it tested this morning?"

Clara held her hands behind her back, swaying. When he did not respond, his lips moving silently as he read, she glanced outside where snow drifted down. A man guided a mule pulling a sleigh, selling Christmas trees. Last night, when Father spoke of bringing a lovely pine from Tahoe, Clara had wanted to stop up her ears. Normally, she adored Christmastime, but she hadn't wanted to be reminded that Tessa, Daniel, and Father had made a family while she was away at finishing school—not even coming home for Christmas.

"What's wrong?" Theo had stopped reading to study her.

"I was just missing my mother."

His features softened. "I understand. Four years—hard to believe. Christmas is just a month away. I know it's a difficult season for you."

Nodding, Clara pushed the feelings away and tapped her article with her finger. "Well, what do you think?"

"It's good." He folded it as though to place it in his pocket.

"And you had the ore sample tested?"

"Sure. Though there was no need. This is the Comstock. A blind man could drill a hole in the ground and find silver."

She frowned and he chuckled. "Don't be a saint, Clara. You're a woman trying to get a foothold in a business run by men. If you were a man, I would refer you to Mr. Goodwin as an ideal columnist for the spot that just opened, but we both know it isn't going to be that easy." He pocketed her article.

"Give that back." Clara extended her hand.

Theo shifted away from her, grinning. "Why?"

"Because I wrote it and will turn it over to Mr. Goodwin myself."

"Clara, surely you know Mr. Goodwin never expected you to do anything. He sent you to punish me for not having the article done by the Thanksgiving holiday."

"I know that, but this is my chance to prove myself. That's why I went into the mine, why I wrote this myself. I would have done it all—if I didn't need your knowledge of the ore. Now, give it back."

Theo blinked, then grinned boyishly as he withdrew the article from his coat pocket, yet he tapped it against the opposite hand playfully. "I didn't mention the column thinking you would get it. I meant that it would be nice if another young fella got it so I could push the mine reports his way. There has never been a female reporter."

"That is not true. Anne Newport Royall owns her own newspaper and—"

"A woman's magazine is not real newspaper work."

"Hers is not a magazine. It is a real paper, printing articles on politics, religion, and news. She is not the only one. Mary Ann Shadd Cary also wielded ink like fire and pressed truth into paper no matter who flinched." She placed her hands on her hips, even when an elderly lady nearby frowned over the top of her book.

Theo barely contained a laugh.

Cheeks growing hotter from his mockery, Clara fumed.

"Truth is truth, Theo, whether spoken by a man or a woman. God gave us all brains, equal capabilities and wisdom."

His smile widened. "You think so?"

"Of course. 'Wisdom crieth without. She uttereth her voice in the streets.' Anyone can have wisdom if they seek after it."

"Still reading Proverbs, I see." He rolled his eyes. "Who am I to argue with the Bible?" Clara pushed her shoulders back and nodded to her writing, but Theo still shook his head. "I should take the article. What if your father hears of you going down to the *Enterprise*? I'm surprised he let you leave the house after yesterday."

She surrendered with a sigh. "Fine."

Theo folded it and stuffed it in his vest pocket. "Why the paper? I thought you wanted to write Bible lessons for young women."

She turned away, the heaviness in her chest dragging her down into the chair behind her. "That was a long time ago." Before Father betrayed her family and Mother gave up on life. Back when God seemed real, close, and loving. Well, even fathers who loved allowed their children to suffer. If that was the kind of father God was, she didn't want to point girls to Him. They would be better off just being good and humble, and hoping God's wrath did not fall on them.

"Clara?" Theo set his hand on her shoulder. "I truly am sorry I left you in the mine. I got scared. You were gone for so long. I kept thinking you must have fallen down a shaft."

As his best friend had, when, years ago, Theo—chasing after riches—had tried his hand at mining. Her heart turning soft, Clara patted his hand where it still rested on her shoulder, and he removed it.

"I have to get this on the press." He patted his coat pocket, then turned toward the door. "I'll see you once your father lets you out of confinement."

She waved him away, yet stayed a little longer. Something

about his dark hair brushing his brow reminded her of Beau Vulpe, and warmth flared unexpectedly. As a girl, she'd admired Theo's boyish charm. Now, at twenty—with her schooling complete and grief still lingering—she found herself drawn to strength, to steadiness. Mr. Vulpe was a miner, rough around the edges and nothing like the sort of man she imagined herself marrying. That was foolish. She'd only begun to write, had not yet earned a byline. Her so-called career was more hope than fact. And she didn't want to meet Mother's end —unloved and undervalued. She needed to become someone first. Someone worth loving.

～

Sunlight glittered off the puddles in the muddy streets and thawed yesterday's snow, except for the patches in the shadows. Beau waited beneath the awning of the Washoe Club in Virginia City, his skin itching from the stiff fabric of a new shirt. He should look his best if he was going to grovel. At least Mr. Peterson was a kind sort. Maybe he would hire Beau back if he understood the predicament he'd faced.

Word about the girl in the mine yesterday had spread, though no one had pointed a finger at Mademoiselle Clara Alexander. The Paiute butler must have reached that Theo Atticus fellow before he alerted the sheriff.

He blew through his lips, creating a cloud before his face. At almost the same time, the seven o'clock whistle resounded from the many mills in the city, echoing off the hillsides. The night shift had ended, and the morning shift would begin. The boardwalk hummed with activity. Restaurant owners would be brewing fresh pots of coffee. The rush lasted for an hour or two, then the town would fall quiet until the next shift change at three o'clock.

Footsteps resounded on the boardwalk, but one particular

clomping set of steps that drew near caused the back of his neck to tighten. Beau turned to face a redheaded man in a knit cap, blue sack coat, and brown bowler hat—Dodge Peterson, foreman of his shift and hot-tempered son of the kind mine owner.

"Well, look what we have here." Dodge wrinkled his nose as though smelling something foul. "Valps."

Beau stiffened. Did Dodge intentionally mispronounce Beau's name?

Easing the pressure on his back teeth, Beau angled himself aside and gestured for the man to pass. Dodge could have easily gone around in the first place but was always asserting his authority over physically superior men in the mine. Beau did not need trouble in Nevada, so he'd let the *malotru* have his way...for now.

Dodge's face slid into a genuine smile before he strode past Beau. "Morning, Pa." He greeted the white-haired man who exited the club from behind Beau, wearing his typical knit cap and sheepskin coat.

Mr. Peterson leaned on his whalebone-handled cane and shook Dodge's hand.

Great—now Dodge was going to monopolize the man's time. Beau was not about to talk to Mr. Peterson in front of his puffed-up son.

"Well, Monsieur Vulpe." Mr. Peterson's face broke into a grin, and he offered his hand, shaking Beau's firmly. "It is fortuitous that you happened by. I've been wanting to speak with both of you. Come on in out of the cold, fellas. Let me buy you a breakfast." He waved both of them into the club with him.

In the dimmer light, patrons sat around tables with matching chairs, the floor glistening from a recent polish, as did the large bar. Behind it, a mirror reflected the goings-on of the room, including Beau entering with the two shorter men.

Across the room, a fire cracked in the hearth where a hog's head was mounted on the stone fireplace.

A tall, stuffy-looking waiter showed them to a table near a large window. Frost laced the wooden muntins framing the busy street outside. Miners wearing narrow-brimmed felt caps and overalls, the latter mostly hidden by heavy coats, swarmed the streets. They would go to the lesser establishments. The Washoe was an elite club and not a place Beau would normally frequent.

"Can I take your coat, sir?" The waiter reached out, but Beau moved back.

"Non. Thank you." It would just be his luck that it would get lost and mistaken for garbage in a place like this. Besides, as a boy, he had picked his share of pockets, enough to know he needed to keep his own.

Beau ordered coffee and a breakfast of steak and potatoes. The coffee arrived piping hot and black. He sipped it and leaned back in his chair, resting one hand on his leg while Dodge and Mr. Peterson talked.

"It is a worrisome time to be mining," Dodge was saying as he rolled out a cigarette. "There was the run on the Bank of California just four months ago, and stocks are falling. Why, every mine on the Comstock had a third less silver just last year. There's no telling what the reports of this year will bring. Virginia City will see its last days. The fire destroyed too much, wiped out our fire department. Why, if we had one more fire, all would be lost. That little department on the Divide can't protect us." He shook his head. "Can you see the writing on the wall, Pa? We need to sell the mine now, get out before the strike dries up."

Beau shifted uncomfortably. Why was Dodge bringing up something like selling the business with him present? It seemed a topic for a private meeting, yet here they were in the middle of the dining room. The man had no sense of propriety, though his patient father did not seem fazed.

Mr. Peterson smiled, sowing wrinkles into his face. "Now, son..." He moved and spoke slowly as he pulled his hat off his head to reveal a tuft of curly white hair. "You worry like a young man. You get to be my age, and you see that the grass withers and flowers fade."

So even if the silver ran out, Mr. Peterson would trust in God? Beau shifted in his seat. The room felt very warm.

He would like to see how the mines did in the future, especially the new Consolidated Virginia which had state-of-the-art equipment. What a shame he didn't typically stay in one place long enough to see the changing of a season. Could he, though? Sooner or later, someone would notice him—a tall, dark Frenchman with the bearing of a brute. He was always running from someone and had been since the start of the war in 1870.

Beau rolled his shoulders, his armpits sticky. Perhaps leaving his coat on was a mistake. He could just drape it over his lap. No. That would draw attention to himself. All the other men had their coat put away. No matter what he did, he stood out. Too big, too poor, and too different.

Mr. Peterson shoved a spoonful of sugar into his coffee, the trembling of his hand sending the crystals over the side of the utensil before he stirred. "Monsieur Vulpe, I heard you had quite the event at the mine the other day."

Before he could respond, Dodge slapped Beau's arm as though they were old friends. "That's right, Vulpe."

Beau tensed, resisting the urge to knock the man's hand away.

"I have to hand it to you. Taking a woman to work with you? What were you thinking?" The redhead laughed and shook his head. "How'd you even get her down the shaft?"

Hot air burned his nose when he inhaled. Beau gripped his fingers into fists, yet turned his attention to Mr. Peterson. "I was pushing the car along one of the shafts when I found a woman. She was near heat exhaustion. I helped her home. That is why I left my shift before it was over. I ask that you not hold it against me, sir. I am always on time, and I work hard."

The elderly man studied him, but before he could respond, Dodge chuckled. "The next thing, you will be claiming that the shaft is haunted and the lady we saw was an apparition." He leaned forward, giving Beau a conspiratorial grin. "Just tell the truth—you brought your girl down to the tunnels, wanting to show off, then you decided you had better things to do with your time. A man who always works so hard must get tired of the grind. Why not just take a day off?"

Dodge was an idiot, but punching him in the mouth would not make him smarter. Beau drew in a deep breath and met Mr. Peterson's gaze. Blessedly, the mine owner continued before Dodge could. "I know you are just poking fun at Mr. Vulpe here, son. Mr. Vulpe has a reputation for working hard and being honest."

The old man leaned back as the waiter returned with heaping plates of johnnycakes, steaks, sausage links, potatoes, and eggs. The rich scent of the food made Beau's mouth water. He had not eaten that morning, and if Dodge had his way, he would not be able to afford to feed himself soon.

"That may be..." Dodge shook his head as he reached for his fork. "But he brought a woman below ground—"

"I did not bring that woman into the mine." Beau leaned forward, his arms crossed. "I would never put anyone, especially someone not familiar with that terrain, in such peril."

Dodge kept talking as though Beau had not spoken. "I just don't feel right about having a man on the crew that we can't trust."

Mr. Peterson raised his eyebrows and waited for Beau to respond.

There was no way to prove himself innocent without

bringing Clara Alexander into this, and he could not do that. She had enough to deal with. Beau firmed his jaw as Dodge sawed off a piece of meat, plopped it into his mouth, then spoke around the bite.

"I can't run a crew with that kind of business going on. It's not safe. If Vulpe didn't take the girl down there, who did?" He looked between Mr. Peterson and Beau. "I want to know so I can fire him."

Beau rubbed his hands on his pant legs, resisting the urge to leave the impossible conversation. He'd worked for men like Dodge before. Men who were greedy and had the boss's ear and trust. His heart was racing, and his muscles tingled with anticipation for a fight.

He inclined his head to his former employer. "If I have done what Dodge says, I am practically a criminal. If not, you're losing a good employee in a failing economy."

"I agree." Mr. Peterson dabbed his mouth with a napkin. "I don't care to lose a good man."

Dodge leaned forward as though about to speak.

"I'll tell you what...Beau, I'm going to have you change shifts. You will work mornings. I know you wanted to work nights so you could go to church on Sunday mornings, but it seems you boys need some space." Mr. Peterson spoke as though Beau and Dodge were kids caught fighting behind the schoolhouse.

"No, Pa. If you're determined to take Vulpe back, he needs to stay on my shift where I can keep an eye on him." Dodge shook his head as though saddened. "Imagine if that girl had been hurt."

"Well, it's not up to you, Dodge. It's up to me." Mr. Peterson glanced back at Beau, his lips parting in a slight smile that showed a few missing teeth. "Mr. Sanderson is in charge of your new shift. He's a good man. He will take care of you."

A strange thing to say, as though Beau—who was stronger

than most and capable in a mine—needed looking after. How did he respond to that?

Dodge looked as though he was about to have an aneurysm. He stood, his chair scraping on the floor, and stalked out of the room.

Mr. Peterson glanced around, likely embarrassed by his son's rude behavior. He cleared his throat. "You a father, Mr. Vulpe?"

Beau hesitated, rubbing his moist palms on his pant legs, his insides turning frigid as a memory took hold...

Père. He could practically hear the precious little voice of his three-year-old son, Martin.

Kneeling in the old stone room beside Amalie, Beau had wrapped his arms around the boy. *Be good for Maman and Aunt Lorraine.*

Behind him, Amalie sniffed as she held his regulation coat and hat. Once war broke out and the Prussian troops invaded Lorraine, Beau had spent the last of his inheritance to move his family to Paris, where he set them up nicely. They would be safe in the emperor's city.

Someone pounded on the door. Amalie startled, then hurriedly kissed him goodbye for the very last time. She had wanted to immigrate to America—to a land of freedom as some of their friends had—but with the war raging, it seemed impossible. But he should have found a way instead of going away to fight.

His boss waited, so Beau managed to push down the grief and respond. "I used to be, sir."

Mr. Peterson leaned back in his chair, his expression relaxing. "You ever thought of settling down here?"

"Virginia City is a mining town." Not the kind of place one wanted to put down roots.

"Sure, but you've seen the land outside town. A woman could mind a house and children there and not worry about the nightlife." He nodded toward a window through which glowed the bright sunlight glinting on snow.

This conversation was too painful. Beau's wife was dead, his son cold in some mass grave in France. He pushed his dish aside. "I appreciate your advice, Mr. Peterson, but I'm not staying in Virginia City. Just as soon as the weather clears, I'm headed out. I only came here to save money."

Peterson nodded, then shrugged. "Fair enough. I just figured if you started courting a decent lady, maybe you'd make a good life here."

Beau shook his head. Yet since parting with Mademoiselle Clara yesterday, his thoughts had drifted toward her more than he liked. But she was an Alexander, and he had been condemned for abducting her cousin. Wondering where she was or what she was doing was fanciful and even wasteful. He had traveled the United States from coast to coast. Nowhere felt safe anymore, and he could not go back to Europe. So once spring came, he would go to Canada.

Beau thanked Mr. Peterson for hearing him out and reinstating his job, then excused himself, leaving the older man to sip his coffee. Outside, as Beau came to the edge of the boardwalk, a coach rolled to a stop beside him, its spoked wheels coated in mud. The shiny black door opened, and out stepped John Alexander, of all people. A newspaper under his arm and a satchel in the other, he raised his eyebrows at the sight of Beau.

"Mr. Vulpe, good to see you. What brings you to the Washoe Club?" He waved to the refined establishment behind Beau, likely thinking that he belonged somewhere else, far away.

Beau squared his shoulders. "I met my employer, Mr. Peterson, here."

"You work for Mr. Peterson?"

Beau nodded.

Alexander handed Beau the newspaper. "You seen this?"

The *Territorial Enterprise* was not a paper he typically chose to read. The editor-in-chief was highly critical of the Volunteer Virginia City Fire Department that had fought the great fire and sustained heavy losses.

"What exactly am I looking for, sir?" Even as he spoke, Beau's gaze fell upon his employer's name. There was an article highlighting the high quality of ore from Peterson's Mine. At the bottom was the initial *T*, then *Atticus*. Not that he was familiar with any of the writers employed by the paper, but wasn't the man who'd been involved in Mademoiselle Clara's mine excursion called Atticus?

"The Peterson Mine report, printed just this morning. Excellent quality of writing, especially for something as simple as an ore analysis." John frowned, studying Beau closely as he brushed his thumb across his chin. "You know, I looked at that claim before Peterson bought it? Hired my own geologist to test the ore."

Atticus had referenced a geologist in his article. A Mr. Phineas Malcolm. Must have been a different one than Alexander's, judging by his frown. Beau forced his features to remain placid, though his pulse sped. "Why didn't you buy it?"

"Because I didn't think it would be worth the investment."

So he was calling into question the richness of the mine. But why tell Beau if there was a problem? And why did the article claim such rich content?

"I'm not sure what you want me to do with this, sir." Beau handed Clara's father the paper.

He tucked it once again beneath his arm. "I foresee trouble in the future, for your employer and possibly my daughter. I wish to know what type of man you are, Mr. Vulpe."

"Your daughter's name is not listed in the paper, sir."

"That doesn't mean blame will not be cast upon her."

"Not by me."

"Regardless, it is my job to protect her. Since you will not allow me to know you better, I am forced to take matters into my own hands." He glanced around, likely gauging who might overhear. "How much for your silence?"

Beau's jaw tightened. "I would not take money from you. There is no need to, anyway. I did not reveal your daughter's identity yesterday. I will not now. Assisting Mademoiselle Alexander home was simply the decent thing to do." And nothing he wanted to gain attention for. Hopefully, the newspapers would not catch on.

"Nonsense. My daughter's life is priceless. Now, if you won't accept payment, come to dinner tonight. I won't take no for an answer." He offered his hand, and rather than disagree, Beau found himself asking what time he should arrive.

CHAPTER 4

He had plagiarized her work—stolen her writing, her creation. True, it was only an article about a mine, and he had secured a geologist to test the ore sample, but she had done all the work. This was her one chance to make it with the *Territorial Enterprise*, and Theo had ruined it. "The sneak thief." Clara spoke under her breath.

"I beg your pardon?" Father looked across the supper table at her, one dark eyebrow raised.

Clara pressed her lips together. She'd not meant to speak aloud, but she'd thought of precious little after rushing out to purchase the paper only to find her work published above Theo Atticus's name. Even when the handsome Mr. Vulpe arrived unexpectedly for supper, Clara had been distracted only momentarily, not enough to keep her from fantasizing about sticking Theo in the eye with a steel-nibbed pen. Now Mr. Vulpe—like Tessa and Father—looked at her as though she'd grown a witch's nose.

"Forgive me. I was caught up in my thoughts." She removed her napkin from her lap, noting that the others present, including her little brother, had eaten more than she.

A maid cleared away her dish, blocking her view of Mr. Vulpe for a moment. Supper was over, and she'd hardly spoken a word to anyone. How rude.

"Well, let's retire to the drawing room." Father stood to pull out Tessa's chair while Daniel balled his fists, crouched, then launched himself off the chair as though leaping from a great height. He landed with a satisfied grunt and took off running, but Tessa caught him by the hand.

Most families did not allow small children at the table, but Tessa insisted Daniel take part in the evening meals. While they were much less quiet, Clara treasured the time with him.

Mr. Vulpe stood behind her, pulling out her chair as well. He moved with surety and even grace, though he was a common laborer. The polite incline of his head also reminded her of the men she encountered in Baltimore, not the miner of a few days ago. He had also known which utensils to use at the table and conducted himself with manners that might impress her etiquette instructor from finishing school. Not to mention, he certainly smelled nice...as though he'd donned special cologne for the occasion.

Father led the way with Tessa on his arm, her clinging to Daniel's hand as he tried to pull away. Clara's little brother was unruly and needed the occasional swat, but his mother fussed about his behavior rather than teaching him how to behave. Shaking away the tremor of conviction—after all, it was not her place to judge—Clara turned her attention to Mr. Vulpe, only to find his stunning dark gaze on her.

"You have been very quiet this evening, Mademoiselle Grant."

Her smile blossomed, chasing away the frown she'd worn most of the day, and she slipped her hand into the arm he proffered. "Well, my father does tend to prattle on." Even as she said it, she blushed. "Politicians." She wasn't in the habit of disrespecting her father. Hopefully, Mr. Vulpe would see it as mere play.

"It is good to see your smile." He lowered his voice when he spoke again. "I wondered how you fared when I saw that the Peterson Mine report was not in your name."

Clara's step faltered, but he kept her going. "How did you know?"

"The report on the mine was published this morning, and you mentioned the *Territorial Enterprise* to your father when you explained what you were doing in the mine."

"I didn't want to tell you the truth in case you laughed at me. Everyone thinks a woman in journalism is absurd—my counterpart included. Obviously, since he stole my work."

"I am sorry. It was a fine piece of writing."

Flooded with emotions, Clara managed a nod and looked straight ahead. When she squeezed his arm, Mr. Vulpe's large muscle hardened, and she tried not to smile.

Daniel broke free of Tessa's grasp when they came to the drawing room. He ran to the bearskin rug and slid across the black fibers to the other side near the fireplace. Hugo, who had been napping by the hearth, jumped up with a whine to move out of the boy's way. Daniel's laughter filled the room as he collided into the wall near the glowing coals.

Clara hurried toward him. "Daniel, be careful. You will hurt yourself."

He jumped up and ran to one side of the rug, repeating the action. Mr. Vulpe tensed when the little boy once again came too close to the fire.

"Daniel, stop." Clara raised her voice, employing the tone she'd used when she'd been in charge of groups of younger girls at finishing school. She looked expectantly at her stepmother.

Fire flashed in Tessa's eyes, though her voice was nonchalant. "He plays here every day and is just fine."

Cheeks burning hotter, Clara avoided Tessa's gaze. Daniel, after all, was her son—and only Clara's half brother. A vagueness entered Father's eyes when he looked between the two of them, his shoulders bending slightly. He seated his wife on a sofa near the window.

Mr. Vulpe saw Clara to the loveseat facing Father and Tessa, the fireplace to his right. He, too, glanced at Daniel. Tessa clung to Father as though she might float to the ceiling like a hot-air balloon without his weight to anchor her.

Silly girl. Clara heard her mother's voice in memory from the first day Tessa came to work for the family nearly five years ago. If only Mother had also known how weak Father was. Clara ground her teeth and turned her attention to their guest. "Were you able to get your job back, Mr. Vulpe?"

He lifted his eyebrows. "I was. Thank you for asking. I am working the morning shift now."

"I'm so glad you were able to retain your employment. It is my fault your job was at risk in the first place."

"Some things are worth more than money, Mademoiselle Alexander."

Meaning she was more important. The kindness warmed her, though Daniel landing once again too near the fireplace gave her a start. She leaned forward, ready to aid the boy, but in doing so moved closer to Mr. Vulpe. He grew still, and so did Tessa in Clara's peripheral.

Father frowned. He must not like her nearness to their handsome guest. Well, she did not like how he'd married his mistress—not that he had ever cared what she thought.

Hugo set his dainty chin on the green, red, and white stripes of Clara's skirt, peering up at her with adoring brown eyes. She stroked his head, then turned her gaze to the side to find Mr. Vulpe's stern face focused elsewhere. A strange twinge of disappointment settled in her, but she contained a sigh.

Daniel slid past Mr. Vulpe, squealing in delight. Hugo

popped his head up and whined, looking between the boy and the fire. Even the dog had sense enough to know what Daniel was doing was not safe—so why didn't his mother? Tessa still clung to Father's arm instead of tending to her son.

Irresponsible. Clara pressed her lips together, keeping condemnation from shaming her even though it flooded her thoughts.

"Tell us about yourself, Mr. Vulpe." Tessa pointed her mousy nose up as though she of all people should look down on others. "Have you lived in America long?"

"Since seventy-one. I am from France. My father was a businessman in the province of Lorraine before it was annexed by Germany."

Father hummed as though understanding something. What was the significance of his statement?

Daniel slid again, and Hugo whined.

"How has your family survived the war?" Father's voice was quiet yet respectful.

Mr. Vulpe gave a shake of his head. "My father's health was failing for years. The demand for metals was high during the war, as you can imagine, but I was in the military, and he could not manage on his own. France lost the war, and remunerations were high. The Germans annexed the provinces of Alsace and Lorraine."

Father nodded slowly. "You were unable to keep the iron works?"

"There were debts. Germany demanded five billion gold francs as an indemnity paid in three years. In addition to the annexation of Alsace and Lorraine, they occupied parts of our territories until the payment was complete."

"That is dreadful." And here Clara thought her life was hard. Amazing that Mr. Vulpe would reveal so much of himself to them. But then he hadn't spoken as much of himself as he had the war and the suffering of his country. "Five billion. A massive sum."

Beau nodded, and Father said, "That would be about..." He tipped his head back as he always did when he was figuring numbers. "1,452 tons of pure gold."

Clara widened her eyes. "My goodness."

Her father grinned, likely proud of his penchant for numbers. "Imagine, Clara, last year the entire Comstock Lode only mined 560.5 tons of pure silver."

All she could do was shake her head. France was a wealthy country, but such a toll must have been overwhelming. And here Mr. Vulpe sat, quiet as could be, humble and kind. He glanced at Daniel, who ran back to the sitting room door and raced past delicately carved furniture to once again slide on the rug.

"The mines provide work. Hard work." Father frowned, his gaze following his son, then momentarily settled on Tessa before returning to Beau. "What did you do in the military?"

"Cavalryman and clerk. I'm good with horses and—how do you say?—numbers."

"Figures. I suppose you learned about the business from your father. There aren't many horses or bookkeepers in the mines. Especially in Peterson's little outfit."

Mr. Vulpe's jaw twitched, his attention shifting between Daniel and Father.

Clara ignored Tessa, who leaned forward as though to say something to her. She needed to tend her son, not make conversation.

"Swinging a hammer pays better." Mr. Vulpe had hardly finished the statement when he darted to his right and stuck out a muscled arm, catching Daniel as he skidded from the rug and into the fire. His little feet slid into the coals, knocking some loose before Mr. Vulpe swung him away.

Tessa screamed, Clara stood helplessly, and Father rose to

stamp out the fiery bits of wood on the carpet. The scent of burned bear hair permeated the air, thick and bitter.

Mr. Vulpe held Daniel in his arms, assessing the leather booties protecting his feet. "He is unharmed."

The boy looked around with bewildered green eyes. Then his gaze fell on Father, and he burst into tears. Mr. Vulpe handed him over. Tessa began fussing about the ugly bear rug in the sitting room.

Mr. Vulpe took a few wide steps to the bearskin and dragged it across the room, away from the fire. No one said anything, but Father's eyes sparked, and his cheeks turned red. He instructed Tessa to take Daniel away, for the boy's wails filled the room. She seemed confused about taking charge of her own son, and Daniel's cries were so tremulous that Clara stepped forward and held out her arms to him.

As her little brother came to her, Clara offered him the gentlest of smiles. "There, dear, you are safe now. You did not realize that sliding toward the fire might cause harm." She pointed to where he'd been so close to danger.

Daniel stared at her solemnly, tears having turned his eyelashes spiky.

Father and Tessa both frowned, but why did neither of them step in?

"You mustn't play around the fire, Daniel." Clara looked into his eyes. "Never. Understand?"

He nodded his round little head, his tears ceasing. "Never. I promise."

Smiling, Clara kissed his cheek and carried him toward the door. She would likely find his nanny in his room.

He wrapped his arms around her neck. "Love you, Clara."

"Love you, Daniel."

Before she could reach the door, Tessa rushed up and snatched Daniel from her arms. Not making eye contact or uttering a word, she exited the room with the door clapping shut behind her. The behavior only served to remind Clara why she tried not to get close to her only sibling. She had been sixteen when Daniel was born and so grief-ridden after her mother's death that the pure joy of the babe had brought her hope. Shortly after, she realized that if she loved the one her father had sired with the witless maid, she would only experience more loss.

Turning around, Clara met Father's gaze. Again, his eyes were glazed and his shoulders slumped as though he suffered from exhaustion. She shrugged as she'd seen common people do. When his jaw tightened, Clara focused on the only other person in the room. "Thank you, Mr. Vulpe. You have now saved both me and my brother from harm."

He only nodded. Both men stared, Father with his mouth seamed tight. Was he angry with her? What if he got another nosebleed? Clara swept forward and sat on the sofa as she continued the conversation with Mr. Vulpe. "You said your family's business in France had something to do with iron. Does that mean your father owned mines?"

Mr. Vulpe lowered to sit across from her, and Father beside her. "Yes. But my father passed before the war due to his poor health. I could not hold onto the business. The taxes were so great. After the war, I sold what was left and came to America."

"That is sad. I have been to Paris once. My mother and I met my aunt there years ago. We went shopping and sailed on the Seine. It was beautiful."

That softened his expression some, and his shoulders also relaxed.

After that, they slid into an easy discourse about the French countryside compared to that around Virginia City, and then of the entertainments Paris had to offer before the hardship of war. Clara especially liked hearing about the parties Mr. Vulpe had attended. If Father had not been there, she would have insisted he teach her a French step she'd never been able to master. The thought had only taken form when Father said, "Ahh, we host a Christmas party every year—nothing too grand. More of a personal gathering. You must come and teach us the latest dance steps of Paris. Of course, Clara always saves me the first dance."

A smile swelled her cheeks. She'd forgotten how, on the eve of any party he and Mother hosted, he came to her room to tuck her in and they danced together. She hadn't thought much about a gown to wear, but perhaps the silk one from last year's winter ball at Grandmother Alexander's house would do. Did Mr. Vulpe have anything proper to wear to the Christmas Eve party?

My goodness. Mr. Vulpe did not look well. He seemed to be turning as gray as he had when he first met Father. "I'm not sure dances that were popular even three years ago would entertain the residents of Virginia City."

Father merely shrugged, then glanced at Clara. "Well, even if that is true, I know Clara would love to learn the new steps. Her mother was fascinated with France, her cousin Melanie having grown up there and Annalise being half French herself. My guess is, Clara is bursting to ask you to teach her here and now."

How did Father know her so well? Clara grinned, and when she met Mr. Vulpe's gaze, he inclined his head, his Adam's apple making a similar motion.

"I'd be honored, of course, Mademoiselle Clara—if you saved me a dance on Christmas Eve."

Not the response she'd hoped for, but his promise to attend was enough for this evening.

CHAPTER 5

Clara climbed down from her buggy and tethered her old gray mare to the hitching post outside of the Crystal Bar in Virginia City the following afternoon. Hopefully, Mr. Goodwin would be here. She stood by the window and hugged her cape closed. Going into the mine was bad enough. She'd dare not enter a place of ill repute like a saloon. It was a shame the *Territorial Enterprise* building had burned in the fire. They printed from the *Gold Hill Daily News* office in Gold Hill, but Mr. Goodwin could most often be found at the Washoe Club—home of the Crystal Bar.

Snow crested the sides of buildings. The sun had risen high enough to melt the center of the street, though it still slid behind large puffy clouds that blocked out portions of the bright blue. Between houses and storefronts, snowy mountains shimmered in the distance.

The minutes dragged, then a familiar man with blond hair and a big coat stepped onto the boardwalk.

Mr. Goodwin raised his eyebrows, his sunken eyes wide. "Miss Alexander, good afternoon. Theo turned in the Peterson Mine report yesterday. You shouldn't have worked so diligently on it. I sent you with him as punishment, yet now he is rewarded for his laziness by taking credit for your excellent work."

Clara gaped at him. "If you knew I wrote it, why did you publish it under his name?"

He blinked. "Honestly, I assumed you were riding out to the Peterson Mine and wrote the report because you desired the young man's attention. I did not realize you expected to have your name in the paper."

"You thought I wished to be alone with Mr. Atticus, and you supported that?"

"Uh..." He frowned, then shook his head. "I meant no disrespect. You must understand the reputation of the Alexanders..."

Clara took a step back. "What about my family's reputation?"

"Nothing. I was mistaken." He waved his hand as though brushing away the entire dreadful notion that her family was anything but respectable. "Do you mean to tell me that you hoped to write for the *Territorial Enterprise*?"

"Yes, of course. I thought I made that very clear. I wish to write for a reputable paper."

"I see." He reached into his pocket and withdrew a number of coins. "I will pay you for your work."

"I do not care about the money. My name should have been at the bottom of that article."

"Miss Alexander...that was at no point agreed upon." He placed the money in her hand. "Now, allow me to show you to your rig." He set a hand on her back and ushered her forward.

She stepped off the boardwalk into crunchy snow and stood beside her mare. "Would you consider accepting other written works from me in the future? I have a reference from a professor at the Maryland State College."

"You attended college?"

Clara patted the sweet mare's brown mane. "No, sir. I

received private lessons from their professors while at finishing school. My father desired that I be educated not only as a lady but as an intellect."

"The article was menial, reporting facts. You had no platform to defend, and even if you did, what reader would seriously consider the opinion of a woman?"

Clara opened her mouth to defend herself, but he just kept talking.

"There is also a practical side to reporting that you do not possess. For example, I need pieces in a timely manner. I have men who work all night when needed and go to all manner of places. Places a lady cannot go."

"I can go anywhere. I spent the last few years in Baltimore, which is a fair sight larger than Virginia City. I have my own buggy and horse. Also, I went into the Peterson Mine. Did Theo tell you that?"

Mr. Goodwin pressed his thin lips together. "No, he did not. I hope you understand I would never ask a lady to do such a dangerous thing. The *Enterprise* has its fair share of enemies. If you were hurt, the public would think that I—that we—at the paper do not care for the ladies in our community. I could not in good conscience employ a woman. That is all I have to say on the matter." He moved aside the wool blanket in her buggy, ready to assist her into the high seat.

The *pop-pop* of a gunshot sent a jolt through the many passersby on the busy street—including Mr. Goodwin. He pulled Clara into a crouch, then helped her rise when no more shots sounded.

"Stay here, Miss Alexander." He squinted toward the Bucket of Blood Saloon while several men rushed for the single door beneath a large painted sign.

Rather than agree, Clara folded her hands in compliance.

Mr. Goodwin nodded, obviously satisfied, then crossed the

street, his long legs eating up the distance. He pushed through the crowd gathering outside the saloon.

Were other reporters headed their way, having heard the gunshots? She was so close. This story might be the one she could use to prove to Mr. Goodwin that she was the reporter he needed. Clara glanced up and down the street, took a breath, and started across. Mud sucked at her shoes, though she lifted her hem high.

As she reached the opposite boardwalk, a sheriff's deputy warned the crowd. "Stand back!"

Another deputy raised his arms to bar two men from the saloon—one frowning, the other blinking stupidly. While they were distracted, Clara slipped past them, her stomach tight with excitement. She would normally never dream of entering such a place, but if she could just stand in the entrance, she could see the goings on.

Wooden beams lined the floor of the main room. The mismatched tables and chairs looked hastily arranged. On the far wall, the bar stood beneath a large mirror framed with photographs.

Several lawmen restrained a struggling man, blood soaking one shoulder. He grimaced, holding his arm as he struggled to speak with a prominent stutter. "H-h-he drew on m-m-me! It was self-d-d-defense."

A fat, bald bartender in a checkered vest wiped his shiny forehead as he spoke to the sheriff. "Then Rankin drew his gun and shot Doug."

"That's a lie," the man shouted, lunging toward the bar. Officers held him back.

"Get him out the back door, lads," said the sheriff, an older Irishman with a bald head and big barrel chest. Sheriff Kelly was not one to be trifled with. Once a boxer in New York, he had proven on more than one occasion that he was deadly.

Now, he stood beside Mr. Goodwin, watchful as a group of men carried the prisoner away.

Clara pressed forward, wedging herself between two onlookers. She stumbled to the very front and stopped behind a large man, peering through the curve of his arm as he stood with his hands on his hips.

There, sprawled across the saloon floor, lay a man. Tall. Broad. A red gingham shirt soaked through with blood. A toppled table blocked his face—but something about him felt... familiar.

Clara rose on her tiptoes, peering over a man's shoulder to see better.

The victim wore denim britches and the same type of red shirt Mr. Vulpe sported in the mine the day before.

Mr. Vulpe!

Clara bolted forward, ducking under the officer's arm and skirting a table. Her heartbeat thundered. Her vision tunneled. She dropped to her knees and grabbed the man's hand.

The face, olive-toned with a shadow of whiskers, belonged to a stranger. Clara exhaled, bracing a hand on the floor. The miner's head turned left, blood soaking his chest. His holster was on the right, yet his weapon lay inches from his left hand. Had he reached across his body to draw the gun on the right side?

Hands gripped Clara's arms and pulled her up.

"Miss Alexander, really. Show some respect." Mr. Goodwin's brows drew down, genuine emotion in his voice. He steered her toward the crowd.

A chortle sounded. One man glared at her while others turned away in disgust.

At the edge of the crowd, Mr. Goodwin exhaled. "Such behavior is unbecoming. Even if you were a man reporting for me, we do not impede the law."

"I thought I knew him." Clara's eyes stung, but her answer seemed only to irritate him more.

"A miner? You, a lady?" He scoffed. "I must say, your actions do not reflect well on the legacy your father and uncle have built. It's bad enough your cousin fell into destitution because of her husband's fraudulent will. Then your father's second marriage produced scandal enough to cost him public office. You'd do well to carry yourself with wisdom, not bring further shame on your family."

Clara reeled. "My cousin is a fine, respectable woman. How dare you?"

He closed his eyes and sighed. "I'm sure she was a victim. Nevertheless, women bear the burden of their men's sins—husbands, fathers, brothers. I'm sorry to be so blunt, but the shame of your father's foolish behavior with his maid—and your mother's sudden death—will fall on you. You must be wise. Modest. Charitable. Not reckless." He gestured toward the scene behind them.

Clara glared at him, trembling. "'Let he who is without sin cast the first stone.'"

"That doesn't change your situation." His tone softened. "You'll have to prove yourself now that you're grown. Exploring mines, dashing into saloons—that's not the way. Your father shielded you from the scandal of your brother's birth by sending you east. You've returned just as the city recovers from the Great Fire, but don't think you're invisible."

He glanced up as a rival reporter darted past them, likely chasing the story.

"Please, make your way home." He nudged her toward a nearby officer, who took her by the arm.

"Come on, missy, no sightseeing today." The lawman ushered Clara past two other reporters who barely noticed her. Mr. Goodwin's words still echoed in her ears. Her family...a disgrace? *Father sent me away to protect me?* No. He sent her away because he didn't want her.

"Now, get on home, girl." The lawman nudged her out of the barroom and into the cold winter morning.

Clara stumbled forward, headed begrudgingly toward her buggy. A staircase led up past the Bucket of Blood and the next half-constructed building with a narrow balcony. A sniffle broke the quiet, then a soft whimper. There, on the stairs, sat a woman not much older than Clara. Snow flurries whipped around her bare shoulders, which were partially covered by tousled curls. She wept into her hands. The poor soul.

Clara moved toward the banister, concern pulling her upward. She tugged a handkerchief from her sleeve. "Excuse me?" She raised the cloth and gently shook it.

The girl startled.

"Are you hurt?"

Red marked the woman's jaw, and strands of brown hair clung to her tear-streaked face. She shook her head.

"I'm Clara." She hesitated. "When I saw you crying, I thought…maybe you could use a handkerchief."

The woman looked down at the offered cloth, then reached for it as if it were something precious. "My sister had a hanky like this once."

Clara tried to smile, but her mouth still felt stiff from Goodwin's rebuke. She should probably go home and hide. But now they were carrying the dead man out on a stretcher.

Another sniffle. The woman cried again.

"Did you know him?" Clara stepped back as Mr. Goodwin passed below.

"Yeah. That was Doug Fitch. Sweet. Not too bright, and a terrible drinker."

Clara placed a gentle hand on the woman's shoulder and, when she made room on the step beside her, sat and wrapped her cape around her.

"I'm Maudy Jane," the girl murmured between sniffs.

"Was Mr. Fitch a friend of yours?"

"Oh no. Us girls always avoided him when he drank. Still, it's such a shame." She sucked in a breath and released another sob.

"Yes, it's awful." Clara gave her a squeeze. Maybe the girl had never seen someone die before.

"Poor Abe. He was Doug's only friend, and now they'll hang him."

"Abe—the man arrested?"

Maudy nodded.

"Why did he shoot him?"

"They were playing cards, and Doug got it in his head that he'd been cheated. He started yelling and cursing. He always had a terrible temper. When he drew his gun, well, what else could Abe do?" She dabbed her cheeks and looked at Clara, tears swimming in her eyes. "It's just what Old Bart wanted."

A breeze swept through the space between the buildings, and Clara shivered. "Who is Bart?"

"The owner of the saloon. He and Abe own the place together, but Abe wanted to sell and move to Reno. He owns over half and could do what he wanted. But now that Abe's been arrested, he will probably have to sell his half to Bart just to retain a lawyer."

Clara tilted her head and pulled a pencil and notepad from her bag. There might be a story in this. "Do you know what happened between Mr. Fitch and Abe? Oh—and what's Abe's last name?"

"What are you doing?" A deep voice struck like a whip.

Clara startled while Maudy pressed close, her bony shoulder jabbing Clara's side.

A few steps below stood Mr. Vulpe—very much alive and clearly furious.

~

*B*eau stood on the stairway leading to the upper rooms where the prostitutes worked, holding his fists so tight, his knuckles popped. He had been running errands on his day off, shopping for a few items like a button for his shirt, when he spotted Clara Alexander sitting on the steps in a blue-and-white day dress with a filthy hem and muddy boots—a far cry from the miner's britches he'd seen her in a few days ago. Her beauty was just as radiant in either form of attire. What was she doing here with her arm around a sporting gal?

Light shone from the space between the two buildings, the sun peeking from between clouds just long enough to set the fine hairs around her head aglow like a halo. Her eyes, still wide from the surprise he'd given her, warmed with a smile.

"Oh, Monsieur Vulpe, just look at you. As healthy as an American thoroughbred." She tapped her chin. "No, you are a Frenchman. Let me amend that. As healthy as a mighty Camargue. It is good to see you looking so alive."

Beau blinked. Her address was so proper, calling him by his surname. Would that he could tell her his legal name. At least, legal in America. And why was she talking about horses? Although surely he compared more accurately with the wild American mustang these days than he ever had the coveted French Camargue breeds of history.

"You know this man?" The pitiful creature beside Clara glanced at him and played with a snow-white handkerchief.

"Yes, though we are only recently acquainted." Clara struggled to hold his gaze, and her tone was less excited, likely because she didn't want anyone to know about her mine exploration. "Monsieur Beau Vulpe, this is Miss Maudy Jane."

Maudy mumbled a greeting, glancing between him and Clara. The woman was probably wondering how a refined lady had come to be acquainted with a miner like him. Instead, Maudy asked, "What is a Camargue?"

"A magnificent horse the French used in the army. It is an ancient breed going as far back as the reign of Julius Caesar. Emperor Napoleon recruited them for the French army. And"—her voice rose a little, and her eyes widened—"they were even used in the construction of the Suez Canal."

"The Suez Canal?" Maudy drew out the name. "Is that in France as well?"

Clara blinked, then looked at Beau and raised her eyebrows.

He kept his features still. Hopefully, she wouldn't guess that he, like Maudy, had no idea where this canal of hers was.

"Actually, it's a waterway in Africa that runs north-south across the Isthmus of Suez in Egypt." She used her hands to illustrate a line—presumably the canal—then she brought them so the backs were facing before drawing them apart when she said, "It separates Africa and Asia and connects the Mediterranean and the Red Seas." Clara gave him a pleased nod, though her smile faded when Maudy blinked at her. "Of course, none of that is pertinent to us here in Nevada or to the killing." Her cheeks turned red, and she giggled nervously. "How did I even begin talking about such a thing? Oh, I remember. The Camargue. Of course, Monsieur Vulpe is not a horse. Terribly sorry. I meant no offense." Her blush rose to her hairline, and she fastened her gaze to her notepad, tapping her pencil there.

What a fascinating woman.

"Egypt." Maudy grinned, a gap in her teeth. "It's from the Bible, and no matter where you go, the Bible is pertinent, so you weren't so far off, now, were you, Miss Clara?" She knocked her shoulder against Clara's.

"Thank you, Maudy." Clara nodded gratefully, as though Maudy had made everything better.

The women shared a smile, then Clara turned her pretty

pert nose in his direction. "Maudy was just telling me that the man arrested was actually innocent and that the owner of the Bucket of Blood Saloon, named Bart"—she lowered her voice—"will let him hang because Abe Rankin, the man arrested, owns part of the saloon and doesn't want to sell." As she spoke, she made notes.

Beau squinted at her handwriting. He could read the print in the paper just fine, but Mademoiselle Clara's scrawling script was difficult to decipher. "What are you doing?"

"I am recording pertinent information, such as dates and times, the names of the men, and their part in the crime." Clara stowed her pencil and notepad in her reticule and looked up. "Mr. Vulpe, would you be so kind as to escort us across the street to the hotel? Maudy has had a rough morning. May I buy you a coffee or some tea?" She raised her eyebrows, as though Maudy might actually turn her down.

"That would be mighty fine, Miss Clara." She stood, and Clara took her arm as though they were old friends.

Beau moved aside, and the women went down the stairs, chatting quietly. Was he supposed to follow? Clara seemed to think he would. But he wasn't at her beck and call. He didn't want to be a tagalong to anyone. Not even Clara Alexander—much as he couldn't seem to resist her company. Besides, he had to go to the barber shop, the launderers, and repair his shirt. Of course, that wouldn't take all day, and it was still morning.

As they neared the edge of the boardwalk, Clara gave her cape to Maudy, who was shivering terribly. Then Clara glanced over her shoulder, raising her eyebrows as though it was strange he had not followed her.

He did, but only because she was alone. Once Maudy was taken care of, he would see Mademoiselle Clara home. Again.

As they passed the Bucket of Blood Saloon, a couple of

miners crashed through the door—their laughter and boots too loud, too careless.

Beau stepped forward, blocking them from stumbling into the women. "Men, watch where you are going. There are ladies out here."

The shorter man reeled, colliding with his companion, who barely had time to curse before catching his friend.

"Sorry about that, ladies." Grimacing, Beau turned his collar up, and gestured for them to proceed him. Maudy bit back a grin while Clara glanced the length of him, a spark of admiration in her gaze. Still, she didn't move. Perhaps he had scared her?

He cleared his throat. "Can't have the president's daughter walking around a mining town without a proper guard."

Her smile bloomed. "I believe I found a bodyguard in you, Monsieur Vulpe."

The rowdy miners stood to the side, hats in hand, nodding to the women as they passed. Beau returned the gesture with a firm nod. They didn't seem much older than twenty. Just a couple of rough kids being reckless.

When Clara remembered she'd brought a horse that would need to be stabled, he escorted the women to the hotel entrance and then parted from them to find a place for the horse and conveyance at the local livery. That accomplished, he met the women at the back of the hotel dining room, where a few tables clustered around a warm cast-iron stove. Maudy sat cutting hotcakes and steak before dipping both into syrup.

When he took a chair across from them, Clara continued scribbling with her pencil, several pages of notes already filled. Was he supposed to wait or leave now that she was settled?

Maudy pointed to a cup of coffee across from Clara. "She got this for you and told the waiter to give you whatever you want. Steak?"

Beau shook his head yet sipped the coffee meant for him.

He'd leave a few bits for the drink. He'd already worked two months in the mines and had savings, more than enough to pay for coffee and that cologne he'd worn to the Alexanders' for dinner. A frivolous expenditure, yet it had made him feel more ready for the challenge of dining with people who would see him as an enemy if they ever found out who he really was.

Focused on her work, Clara reached for her coffee, only to wrap her fingers around his mug. Beau let go of the handle, and she lifted it to her lips, which moved as she read. Then Mademoiselle Clara's eyes grew large. She moved the cup away, grimacing and swallowing. "Oh, what terrible stuff."

He grinned while she tried to gather herself, touching her throat as she searched the table for her cup. Finding her creamy brew, she shook her head. "I don't know how you drink it black, Mr. Vulpe. So bitter." Then she lifted her own drink to her mouth.

Warmed through, Beau looked away. His thoughts stayed on Clara and her pouty lips, so quick to smile. He rubbed his hands on his pant legs. "If you are all set, I will be heading out. Just remember, the sun sets early this time of year. I suggest you not linger too long, Mademoiselle Clara."

"Thank you." She tapped her chin with her pencil. "Did you witness the shooting, Mr. Vulpe?"

Wincing internally at the use of his legal name, the one given by his father and which he had never been worthy, he said, "Call me Beau, and no, I saw nothing. Why do you ask?"

"Because they arrested the wrong man. That is big news, likely enough to shed doubt in the minds of the citizens or at least prompt the sheriff to investigate further. I intend to sell this article to the *Territorial Enterprise* and show the editor that even though I cannot go to places men go, I can still get the truth." She nodded firmly. "So what *did* you see?"

"Nothing." And even if he did, he would not tell her or Mr.

Goodwin. The last thing he needed was attention from the press or the law.

Maudy set her knife down. "You are going to tell the paper what I saw?"

Clara became still, the top of the pencil between her teeth. She removed it, setting it down beside her notepad. "I planned to. Is that a problem?"

"Well, a girl like me...mentioned in the papers. That will bring me the wrong sort of attention. Us working girls haven't had it so good lately. You know the fire started at Crazy Kate's house. Besides, they never believe us working girls. I could lose my job. It's an awful time of year to be on the streets." Her bottom lip trembled.

Clara squeezed her arm. "Oh, I didn't know. I don't want to make things hard for you, Maudy."

Eyes pooling with tears, Maudy tried to smile. "A whore's life is hard."

Beau shifted in his chair, though Clara seemed unaffected by the term.

"You realize that if you say nothing, Abe will hang, though he is innocent?"

"He'll hang whether I speak or not. Folks don't believe me about nothing. You're a fancy lady, so you don't know what it's like." She pressed her trembling lips together.

Clara glanced over her writing, then seemed to stray in thought. With her shoulders back and slender neck framed by a black velvet choker, Clara resembled one of the Nordic paintings Beau had seen of a blond Madonna. Completely inaccurate because Jewish people looked more like him than any Norseman, but still, it was beautiful. As was Clara.

She snapped her gaze back to Maudy. "I won't name you as a source. I saw the body. Mr. Fitch's left hand was near his revolver. If Abe drew first and killed him, he wouldn't have had time to draw. He was left-handed, was he not?"

Maudy adjusted her shawl to cover her cleavage. "He often held his drink in his left hand. Sometimes his cards too. But sometimes his right."

"He was probably trying to hide that he favored his left hand. I knew someone who did so." Clara's gaze drifted to Beau. "Mr. Vulpe, would you be so kind as to go back into the saloon to hear what talk there might be about the shooting?"

She wanted him to go poking around, possibly drawing attention to himself? "I am no reporter. And neither are you."

She lowered her shoulders and sighed. "Yes. I know. You are not the first man to remind me of that fact this day. I only need some corroboration that what Maudy says is true. I don't have to name sources, though I would like to. The papers just want a good story, and I need to show reasonable doubt if Mr. Rankin is to be acquitted of a crime he did not commit."

Maudy brightened and leaned forward with Clara, both women looking at him imploringly. If he went to the saloon, he could purchase his own meal. He stood and Clara smiled. If he heard something about the shooting, that would be all right too.

CHAPTER 6

The gray clouds turned black when the sun set over the side of the mountains and the moon rose into the heavens the night of the shooting. Below, Gold Hill was alive with song and laughter. Warm lights glowed through saloon and hotel windows, though thick shadows closed around Clara and Theo as they stood before the *Gold Hill Daily News* office, where the *Territorial Enterprise* did its printing. Shivering from the cold after waiting outside for Mr. Goodwin because the clerk would not let her into the office, Clara offered Theo her article when no one else came out.

He took it, looking from it to her. "I didn't think you would talk to me after the printer slapped my name on your mine report. I am so sorry, Clara."

"Mr. Goodwin explained as much, though if you are truly sorry, you could correct the oversight."

"Oh, that would make the paper look very clever."

She didn't answer. What he said was true. She had lost the report and that was that. The shooting article offered her hope, so she would let the matter lie.

Clara folded her arms and glanced down the dark street

toward the livery. Mr. Vulpe—Beau—was supposed to be coming down the road at any moment. It was strange calling him Beau, which essentially meant beautiful. Every time she did, she felt a little tight in the stomach. Did he know she found him comely? Likely.

He had not been willing to go by his surname once he'd returned from the Bucket of Blood Saloon with new information for her. Sure enough, Maudy spoke the truth. Mr. Fitch had drawn first, according to three other patrons, none of whom were brave enough to cross the portly barkeep, Bart Masterson, who had lied to the law.

"What is this? Fitch was left-handed? He drew first?" Theo looked up from her article, his eyes wide.

"Y-yes." Clara's teeth chattered as her breath turned to fog. "I have two witnesses who'll corroborate this evidence. Mr. Masterson lied to the sheriff. I just need you to give this to Mr. Goodwin. And this time, it should be printed under my name, Theo."

"Witnesses not named."

Her shivering paused for an instant when a burst of irritation rushed through her. "You know me to be honest."

He flicked his eyebrows upward. "I know you want a job at my paper."

"So what kind of reporter would I be if I fabricated stories? Why, that is fiction."

He grinned, reminding her of the old Theo who quoted Shakespeare for her and dreamed of being a senator. "Mark Twain made his way at the *Enterprise* with works that were wholly fiction. Remember the petrified man and the sack of flour?"

Twain's tall tales had brought entertainment, to be sure. "That is not the kind of writing I want to create. Now, tell me you'll add this to tomorrow's issue. It's a great article, and it's true. Someone has to tell Mr. Rankin's side of the story."

The steady trot of a horse on the road signaled Beau was approaching.

"All right. I will add it, but I cannot print it until Goodwin gives the command. And..."—he tipped his chin, eyes narrowing—"this doesn't mean you're getting that column. You need to let it go, Clara."

"If my writing is good enough, Goodwin will hire me." She gave a firm nod, but he only turned away, shaking his head.

His hand was halfway to the door when he paused and scowled at the sight of Beau stopping her buggy. "Who's he?"

"A friend. Have a good night, Theo." Clara rushed forward as Beau grabbed her lap blanket and hopped down to meet her.

He wrapped wool cloth around her, along with the sense of safety. He muttered something in French that was surely a complaint, then lifted her into the seat. Clara sat back, tucking her nose into the scratchy material.

"I suppose you gave your shawl to Mademoiselle Maudy." He hoisted himself into the narrow seat, pressing against her, then flicked the reins so the mare plodded forward.

"I have more than enough at home, and she needs it more than I."

"If you get influenza, you will not need any."

She snickered at his dramatics. "If I get influenza and die, you may give my things to the poor."

Beau jerked his head around, his dark eyebrows bent fiercely. "You joke about death?"

She shifted her head back before saying, "Why does it matter? My joking changes nothing. All living things die."

His expression darkened. "If you ever lost someone dear to you, you might not be so flippant."

An iciness like that stinging her nose crept into her chest. Perhaps he was right. She spoke too freely of death, but what good had it done anyone not speaking when Mother died?

Regardless, she should consider those around her with more sensitivity.

Clara settled her chin on the fold of the blanket to ensure he clearly heard her. "It was an insensitive thing for me to say. Forgive me."

"Forgiven. I should not be so quick to anger. Will you forgive me?" His voice was softer, and Clara nodded.

"I lied to you, when you found me in the mine. A young man did take me there, but it was not for something untoward, as you suggested."

"Which young man? That dandy you met back at the paper?"

"Yes."

He made a low sound of protest, watching the road ahead. "Why newspapers? Why not pursue lecturing at ladies' aide societies or Sunday school teaching? Something more befitting a lady?"

"Susan B. Anthony and Elizabeth Cady Stanton founded a newspaper for change. Jane Swisshelm printed justice even when it cost her everything. Anne Newport Royall turned the press into a weapon sharp enough to crack the senate's silence. If they could do that—if they could write even through persecution—why shouldn't I?"

Beau held the reins with a white-knuckle grip, poised as the mare struggled up an icy hill. "We should not have stayed out so late. The roads are not safe."

His change of topics stole her gusto. "That is my fault. I waited, hoping to speak with Mr. Goodwin myself."

"There is no fault. I could have just tossed you over my shoulder and carried you home if I wanted." A grin pulled his lips, though it vanished as quickly as it appeared, his focus on the horse and road.

She leaned back against the cushioned seats, content to let him tend to the driving. Snow was falling again, and though it

THE CONVICT'S COURTSHIP

was only near suppertime, the night was already dark. By the time they reached B Street, the snow was stacking up, and Beau Vulpe's frown was back in place. Clara sighed. Best just get inside so he could have his time free. For some reason, he had stayed at her side all day, drinking coffee and reading the newspaper while she wrote. Even once Maudy left, Beau had remained. Mining was backbreaking labor, with long hours. Surely, he needed to either be at work or at rest.

A groom took the horse and buggy. Beau helped Clara down from the carriage as though she weighed little more than Maudy might. She smiled.

Beau set a brisk pace across the snow-blanketed yard, uphill toward the house. Clara had to practically run to keep up. Typically, she was left at the entrance, but she'd not protested when Beau drove to the stable behind the house.

"Which door?" he asked, glancing back.

Clara sucked in a breath, a bloom of fog forming before her face when she said, "I'd prefer to enter through the servant's entrance than draw attention to myself."

"Once through the front door with me was one time too many, I suppose." He stopped, and so did Clara, holding her side where a stitch pained from her jaunt toward the house. "Why did you not tell me to slow down?"

A sinking feeling in her chest, Clara frowned. "Because it would be impolite." She slipped her gloved hand from the blanket she'd kept for warmth and grasped his arm. "I sat at your side most of the day in a public place. Why would I be embarrassed to have you enter my home?"

He shivered, the house with multiple windows glowing behind him and the gentle snowflakes catching on his shoulders. "I am poor and a foreigner. This is not a place for me." He gestured around them, at the two-story stable with groom's quarters, paved walkways and high walls, and the three-story Gothic mansion Mother had loved so much. "Your father

65

invited me to supper because he fears I may speak of your excursion to the mine." He gestured for her to lead the way, not taking her arm as he had before.

"I believe he likes you, actually, and you did rescue me from the mine," she offered meekly, but Mr. Vulpe's granite-like jaw and arched eyebrows remained unchanged. Arguing was useless, so she just led the way through the yard.

Light spilled from the lattice windows of Mother's library and cascaded across them. Who would be there at this time of night? Above, a balcony led to one of the upper rooms. He used to lean over the edge to speak with Mother or drop her a love note. She veered away from old memories that stung like salt in a festering wound.

Clara started up the few steps and passed a sparkling white column. "My father is not like other men. Of course, he is not perfect. No one is—at least, not on earth because we still have our sin nature, unlike those who have died and gone to be with God."

Beau glanced at her in confusion, likely because she was babbling.

"But, I digress. He admires honesty, hard work, and honor. I think it is because of my uncle Titus. He is very rough around the edges, but a hardworking man. A courageous man. You remind me a lot of him."

Beau snickered as they came to a side entrance. "I am like Titus Alexander?"

There was something in the way he said that—as though he believed something particular about Uncle. But he'd never met him, so how could he make such a judgment?

Clara carefully navigated the icy patio, withdrawing her keys from her purse and nearly losing her balance on the slippery surface.

"This isn't the servants' entrance." He scowled at the double doors with the swags of cedar hanging from them. A glowing wall lamp created a tangerine hue of light around them, warming the snow and brick steps.

"I have a key to this door, and since it is closer than the servants' entrance, I'd prefer to use it."

"Clara?" Beau crossed his arms, glancing around as though in search of something. He swallowed, the lump in his throat pushing against the red knit scarf he always wore. Below, the top button of his shirt was missing to reveal smooth skin, a shade lighter than that of his muscular hands.

Throat tight, Clara glanced away, yet caught— out of the corner of her eye—Beau closing his coat more securely to cover the garment's damage.

"*Eh bien...*" He hesitated, scratching his chin. "*Dis*, what is a troglodyte?"

Ah, he must be remembering her comment regarding the half-naked miners working underground. "I should not have said that. It was unkind."

His dark eyebrows crowded even closer together. "Now I am more curious." He gestured for her to continue.

"A troglodyte is a cave dweller, like in ancient times. The etymology of the word *troglodytes* is from ancient Greek. *Trogle* means *hole*, and *dyein* means *to dive into*."

He snickered, then shook his head.

Wait, was he laughing at her? Clara turned back to the door, fumbling with the keys. Of course he was. What young lady spoke of ancient cave dwellers? She worked the key in the lock yet glanced back at her companion.

Beau crossed his arms where he stood on the brick steps in the darkness. "I will not attend the Christmas Eve party."

Heart sinking, she frowned. They had been talking about cave dwellers. Why the sudden change of topic? Unless he was just stalling when he asked. "You do not want to attend the party?"

He glanced away. "I have a previous engagement."

She stepped toward him, closing the distance between them. "Did you just lie to me?"

Beau snapped his gaze up from studying the patio. "Yes, foolish woman. Stay away from men like me. Girls like Maudy. Ruined people ruin people."

"Yes, and wounded people wound people. And I am not foolish. Maudy was all alone and needed someone."

"Non, *ma belle*, you misunderstand me." He retreated, one hand extended. "You are young—"

"I understand that you are hurt, perhaps grieving, but you needn't lie. Tell the truth. You do not wish to be in my company because I babble about stupid things like heaven and earth, the Suez Canal, Tommy Knockers, and Camargue horses. Do not think you are the first man to dismiss me because of the way I am." Even Father occasionally seemed annoyed by her ramblings.

Beau retreated a step so he was nearer eye level when he clasped one of her shoulders. "You are beautiful, smart, fascinating. But you must see, too—I don't belong here."

"That is nonsense. My father has welcomed you. At supper, you knew which forks to use, and you have perfect manners. I've surmised that you were likely raised by a notable family and received professional education."

"Which I did not finish. I ran away from school, my duties, my father." His voice cracked.

Clara crossed her arms. "I think you see yourself differently than others, Beau. You know, you are a fine man."

He blinked, cocking his head to one side as though not sure if he heard correctly.

Unfortunately, at that moment, powdery snow swirled in a stinging breeze, and Clara shuddered, closing her eyes.

Warmth swept her face. When she opened her eyes, he was so near, she could see the shards of gold in the dark of his eyes

—and the clean line between a day's worth of whiskers and his bold lips.

She glanced away, her heart racing. My goodness, what was she thinking, speaking so forwardly to a man she hardly knew and allowing herself to stand so near him? This was attraction, like something she'd only ever read about in books. Regardless of the gentle tugging she always felt toward him, wisdom and caution were needed.

"I am not a fine man. You do not know me." He gripped the sides of the blanket, wrapping it more snugly around her, then stilled. "Besides, I am leaving Nevada in the spring. You will never see me again."

Clara stepped back, and he let her go. She gripped the chilly doorknob behind her. "You work in the morning, do you not?"

For a moment, Beau stood like marble. "I do." He gestured toward the door, and though it behooved her to simply obey, Clara hesitated. They'd had such a fine day. Might he change his mind? Stop her from leaving? Say something. Even just give her a proper goodbye?

She pulled the door open slowly, giving him time to call her back. When she spoke a farewell over her shoulder, he didn't respond. He just stood there, darkness behind him, snow falling softly, light from the doorway casting across his resolute jaw. But he wasn't going to stop her. Her time with Monsieur Beau Vulpe was over.

∽

The bell above the door to the *Gold Hill Daily News* rang like the tweet of a bird—too cheerful for Clara's mood—as she pushed her way into the newsroom. The familiar scents of parchment, ink, and machine oil curled around her, but today they felt cloying. Her jaw tightened. Behind the counter and in the next room, the press pulsed with its steady thrum, rhythmic as a heartbeat, indifferent to her presence. She passed towers of newsprint bound with twine and sidestepped a paperboy who didn't bother to look up before vanishing out the door again. No one noticed her. Of course they didn't.

Cheeks hot from brooding over the newspaper now tucked beneath her arm, she marched to the front desk. Behind it, journalists bent over their work in a brightly lit room fogged with tobacco smoke. A tall man with dark brown hair matching a thick beard stood and walked toward her. When she met his gaze, he cocked his head to one side.

"Clara." Theo darted in front of her, blocking her view. "What are you doing here?"

A flash of red lit her vision at the sight of the two-timing sneak thief. "You said you would speak with Mr. Goodwin on my behalf. Instead you stole my work."

He gripped her arm, pulled her toward the door, then pushed her outside.

She tugged her arm loose and thrust the newspaper against his chest. "I wouldn't be surprised if you told the printer the mine report was yours as well. You're a fraud."

Theo brushed the pages away, his eyes flashing wide. "Shh. Do you want to get me fired?"

She nearly laughed. "Yes, you should be fired for plagiarizing my work."

He tensed, his fists tightening for a moment. "You go accusing me of plagiarism, and I'll be run out of this town on a rail."

"My, what a splendid idea." She patted his shoulder. "Do wait here while I fetch Mr. Goodwin."

He dodged in front of her again, this time taking her by both arms. "That man who just approached you was Mr. Alf Doten, the owner of the *Gold Hill Daily News*. The only reason we are afloat is because he allows us to print here, on his press. If you endanger that, Goodwin will never give you a chance."

"As if he ever would when you're taking credit for my work." She fumed, but Theo crossed his arms and shook his head as though she were the foolish one.

"Don't be stupid and ruin your only chance of becoming a reporter, Clara."

"You—"

"Would you rather not have the article about Rankin printed at all? Goodwin would have tossed it out if he knew it was from you."

"That's a lie. It is a fine piece of writing. Front-page news."

"The print was set for the night." Theo shook his head in frustration, the pungent scent of old tobacco on his breath. "If I told him it was from you, he would not have even looked at it. The only way to get it in the paper was for me to let him believe I wrote it. Look." He reached into his pocket and drew out a bank note. "I went to the bank this morning. Here is your payment."

Teeth pressed together, Clara studied the bank note with its green ink and elaborate illustrations. "Thirty-two whole dollars?" A decent amount. She accepted it. After all, this was her money. She could buy Daniel a Christmas present at the mercantile and maybe secure a shawl for Maudy. If she had enough left, she could purchase a button and give it to Beau for his red shirt. Oh, no, that would not be fitting. Besides, she wasn't going to see him anymore.

Her shoulders suddenly became weighty as the fight drained from her.

An exasperated gust rushed from Theo as he rubbed his arms in the cold morning air. "Listen. You can write. I will give you that. The paper sold more copies than any in months. We even increased our subscriber list. When I tell Goodwin that was you, he might actually consider hiring you."

"I tire of your games." Clara cocked an eyebrow. "Let us speak to Mr. Goodwin directly."

He put out a hand. "One article is not enough?"

"I had the ore article as well."

Theo laughed, and Clara sighed. He was right. A simple analysis of the ore was nothing. Cheeks burning, she tried to keep her chin high. She just needed to write more significant articles to prove her worth. Ones like the shooting.

"I know this is important to you, but you can't change the times, Clara." Theo touched her shoulders, massaging her upper arms for a couple of squeezes. "Goodwin is an old man with old ways of thinking. I tell you what. If you write articles and give them to me, I can get them into the paper."

Clara jerked away. "No."

"Not under my name. Under a pseudonym. Once you're established, we can tell him it was you, and then he'd surely hire you."

She shook her head. "How stupid do you think I am?"

Theo rolled his eyes and, slipping his hands into his pockets, shrugged. "Fine, do it your way. Keep begging the old men in this town to hire you, but it won't work. There just isn't room in the world of newspapers for women."

"I will see about that myself." Clara reached for the door.

He blocked her. "If you say anything, I will tell them you are lying. No one will believe you. You have no choice except to write my way or not at all."

She jerked her hand back, glaring at the blighter she'd once considered a friend. "How dare you?"

A shadow crossed his face, though he'd conducted himself with a note of congeniality thus far. "How dare I? I didn't want any part of this. You're the one pushing your way into my place of work, insisting on being a nuisance." He grimaced, his voice deep and serious. "You need to give up on this ridiculous dream that you can be a reporter. Marry and have children, like normal ladies."

"And be insignificant? Nothing in the pages of history? Never have my work in print where I can make a difference?"

"It's just the way God made mankind. Plenty of powerful men have virtuous, brilliant women behind them. It is the destiny of your sex to work in the shadows." He cocked an eyebrow. "Why do you crave the limelight like some brazen actress? The Bible says a woman of a gentle and quiet spirit is precious in the sight of God." He headed for the front door of the *Daily News*, tossing over his shoulder, "If you change your mind and want to do this my way, let me know."

Clara's heart raced. Had Theo just chastised her with the Bible?

Lord, am I prideful? Sinful to want to make a difference with my words? Have I missed my calling?

Was she wrong, sinning by pursuing writing in a professional capacity?

CHAPTER 7

Beau lowered the pick, his muscles shaking from holding the four-foot metal bar while the hammer-man pounded it in. The rest of his team also lowered their tools, some sitting on beams used for framing the tunnels they dug. They took out lunch pails and passed around canteens of water.

He leaned against the dirt wall, the earthy scent pungent and warm. The Peterson Mine wasn't as deep or as well built as other mines. This was the deepest shaft at only four-hundred feet. Others in Virginia City went down double and triple that depth.

"Water?" Sanderson, Beau's hammer-man, tossed him a canteen.

He caught it one-handed, then tipped it back, gulping down the icy yet bitter liquid. Beau lowered to the timber, resting his elbows on his bare knees where he'd rolled his pants up because it was so hot. Remembering Clara's wide eyes and her attempt not to stare when they'd been in the mine together, he smiled. The expression faded.

In the last two weeks, he'd worked tirelessly, trying not to remember the intelligent blonde who had trusted him so readily. He had hurt her, yet she had been graceful in the end, accepting his decision and bidding him goodbye.

Would Clara someday learn his true identity? The other Alexander family would not recognize the name Vulpe, but Lorraine—if she visited Virginia City—certainly would.

Beau sighed and stretched out his neck, letting his head hang loose. *What else would You have me do, Lord?*

"Some of the boys said they heard ghosts in the tunnels last eve." One of the miners spoke to the group before God could answer Beau, so he raised his head. The man looked around with wide eyes, his thick accent and black hair setting him apart as one of the Cornish men.

"I say it was just blasting," his friend replied, squatting on the floor with a meat pie in one hand.

Several large rats scurried along the tunnel to perch on a timber that had been left by the building crew. The biggest one looked at the miner eating his pie and squeaked, its pink nose wiggling and clear eyes shining. The miner tossed him a few nibbles of crust, which he had to defend from his furry friends.

One of the men chuckled, his dirty skin shiny with sweat and white teeth flashing in the lantern light. "As friendly as cats, I'd say."

Beau focused on the dirt between his feet. Something metallic caught the light from the lamps. Was it a coin? He picked it up and pinched it between two fingers. The metal cap of a buckshot.

"I thought this vein was drying up, but look at this." One of the other men ran his hand in the loose gravel at his feet. "Silver." He grinned, but Beau frowned.

Silver couldn't last forever, as much as the Bonanza Kings wanted it to. There were many ways to salt a mine—make it appear the ore was of a richer content than it actually was. By taking apart a shotgun shell, removing the buckshot, and replacing it with silver nuggets, one could then shoot the precious metals into a cave wall.

Beau stood, followed the scattered patterns of silver flecks in the tunnel, and then squatted to inspect a handful of ore. He was no geologist, but there didn't seem to be as many of the shiny bits within the clump of earth. Shouldn't there be? When John Alexander showed him the article Clara wrote, he also said he hadn't purchased the mine because of the low ore content. If the mine's false reputation led to financial loss or public harm, Theo Atticus might shift the blame onto Clara. Beau had to warn her.

~

Standing on the Alexanders' porch steps once again, Beau raised his hand to knock, yet he could not force his knuckles to meet the hard wooden surface. *What am I doing here?* When last he'd stood here, it had been beside Clara. He'd tried to set a boundary, yet here he was at her doorstep again.

The door sailed open, and Mr. Hancock stood in the threshold, his solemn features as unreadable as ever.

"*Bonjour*, I am Monsieur Beau Vulpe." He cleared his suddenly tight throat. "Is Miss Clara at home?"

"Does her father know you're calling on the lady?"

Beau shifted his head back. Apparently, the hired help had no problem being nosy.

"No." What else could he say? He wasn't going to tell Clara's father about his suspicions and embarrass her. She deserved to know first.

Beau met the butler's gaze and frowned. What was the old fella waiting for?

"Hancock?" Mr. Alexander's voice sounded nearby, followed by the tread of shoes on a wooden floor. Hair neatly combed and dark gray suit pressed, John Alexander grinned as he came around the corner.

Beau stepped forward before the nosy butler could protest. "Bonjour, Mr. Alexander."

"John. My name is John. No 'sir' to it. No 'mister' either." He offered a handshake. "Welcome. Come in out of the cold."

Only then did the butler move aside with a dip of his head.

Beau stepped onto the glossy floor, his mud-caked boots leaving chips of hardened soil behind. The butler glared as though he had defecated on the hardwood. Beau turned to Mr. Alexander, who ushered him toward the front parlor. He walked as lightly as he could, but to no avail.

The front parlor was as bright and cheerful as he remembered—only now, a grand Christmas tree was featured like royalty in the center of the room. The black bear rug shimmered in the light, and there, before the hearth in a wingedback chair that seemed to swallow her up, sat Clara with her little brother in her arms.

Unable to move or breathe, Beau halted, flashes of his own young son flitting through his memory like leaves in autumn, blowing past, then away. Martin hadn't looked like Daniel. Beau's son had been far darker, yet he'd slumbered as peacefully as Daniel did now, his face angelic. Martin's fingers had been so small. His smile oh so bright. Frozen inside, the blackness of grief stilling the world around him, Beau fought to return to Virginia City.

He blinked, and the room cleared to show the warm glow of the gaslights and a rosy-cheeked Clara peering not at him but at her father. Had Mr. Alexander asked her something?

"Sorry, Beau. A friend just dropped by. I won't be long." Mr. Alexander smiled between the two of them.

"That is all right. I was actually hoping to speak with Miss Clara."

"Ah. I see. Very well." He lingered a moment, then turned and strode through the doorway and out of sight.

Beau turned to Clara and stilled at the sight of her. The boy's brown head rested against the white cotton of her blouse, her chin nestled gently on his forehead. Someday, Clara would be a gentle, loving mother.

Eyes of deepest blue met his, just as lovely as the last time he'd seen her, yet lacking her spark. Was that because she was unhappy to see him? How much more unhappy would she be when she learned the true reason for his visit?

She curled an arm around Daniel's back. "Please take a seat." She pointed to a sofa and, when he complied, said, "How is your day thus far, Monsieur Vulpe?"

He scooted to the edge of the sofa. "My morning has been fine. Not very productive, though."

"Oh?" She raised feathery eyebrows below soft golden bangs. The hair there was so fair against her skin, like sunshine on freshly fallen snow.

Beau looked away, trying to put his thoughts to rights. "I finished my shift and went to see Mr. Phineas Malcolm, the geologist who consulted on your article. Unfortunately, he wasn't home. He is out of town for the holiday and won't be back until after Christmas, weather permitting."

She cocked her head. "Why, Mr. Malcolm tested the ore I took from Mr. Peterson's mine."

"Oui. Did you see him run the test?"

A shadow crossed her face. "I never met him. Theo, the reporter I was working with—or thought I was working with—contacted him. He added his comments to the article I had written." Her frown deepened, and she hid behind her lashes when she focused on her brother, gently rubbing his back.

She seemed different. Sad or maybe discouraged.

"I saw the article on the Bucket of Blood shooting. It was a real fine piece of writing."

"If you read it, then you know that Theo took full credit for it." Her eyes flashed with anger, though once again, she tried to hide her emotions.

"I am sorry he stole that from you."

The muscle in her jaw twitched. Still, she hugged Daniel.

"I am sorry to have to bring bad news to you, Clara, but I think he has got you into some trouble."

"What do you mean?" Clara shifted her slumbering brother, but before he could answer, men's voices sounded from around the corner, and Mr. Alexander and another man walked into the room.

~

Clara stood at the sight of her father's visitor. Why, it was the man she'd seen earlier at the *Gold Hill Daily News*. What had Theo called him? Mr. Doten.

Father smiled wide when Clara and Beau reached his side, his features growing tender as his gaze dropped to Daniel. "Mr. Doten, allow me to introduce you to my daughter, Miss Clara Alexander. She is minding her brother, Daniel, while my wife is indisposed."

Clara managed a semi-curtsy to the man with equally dark hair and beard. His simple sack-coat suit hung on his tall, thin frame.

"Pleased to meet you, Miss Alexander." He smiled with a kindness that made her wonder if he was a father as well.

Father actually clapped Beau on the shoulder. "And this is an acquaintance of ours, Mr. Beau Vulpe."

"I have read your defense of the fire department in the *Daily News*, Mr. Doten. You are well-spoken." Beau offered a handshake, his long arm stockier and his tanned hand larger than Mr. Doten's.

"Our community needs to come together, not be torn apart

by political drama." He referenced the well-known criticism against the fire department. "I am a fireman as well. You should come by the station for our yearly meeting. There is a lot still undecided regarding the future of the Virginia City Fire Department."

The slightest smile eased Beau's stern features. "I will if I can."

"Well, you were there that day. We all were." Doten squared his shoulders and looked to the others. "There was nothing more anyone could do with the winds blowing on the mountain and the water supply so inconsistent. We shouldn't crucify men who fought bravely and sacrificed much simply because a hurt city needs a scapegoat."

"Agreed." Father and Beau spoke in unison, sending a strange twinge of warmth through Clara.

The way Father smiled at Beau and had introduced him, welcoming him into the house—he liked him. And Beau was not afraid of Father as Theo had been or like any of the other young male friends Clara had. Then again, Beau was not so young. But he was not old either.

Mr. Doten turned to her, his smile one of resignation. "Well, this is hardly a topic for a lady. I don't want to bore you, Miss Alexander."

"You needn't fear boring Mademoiselle Alexander with such talk." Beau turned his midnight-dark eyes on her. "She is a thoughtful, modern lady."

Heat entered her cheeks. What on earth was he saying?

Father blinked hard. Mr. Doten tilted his head as though he'd misheard, but Beau rambled on. "She is well-versed in history, current national happenings, and science."

Father rubbed his chin. "That's right. Your professor of history was impressed with your ability to recall events. As bright as any young man he ever taught, I believe he said."

"It is true—I am not easily bored." Clara managed a smile, rocking from side to side.

"She has even written for newspapers under pseudonyms." Beau's words sent her ears ringing.

Father's smile fell, and Mr. Doten's eyebrows shot high on his tall forehead. The editor and owner of the *Gold Hill Daily News* studied Father, obviously monitoring his reaction, but Father—while frowning—did not seem especially angry.

So Clara raised her chin and said, "It is true. In Baltimore, I wrote for a ladies' magazine, but since coming to Virginia City, I have written—under a pseudonym, of course—for the *Territorial Enterprise*." Her voice quaked a little, and she struggled to hold Mr. Doten's gaze. After all, her experience with Mr. Goodwin had not been encouraging, and Theo would see her writing in obscurity while he took credit for her work. But she was smart and had written good work. She forced her chin higher. "The truth is, I am intelligent, educated, analytical, and intuitive. I am a credit to any literary establishment."

"Clara." Father's voice sounded in exasperation, but Mr. Doten laughed.

"My goodness, Miss Alexander, if I didn't know any better, I would say you were looking for work. However, not all fathers approve of their well-bred young daughters working. In fact, I believe few do."

"I can agree with that. However, Clara has never been satisfied by simple home life." Father sighed. "She's been writing stories since she could hold a pencil. I didn't mind her writing for ladies' magazines where she was always in polite society." His features tightened—likely, the result of him remembering her mine escapade.

Here she was again, being told to write for a ladies' magazine when entertainment was not the change she wanted to effect in the world.

"Well, then, Mr. Alexander and Miss Alexander, I think I

can offer civilized opportunities for the young lady to exercise her talent. There are several Christmas and New Year's celebrations on the calendar in Gold Hill and Virginia City. I imagine it will be easier for you to gain an invitation than my reporters, and I wager your intuitiveness and attention to detail would make you a better candidate for the job. If you are interested."

Clara had been swaying with Daniel, but she slowed the pace. "You want me to..." She looked to Father, who could ruin her chance with one word, but Mr. Doten wanted her to work for his paper. Would Father be ashamed if she did? And what about making a difference? This was just writing for entertainment. For the society pages. That wasn't serious journalism. Theo's offer to write in obscurity and then reveal to Mr. Goodwin that she was the talented person had an appeal. She just couldn't trust Theo to do his part or Mr. Goodwin's temper to not backfire on her. "Would I publish under my name?"

"I think..." Doten again looked to her father, not her, but really, what else could she expect? They were friends, and Mr. Doten would not want to do anything Father would disapprove of.

"Yes, I think that would be fine, Clara." Father lifted his arm, and she swept under so he could hold her to his side. "I'd rather you work hard and earn what is due to you than be taken advantage of by greedy men."

Throat tight, Clara smiled so wide, her cheeks hurt. She clutched Daniel a little closer, as if the warmth of his small body could anchor her in the moment. Mr. Doten chuckled, the sound low and genial, while Beau rocked on his heels, hands tucked behind his back, clearly pleased with the opportunity he had helped to create.

Was this God's answer to her prayer from earlier, reassuring her that she hadn't missed her calling and was not craven and vain for pursuing notoriety in the current literary landscape?

She certainly hoped so, and it seemed as if Father might have realized she wasn't just some foolhardy girl. That she was more.

"Wait..." She cleared her throat, voice barely steady. "What happens when Christmas is over?"

Mr. Doten's eyes twinkled. "We may speak about it then."

Clara nodded slowly. After all, what else could she do?

"It's been a delight meeting you, Miss Alexander." Mr. Doten offered her a real handshake—firm, respectful.

Once he had left, Father stepped forward, gently taking Daniel from her arms. "Beau, will you be joining us for supper?" he asked quietly, rubbing the little boy's back.

Beau opened his mouth for a moment, then shook his head. "No, sir, thank you."

Father's footsteps were fading, and Clara was still reliving her happy moment when she turned to Beau. He smiled, bringing youth to his rugged features.

Clara clasped her hands together, resisting the urge to kiss both his cheeks. "It was kind of you to speak so highly of me to Mr. Doten."

He shrugged one shoulder. "You're intelligent, and those fools at the *Enterprise* aren't worth your time."

She stood on her tiptoes and brought her fists up beneath her chin. "Thank you."

His broad shoulders relaxed a little, and a softening around his eyes turned her heart to mush. For a moment, he studied her, then he took a deep breath. "I wish I could end our visit on such a sweet note, but soon your father will return, and I need to speak with you privately."

"Oh." What on earth would he say to her that he could not say with Father present? "What is it?"

He slapped his miner's cap against his leg. "I suspect the Peterson Mine was salted."

"Salted? You mean the claim is not rich?" Clara released her clasped hands. "Why do you think that?"

"I found evidence of a method of salting with silver. Some of the local mines are drying up. And someone told me they had a geologist test a sample of the ore and they chose not to purchase the mine when it was for sale, before Mr. Peterson purchased it."

"That is strange since the geologist..." Theo's geologist whom Clara had never met had said the mine had rich ore content. "You believe the report was wrong, don't you?"

"Oui." He crossed his arms and leaned against the frame of the large open doorway between the main parlor and the foyer. "I'd like to get some answers before I go to my employer."

"But Mr. Malcolm was not in town. Who had a sample tested before Mr. Peterson?"

Beau looked pointedly in the direction Father had gone.

"My father?" Clara whispered, leaning closer, grimacing when Beau confirmed with a nod. "Oh, if he knows I wrote the Peterson Mine report and didn't have the details of the geological test validated myself..." She shook her head. All the respect and admiration she'd sensed in him when Mr. Doten offered her the job would fade. "Please don't tell him, Beau." There she was, using his Christian name when he'd made it clear he wanted to be on less personal terms with her. "Mr. Vulpe, I mean. Please, if we can find the geologist, we can try and get this figured out. Poor Mr. Peterson."

"It's not your fault." He touched her arm briefly, squeezing for an instant and warming her through. "Besides, we do not know anything for certain. I could be wrong. I just wanted to warn you...in case. I think we need to talk to your father."

Clara shook her head, wishing he might clasp her arms again. Reassure her that all would be well—a foolish notion considering she had only met him two weeks ago. She crossed her arms. "Of course, it is my fault. I wrote the article, so I am responsible."

"Your name wasn't on the paper."

"A blessing, in hindsight."

"'The eyes of the Lord are over the righteous.'" His dark eyes focused on her, conviction in his voice lending her courage.

"'And His ears are open unto their prayers.'"

Beau reached across the space separating them, and when Clara squeezed his hand, the warmth of his touch sent a hush through her worry. "'But the face of the Lord is against them that do evil.'"

"Psalm chapter thirty-four?"

His thick eyebrows arched. "I thought it was First Peter chapter three."

She gave a soft shrug, her smile blooming despite the weight of the evening. "The writers of the New Testament were familiar with the Psalms. It isn't uncommon to find those verses in the New Testament."

"Really? I didn't know that." Amazement filled his eyes, and for a moment, the mine and Mr. Peterson's schemes faded into the background.

But as the night wore on, Clara's doubts crept back into her mind. What would they do if Mr. Peterson's mine was salted?

CHAPTER 8

Clara guided her buggy around the curve where the road split into B and C Streets—B leading to Millionaire Row and C to the business district. Having just submitted the first of her holiday articles, warmth filled Clara's chest. She was on her way to becoming a columnist. As she shifted the reins to head home, a woman a block away waved her arm wildly. Clara squinted. It was near the edge of the red-light district. Who would be signaling from there?

The woman's face came into view, and Clara smiled. "Maudy?" She reined in beside her.

"Hello, Miss Clara. So good to see you on this fine day." She huddled in a worn blanket, visibly shivering.

Clara didn't dare ask what had happened to the cape she'd given Maudy. Hopefully, it had not been stolen. Perhaps Maudy had sold it to get by.

"Good to see you." Clara scooted over on the seat. "Allow me to drive you to your destination."

After a moment's hesitation, Maudy climbed up beside her. "Thank you kindly. You are an answer to prayer. I'm late delivering these baked goods for my landlady."

"Where are you going?"

"Corner of Union and F Street." She grinned, showing a gap in her smile, though her teeth were clean. "I thought that was you, driving along by yourself like no proper lady should." She laughed and shook her head. "Where's your handsome friend?"

"Mr. Vulpe?" Her stomach tightened just thinking of Beau and the last time they'd spoken—his warning about her inaccurate report. Some newspaperwoman she was. Even if the public never knew, she did, as did he. She pushed aside the thought. "I don't know where Mr. Vulpe is. Working, I imagine. You said you're delivering these for your landlady. Does that mean you no longer live near the saloon?"

"Not anymore. Bart sold his half to Abe so he could pay for a lawyer. The sheriff is none too happy that he lied in his original statement. Abe turned around and sold the Bucket of Blood Saloon back to the original owners. He and Bart had won it in a card game and only owned it a short time. Abe's gone into the mercantile business with a laundry service on the side. He even let the girls who worked at the saloon work for him, provided they peddle nothing except clean duds." She shivered, her eyes darting away. When she turned back, her smiled seemed forced. "O'course, most decent folks won't let us wash their linens, but the miners always need their clothes cleaned."

"That's wonderful." When another cold wind blew through the gully, Clara adjusted her lap blanket to cover Maudy as well. "Are you happy?"

"Very." Maudy shrugged, her cheeks ruddy from the chill as she offered a cautious smile. "I, ah—when Abe was in jail, I took him some food and told him about the article you wrote. He didn't really believe me. Then Bart found out and roughed me up. Lied about me and got me kicked out on the street. After Abe was released, he found me. Helped me get a place to live and a job." She tilted her chin up, a gleam of pride in her eyes.

"That's wonderful, Maudy. I'm so proud of you." Clara bumped her shoulder gently.

"Yeah, it's real good, and Abe comes by to see me. Like a real courting fella."

"Abe is courting you? Maudy, is that wise?"

All the sunshine faded from Maudy's face. "This is the house." She pointed to a Second Empire-style home with bay windows on the bottom floor, arched dormers on the second, and the signature mansard roof—hardly allowing Clara time to stop the buggy before she jumped down. Maudy crunched over the snowy ground, through the gate, and around the side of the house without a backward glance.

Clara had better wait and give her a ride back, especially since she'd hurt Maudy's feelings. But really—could the woman believe entertaining a beau who knew her past profession was wise? What if Maudy didn't know better than to yield to a man's desires? After all, he gave her a job and a place to live. That gave him power. How dare he use her situation against her?

Maudy returned, closing the gate behind her and waving to three little girls who peeked from a window. Her smile was back in place as she climbed up beside Clara again. "I'm working at the Tahoe House Hotel. If you want to drop me back on C, I can make my way from there."

"I can take you. Do you board there as well?" Clara flicked the reins, and the horse pulled them forward.

"Yes, I enjoy working there. No—I board down on B Street in Mrs. Mary Matthews's boardinghouse. It's a bit of a walk to the Tahoe House, but I've walked farther. Abe and the owner are friends. With Abe owning the saloon, they both know what it's like to run a business. Of course, Abe's gone straight now, and isn't in the saloon business." She jutted out her chin and gave it a firm nod.

"I'm glad to hear that." Clara shifted on the seat. How could she broach the subject without offending? "Maudy, you said Abe provided a place for you to live, and that you're courting?"

Completely still, Maudy simply waited.

"Are you sure that's wise? I mean—with your past and his elevated situation."

Maudy screwed up her face. "Elevated situation?"

"Yes, he has money. He's a successful business owner, and with his influence and connections to your employer...he could see you put out on the street if you were to displease him."

Maudy put up a staying hand. "Abe's not the kind of man to take advantage of a woman. All the months I worked at the saloon, Abe never engaged any of the girls, and anytime a girl propositioned him, he refused. Just like your handsome friend, Mr. Vulpe."

Clara's insides froze like the ice crystals clouding many windowpanes on C Street. "Mr. Vulpe frequents the Bucket of Blood?"

"No. I saw him there once before the shooting. He had just gotten off work. None of the eating houses are open that late. He ate a huge supper, then left. Didn't take a sip of spirits even though the night was cold." She patted Clara's knee. "He seems like a real fine man, and so is Abe. He never took services at all —even though, as part owner of the saloon, he could have." She grimaced. "Bart sure did."

Cheeks growing hot, Clara focused on Hattie's head. Thank heaven Beau was a righteous man. She tried not to think of the worldly things men engaged in here in Virginia City, always worrying that if she did marry, her husband might fall to sin. She shouldn't even be thinking about herself, though. Here Maudy was shivering and cold, working herself to the bone. But who was Clara to give advice? Her own romantic experience amounted to a kiss. Even the idea of Maudy's former work twisted her stomach.

"Listen, Miss Clara, I owe you for helping get Abe out of jail and being a friend to me, but I don't need your goody-two-shoes opinions. You live up there on Millionaire Row with your rich daddy who'll get you anything you want." Maudy pointed up the slope where mansions sat in rows—beautiful in the light, until one reached the blackened rubble of those that burned.

"I'm not a goody-two-shoes, Maudy. I'm trying to warn you. Men always pursue the flesh. They can't help it. Even in the Bible—King David, a man after God's own heart, took another man's wife. Abraham, Solomon, Moses—even brave Gideon—weren't satisfied with one woman. Men are different from women. We want to love and devote our hearts to one man. They don't love the same way."

"By that logic, I'd never want to be married," Maudy said low, brushing away tears, her lips trembling. "But what if you're wrong? That pastor at the Presbyterian church said men should love their wives like Jesus loves the church—and gave His life for it. There's only one church. One bride of Christ, right?"

Clara nodded slowly. And the New Testament standard for elders said such a man must be the husband of one wife. But even if the Bible said that was best, men always strayed.

"If Abe was like that—a man who couldn't help chasing lust—I'd know. I think he's a good man."

Clara found herself shaking her head. "You can't know that for certain. Even if he hasn't strayed in the past, there's no guarantee he won't in the future. He's a man."

Maudy looked down, her expression hesitant. "I suppose a girl like me can't be too picky. Abe deserves better. If we were married and he did stray...well, I guess I'd just have to remember not to cast stones. Someone like me's got no business hoping for love, let alone faithfulness."

"Maudy, no—that's not what I meant—"

"This is it." She pointed to a brick building with *Tahoe*

House Hotel painted in large white letters. Its second-story balcony wore a fresh coat of snow, and red bows with cedar boughs decorated the windows.

Clara stopped the buggy close to the sidewalk so Maudy could hop down without getting mud on her shoes. "I didn't mean to discourage you, Maudy. You deserve faithfulness and love. If a man could just obey what the Bible says—to love one wife..."

Maudy turned back, forcing a smile. "They serve the evening meal at six o'clock every night at Mrs. Matthews's house. Five cents a meal if you ever want to stop by. I attend the Presbyterian church on C Street every Sunday. You should come. You could use some hope and healing too."

Clara blinked. Even after her forward remarks, Maudy still welcomed her. She smiled. "I'd like that very much. I'll see you Sunday." Maybe the hope and healing Maudy spoke of could be within reach. She turned her buggy around, her heart heavier than ever. Was there something waiting beyond men who always chased the flesh and a God who seemed so distant?

~

Sunbeams poured through the white muntins, fading only when the maid came to fix Clara's hair, cinch her into a corset, and finally lace her into a ruby-red-and-white silk ball gown. She needed to leave if she was to welcome guests with Father and Tessa as expected. But Clara lifted the bustle enough to sit at her writing desk, her skirts rustling softly beneath her.

The desk was ordered—papers stacked neatly, identical inkwells spaced evenly across the polished marble top. From a drawer, she withdrew the rough drafts of reports she'd submitted to the *Gold Hill Daily News*.

The parties she had covered had been beautiful. The latest music mingled with timeless carols like "O Christmas Tree." Glittering lights, tree boughs, and an endless flow of champagne brought joy, at least for everyone else. For Clara, each gathering only deepened the ache. Watching couples—young and old—twirl across dance floors or lean close together near frosted windows reminded her of what she would likely never have. Her heart remained heavy, not only from missing Mother but also from the sting of her conversation with Maudy.

Could men really love the way the Bible described? As Christ loved the church?

Her teeth clenched. "Never," she whispered.

A knock sounded at the door. Likely, the maid again, bringing her a reminder of duties as daughter of the host. The door swung on silent hinges, and Tessa entered, dressed in a green silk gown with enough braided gold trim and glittering beadwork to pass for a Christmas tree.

"Hello, Tessa." Clara rose, her slippers sinking into the wool rug. The train of her gown whispered as she stepped forward.

"Good evening." Tessa clasped her hands together. Her pretty smile revealed perfect teeth that would be envied by any girl at Clara's finishing school. "John asked me to fetch you. He'd like us to come down together."

Clara froze. Her mind flitted back to the only Christmas ball she'd attended with Mother, when they had readied together with Aunt Melanie and Cousin Aubrey. How fun it had been, sharing stories, laughing. Now—Tessa wanted to walk down the stairs as if they were the best of friends.

"I told John you wouldn't want to go down with me," Tessa added with a forced chuckle. "He's always so hopeful, especially since this is your first Christmas home in so long..." She nibbled the tip of her gloves—a habit Clara suspected would have transferred to her fingernails had she not been wearing them.

Clara looked away, ashamed of the bitterness swelling in her chest. When had she become so petty? So judgmental? She didn't want to be like the Baltimore socialites who tripped maids for amusement or mocked street women from the comfort of their carriages.

Tessa moved toward the door, hand brushing the knob. "I just thought, with this being your first year back, I'd try to..."

"Wait." Clara's voice caught even her by surprise.

Tessa paused with her hand on the doorknob, turning enough to meet her gaze over one shoulder.

"It will bring Father joy if we go down together."

Light flickered in Tessa's eyes, a breathless, hopeful shine.

Why did she care so much about the opinions of others? Clara's stomach clenched. "Well," she said, stepping forward and dimming the gas lamp near the door, "we'd better go."

Tessa sighed in relief. "That would be nice. You know, Clara, I had hoped when you returned, we might become friends."

Clara paused, unable to meet Tessa's gaze. Why would she want to be friends? Perhaps she was lonely. Maybe Tessa bore more shame over Daniel's conception than Clara realized.

"I..." Clara couldn't forget who Tessa was, what she'd done. And yet, when Tessa looked at her with such hope, Clara nodded for her to lead the way.

"I was afraid you'd hate me forever," Tessa said, looping her arm through Clara's.

Unwilling to be so cruel as to shake her free, Clara walked along. They reached the top of the grand staircase. Below, a few guests milled about near the door.

Tessa paused. "I have to warn you, Clara. You are in danger."

Clara blinked. "Oh?"

"There's someone you've encountered who isn't safe," Tessa whispered, eyes scanning the hall. "I think you already suspect."

"What are you talking about?"

"Mr. Vulpe. He's a thief. An escaped convict."

Clara stepped back, touching the pendant dangling at her collarbone. "That's not true. He's a miner from France."

Tessa leaned in, voice hushed. "Don't judge the heart by the outside of a man."

Clara pulled away. "So now you insult my intelligence?"

"No—Clara, you're smart. But you're young. You don't know how men manipulate emotions. They say things...make you feel things...just to get what they want."

Clara's chest burned, as did her cheeks, and her voice lowered when she spoke. "I am not like you."

Tessa's face flushed crimson. "Putting on airs, as usual. I told John that letting you return would cause trouble—and I was right. First, the mine. Now, this French convict."

"'Let' me?" Clara hissed.

"Yes. Your grandmother wanted you to stay in Maryland."

"I suppose you wanted that, too," Clara snapped. "And now you think we'll bond over gossip and slander?"

Tessa shook her head, continuing on as though not even hearing her. "It's been hard enough building a good life for Daniel. Now you come back and push John toward drinking again." She stormed down the stairs, skirts whipping around her. Father met her at the bottom, gently gripping her arms.

Clara stood frozen at the landing. What on earth had possessed her stepmother? And how could Father comfort her like that? Tessa was a snake in the grass.

Men can't help themselves. Mother's voice echoed in her mind. The words turned Clara's heart to ash.

Her assignment to report on the party for the *Gold Hill Daily News* loomed. She was expected to chronicle the festivities with precision and charm. The rustle of silk gowns and the shimmer of jet beads, the whispered alliances formed over punch bowls. Even the orchestra's selections and the quality of the champagne would be scrutinized by readers hungry for society gossip. So much for making a difference.

Regardless of her desire to flee down the opposite hallway away from the frivolity, she remained focused. If Beau did attend, Tessa might mistreat him. Clara could not conceive of that, so she steeled herself to fulfill her duties.

CHAPTER 9

Floor-to-ceiling windows mirrored the goings-on in the ballroom, the slightest outline of the moon making it through the reflection and frost. Outside—that was where Beau would like to be—but instead, he was standing shoulder to shoulder with Virginia City's elite. Crystals in the chandeliers twinkled with the gaslights aflame, the light settling on the inhabitants of the room, dulling every gray and blue and causing the oranges and reds to practically glow.

John Alexander gripped Beau's arm and pulled him through the crowd. "I want you to meet someone."

Stomach still cramping with nerves at the sight of the rich environs where he did not belong, Beau resisted the urge to dig in his heels. He had told himself that morning he would not come but after thinking far too often on Clara during his shift, and the disappointment she would feel if he did not attend, Beau had donned the only suit he owned and hiked up to Millionaire Row. They needed to speak of the salting and see if she had changed her mind about speaking to her father, anyway.

John waved to a man ahead, his manner so congenial that

Beau found himself following. Clara's father—Titus Alexander's brother—was a kinder man than Beau ever expected.

The tall man John had acknowledged possessed light-brown hair combed neatly back, a straight nose, a thick mustache, and direct eyes. His frock coat was the finest silk with a gold fob hanging from one button to his pocket. Beau's own workman's timepiece suited his store-bought jacket, which was a little tight on the shoulders. It fit him about as well as the room. Too small, overly warm—and worst of all—foreign.

John Alexander brought them to a stop in the middle of the crowded ballroom, passing Beau a confident grin when the man greeted them with an Irish accent that curled around every word. "Good evening, John. It's a grand party you've hosted."

John gripped the Irishman's hand, wishing him a Merry Christmas, then gestured to Beau. "I want you to meet Mr. Beau Vulpe of France. Beau, this is my good friend Mr. John MacKay—one of the Bonanza Kings, as it were."

MacKay shook his hand firmly, his palms as callused as Beau's own. "A pleasure to meet you. France?"

"Yes, sir. Lorraine, originally. My father owned ironworks there." It was strange to even think of that time, before the war, and his life with his father. Stomach tight, he mentally withdrew from those thoughts.

"Yes, I have heard Alsace and Lorraine have a wealth of iron deposits. A valuable region, to be sure." MacKay did not need to comment on the war, or that those two important economic areas now belonged to Germany, nor the losses suffered by citizens. He glanced at Beau's rough hands, likely guessing he worked and did not own a mine. Still, he tasted the name as though trying to weigh its solidity. "Vulpe? A good French name. I imagine you attended university?"

"Yes, sir, I did. The École Impériale Polytechnique. I studied engineering, mathematics, and industrial analysis."

"Aha." John's eyebrows jumped to his hairline. "You are a polytechnicien?"

Nearly cringing at the term, Beau straightened his shoulders. "Not quite. I did not complete my studies."

"How long did you attend this fancy French university?" MacKay unbuttoned his tailcoat to settle a hand in his vest pocket.

"Three years." He'd offer no explanations about his father's failing health, the struggle of being a half Roma among the sons of France's military leaders and intellectuals, or the restlessness constantly crawling up his spine while he lived away from his mother's people. He'd been too wild for such a place, as he'd tried to explain to his father.

"Well, education isn't everything. I barely passed my language arts studies, and MacKay here has one of the wealthiest strikes in these parts, though he has little formal training." John gave his friend's arm a shove, to which MacKay grinned. "You wouldn't know it if you met him on a regular day. He still goes down into the mines, working with the men. Just trying to make the rest of us look lazy."

MacKay shrugged. "You don't need my help with that."

Both men chuckled, then MacKay shifted his attention back to Beau. "John tells me you work at the Peterson Mine. With your experience, why work for such a small outfit?"

"Peterson is a good man," was all he could think to say, even though he might not be working for him much longer.

"That is true, but there are many mines in Virginia City." John narrowed in on him with squinted eyes, likely doubting the future of the Peterson mine. "If you ever have need of another job, you may call on me."

"Or me." MacKay offered a handshake.

"Thank you. It was nice meeting you." He shook both the men's hands and moved on through the crowd, slipping on his gloves. The scents of lavender and bergamot from pomades and colognes mingled with the rich aromas of hors d'oeuvres and beverages. Couples ambled across the polished floor, some swaying in slow, practiced waltzes, the ladies' gowns sweeping the hardwood.

Over the heads of other men, he caught sight of a woman in a red silk dress descending the grand staircase across the room. There she was. Clara paused like royalty overlooking her subjects. Keen eyes searched the crowd, her brow slightly furrowed and cheeks pale despite a modest application of blush.

Was she looking for him? How he missed her random facts and the banter they'd shared before he told her he'd not attend the Christmas party because he didn't belong in her world.

His heart rate sped as Beau moved like an ore car on iron tracks. The nearer he drew, the more radiant she appeared. Her golden hair lay plaited high, adorned with a ruby-and-diamond tiara set with emerald leaves. Soft curls cascaded down one side of her neck to hide the birthmark he'd seen the first time they met. Down the steps she came, her dress trailing behind her. He met her there and took her hand.

"Hello, Beau." Her voice sounded small, and it was all he could do not to draw her a little nearer.

He didn't even think to return her greeting—just ran his thumb over her fingers—covered with satin gloves. "You are beautiful, Clara."

That brought some color to her cheeks, and she blessed him with one of her full smiles. "I didn't think you were coming tonight."

"I needed to see you."

Fine brows lifted, then she pressed her lips together before saying, "Do not tell me the infamous Monsieur Vulpe, adventurer extraordinaire, missed a simple lady of letters."

"'Lady of letters.'" He cocked his head to one side, leaning near enough to hear the subtle change in her breathing when he whispered, "Is this a new disguise?"

She giggled, squeezing his hand so she tugged him even nearer. Arms aching to be around her, Beau resisted the allure between them and nodded toward the dance floor. "Care to dance?"

"I think I have room on my card for one so handsome, but you mustn't tell my father." She lowered her voice to a whisper. "He might not like for me to dance with one of my guards."

"We best move quickly, then." He pulled her onto the floor as the band struck up a lively tune for a quadrille. Couples hastened to the middle of the floor, forming sets of squares.

Together, they weaved through the set, the moves straightforward, the rhythm quick and joyful. The dance ended as quickly as it began. The band swung into a slower waltz, the melody of "Meet Me by the Moonlight" carried by a sweet little fiddle. Behind Clara, that spindly reporter, Theo, headed toward her as though to ask for a dance. Unwilling to let the snake near her, Beau defied societal decorum and drew Clara close for a second dance, not even glancing to see the man's reaction.

Her movements were easy, as though they'd partnered in dances for years. "What are you staring at?"

"That." He pointed his eyes toward her crown. "Who are you, the princess of Christmas?"

She laughed, the sound sweeter than sleigh bells. "No. I am the *queen* of Christmas."

"Is that so?"

The soft glow of the gas lamps gleamed on her smooth shoulders when she shrugged and nearly caused him to lose his step. The fading of her smile sobered him, though. "If anyone was the queen of Christmas, it would have been my mother. She loved decorating the tree and going to parties.

Hosting the Christmas Eve Ball was her special event. She made every year magical, but I haven't much of the holiday spirit left in me since she passed." She glanced at the grand pine tree in the next room when they neared a doorway.

Then her eyes focused on him, bright as though having just awakened. "I apologize. Such talk does not make for very happy conversation, especially on Christmas Eve."

"You lost your mother. It makes sense that you would miss her. I have lost many loved ones. It is hard." The constant pain in his chest deepened, and, with Clara looking into his eyes, her gaze so open, he allowed the admission. "My *maman, père*, wife, and son."

"Son." Nearly inaudible, her whisper preceded the pooling of tears in her twilight eyes—blue like the hour when everything softens, and even the truth feels gentle. A tear slipped over honey-colored lashes and left a streak down one of her cheeks.

"Sometimes I don't know which is more painful, the loss or just living." She looked down then, defeat in her demeanor.

He held her a little closer. "Life is a gift many do not hold for long. We are blessed." It felt good to make the statement with such conviction.

That seemed to warm her, and she nodded ever so slightly.

Would that he could fix this trouble with the mine and newspaper, and resolve the issues that so deeply hurt the Alexander family. For now, he'd simply sway with her. He missed being close to a special woman. Brightening her day and making her life a little better.

Staggered by his thoughts and how they had run to such deep emotions, Beau nearly missed the last few steps. The dance was over.

His breath caught when he met her gaze, a flicker of something unspoken passing between them, long enough to stir a storm inside him. Here was something sweet and tempting. Something he was not worthy of. But he'd already learned he couldn't bow out when the issues at the salted mine were still unresolved, and he had actually made Clara's life better speaking out in front of Doten so she'd get the job. He had also kept her safe the night of the shooting, and somehow, every time he drew near, she lit up—as if he brought a quiet warmth to her world. But how long could he stay for her?

~

*H*eart aflutter, Clara kept her hand in Beau's arm as they wended through the ballroom. Off to one side, where red velvet drapes hung near a frosted window, Alf Doten and Mr. Goodwin conversed in a lively manner, hands waving elaborately. They likely argued some political point, reminding her of Mr. Peterson's predicament and the possible backlash once the truth of the mine was known.

Clara leaned closer to Beau so he could hear her amid the frivolity. "Have you discovered anything more about Mr. Peterson's mine?"

"No. I stopped by Phineas Malcolm's office again. He is still gone. An associate of his said he would be happy to check a sample. I cannot smuggle one out. I have not told Mr. Peterson of my suspicions because we had not spoken in some time. I do not want to betray your trust."

"I appreciate that." Her voice sounded steadier than she felt. "You must tell him, though. Poor Mr. Peterson." She fidgeted with the edge of her glove. "I think I will go and look in my father's study now. He may have kept the report. Will you stay here as lookout?"

"Lookout for what?"

"My father, of course. Or Tessa." He started to shake his

head, but Clara gripped his arm. "Please, Beau. If I ever hope to write professionally, I cannot have this weighing on me, and when you speak with Mr. Peterson, you need to know as well. I won't be long." She turned away before he could respond and swept through a nearby doorway and down a hall—away from the partygoers to where the gas lamps shone dimly.

At last, she came to Father's study. She lit a lamp mounted near the door, and the light glanced off the wood-panel walls. Clara crossed to the cabinets where Father kept business files. She'd just begun her search when a familiar male voice sounded behind her.

"What have we here?" Clara turned with a start to find Theo leaning against the doorjamb, his arms crossed and a smile on his handsome face. "Clara, I know you want to be a reporter, but really—snooping through your father's study?"

Letting out a sigh, Clara waved him away. "This part of the house is off limits to guests. Kindly show yourself out."

He slapped his fist to his chest and grimaced. "Ouch, that hurts. I thought we were friends."

She shook her head and headed his way, ready to usher him out when he caught her hand and spun her around. Then his arms were around her, and he sang "Goodbye, Liza Jane"—a song from their youth that swept her back to happier times and summer-time parties.

She tried not to smile, yet she let him lead her for a couple of steps. Then, with a shake of her head, she pulled back. "We are not friends. You lied to me and—"

"I never lied to you. I did what I had to, to give you a chance at the paper. Why can't you see that?" He shrugged, hands open and eyebrows raised. "I thought I was helping you. Honestly, Clara, don't you think you'd be happier married, with children, and a good man to love you?"

Her face warmed for how much she'd confided in this man

when she, in her youth, had trusted him a little too much. Clara clasped her hands. "You need to leave. You sneaked back here, and you know my father would not approve."

He snickered. "Since when do you care about your father's approval?"

Flexing her jaw, Clara motioned toward the door.

Theo glanced toward the cabinets she'd been searching, but before he could speak, Beau stepped into the light, holding the door open with one long arm. "The lady said to leave."

Theo's expression darkened. "First, you steal all Clara's dances, and now you follow her into the private rooms of the house?"

Beau struck an intimidating pose with his thick shoulders flexed and gaze as sharp as a razor blade, black brows hovering over piercing eyes.

"I've heard about you, Vulpe. A liar who hides down in Gold Hill, working for a shoddy outfit like Peterson's."

Clara stepped before him, her hands on her hips. "For your information, Mr. Atticus, Beau Vulpe is welcome in my house and has reasons to remain with Mr. Peterson—reasons that are a sight more honorable than you could understand."

He turned on her. "Are you seriously vouching for this man, Clara? He is a foreigner no one trusts. You don't know anything about him."

"I don't know what gossip you've been listening to, but you're wrong." She stepped aside, gesturing toward the door. "And you need to leave."

Beau allowed enough room in the doorway for Theo to barely squeeze through, then he grabbed him by the upper arm and pulled him close.

Theo flinched and squirmed, color climbing up his cheeks.

"If any harm comes to her, I will find you." Beau let Theo go so suddenly, the smaller man stumbled away, casting a hateful glance back—not at Beau but at Clara.

After he left, all was quiet, then Clara rubbed a shiver from her arms. "I don't think he means me harm."

Beau turned his narrowed gaze from down the hallway. "How long have you known Theo Atticus?"

"He came to work as a stable boy about a year before my mother died." She returned to the cabinets. "I used to fancy him, but since I've returned, he doesn't seem as impressive." Not like the man behind her. What a shame she had foolishly given Theo her first kiss—a goodbye gesture that had seemed the most romantic thing in the world but suddenly seemed stupid.

Beau's footfalls told her he approached. When he spoke over her shoulder, his nearness warmed the skin on her neck. "What will we do if we find the report? I will not steal it from your father."

"I..." Clara started to turn, but her dress caught on the side of the cabinet. "I do not want to steal it."

"Good." His voice was raspy.

The same tug of attraction that had teased her senses throughout the dance strengthened, and when his knuckles gently brushed her cheek, she let her eyes slide closed.

"You're so beautiful, Clara. Thank you for defending me to Atticus." He cupped the nape of her neck.

Before he could draw her close, she shook her head. The rough skin on his palm grazed her cheek. "Beau, you said you are leaving."

He sighed, his gaze lingering on her lips. "I don't want to."

"Then kiss me." She leaned against him, offering her mouth, and he touched his lips to hers, softly, cautiously. Clara sighed and leaned into him, clasping the hand he laid upon her neck.

Angry voices sounded down the hall, and Clara drew back. "Oh, no. My father must have caught Theo in this part of the house."

Beau grimaced, his breath leaving him in a compressed hiss as he pressed a hand to his mouth.

Her heart thundered, and she stepped back. "Oh." He regretted kissing her. Shaking his head, he reached for her, but she put out a staying hand. "It's fine."

Men always leave. Mother's words kept her rooted in place. All that was warmth and life bound into a cold stone that sank into the pit of her stomach, yet she had the wherewithal to move back toward the cabinets as Father's steps approached the study.

He stepped into the room, his gaze landing on Clara. "Did Theo upset you?"

"No. Beau sent him away." She sifted through the files, no longer caring that he had caught her nosing about. Indeed, the notion seemed trivial in light of Beau's rejection, and hiding the truth from Father would accomplish nothing.

Father offered Beau a handshake. "You looked after my daughter. I thank you." His voice softened a little when he addressed Clara. "What are you looking for?"

Unwilling to hide her flaws, and numb after Beau's regret over kissing her, Clara turned, shrugging her shoulders, then clasping her hands. "I was looking for the geologist report you had done on the claim Mr. Peterson bought."

Father raised his chin, then nodded as he strode across the room to her. "You learned that the geologist test Mr. Atticus obtained read differently than the one I received?" He glanced at Beau, likely guessing he had told Clara as much.

"Yes, Father. Do you have the report?"

"No. I saw no reason to keep it once I learned the value. Once I read your article, which I believed to be falsified, I disposed of it on the off chance that blame might later fall on you. I want you to have success in everything you do." He closed the cabinets. "Clara, you were right when you told Alf Doten that you are a talented writer, and I know you to be above reproach—one of the most honest people I've ever encountered. When it comes to the Peterson mine report, you trusted the wrong person, and you shouldn't have to pay for that."

She frowned, looking between Beau and Father. "That's not true. I am responsible for every word I've written."

"You are young and should be protected, not preyed on by men like Theo Atticus."

Still, this was her fault. She'd allowed her need for success to drive her to go down into a dark mine alone and collect ore samples—a reckless decision because she wanted to impress Mr. Goodwin so much. That same desire pushed her to trust a man she hardly knew anymore.

Father wrapped an arm around her, hugging her. "You should be protected, even when you chase a career like newspaper reporting that is far beneath your capabilities." She opened her mouth to protest, but Father raised a hand. "I know, this is important to you. That is why I did not object when Alf offered you a job for the *Daily News*. So you could get a taste of the life of a reporter."

So he didn't trust her to be intelligent. He was just looking out for her. She deflated like a hot air balloon as it cooled.

"I couldn't have you tagging along behind Atticus." He ushered her toward the door.

"And here I thought I got Clara the job." Beau slipped his hands into his pockets. "It seems you are very generous, trying to find employment for others everywhere you turn."

"Neither of you got me the job. Just because you agreed, Father—and Beau, because you brought up my interest in reporting." Clara placed her hands on her hips. "I am smart and can get by on my own merit, you know. I am not just some dumb female."

Both men stopped in the hall and stared at her. Beau was

the first to respond. "At no point since meeting you did I believe you were anything but intelligent."

"Unwise, at times"—Father chimed in—"but no one can deny your intellect, Clara."

Nodding numbly, she started down the corridor again, and the men followed, the muffled hum of Christmas cheer echoing from the grand rooms ahead. "What did you mean when you said Father is trying to find employment for others?"

Beau made eye contact for just a moment, his features hardening. "He tried to convince MacKay to hire me as an engineer."

Father frowned. "Beau, your talents and education would be best used in another mine. You've been educated as a polytechnicien."

Clara's lips parted, and her eyes widened as she slowed and stared at Beau.

He shifted and avoided her gaze.

Father stopped with his back to the well-lit rooms where the warmth of lanterns mingled with the lively strum of guitars and the harmonious blend of the band playing "The Holly and the Ivy." "By the way, Beau, I would like to speak with you soon —on a personal matter."

"When?" Beau asked, seeming undaunted.

"Come find me when you're ready."

Beau met Clara's gaze. "I'm afraid it is time for me to be going. Mademoiselle Clara, thank you again for defending me to Mr. Atticus."

"No need to thank me." Her voice softened. "I only spoke truth."

As he inclined his head and shook hands with her father, Clara's fingers fidgeted at her sides, her stomach twisting with unease. Her thoughts like a snow storm, she hardly responded as Father accompanied her back to the ballroom.

Beau would speak to Mr. Peterson now that they knew the

mine was salted. The poor man. What did that mean for Clara's future in journalism? And for the shareholders who had bought stock because of her recommendation of the mine? Was it wrong to let Theo take all the blame?

Even more upsetting...Beau regretted kissing her, which hurt far worse than it should.

CHAPTER 10

Beau's throat tightened where he sat in Mr. Peterson's parlor, rubbing his cold thighs after having come in from the chill. He'd walked directly from the Alexanders' to the old man's house, wanting to get the conversation over with, and completely forgot that it was, in fact, Christmas Eve. Since Mr. Peterson was alone, though, Beau had decided to accept his employer's offer of coffee and pie despite the late hour. Dodge was probably out gambling or at a house of ill repute. The imbecile didn't have the good sense to be around family on Christmas Eve.

Once Mr. Peterson brought out pie and coffee, he smiled like a kid peering into a candy jar, yet motioned for Beau to partake ahead of him.

Beau took a bite of the apple pie, its sweetness mellowed by a gentle warmth that lingered on his tongue, while the flaky, buttery crust melted in his mouth. He nodded his approval, and then, after taking a single bite, the mine owner regaled him with memories of Christmas Eve with his family. Mrs. Peterson had died of typhus fever, which she caught nursing sick children back to health.

"We had a daughter. She lives in Salt Lake City. Married a farmer, but he is good to her and their children." Mr. Peterson reached into his pocket, the amber light in the room catching on a pair of spectacles that perched on his nose. "Here's a picture of them." He held up a stereoview of a pretty lady not much older than Clara with two fat tots on her lap.

Beau grinned at the boys, one with a huge smile and the other with his face wrinkled as though about to cry.

"That is where I want to be, with my grandchildren, not in this godforsaken mining town."

"Why are you here, then, sir?" Beau set the mug down on the small table between them.

"Dodge was working here when the fire swept through and took three houses and two of my businesses."

Beau rolled his suddenly stiff shoulders. "Sorry to hear that. The fire devastated many a businessman."

"Indeed. He lost a good friend too. I didn't want him going through that alone." He sighed long. "I'll tell you what...I don't always know the right thing to do as a father. I wonder if my papa ever felt that way."

"I'm sure he did. No father is perfect, and a good père knows it—but that is all right. If we were perfect, our children would never need God. When we fail, they can turn to Him."

Mr. Peterson leaned back in his overstuffed chair, the furniture nearly swallowing him up. "So what brings you to my door on this holy night?"

"Well, sir, I am afraid I have bad news." He gripped his hands into fists, his left heel tapping. "I found something in the mine about two weeks ago." Beau fished the buckshot cap out of his shirt pocket and handed it to Mr. Peterson. "I suspected, in November, that the ore quality might be going down. That we were digging in the wrong place. Some boys said they heard a ghost in the mine, something that sounded like thunder.

When I found this in the new tunnel, I thought it might be salted."

Mr. Peterson turned the metal between his wrinkled index finger and thumb. "You tell anyone about this?"

"No, sir. I didn't want to cause a fuss for no reason." Wait... he'd told Clara. Well, he wasn't mentioning her and then have to answer questions about her involvement.

"Why did you wait two weeks to show me this?"

"I had hoped to find proof that the mine might contain rich deposits of precious metals."

"And you found proof it does not." Mr. Peterson pocketed the cap, then buttoned his vest. "The mine is bust. No good. Probably never was."

"It would appear that way, oui."

Heaving a great sigh, Mr. Peterson leaned back in his chair. "I appreciate your honesty." He sat there for a long time, quietly staring into the fire, the lenses of his spectacles glowing. "You know, sometimes things don't go the way we'd like."

Beau wasn't sure what to say, so he just nodded.

"I served on a jury in Salt Lake once... Ugly business—juries."

That stilled him. He blinked, and the air around him seemed to press in, colder than the winter beyond the windows. *Salt Lake.* The name scraped across a scar he didn't like to touch.

Could Peterson have seen him then? He'd been paraded like a criminal in a circus—shackled, half starved, his name smeared across every newspaper west of the Colorado. The Alexander abduction trial was no quiet affair, and he was the last gang member caught. No man could sit through that and not remember his face.

No—Peterson could not have. Otherwise, Beau wouldn't be sitting at the man's table eating pie. He'd never have offered the job at the mine or welcomed him into his home this Christmas Eve night.

He cleared his throat, voice taut. "What do you plan to do, sir?"

"I, ah, I don't know." His frail shoulders stooped, thick white eyebrows blocking the view of his face. "I wouldn't blame you if you went looking for work elsewhere, though."

"I will probably leave town."

"Why, there are plenty of places out there to work." He gestured toward the window, the distant tapping of the stamp mills confirming the mining towns were thriving.

"I always planned to leave. Your kindness when I arrived..." Suddenly unable to speak, the feel of inadequacies and gratefulness building inside him, Beau shrugged. "Is there anything I can do?"

"No. No. Nothing to do." Mr. Peterson offered a handshake, rising and gesturing Beau toward the door. "It was good of you to stop by. You have a merry Christmas, now."

Beau bid his employer goodnight. What else could he do, when the man clearly wanted to be alone? As he stepped out into the slow, softly falling snow, along the road that curved near Mr. Peterson's house and the neighboring property, Beau's heart felt heavy. Perhaps the man would move to San Francisco, where his daughter lived. He might find happiness there, especially if Dodge remained in Virginia City.

One thing was certain—Beau had a choice coming. He could work for one of the other local mines or move down the mountain and finally sever ties with the Alexanders.

~

Clara turned over in her bed once again, the memory of Beau kissing her a delight and a torture. She understood his regret. After all, the kiss had been rash. They had no commitment between them. What a shame it had not the opposite effect on him, prodding him to stay in Virginia City. To gain permission from her father to court her. But he did not want that.

Clara sat up, her room dark except for the glow of coals in the hearth. Casting her covers aside, she swung her feet out of bed. She had to ask Father what he thought. If he approved of Beau, maybe he could get the man to stay in the area. Offer him a job, since Mr. Peterson's mine was bust.

She snatched her wrapper from a chair near the bed and swept it around her, an internal voice stilling her as she slid on her slippers. *What happened to "men can't be trusted?" Do you think Beau is any different than Father?*

Yes. Hopefully. Maybe. Clara's shoulders sagged. "I will never find out if he leaves." And with that, she tiptoed out of the room, heading for Father's study. It was Christmas Eve, but hopefully, he'd follow his usual habit of passing late-night hours there before turning in.

Light shone beneath the door of Mother's old library. Who would be in there?

Clara drew near the door and leaned close, listening, but no sound came. She turned the knob. Warm light and the sweet scent of pine and wood smoke invited her inside. Clara peered past Empire-style mahogany furniture with inlaid bronze and gilded edges. The table with a lacquered finish reflected the firelight, a vase full of holly standing behind the couch—its dark-green leaves and crimson berries a splash of Christmas cheer. A limestone fireplace, carved with delicate motifs, sat proudly against one wall, its hearth ready for a winter's eve.

The crimson fringe of a velvet skirt draped around the edge of the couch with the sphinx carvings. As though lurched back in time, Clara imagined Mother lounging there, reading Christmas correspondence. With a wisp of mistletoe in her golden hair and a gentle smile on her lips, she looked so serene, so alive.

Movement near the fireplace caught her eye. "Mother?" Clara eased farther in, memories fighting for a grip in a reality where Mother did not exist anymore.

But it was Tessa, not Mother, who sat upright with a gasp. And she wore Mother's lovely Christmas gown. Beside her, Father sat with his collar loose and cheeks dark.

Realization that she had interrupted something intimate crashed in with embarrassment. "How dare you? In Mother's library!" She hurried to the portrait of her parents on the mantel, the one she'd brought back from Maryland when she returned home. Taking the photograph, she turned it toward her breast as if to shield her mother's eyes from the goings-on in the room.

Father stood, extending a hand. "Clara, please listen—"

"Listen to what? The lies you told Mother? That she was the love of your life?" Tears spilled down her cheeks, and her voice cracked as she strode toward them. "That the attention you paid the silly maid was a drunken mistake? That your heart would always be hers?" She repeated the words she'd heard when, as a nosy sixteen-year-old hoping to overhear Christmas plans, she'd witnessed her father's confession of infidelity.

Red infused Father's face. He clenched his jaw and stood straight and tall. "You have no right to intrude on a private conversation, Clara Leann. What I tell my wife—"

"Was a lie, and she believed you!"

"You have no right to make that judgment." He advanced, glaring until the black of his pupils nearly covered the green of his irises. "To speak of things about which you know nothing."

"John..." Tessa stood, reaching for Father's shirtsleeve. "Perhaps it would—"

"You're claiming I know nothing?" Clara took a step closer, despite his anger as palpable as the heat of fire. "I know how she waited for you. Stayed on the patio there"—she pointed toward the door and the veranda where Mother had breathed her last—"refusing food or water. Watching the drive for your return from San Francisco, where you took this whore." She pointed a finger at Tessa when she unleashed the nastiest word she'd ever uttered.

Tessa gave a sob and ran from the room, her wails carrying down the hallway.

Clara heard another's cry, though—that of her mother, when Father had held her in the very same room he now used to rendezvous with his mistress-turned-wife.

"You killed her." Clara spoke the thought that had taken root when Father cast the first handful of dirt onto Mother's coffin. "This is all your fault, and you don't even care."

Father's face was dangerously red now. Sweat formed in beads at his temples amid black and gray hair, and he held his hands in large fists. "How dare you, Clara?"

"I was there when she died. Where were you?"

"Enough!" He grabbed her left arm, his shout filling the room. "I will not be chastised by a girl who has no idea what the world really demands."

Clara trembled, her emotions swinging between fear and anger. Though survival begged her to stop, she could not. "You're not even sorry."

He shoved her onto the couch and swiped the lovely vase of holly from the table behind. It shattered on the floor. Next, he swung around, grabbed a lamp, and threw it into the fireplace. When the oil font of kerosene broke, flames exploded from the hearth.

Clara scrambled away from the sofa, but Father ripped the drapes from the tall windows and shoved them in the fireplace. Flames licked the gold-and-burgundy Aubusson rug, sparking when they seized the fringe. Father hoisted a side table over his head and slammed it into the stonework, breaking off the legs.

"Stop, Father. Stop." Clara called to him in a shaky voice. "Mother's things."

Roaring in rage, his face twisted, he knocked the books off the shelves, throwing a first edition of *Emma* through a window. He did not form words or curses but sounded like an attacking animal.

Clara covered her ears. "Father, stop!" He was losing his mind.

She backed toward the doorway as he picked up a lovely pair of kissing figurines on the table and pitched them against the mirror above the marble mantel. Glass shattered and rained down onto the flaming carpet.

Sobbing, Clara ran out as the butler and another servant rushed in to help with the blaze. Hopefully, they could keep her father from burning down the house.

CHAPTER 11

Beau ducked behind the side of a building to avoid the stinging wind, then turned in the white light of a near-full moon to follow John Alexander down C Street. After noticing Clara's father with no coat to ward off the cold, Beau had felt he had no choice but to follow him. What was the man doing outside this time of night in such a state? Something must be wrong.

After his conversation with Mr. Peterson late that night, Beau had been unable to turn in. He'd gone out for a cup of coffee at one of the saloons that stayed open all night. The temptation to drink as he had in the past was there, but it no longer ruled him. And how glad he was that it did not as it did John Alexander.

Striding past the saloons with their outside lamps showing patrons the way in, Beau followed John until he reached a brick building which housed the elite Washoe Club. There was no way they wanted the likes of Beau inside, but if Mr. Alexander left the club drunk, he might not make it home safely. Should Beau intercept him now—possibly earn his ire—or leave him be?

John stood before the back entrance, a single doorway at the corner of the building. He hung his head, his shoulders rising and falling.

Beau paused a few feet behind him. "John?" It still felt strange not to call the man Mr. Alexander.

He turned and stared at Beau with a blank expression. "Beau, what are you doing in this part of town?"

Beau forced his shoulders to remain straight despite the insinuation that he was not welcome at the distinguished club. "I was coming back from visiting a friend when I saw you walking around without a coat. I thought you might be in trouble."

"Trouble. Indeed." He shivered, then glanced toward the doorway. "Care to join me for a nightcap and a game of billiards?"

"It's been years since I played billiards, sir, and I don't drink."

"Just the same..." John nodded toward the door. "It's cold. Come on in."

Beau followed, not voicing his hesitation further, but he couldn't very well stay out in the cold and wasn't willing to leave John until he was certain the man was well.

Inside, the warmth and pleasant sounds of conversation wrapped around him. A carpeted stairway led to the second story and the upper hall. John remained quiet, as though he'd forgotten Beau accompanied him. He led the way through a door and into a card room with billiards tables. The room measured about fourteen-by-fourteen feet, with a wine and dining space toward the back. A sidebar of black walnut ran along the wall, elegantly and elaborately carved.

Fancy paintings of storms hung on the walls, and blue-and-gold drapes framed plate-glass windows. His feet sank into the thick carpets, his dark, scuffed boots as ugly as donkey hooves against the woolen threads. A tight knot formed in his gut.

At the age of six, he'd been delivering quail eggs for his mother. The woman buying them had taken one look at his filthy, bare feet on her spotless floral rug and screamed at him. It was the first time he experienced the slur of *Gypsy*, but not the last—and the same for the slap she delivered. Maman died less than a year later, and Beau moved to his French father's home, but he never forgot what it felt like to be turned out of the house like a filthy animal. He didn't belong here.

"My older brother taught me to play." John bent beneath silver-polished chandeliers. He rammed a long cue into the white ball. It shot forward, connecting with the group of balls at one end of the table. They snapped and clattered into one another, rolling into various positions.

John took a deep breath, obviously gaining calm. So did Beau. The crack of billiards brought to mind long, warm nights with his père—a life dead now. He hadn't spoken of his père in years—it hurt too much—but the scent of cigars in the air, the sound of the game, and the expectant look John gave him brought forth a wave of loneliness.

John handed him a cue, and Beau smeared chalk on the tip, then chose his shot. He bent to line up his cue ball with the solid red. Breathing out, he thrust the stick forward. The white ball surged into his target, sending it into the nearest pocket. He set his sights on his next goal and made his way around the table.

They had played five games when John racked the balls a final time. "You still objecting to a nightcap?"

"Yes, sir. Some can drink and some can't." Not and keep themselves. Beau had indulged in drink and dangerous living when he first came to America, and he'd lost himself. He couldn't risk even one drop of liquor touching his tongue.

"A wise statement." John waved to a waiter. "Two cups of coffee."

Soon the man had them settled near the fire, above which a marble mantel supported three bronze statuettes, the one in the center bearing an elegant clock. Above them hung a French plate-glass mirror. Beau sat on an upholstered chair that matched the carpet, listening to John talk about learning billiards from his father as a boy and the competition between him and his brother.

Beau's skin tightened just thinking of Titus Alexander. The last time they met, Titus kicked Beau through a window—which would never have happened if Beau hadn't been fighting another man. Still, he couldn't blame him. After all, Beau had stolen his son. If he had been able to find the men who took his son during the Franco-Prussian War, he'd have killed them.

Shaking away the thoughts, Beau looked up to find John watching him. "You a father, Beau?"

Beau tightened his fists and remained silent.

"I'd say you are, judging by the way you grabbed Daniel the other day."

Beau drew in a deep breath. "I could have just as easily missed. God provides when we fail." Because He knew how very helpless Beau was when it came to keeping others safe.

John swallowed, turning his focus to the crackling blaze in the hearth. "You think so?"

"Yes, sir. I know I'm weak and can't do anything good. Not really. I'm a born failure." A statement that seemed especially true amongst the elite of Virginia City.

"None are born a failure." Anger tinged the older man's response.

"Oh, no?" He chuckled and shook his head. "I suppose when you're born into wealth, that is easy to believe."

A certain calm fell over the other man's face, and he nodded, leaning back in his chair and waiting until the coffee was delivered and two mugs poured to speak again. "Wealth is fleeting. It can be gone in a day, destroyed by natural disaster or people. We are all made in God's image. We can all work to make ourselves better."

"I was born in '45 to a Roma woman in France. When she died, I was sent to a Frenchman I did not know—my father—to live a very different lifestyle."

John stilled with his cup halfway to his mouth, still looking unconvinced.

"John, the final emancipation of the Roma was in '65, same year Confederate General Robert E. Lee surrendered at Appomattox Courthouse."

John seemed unsurprised to learn that Beau had been born to an enslaved woman, simply nodding. Beau shifted slightly, his shoulders tightening. Why had he mentioned his parentage? Even if John was comfortable with the conversation, he wasn't. Best to change subjects. Americans loved to talk about wars. "Where were you that day, in '65?"

John groaned and massaged his temples. "Commanding the 1st Maryland Infantry. Annalise had just been diagnosed with tuberculosis. I was so scared she would die before I could make it home. Clara was only nine. I just kept thinking, I never should have gone to war."

"Why did you?"

He rolled his eyes and pushed a mug toward Beau. "My younger brother enlisted. He said it was a matter of principle. I thought he was just trying to be better than me. He always was." Beau grinned, and so did John, though his faded some. "I don't suppose you have a brother either."

"'Fraid not. My mother died before I reached ten."

"Clara was sixteen when she lost her mother." His gaze wandered again—only this time, a darkness filled his eyes. He was sinking into black thoughts, a dangerous place to go. "Waiter." John sat up, looking around. "Bourbon and a glass."

The young servant nodded and quietly walked to the sidebar on the other side of the room.

"You sure you want to drink when you still got the walk home?" Beau asked casually, earning John's dark stare.

"What business is it of yours?"

Beau shrugged and sipped his coffee. If the man wanted to be a fool, that was his prerogative. Beau wasn't above leaving a fool to his ways—except this was Clara's father. Kind, hopeful, honest Clara who, despite her persistence and courage, had a deep wound. If John drank and, on his way home, fell down one of the many steep inclines or was assaulted by thieves, Clara would be further scarred.

John stared into the fire, playing with his wedding ring. Unfortunately, Beau had heard the rumors surrounding the Alexanders, including the hints that young Daniel was conceived in adultery. That was a fiercely personal thing for strangers to talk about. How it must weigh on John, if he was a good man as Clara claimed.

"I was married to a girl I hardly knew. She was..." Beau's chest tightened so he could hardly breathe, but John focused on him with keen interest, and the waiter would soon return with the bourbon, so he continued. "She was the gentlest, most compassionate woman I've ever known. When war broke out between France and Germany, I moved her and our son to the city where I thought they would be safe." He shook his head.

John placed a hand on his shoulder, and the weight of grief intensified for a moment, then relented enough so Beau could speak again. "You have your children. A wife. You are not alone."

John withdrew his hand, watching the waiter return with the alcohol and pour for him, yet he sipped his coffee. "Clara blames me for her mother's death. She doesn't know that Annalise's tuberculosis had gotten worse that winter. She was so weak. I couldn't stand to hear her cough. Watch her die. So I threw myself into my work. I was exhausted, and I drank too much." He bowed his head, shaking it. "I wasn't there for her as I should have been."

Had he, in his absence and drink, been weak in other ways? Not that it was any of Beau's business. He looked out the window that faced Mount Davidson, only to glimpse his own reflection and the shadows of falling snow on the other side of the glass pane. It must be past midnight, and Beau had to work tomorrow morning. "I think I should be getting you home, sir."

Slowly, the man nodded in agreement, leaving the bourbon untouched. They started home—John in a borrowed coat.

When they came to a corner a few snowy streets down beneath a freezing sky, Clara's father reminded Beau there was still a subject they needed to discuss. Judging by the expression he'd given Beau when he entered the study earlier that evening, moments after Beau had kissed Clara, John had seen something of the interaction. He would likely tell Beau that Clara was too good for him, and he'd be entirely right.

If that was how John Alexander felt, why had he offered Beau friendship—insisting on the use of Christian names rather than surnames? Perhaps he did not want Beau to keep his distance. Perhaps he favored a courtship. John had been impressed by Beau's education. Had that been the reason MacKay and John offered Beau jobs that night?

If so, it would do little good. Beau would not work for an Alexander. But Peterson's mine was bust. Beau had to work somewhere, but did that mean he had to work in Virginia City? Was it time to move on?

~

The following morning, tears wet Clara's pillow. She drew a deep breath, hiccupping on a sob. Her throat was raw and her head and heart aching. She straightened her legs, pushing them from her blankets. Her stocking-covered feet set down on the cool floor, then the rug in the middle of her room. She passed her white armoire with gold inlay and delicately carved angels. Beside it hung her freshly pressed white-and-red silk ball gown. The delicate lacework around the bodice and shoulders was like something Christmas fairies might weave.

The Christmas Ball, with its lovely music and dancing, seemed far away now. Eyes swollen and throat scratchy, she pushed the dress out of the way and opened her armoire. She grabbed a traveling suit and dressed herself. Next, she dug into her chest and unearthed her carpetbag. Normally, for shorter trips, she loaded it with snacks, gloves, handkerchiefs, an extra shawl, and her money—but today she carefully rolled some underthings, a simple skirt and shirtwaists, and candied ginger to help with the wooziness she experienced on trains. Next, she stuffed blankets beneath the covers where she usually lay until it appeared she was still abed. That should keep the maid at bay until at least ten. Finally, she placed a note underneath her pillow where it would be found.

Father would never let her leave in the dead of winter, but she wasn't staying here. Not after last night. She covered her arm where he'd grabbed her, tears once again overwhelming her.

With her chin to her chest, a sob shook her to her core. She'd cried so much last night, she didn't think her body could make more tears. How could Father grab her, scream at her, throw the lamp into the fireplace? Did he want to burn down the house? Even if he didn't care about her, how could he have been so careless with Daniel but a few doors down? Not to mention, another fire in Virginia City might decimate the town.

Tessa's criticisms from the night before returned, reminding Clara that the family was better off without her. Clara forced the clasp on her bag closed, her hands shaking. She was bad for

Father. He was happier without her. Likely, he would not have even gone into such a rage with Mother.

It was better if she just left. But what about her brother? What if he grew up not knowing her? Did it matter if his home was a happier place without her?

She turned to the door, snatched up her cape on the way out, and slipped into the dark hallway. No one was awake except for a few servants whom she dodged. If she was going to make it to the train without Father stopping her—or coming after her—she had to leave unseen.

The side door gave a soft groan as she slipped outside. Cold met her like a breath to the face—sharp, uninvited. It stung her cheeks and sliced through the layers she'd barely noticed putting on. The sky had warmed with a glow of yellow on the eastern line, down the mountain and on to the valley, which was surrounded by rugged mountains.

Clara made her way through the town's sleeping streets. A crow called overhead. The world was quiet—but not empty. Houses stood watch with drawn curtains. Smoke rose in lazy ribbons from chimneys.

The ache in her chest a constant now, she pressed on toward the train depot. She would head back to Grandmother and Grandfather Alexander's house in Maryland where she knew she was wanted. There was nowhere else for her to go.

What would Beau say if he saw her, knew what she planned? He'd not like it, but what could she do? They had no commitment between them, and he kept saying he would leave. How ironic that she would be the one to leave him behind. She should have at least written him a note.

Her heels tapped on the wooden boardwalk, and Clara wrapped her cape a little closer, breathing into the fabric.

A figure wrapped tightly in a blanket hobbled forward with matted black hair and wrinkled face—one of the Paiute natives who lived on the outskirts of town. At the far end of C Street, past the quiet shops closed for the holiday, several women carried bundles of juniper and pinyon pine branches. Suddenly, Clara's life didn't seem so bad.

As she stood watching the people forging before sunup, someone grabbed her arm. Clara spun around, her eyes rounding with recognition.

CHAPTER 12

Beau rolled onto his back, one arm stretched above his head. The scent of woodsmoke and clean linens filled his nose. Shadows hid the boards in the ceiling above, though he could just make out the supportive beam running the length of the room as hints of daylight crept beneath the curtains. Across the small space—so near he could nearly reach out and touch the other bed—his roommate, Mr. Sanderson, snored, taking great big snorts of air. When first they boarded together, they had worked different shifts in the mine, so they seldom spoke—let alone slept at the same time. It had been a great setup...then.

He rolled so his feet hit the floor, one long sock loose around his toes. He adjusted it so the two were equal, then sat, head in his hands, heaving a breath. His chest ached as though a great weight sat upon it. Sleep had evaded him for most of the night. Memories of Clara plagued him, as did thoughts of a future absent of her.

He had rejected her. Clara was kind, honest, strong, intelligent, good-humored, and heart-stoppingly pretty. What he'd give if she could be his wife...

Impossible. In his twenties, before he quit school and disappointed his father, Clara was just the type of prospect for him. Now, he was a thirty-year-old widower with a criminal past, on the run from the law, and she was the last woman he could consider. He'd had no business kissing her, but when she'd offered, he'd not thought. He'd acted, and what a kiss. Never had so brief a touch ignited such a flame, verifying what he'd suspected and hoped to deny. Clara was not like other women.

Beau splayed his fingers into his hair and pulled the strands taut. He could no longer stay in Virginia City. Peterson's mine was bust. It was time to leave for Silver City.

He stood and pulled on a clean pair of pants, then began stuffing his few belongings into his bags. Silver City was just a few miles away. If he left with the morning train, he might round up work by the end of the day. But what about Clara? If he said goodbye, she would want to know why he didn't just work for her father. He couldn't actually tell her why. Neither could he tell her the truth. One thing he knew—he had to leave. This was his life now—working, running, surviving.

A knock thundered on the door, stilling his movements. His roommate coughed and rolled onto his side, only to recommence the cacophony of breathing.

Beau stepped past the slumbering man and reached for the door, his gut clenched. Any day, those he ran from could hunt him down. He should not have stayed in Virginia City so long.

"Hello? It's the landlady. Do open the door...please?" The woman's muffled voice came through the wooden barrier.

Beau heaved a sigh and reached for the knob. Sanderson must have forgotten to pay his share of the boarding fee again. The door swung on squealing hinges.

The sawed-off barrel of a shotgun pointed at his face froze Beau in place. Behind it, the city sheriff glowered from beneath a stiff new hat.

"Mr. Vulpe, you are under arrest for the murder of Mr. Andrew Peterson."

∼

"I did not kill Mr. Peterson!" Beau repeated, his voice steady despite the frustration in his words, as he sat cuffed to a chair within the unfinished walls of the Storey County Courthouse on C Street. Around him, cells with barred doors loomed, a stark reminder of his impending imprisonment. He had explained that he visited his employer the night before—telling Mr. Peterson about the mine salting and offering proof to support his claim. The information made little impression on the lawman.

Sheriff Kelly, a sweaty, bald man with the scarred face and knuckles of a prizefighter, leaned across the table, both hands planted on the wooden top. "The witness says ye was there at the time. And by yer own words, ye admit it. I also hear ye had trouble with the Petersons before now."

"I was on good terms with the elder Mr. Peterson." He'd had enough of listening to this man cast blame on him. "And yes, I wished him a Merry Christmas last night, but I did not kill him."

"Mr. Peterson was struck down last night, a blow to the head. Someone saw ye go into the house. No one else visited him that night, and his son was not home." The sheriff stepped back from the table, shaking his head and pacing. "If not ye, then who?"

Beau hung his head. Poor Mr. Peterson murdered. *Lord, why him?*

The place was made of cold stone. They occupied a large room with a table in the middle, each connecting room a cell with barred doors—a stark contrast to his room in the boarding house, Clara's fine home, or even the Presbyterian church he occasionally attended. What would those people think when they learned he'd been arrested for murder? Would they believe him guilty? Was this God punishing him because he'd run from the penitentiary?

Lord, I believed it best at the time. Was I wrong?

Obviously so, since he now had a murder charge looming over him. He had to think. Be smart and not emotional. A single breath barely helped to clear the stars from his vision or the ringing from his ears, but after five deep breaths, Beau crossed his arms and spoke. "Who supposedly saw me at Mr. Peterson's? His lazy son, Dodge? That man is a liar and a cheat, and anyone in this town can tell you that."

"And what would the folk of Virginia City say about *you*, Mr. Vulpe? Hmm?" Sheriff Kelly stopped his pacing long enough to angle a narrowed stare at him. "Nothing. Nobody knows ye here. There's no one to vouch for a French miner passin' through Virginia City — no friends, no family, no roots."

A fire in his gut, Beau shrugged. He didn't have anyone. Mr. Peterson was dead.

John thought Beau was honest, but how could he set John in the limelight when his family was still recovering from the scandal of the affair and death of the late Mrs. Alexander? Beau couldn't drag good people into his trouble, and so when Sheriff Kelly had finished his questioning, Beau entered one of the cells without protest. And there, he spent the night with restless dreams and warring emotions.

The sun was just coming up when the big door to the main room of the courthouse opened, letting in enough light to shine through the crisscross pattern of his cell.

"Mr. Alexander. Top of the morning, sir." Sheriff Kelly's cordial greeting seemed out of place in the jail.

Beau resisted the urge to hide his face. What if John thought Beau was a murderer?

"I heard that Mr. Vulpe was arrested for the murder of Mr. Peterson?" John's voice held a concerning note of weariness.

Beau sat up and walked to the door, the stone walls preventing him from seeing anything more. The men's voices were muffled, then John's made it through. "...impossible. He was with me at the Washoe Club playing billiards well into the night. A waiter there will corroborate for me."

"There was still time between the party and when he joined ye at the club. He was at the old man's house."

"It could not have been that long, sir. Besides, didn't the article say that Peterson left the house alone after Mr. Vulpe visited?"

"Blasted reporters, printing things before a lawman has time to conduct a proper investigation."

Keys jingled, then came the scuff of boots on the floor outside.

Beau stood frozen, hardly believing what was happening. Was he being set free? The door swung open, and the Irish lawman set a bulgy pair of eyes on him. "Seems your luck has changed, Vulpe, but do not leave town."

Beau stepped into the sunny main room, meeting John's gaze where he stood with mussed coat and day-old whiskers on his cheeks. "You're coming home with me, Beau."

His first step felt particularly heavy, yet with each one, he sensed himself growing lighter, until he moved toward the door, following John Alexander. A single thought echoed through his mind. Soon, he would see Clara, and then—all would be right again.

CHAPTER 13

Beau dozed in an overstuffed armchair near the fire in John's study. The ambient warmth from the hearth soothed his aching body after being in the hard, cold cell.

Gas lamps glowed softly against the bookshelves and a portrait of a man bearing the Alexanders' striking features. Two boys stood beside him—one a young teen, the other maybe five—presumably John and Titus Alexander with their father.

A light knock on the door brought his head up. Was it Clara? Instead of the fair-haired beauty he hoped to see, John stepped in, his countenance wearier than ever.

"Sorry to keep you waiting, Beau. I have told the maid to prepare a guest room." He ambled forward, his hands in his pockets. "I vouched for your whereabouts that night, but if the law turns on you again, you need to let me know right away. I will see you get a lawyer."

"I shouldn't need one. I did nothing wrong, which I told Sheriff Kelly. The man didn't want to listen to me." He leaned back in the chair, breathing shallowly.

"Sheriff Kelly was following leads, but I will vouch for your character."

Just as the sheriff had said—Beau needed someone to speak on his behalf. He clenched his jaw, pressure building until his molars ached. He stared into the fire, its steady crackle offering no comfort.

John sank onto the sofa across from him, his hands clasped. Gray and black whiskers outlined his jaw. Strange...Beau had only ever seen the man clean shaven.

"You look worn. Is something wrong?"

John stared at the carpet and nodded. He clasped and unclasped his hands, drawing in a shaky breath. "Clara is, ah..."

Beau's blood turned to ice. "Clara?"

"She left a note. She's gone home to Baltimore to live with my parents."

"In the middle of winter?" Beau sat up straighter, pain blooming in his ribs after the night on the hard floor, but he ignored it. "I didn't know that was something she planned to do."

Had she left by choice? Or had the tension in her home—a quiet undercurrent every time Beau had visited—finally snapped? And yet the last time Beau had seen Clara and her father together, they had seemed close.

"The two of us...we had a disagreement," John admitted. "A conversation about her mother. Clara left without notice. I only just came from down the mountain, looking for her."

Beau gripped the edge of his chair, knuckles popping. "She's traveling across the country alone?"

A beat of silence hung heavy between them. Then Beau shoved to his feet, breath sharp, vision swimming. He had to go after her. Find her and keep her safe.

John waved his hand, gesturing for him to sit. "I could report her as a runaway, but, for goodness' sake, she is a woman of twenty. I am afraid doing so would only make a bad situation worse."

"But if she is caught by the authorities, she is safe. They would contact you. Then you could go to her and escort her the rest of the way, if being in Baltimore is really what she wants."

John shot him a bloodshot gaze. "Of course. I should have thought of that. I didn't want Clara to hate me more, but, as you said, her safety…"

Beau looked away. What could Clara have been thinking, trying to cross the nation by herself? Didn't she know how dangerous it was? What if she was set on by men of nefarious intent? Beau knew a thing or two about that, having his own background in crime. How many times had he turned a blind eye while an accomplice snatched a purse, necklace, or an item of jewelry from one such as Clara? Too many. And some might intend much worse…

Throat constricting, Beau walked to a nearby window. The cool air off the glass bathed his hot face. The sky outside was so far away, scattered with clouds and a bright sun.

John stood, rubbing his hands on his pants. "I hope you will accept my offer to stay here tonight. I have to speak to Sheriff Kelly about Clara running away, anyway. Go see Mackay tomorrow. He'll give you a job in one of the richest mines in Virginia City. I hope you will accept the advice offered to you, Beau." John extended a handshake. "A wise man would."

Wisdom—in that, Beau was lacking, as he'd found out that spring when he'd followed the wrong men into a criminal journey that lost him what little of himself he had left after the war in France.

Perhaps here, in the handshake John Alexander offered, was the type of life he'd always missed. Perhaps it was wise to stay when his instincts told him to run. And by staying, at least he would know when or if Clara was found and returned to safety

~

Sunlight spilled through the window of the second-story room Clara had taken shelter in for the past two days. The boardinghouse room was barely wide enough to hold two people, yet Maudy had taken her in when she'd found her in the cold, exhausted and wandering the streets. Her lavender tea gown spilled over the cane chair, its hem brushing Maudy's boots tucked neatly beneath the bed. The air smelled faintly of rosewater.

Her thoughts drifted to Beau, wondering what he'd think if he knew of her father's hurt and her escape, but his regret after kissing her haunted her. When she finally rose that morning, she pulled out her journal and began writing, pouring out her heart in jagged lines between breathless prayers. Tears blurred the ink as she searched the Scriptures, not for a tidy answer, but for something solid to stand on.

"What are you writing?" Maudy asked over her shoulder, making Clara jump. "Didn't mean to startle you. Thought you might be hungry, so I brought you a sandwich." Maudy set a newspaper-wrapped bundle beside her.

Clara scanned her writing, then hesitantly read, "'Sometimes in this dusty corner of the West, I think love must be a quiet work—a bit like laundry done in creek water or prayers stitched into patchwork quilts. It doesn't always come loud, but when it's real, it changes everything.'"

Maudy's mouth fell open. "That is beautiful!" She peered at the words as though devouring them.

Clara moved a hand over them protectively.

"Oh, you needn't worry, miss. I can't read. I could never get the letters quite right on account of my bad eyes." She raised her chin. "But I can quote almost any verse in the Bible for you."

"Is that so?" Clara set aside her quill and picked up her Bible, meeting Maudy's challenging smirk.

They made it a game—Clara opening the Bible to random scriptures and Maudy quoting them with little to no effort. She finished the memory exercise with the parable of the talents from Matthew chapter twenty five. "'And unto one he gave five talents, to another two, and to another one; to every man according to his several ability; and straightway took his journey.'"

"That's amazing," Clara told her between bites of venison on sourdough. "It's a wonder you struggle with letters but remember so many verses."

"That's just my eyes going. My memory is fine. A good thing, too, 'cause those Bible verses got me through the hard times."

Clara brushed the soft fabric of her tea gown. "You know that the talents are not actual talents but money. One talent was roughly equal to six thousand denarii, and since a single denarius was considered a fair day's wage for a laborer, that totals about twenty years' worth of pay for just one talent."

"I didn't know." Maudy bit into her sandwich, then spoke around the food as she chewed. "You should send that there writing off to a magazine that publishes religious articles."

"Maybe. But I want to write something great."

"'Maybe...' Is that what the servant who was given five talents said? No. He traded them and gained five more. And the one with two doubled his as well. I betcha they didn't say 'maybe.' They said, 'Yes, sir.'" Maudy poked her, tickling her side, until Clara laughed and dropped her sandwich.

Waving her friend away, Clara stooped to pick up the food, her gaze catching hold of words on the paper that had served as the wrapping for her sandwich.

FRENCH MINER ARRESTED FOR PETERSON MURDER!

Clara snatched the newsprint from the bed and sat upright, speed-reading through an article. "What is this? Beau..." Her breath stopped as though someone reached in and grasped her lungs in a fist. She'd tried not to think about him, but his absence had been its own kind of ache, humming beneath everything she did.

"Oh, no." Maudy gripped her arm. "No, honey, that French fella of yours is just fine. That was a bad article. Now, just you sit down here." Maudy guided her to the bed, and she sank down, only to nearly slip off. "Monsieur Beau is safe. And innocent. Your daddy vouched for him. Probably saved his life."

"Mr. Peterson." Clara scanned the article again. "He was killed?"

"I'm afraid so, but it wasn't Mr. Vulpe. There was talk of it at the breakfast table this morning. Some randy young reporter down at the *Territorial Enterprise* got carried away. None of what he stated was factual. He got himself fired, and the *Enterprise* has issued a retraction."

"Poor Beau. I can't believe I slept through all of this." Clara stood, her knees still wobbly when she paced the scant space. "Who was the reporter?" She snatched up the paper again and read the culprit's name. "Theo Atticus."

"Who's that?" Maudy gathered the sandwiches, offering Clara hers, but she waved it away.

"He used to be a friend of mine." Beau had warned Theo not to hurt Clara, and she'd thought it strange at the time. Perhaps he knew more about Theo than she did. Likely, since she seemed to know so little these days.

"Well, I'll take the rest of this sandwich down to the Paiute boy who comes around for scraps this time of day. He'd love to sink his teeth into something so fine."

Clara paused, remembering the Paiute people who drifted like shadows through the town in the early dawn hours. "Maudy, what do the Paiutes do?"

"What do they do?" Maudy screwed up her face as though not understanding.

"They were out the morning you bumped into me and then yesterday morning as well."

"Ah, I suppose you don't see them much up on Millionaire Row."

Clara had to duck her head even as she shook it.

"They forage for anything they can find. Wood for fire, scraps of food thrown out the night before. Anything to carry off to their huts to survive."

"What a miserable existence."

"Well, this sandwich will make a difference to one of them." She waved the food, then added hers with a sigh. "I'll be going now. There's a meeting at the fire station on the Divide, and many of Mrs. Matthews's dinner guests want to finish with the evening meal and leave early."

"The meeting is tonight?" According to Theo, Mr. Goodwin had actually asked her to report on that meeting, but what if Father was there? And what if the men turned her out, as they had at the saloon? She tightened her fingers on her knees. "Maudy, I have something important for you to do for me, if you will."

"Oh, what is that?" Maudy spoke slowly, as though knowing Clara was scheming.

She stood and crossed her arms, only to spread them wide when she said, "I need pants."

~

The firehouse smelled of scorched wool, pipe smoke, and stale bread—not the most appealing scents, but Beau had nowhere else to go since the mine closed. Clara was gone, and though he should have headed to Silver City or contacted Mackay as John suggested, he hadn't. He was in limbo, unable to move forward. So he stepped into the firehouse meeting to get warm and catch the latest news.

Beau stood with other men who had fought the blaze two months before, many still wearing the scars. They packed into the firehouse by dozens—once the city's defenders, now called vagrants, thieves, drunks. Last year's muster had been twice this size. Tonight, they'd decide whether they'd keep standing or leave the misguided townsfolk to their own fates.

A grimy miner with a tattered gray beard shuffled past Beau, peering at his face as though trying to recognize him. Beau held the man's stare, offering him a nod. He'd not cower, though that feeling of being hunted skittered up his spine. The man walked past, a friend in similar condition close behind him. Beau hated having them at his back, but to watch them would only make him more conspicuous.

Chief Frank McNair stood at the front of the group. Though not a big man, he possessed a commanding presence, and his voice reached the rafters when he spoke. His face was weathered from years of smoke and sun, and his sharp eyes missed nothing. "Men, we are gathered here tonight to discuss what to do in case fire strikes our town again."

"Why?" A tall man with a burned ear stood up. "So the *Enterprise* can slander our names? So the city council can wag their tongues while we haul steamers through snow to save their blasted parlors?"

"Let it burn, I say." One man spoke up loudly. "Men lost their lives fighting that fire. Others will forever be scarred. But all we've gotten from this city is grief."

The din rose as more men started talking at once. Thomas Alcorn, captain of company one, came to the front of the fire hall to stand beside Chief McNair, his coat still damp from snow. "I say we walk. We gave all we had. Now we're met with contempt. Let those who spit on our boots pull their own hoses. Let them see what real danger feels like."

A man nearby muttered low, "Funny how the Frenchman's always around when something goes sideways."

The hair on the back of Beau's neck raised. Heads turned. Not all—but enough. His face heated.

"Too smooth by half," another man added. "Bet he knows more than he lets on."

This time, he did glance back in time to see the two miners holding a new script from the *Enterprise*. Light spilled across its headline smudged in grease—

FRENCH MINER ARRESTED FOR PETERSON MURDER.

Beau's stomach turned. The slanderous article by Theo Atticus was bad enough. At least the reckless reporter had finally gotten his comeuppance when he'd been sacked. But if this angry group of men turned their attention elsewhere, on him, he'd likely be swinging from a rope by night's end.

Around the hall, some men shouted while others stood silent. One unit disbanded, the captain walking away with his men. The chief promised change and outlined a plan for hydrants every other block and a paid fire department.

Near the back door, a slender young man with a derby hat leaned against a wall, scribbling in a notebook. Strange. The meeting was supposed to be closed to all except the firemen, yet that person looked like a reporter. He better not be that wily Atticus. Beau shuffled through the crowd to better see the man's face. Though his hat was pulled low, wisps of golden hair contrasted with the dark fabric. Something about him—

His heart jolted.

No. That could not be Clara. She was on her way to Baltimore, far away. He'd likely never see her again. But what if it was her, on one of her wild escapades in men's britches? Someone passed between them, and the scribbling man was gone.

Beau blinked. He must be losing his mind.

At last, the crowd dispersed, some leaving with a quick pace while others lingered near the big black stove in the corner of the room. Beau headed for the rear door.

Outside, snow fell in subtle, fluttering waves—so opposite the turbulence in the fire hall. Beau lengthened his stride, eager to be away from the tension of the meeting. Through the snow up ahead, a slight figure came into view, picking a course among puddles of slush.

Memory collided with the vision before him. When he'd walked Clara home that first day after finding her in the mine, he'd thought that even in the pants, she moved like a woman of breeding. Likely because of her time in finishing school.

Hanging back, he stayed close enough to see, yet far enough to duck into cover and remain inconspicuous. It couldn't be her. Not only had she left the note stating that she was going to Baltimore, but John had looked for two days for her. And yet Beau couldn't stop following her nor stop his heart from racing.

CHAPTER 14

The mysterious reporter entered a well-lit, two-story lodging house on B Street, farther north than polite society would venture. Beau waited, then opened the gate, which swung on creaking hinges, and trudged through the slushy snow up to the porch. He knocked on the front door, and it was opened by a tall lady with a severe-looking face and black braids that looped on either side of her head.

One hand landed on her hip, the stance firm and unyielding. "I don't accept male boarders, and I am all full, anyway."

"A friend of mine boards here. He just entered the house a moment ago."

She raised thin black eyebrows to her severe hairline. "That cannot be since I only board women. Goodnight, sir." A final glance—brief and dismissive—was all he got before the lock clicked into place.

He backed down, forcing his hands deep in his pockets, and turned away. Had he imagined Clara being here? He must have. Man, he was truly lovesick.

"Beau?" came the hissed call of a woman.

Upon hearing his name, he looked up to find Clara leaning

out of a second-story window, a mere shadow against the moon-cloaked side of the boardinghouse. When she waved wildly, Beau stifled a relieved laugh. It was Clara, here in Virginia City.

"Go around." She pointed around the corner of the house.

He jogged in the direction she indicated, climbing when the slant of the yard became severe. A small window glowed, then swung open. Light shining behind her tawny hair, Clara appeared in silhouette.

Beau eyed the tree growing beside the house. He took a running leap and landed in the branches, then climbed his way up until he gripped the windowsill and sat on the ledge as silently as an owl alighting on a branch. And there she was, wearing a modest wrapper and standing in a small washroom. Her eyes widened at his sudden appearance in the window, and she swept forward, right into his arms, a giggle in her voice. "What are you doing here?"

He trailed his fingers through her half-undone braid, her tresses gleaming like starlight spun into gold. "Looking for you. I thought I had lost you."

She blinked in surprise, searching his eyes, then she angled her head to one side. "And this from the man who plans to leave Virginia City. Who cannot stay for any reason." The sweet turn of her mouth hinted at kindness, even joy, though he'd rejected her kiss.

"Yet when I believed you were gone, I could not leave...for fear of never knowing what happened to you." He cupped her chin gently, tilting her face up so he could look into her eyes. "But something...someone...I saw tonight at the fire hall meeting made me think you're not quite done with adventures."

She gave a little gasp, her blush confirming his suspicions, though she lifted her head stubbornly as she said, "There are other things to discuss as well, Beau. You are here, holding me, yet you regretted kissing me before."

"I was a fool." He eased closer, careful on his precarious perch, giving her space to pull away.

Her eyes widened briefly as they searched his. "I thought..."

He tipped her chin and brushed his lips over hers—soft, intoxicating. The brittleness in his chest cracked wide when her mouth answered his with quiet certainty. He slid his arms around her waist. For a moment, he teetered on the edge of the sill. He steadied himself—and her—as a voice chided him. *She is young. Naive in love and men.*

Then I will show her, he answered back and kissed her jaw, then the pretty birthmark on her neck.

How will you show her? By marrying her as you did Amalie? Then leaving her behind?

That stilled him.

Beau pulled back, breath shallow, heart tight. The past clawed its way up his spine—too many ghosts, too many regrets. He hadn't expected sorrow to follow so closely on the heels of tenderness.

Clara pressed her face to his chest, arms tightening around him, a gentle shake of her head brushing against his collar.

Had he upset her? Gone too far? He cupped her cheek, lifting her chin to meet his gaze. "What's wrong?"

But it wasn't hurt he saw in her eyes—it was tenderness. Embarrassment. Something soft and unsure, as if she hadn't expected to feel so much.

"I just never..." She tucked her hair behind her ears, trembling when he reached for her hand. "I won't be like her." Her voice dropped, taut with something too personal for the cold night. "I won't lose myself just to please a man."

He blinked, heart jolting. Her mother? Was that who she feared becoming? A woman wounded by a faithless, foolish man?

"I want better than that for you too." He should never have brought her to such a vulnerable state.

Still, confusion marked her brow. "Is this why girls like Maudy do what they do?"

He groaned inwardly. "Non, *ma chérie*. That is something different."

She crossed her arms, leaning away from him—though not so far as to move from his embrace. "Why, then, did my mother just stand by—even try to justify my father's infidelity? Her only explanation was that she loved him."

"I cannot say—and neither can you. Listen." He gently cupped her jaw, looking into her eyes. "What you felt was desire. It leads to two becoming one." Hopefully, with her love of the Bible, she would recognize the phrase.

"'Stir not up, nor awake my love, until he pleases.' That verse played in my mind when we kissed, yet still... Beau, you're the first man I've cared about in a way that scares me—in a way that matters, but I don't trust myself to make decisions, a commitment." She shook her head, lips parting yet no words coming until she choked, "My father..." She looked away, hunching her shoulders as though ashamed.

Beau straightened, a warning pounding through him. "What about your père?" When she did not respond, he ran his hands up her forearms, gently squeezing. "Clara?"

She gasped and pulled her left arm from his grasp, a flash of pain in her eyes.

"He hurt you?" He kept his voice low, leaning close to better gauge her reaction.

She nodded, tears burgeoning again. "I brought up my mother—his past sins. I was most disrespectful—intrusive, even crude—and he lost control."

"Do not ever excuse a man for crossing a physical line during a verbal conflict." He'd switched to French, unable to find English words. Drawing a deep breath, he tried again.

"Those with power, strength, have a greater need—even a debt—to be better. Self-controlled."

Her eyelashes fluttered as she tried to blink away tears that streamed.

Beau gathered her close and tucked her under his chin. "Would you like to tell me about it?" He caressed her hair away from her face, and she nodded.

"You've heard of the scandal surrounding poor Daniel's birth." She pressed a hanky to her nose. "My mother was ill. Father took Tessa to San Francisco—just left us here. I tried to take care of Mother, but all she wanted was him. She didn't care that I was there, so I left her on her veranda. When I came back, she was gone."

More tears overwhelmed her, and Beau waited, running his thumb across her knuckles.

"I didn't say goodbye, Beau." She returned to her story, having gained composure. "Mother was barely cold in the ground when Father married Tessa, and I hated both of them so much. I thought perhaps things had improved after I went away to finishing school. But every time I look at Tessa, all I can think is—why didn't Father love Mother enough to remain faithful? And now, I can't even be happy for Maudy and Abe. I think I've become so bitter, I don't believe in honor or love." She looked at him, pleading in her gaze, as though he held the answers she needed.

"I have no great wisdom for you, Clara." He shrugged, frustrated by his own inadequacy. "Everyone you meet will disappoint you. God's the only one we can count on to be perfect. But if we're willing to forgive, we can still build something beautiful."

Her eyes widened, as if his words had struck a deeper chord than he'd intended. Yet even if she'd read more into them, she wasn't wrong. Whether offered in friendship or something more, he'd meant every word.

"I don't trust myself just now, Beau, but I'm glad you're here." She forced a hopeful smile, her light eyelashes darkened with tears.

"I'm not perfect."

"Really?" A smile toyed at the edges of her mouth.

"If you could forgive me, I'd..."—what was he even saying?—"I'd give you everything I have."

"That's a strange offer," she said softly, tilting her head. "Are you hiding something from me, Beau?"

He nodded, selfishly wishing to be free.

She leaned back yet kept her hand intertwined with his. "Like what? A secret second life? You're not married, are you?"

He flinched, and Clara's expression fell. The shadow in her eyes tightened his chest. He hurried to explain. "No. I was married at nineteen to a Roma girl. We had a son and lived with her troupe, but France had universal male conscription under the Jourdan Law of 1798—'Every Frenchman is a soldier and owes himself to the defense of the nation.'" He repeated the phrase, long ago drilled into him like a soldier's march, though every beat of his Roma heart rebelled, urging him toward the wild hills and freedom.

"Because I was my father's legitimate heir, I had to fight. Before I left, I moved my family to Paris, hoping they would be safe. They died during the Bloody Week in 1871." He paused, his voice tight, the memories clawing at him like a nightmare. "After that, I was lost—what the Bible would call a stranger in a strange land."

Clara squeezed his hand, but Beau stared into the past.

"I came to America with Lorraine, a woman who was like a sister to me." Beau's memory took him back to that moment he stepped off the gangplank. The air, thick with coal smoke and sea brine, clung to his coat. Castle Garden loomed—a circular stone structure at the edge of Battery Park, its walls weathered and echoing with the voices of thousands. Inside, the rotunda buzzed with chaos—languages clashing, children crying, officials barking orders.

"Beau?" Clara's fingers tightened around his, grounding him in the here and now.

He blinked, memory loosening its grip. "There were so many faces, languages. Their chatter was foreign, their customs unfamiliar."

He had clutched his satchel tighter, and Lorraine slipped her hand into the crook of his arm, her dark eyes and gaunt face reminding him why they came to America. The one person there to lead them was Emil Willot—a man he had known in his teens, the man who had helped smuggle him and Lorraine out of France.

"I realized then that I would never belong anywhere."

"Beau, that cannot be true." Clara placed her palm against his cheek, her eyes pleading. "Everyone has a purpose, and there is belonging—real belonging—when we turn our hearts over to God." She leaned in, her voice tender yet resolute. "The Bible says, 'For our conversation is in heaven; from whence also we look for the Savior, the Lord Jesus Christ.'"

Beau frowned. "'Conversation'?"

Clara's eyes brightened in that familiar way, as if she were about to share a secret only she knew. "When the King James Bible was translated in 1611, conversation didn't mean just talking. It meant one's entire manner of life—citizenship and conduct. The original Greek word is *politeuma*, connected to *polis*, which means city, and *politeia*, which means citizenship or commonwealth."

Beau sat back and rubbed his chin.

"So Paul was really saying our true citizenship—our way of life, our allegiance—is in heaven. Not here."

"I know that to be true. I believe the Bible, but you don't understand." He thumped his chest with emphasis. "After I lost my wife, Martin, my père, my people, I lost myself.

Followed bad men. Displeased God. I did things that cannot be undone, no matter how I have tried to atone for my wrongs."

The words hung in the space between them.

"Only Christ can atone for our sins." Clara's voice was soft but steady, her clear eyes so hopeful.

He shook his head. "The law requires atonement."

Clara blinked, then swallowed. "I think I know what you mean."

She didn't—but maybe one day, when she learned the truth, she'd remember this conversation.

"That is why I tried to leave Virginia City—to stay away from you." He released a shallow breath, a vise tightening around his lungs again. "And I was right to do so—except I keep finding myself with you again."

A smile bloomed on her face, gentle and unguarded, as if hope had surprised her. "I am glad you are here with me. Oh, and I have something for you."

Feeling like a man watching a bridge collapse beneath his feet but spotting one beam still holding, he took her hands. "What is it?"

Clara gave his fingers a lingering squeeze before pulling away. She knelt by a pile of clothes on the floor—the men's attire she'd worn at the fire station—and plucked a white piece of fabric from the pocket. Then she laid a handkerchief on his thigh, his initials embroidered on the corner. "This is for you. Merry Christmas. Sorry it's late."

"You did this?" He ran his thumb across the letters. It had been years since he'd had anything so fine.

"I did."

"I must give you something." He unwound the soft knit scarf he always wore and draped it around her neck. The scarf's deep red settled against the pale gold of her hair, which gleamed as if morning light had ignited embers.

She nestled the fabric against her cheek with a contented sigh. "It's warm...and it smells like you."

He cracked a grin. "I hope you consider that a good thing."

"I do." Clara brushed snowflakes from the stubble along his cheek, yet followed his glance at the men's clothes on the floor. "I'm doing some freelance work, and I've written a devotional and sent it off to *The Sunday Magazine*. It's a British publication widely circulated in the U.S., especially among Protestant readers. They include sermons, religious essays, poetry, and serialized fiction with moral themes."

He smiled, his chest feeling lighter at the mention of safe journalism. "That's amazing. You are so smart."

Footsteps in the hall alerted him that they were soon to be interrupted.

"Oh, hurry, hurry," she whispered fiercely. "You must get down before we are caught."

Repressing a chuckle, he shrugged. "Just tell them you are busy."

"I cannot do that. How unladylike." She gave him a little push, and Beau grasped the wall to keep from falling.

"Clara." This time he did laugh, low and quiet.

She tried to haul him back in, so he wound his arms around her and leaned back as though to take them both through the window.

"Beau, no." She wrestled from his grasp, yet froze as someone knocked on the door.

"Is anyone in there?" came the muffled call of the waiting tenant.

Her eyes, like large moons, flashed, then she gave him a smack to the chest. "See what you've done."

Beau hung at an odd angle, still clinging to the sill. He softened his grip, yet she did not step away. There was an offer in her lifted chin, open arms, and wide gaze—though she likely didn't even know it.

"Ah, mademoiselle, you tempt me." He brushed a knuckle down her cheek, tender and reverent. "But I dare not take what you're not yet ready to give—even a single kiss—not when your heart matters more to me than a moment's desire."

Clara swallowed and let him go. "Will you come to the evening meal tomorrow, after your shift?" she asked, her voice unsteady. "Some guests stay by the fire reading and such."

A knock sounded again.

"For as long as you will have me."

Then he dropped out of sight, landing lightly on the ground not far below. He dared not glance back at her. The lovely woman in the glowing window was too tempting. He was better off calling on her tomorrow—courting her, for lack of a better term. His step faltered when he came to the snowy street, and he glanced up at the far away heavens instead of the house behind him. *Lord, why did You bring Clara into my life? I don't deserve her.*

As he stalked his way home, his hands buried in his pockets, his thoughts drifted back to that precious kiss and the notion of a future. His prayer changed. "I'm glad You brought Clara into my life, God. But what should I do now?"

CHAPTER 15

Morning light swept through a window as Beau waited in John's study. The room smelled of tobacco and old books. A grand mahogany desk sat like a throne on the far side, its polished surface scattered with correspondence and ledgers. Behind it, tall bookshelves lined the wall, flanked on one side by heavy filing cabinets, while a fire crackled in the hearth to the right.

He'd been waiting for a few minutes now. John would think him out of line, and maybe he was, but something had to be said. He couldn't shake the image of Clara cupping her arm, trying to take responsibility yet so obviously hurt.

And who was Beau to call a man out for violence? He'd bloodied his fair share of men.

But...men. That was the resounding difference. Not a woman—let alone a daughter meant to be protected and loved.

"Sorry to keep you waiting, Beau." John walked into the study, looking as tired as ever. Not for the first time, Beau caught the scent of brandy on him.

John sat down across from him in the leather chair, moving a few papers around on his big desk. "You talk to MacKay about work yet? He can get you a job at the Consolidated Virginia & California Mine."

"I did, sir. I start this Monday, but that is not why I am here." Beau clasped his hands to keep himself calm. Tension made his muscles coil tight. He did not want to provoke John further. The man had been drinking—that much was clear. Still, his step had been sure when he entered, his gaze steady. Hopefully, his mind was clear too. "What would you say if I told you I ran into Clara yesterday?"

John's eyes widened, and he leaned back in his chair. "Where is she?"

"Safe. Still in Virginia City." He gauged the man's reaction, but John just rubbed his chin. "Are you going to force her to return home?"

"No. She would just be unhappy, and I..."—he shook his head—"I don't believe I can live at peace with her and my wife. Clara hates Tessa and me for what we did. I thought, now that she is older, she might understand that adults make mistakes." He rubbed his face hard. "It was too much to hope."

Beau clenched his jaw, reining in his temper. "She said you hurt her."

John's face turned red. His eyes darkened. "I don't believe that is your business. You are not her fiancé. Not even her beau."

"I am your friend, John."

Confusion flickered across the man's face before his voice grew stiff. "I don't have many friends."

"Maybe if you had more, you would not need drink to cope."

"You trespass again, Beau." John stood abruptly, his chair thudding against the side of the desk. He strode past the fireplace, then rounded the desk to face Beau head on. "I don't know why I let you speak to me this way."

Beau stood too. "I might be just a poor miner, but I am a

man of values." The words felt foreign coming out of his mouth. He had not held to his values after the war. He had never belonged anywhere or with anyone long enough to establish values, an identity. But he had done right in San Francisco with Aubrey Willot and Nathan Reed. And he had stayed here—for Clara. If he ever hoped to be a good man again, like God wanted, he had to speak the truth. Follow it.

"You lost your temper and hurt your daughter. You need to guard yourself against further outbursts. Protect your family because you love them. Because you do not want to be this way."

John's face deepened from red to purple.

Beau breathed deeply, trying to defuse the tension in the room—but he braced himself, anyway, fists clenched, muscles taut.

Still, he was barely prepared to block John's quick left jab to the gut. He swatted the next blow aside, stepping back to give the man space. John charged—nose bleeding again, just as it had that day Clara entered the mine. The old warning sign—anger too hot, pressure rising too high. Veins in his forehead pulsing as he swung wide.

Beau shoved him away. John stumbled into the cabinet, papers spilling as a drawer snapped open. Beau backed toward the fireplace, using the leather wingback chair as a barrier, but John came at him again, knocking a pile of ledgers to the floor.

Beau moved in a slow circle, dodging the worst of it and taking the occasional hit to his side. Desperation carved lines into the older man's face as he cursed. They circled past the bookshelves—Beau sidestepping a low stool, John knocking over a coal bucket by the hearth. A painting on a wall wobbled on its hinge from the vibrations of their fight.

John landed a few solid punches.

Beau countered—hard enough to sting but not injure. He had not come here to fight. But clearly, John needed to let something out. They went round after round, until the older man began to slow.

Then Beau slammed a right hook into John's jaw, dropping him flat on his back.

The man lay there panting, chest heaving.

Beau squatted beside him and set a bandana on his chest. "Clara would be heartbroken if she knew you were bleeding."

John sat up slowly, sweat rolling down his temples. Around them, the room bore witness to the violence—chairs askew, papers scattered—though the fire crackled cheerily behind them as if nothing had happened.

John took the cloth he offered. "I've always had nose bleeds. My little brother thought that was so funny. But Kingston…"

Oh, no. There was another Alexander brother? *Lord, preserve me.* Sitting cross-legged, he joined John on the floor. "You have another brother?"

"Yes. My father's from his first marriage. No one talks about him. He was wild. Put the family to shame."

"Where is he now?"

"Dead. He died in some opium den in the city when I was ten. Titus—my younger brother—was six. He doesn't really remember him. I always figured, if someone had given Kingston a chance—told him that men make mistakes and can start over—maybe he would not have run from the people who cared about him."

Beau arched a brow. "Say, he is not the reason you took me in, is he?"

"No. But you sure remind me of him." He smacked Beau's knee. "Now help me up. I'm an old man."

Beau hauled him to his feet with one hand. "An old man with an iron fist."

That drew a smile, though it faded quickly. "I know I'm not perfect. But if I let myself sit and feel bad about Annalise, Tessa, Daniel, and Clara…"—he shook his head—"I'll never do better.

Too many people rely on me for me to stay stuck in my mistakes. You know what I mean?"

"I do. I have my own past I want to be free of."

John nodded and returned to his side of the desk, flopping into his chair. "I cannot believe I got whipped by a kid. Titus will be amused."

Cold crept down the back of Beau's neck. "Oh?" He made his tone light. "You expecting a visit?"

"He always comes in the spring. Likes to drop by unannounced as though he's going to catch me doing something foolish." John made a sound between a laugh and a grumble. "He's happy now, though. His wife died about a year after Annalise. Both his children went through hard times, but they're doing well. He's a grandfather, so he's going to bring those babies up here to rub it in my face."

Despite the topic, John grinned—until his expression darkened again. "I know I lost your respect, Beau. But believe it or not, I'm trying. Trying to be a better husband to Tessa and a better father to Daniel and Clara. I'm sorry you had to see this side of me." He kept his chin high, jaw firm, though it seemed like a battle to meet Beau's eyes.

"It is against God and Clara that you sinned, sir, not me."

John leaned forward, pointing a finger at him briefly. "What did I tell you about calling me 'sir'?"

They shared a smile before John drew out a piece of paper. "Where is Clara staying?"

Beau didn't flinch. "Since she is twenty and left of her own free will, I think perhaps she should be the one to tell you that... sir."

John slammed the paper on the desk. "Are you going to cross every line today?"

Beau said nothing.

"Then, since you will not tell me where she is living, I'll count on you to check on her. Make sure she is safe. It might be good for Clara to learn what it is like out there, paying her own way. But I do not want her hurt."

"You trust me with this? After the arrest?"

"I do. You are not the only one who can read people, Beau. You are hiding—from your education, your father's legacy. I know what that's like. No matter how hard we try, we may never carry that weight well. But a man cannot live in fear, running from the things that are too much for our loved ones. Can he?"

"No." Though John had no idea what Beau was really running from, or how it affected his brother. "I thought, for a minute on Christmas Eve, you were going to speak to me about courting Clara."

"I thought we might need to straighten out the details. Turns out, we did that today." He grinned dryly, and Beau had to nod.

"There's just one more thing. You're cleared of murder, Beau. But people don't forget. Clara's vulnerable. She doesn't need false hope."

Beau shifted his weight, his gaze drifting to the quiet street beyond the study window. He would stay for Clara, keep her safe while she was at Mrs. Matthews's, but sooner or later, Titus and his family would come. And when they did, everything in Virginia City—his place in this town, his safety, his future—would be over for good.

~

"What are you staring at?" Maudy asked as she pulled on a long stocking where she sat on the edge of the bed they shared.

Clara faced the window, the warm rays of sun streaming past the buildings on the lower streets and setting the town aglow. "Virginia City is one of the most beautiful places to view a sunrise."

"It is, indeed, and the sun is rising. Are you?" Maudy wiggled into a petticoat, casting Clara an expectant glance.

"What do you mean?"

"I mean, you need to get to work. You dressed up like a man and went to the fire station. Don't tell me you wasted your time."

"I think maybe I did. The writers of the *Territorial Enterprise* have been downright cruel to the firemen. After what I witnessed last night, I don't want to work for them. Not only that, but I overheard some of the men at the firehouse mentioned that the *Territorial Enterprise* was bought by William Sharon to print a narrative that will support him in his run for Congress. I want to make a difference, but not that kind. Serving a greedy man who cares nothing for the pain and scars of our community. I want to write truth, not polish the boots of a politician."

"So send your devotional off to that magazine we talked about. The one for Sunday schools."

Clara sighed. Plenty of women wrote for magazines. She wanted to write where the general public would read it. "What use is writing if I don't make a difference?"

"You think you don't make a difference?" Maudy placed her hands on her hips. "Oh, honey. I sure am glad the Apostle Paul never said such a thing." She chuckled, shaking her head. "Well, at least don your reporter outfit and head on down to the paper. If you just stay in this room moping, you'll never do anything great."

"Beau asked me not to wear the pants." She sighed yet again, remembering the way his hand cupped her face, his voice low with concern when he explained trouncing around town in pants was not safe. Not that she trounced anywhere. He hadn't told her to stop being brave—just to be careful. But how could she do one without risking the other?

"Hah. Chances are, you are a heap safer looking like a boy

than walking around town with your hair pinned and your waist cinched. If I could pass for a lad, I'd be climbing up and down the mines myself. But alas..." She gestured to her ample bosom and heaved a great sigh.

Clara laughed despite herself. Maudy's irreverence always caught her off guard, like a hymn with an unexpected key change. "Did you know that in Greek mythology, a woman's ample bosom was seen as a symbol of divine femininity?"

"Greek mythology? I thought you were a Christian lady."

"I am. It is merely history, Maudy. I know those goddesses were false."

"Good. Now have a look at this." Maudy reached into her coat and withdrew an item wrapped in a handkerchief. "I found this on the bathroom floor when I was working at the Tahoe House Hotel." She held it out to Clara as though giving her a gift.

"The bathroom floor?" Pulling back the folds of cloth, she revealed what looked like a rat pelt. "What is this?"

"It's a mustache. Don't worry. I washed it and combed it proper." Maudy grabbed the thing and held it up to her lip. "You see, Monsieur Vulpe is correct. You are far too pretty to pass for a man, but with this beauty..."

Clara laughed and wrinkled her nose, but upon taking it to the mirror was surprised by how different the light-brown fake mustache hid her face. "I could go anywhere with this."

After applying glue to her face and setting the mustache on her top lip, Clara made her way down to the *Gold Hill Daily News*. It took two whole cents to ride the omnibus there, but she had time to think of what she would say. The article she'd written late the night before was solid—about Captain Alcorn's decision to disband Liberty Engine Company No. 1—and her writing had never felt sharper. Lord willing, Mr. Doten would read it without recognizing her. She'd worked on using a lower voice and changing the way she walked since Beau admitted that was how he'd spotted her—an idea that both alarmed and thrilled.

Taking big strides and landing her heels with impact—though honestly, she just felt like she was stomping everywhere—Clara made her way to the *Daily News* receiving room. A gust of wind hit the door when she entered, and it banged shut. Several men working on the press room peeked over the high desk to see her. The scent of parchment and ink greeted her like an old friend—sharp and earthy, with a touch of oil.

Clara adjusted her hat, tilting the brim low to hide more of her face. The mustache tickled beneath her nose, but it only fueled the thrill of the moment. This was where stories came alive. And she was about to become a part of that process.

Behind the counter, Mr. Doten leaned against a column of ledgers, flipping through a stack of envelopes. His brow was furrowed, but when he looked up, he smiled. "Good morning, young man. Are you here to place a notice?"

Clara cleared her throat and pitched her voice down. "I have an article I'd like to sell you. About the disbandment of Liberty Engine Company No. 1. Captain Alcorn's decision."

Doten tapped the envelope against his palm. "Mmm. Timely. Tragic. And unexpected for someone who doesn't work here." He paused, lips twitching. "Tell me, Mister…?"

She swallowed a surge of nerves. Lucky she had a name figured out. She'd flipped her first two initials and added the last name of one of her idols. "Mr. L. C. Royall."

He looked at her again, longer this time. She couldn't tell if it was suspicion or something quieter—curiosity, maybe. She forced her hand forward, offering the article to Mr. Doten. "I need work and can deliver. If you have something in particular you want me to report on, just let me know."

Would he believe her? Or did she sound like a fool in borrowed boots?

Doten turned his head to the side, reading over the paper

she'd written up. "You have a flair for capturing the spirit in that room. How did you get in? The meeting last night was supposed to be private."

What would Maudy say? "I'm small enough that people notice me less, and I get in more places." She gave him a smile, not showing her teeth and pushing her bottom lip out a bit.

He flicked his eyebrows up, then sighed like a man half impressed and half resigned. "I was at the meeting as well. However, some citizens are tired of hearing from me. And..."—he grinned—"I haven't got time to write about it. We're always in need of new blood here at the *Daily News*. And I appreciate your sentiment toward the Liberty Engine House. Go on in the back and work on the latest print. Check for spelling and layout errors before press time. I want to see your work when you're done."

Clara blinked, stunned. Then nodded and shuffled toward the print room, her heart thudding in time with the press. She shed her coat, kept her cap on, and returned every curious glance with a glare. No one scolded. No one asked. They simply looked away and left her to it.

Was being a man so easy?

CHAPTER 16

She had been a reporter for only two weeks, still new to the rough-and-tumble world of local journalism, and had managed to avoid saloons—until today. The muddy streets of the town had been quiet as she walked from the Divide, an overlook where she had gone to interview Mr. Tibbons—Mr. Peterson's neighbor and the only witness related to the unsolved murder. Unfortunately, her visit turned up nothing, which was why she was headed to the saloon. If she was going to help Beau clear his name, she needed to push herself further.

The double doors of the Delta Saloon loomed before her. She glanced over her shoulder and caught a fleeting glimpse of a man in a brown bowler hat ducking into an alleyway. She'd only seen his reddish-blond mustache. Had he been following her? He must have been—moving out of sight so quickly—unless it was pure happenstance. She'd need to be more vigilant about her surroundings.

Clara pushed through the heavy doors into a bright room—chandeliers casting a warm glow, cigar smoke curling in the air, and a delicate piano melody by Chopin drifting softly. Because the miners worked all hours—day and night—there was always a crew free to drink, gamble, and socialize with the paid women who worked there.

She strode to the back of the building, where the dark stairs she recognized led up to the office spaces. With a quick, practiced motion, she tucked her braid into the collar of her shirt and adjusted her derby cap.

Reaching the landing, she knocked on the sheriff's door, which swung open almost immediately—revealing the burly, big-nosed man who served as the peace officer of Virginia City.

"Hello, Sheriff. My name is L. C. Royall, with the *Gold Hill Daily News*." She held out her hand and shook firmly. "I was hoping to get a quote on Mr. Tibbons leaving town in the wake of the Peterson murder."

His red eyebrows shot up high, creasing his forehead—save for his shiny bald scalp. "And how would ye know he's gone, lad?"

Suppressing a gulp—along with her worry that he'd just been out for a ride—the honest answer spilled out. "I don't. I only assume so because I've been unable to locate him myself."

He swept his hat off a nail on the wall, then stepped forward quickly with his coat over his arm, nearly causing Clara to jump back. "We'll just have to go and see," he said as he stooped to lock the door, then trotted down the stairs with Clara close behind.

By the time they reached the Divide, Sheriff Kelly was speaking like a man who'd been gagged for a week. He gave her the entire account of arresting Beau, then pursuing other leads.

Breathless from the brisk pace, Clara dragged her feet up the porch steps of Mr. Tibbons's house behind Kelly. "Did you discover anything from your other leads?"

"There aren't many other leads. I questioned Mr. Tibbons, and he spoke openly. I had no cause to doubt him until that Frenchman mentioned he and Dodge Peterson had bad blood between 'em, and that the lad wanted his father to sell the mine. I questioned Dodge, and he said he was at a tavern that night. Witnesses seen him there."

Clara filed this away mentally. She didn't dare note it in a real notepad. Men like Sheriff Kelly could be flighty when talking to the press.

Sheriff Kelly knocked on the door—his pounding like that of the stamp mills.

"Now, this is where it gets interestin'." He squinted one eye at Clara. "Mr. Peterson died from a blow to the head. His fingers were frostbit, so he likely perished outdoors, away from his house—but they found him in his nightshirt, sittin' by the fire with a plate of pie and tea for two, can ye believe it?"

"Just as Mr. Vulpe said. So why would Vulpe admit to having tea and seeing Mr. Peterson in the very spot his body was found, if he was guilty? He wouldn't."

He gave the doorknob a yank and it shook in its frame. "And ain't that the truth? None of it make sense."

The door creaked, enough for the lawman's shaking to cause it to slip open. Sheriff Kelly stepped into the house, calling for Mr. Tibbons. A cold draft filled the space. He must have been gone some time. A neat parlor featured the usual furniture. Worn but clean. The coals in the hearth were black and cold. Strangely, Mr. Tibbons hadn't swept them clean. He seemed a tidy sort, as her fingertips attested when she ran them across the mantel and found it spotless. Likely, he'd left in a hurry.

"Where would he go in the dead of winter?" she asked softly.

Sheriff Kelly's big boots sounded as he moved through the house, his gruff voice calling for the elderly man. Clara walked down the hallway until she reached the kitchen. The room was warmer than the rest of the house. In the corner sat a small cast-iron cookstove. She extended her hand, though she already felt the heat.

"What did ye find, lad?" Sheriff Kelly stopped in the doorway behind her. He spoke as though she were a child—a frequent assumption since many thought her young because of her voice.

She did her best to lower her tone without making it seem obvious. "The stove is warm."

He shrugged. "Maybe he had a housekeeper come back to check on the place."

"Mr. Peterson lived with his son, did he not?"

"No. The boy has a house in Virginia City. Maybe if he'd been there that night, the old man wouldn't be dead now."

Unable to find any sign of the neighbor, Clara offered to buy Sheriff Kelly a cup of coffee at a nearby café. He agreed to give her a few quotes for the article she intended to write about Mr. Tibbons's disappearance. If anyone knew of his whereabouts, perhaps they would come forward. And even if they did not, the guilty party—or parties—might still be reminded that justice always demands payment.

～

Deep in the Virginia Consolidated Mine shaft, where heat rose in waves of steam and the coppery stink of minerals hung thick in the air, Beau positioned himself at the Burleigh drill stand. Even through his leather gloves, the metal scorched his hands. He angled the drill—a three-foot cylinder with a two-foot bit—and pressed the star head against the rock wall, just two feet off the ground. Around him, men of all different sizes and colors hauled rock into cars, which they pushed away to a main drop-off spot.

This crosscut intersected with the main shaft, and once they finished it, it would improve ventilation for that section of the mine. Only minutes now until someone took over and he could breathe.

The compressors hummed loudly, drowning out the hissing of the vents and groaning of the pumps echoing through the shaft. Beau checked the valves, then pressed the power lever. The bit began to turn. He gripped the drill tight as the vibration pounded like a mule's kick, the grinding shriek echoing through his skull—as it had most of the day. It was just a matter of time before his hearing suffered, like that of so many of the miners. Still, he kept pressing until Sanderson came to relieve him.

Joints like jelly and muscles shaking, he trudged toward the cooling room, where massive pipes sucked polar air from the surface and blasted into the chamber. The crew picking up rock went ahead of him, the relief crew taking their place with Sanderson.

The compressor's growl faded, but the air blowing from the pipes still howled like a storm on Mount Davidson. Beau pushed through the crowd and grabbed a pick and hammer. He broke off a chunk of ice from the slab before sinking onto a pile of square beams that would later be used to brace the tunnels.

They'd worked all day at the two-thousand-foot level, taking turns in the cooling room to avoid heat exhaustion from the 115-degree temperatures.

Breath ragged, he rubbed the ice along his neck. Water trickled down his skin, warming before it rolled to his waistband. No wonder many believed hades was underground. MacKay's interest in utilizing Beau's engineering background appealed more with every passing day.

He breathed deeply, the briny taste of sweat sticking to the air. When he peeled off his leather gloves, he found his hands bruised and blistered.

"Ol' Frenchy didn't know what he was signing up for when he left that rinky-dink outfit in Gold Hill to work for the kings," a burly miner bellowed with laughter. He had more muscle than a bull bison and just as much hair on his bare chest.

Beau grinned and waved him away, too exhausted to reply. George Halman—called Bear by the men—always seemed to be talking, singing, or joking with someone. It made hell a slightly more tolerable place.

"You got mines in France, Frenchy?" Bear sat down beside him, working his own piece of ice in a similar fashion.

"Oui, some." Beau had to practically yell over the blasting cold air. "You know I am only half French?"

"I figured. But since you didn't go work at the Mexican mine, I thought you owned your French side."

Unwilling to hide his roots any longer, Beau pushed his shoulders back. "I'm not Mexican either. My father was French. My mother—Roma."

Bear raised his burnt-red eyebrows nearly to his frizzy hairline. "A Gypsy?"

"No. I am a Rom. Half, anyway."

"Do you believe in spirits? Mystics?"

Closing his eyes as he pressed the chunk of ice to his cheek, too hot to argue religion or superstition, Beau just breathed for a moment, then said, "I believe in God."

"Me too." Bear jabbed his chin down, cheeks red as charbroiled salmon. "You know, some say these shafts are haunted by the men who died digging this portion. The flooding was something terrible. Had to bring in two Cornish pumps. They average about five million gallons of water a day. Still, it isn't enough. My daddy was a superstitious man, to be sure. He'd walk two whole blocks around a black cat, if he sighted one."

"Oh?" Beau massaged his throbbing wrists, trying not to count the hours left in his shift. The thought of stepping out into the cool, snowy air stirred a deep ache inside him.

"Yeah. Funny thing is—I saw a black cat on my way to the

mine today. Darted right in front of me, faster than I could blink." Bear fell still, staring at the floor.

"You a Christian, Bear?"

The big man jumped, then glowered. "Yes, sir, I am!" he practically shouted.

Beau grinned, clapping him on the back. "That's good... because God made the cat."

And with that, he rose to drink his fill of water before returning to the drill. The heat met him like a wall when he left the cooling room.

Bear walked at his side. "I sure would love to be home with my girl about now."

Clara's face flashed before Beau's mind's eye—her cheeks bright from the cool snow. She was his clear sky above the dark mines. Every evening, he dined with her at Mrs. Matthews's boarding house, known for its hearty stews and shared laughter. Afterward, he stayed as late as the proprietress allowed—reading worn novels by the flickering lamp and engaging in quiet conversations that stretched into sweet memories of simply getting to know Clara better.

Only three more hours until his shift ended. Five hours until he would see her.

At the end of the crosscut they'd been laboring on all day, Sanderson faced the rock wall. He paused his work but left the compressor running as he gave Beau a haggard look. He mopped his red face with a neckerchief, eyes bloodshot and skin dry.

"You don't look too good, Sanderson." Beau handed the man the little bit of ice he'd carried from the cooling room.

"Thank you. I don't know how much more of this I can take." He pressed the ice to his face.

"Go on and make sure you drink lots of water."

The man stumbled away down the tunnel without a backward glance.

Beau took his position at the drill and went to work on the hard rock wall. The drill ate away at the stone, and Beau mastered its path. On a good day, he could gnaw through twelve inches of rock per minute. He'd only made it two feet when a deep crack rang out and scalding-hot water spewed from the place he'd been grinding.

Beau shouted and slammed against the wall to get away from the water that shot straight out, trapping him in the corner of the crosscut. Steam hissed around him like the breath of hell. Hands still locked on the drill, Beau released the exhaust valve, allowing the full head of compressed air to rush out in a steady stream, saving him from the steam. He turned against the rock wall, pressing as hard as he could while the heat tore at his back.

"Help. Somebody help!" He tipped his head back, but the roar and rush of water drowned him out.

Water began to pool around his shoes. Beau tried to gain footing on the rocks, but it was useless. He found no purchase. Everything was slick and too hot. When he tried to climb, he slipped and slid into the hot spray of water.

He was trapped, the air compressor still blowing on his upper body and head while his feet burned in the rising water. The hot rocks tore at his flesh. There was nowhere to go.

He shouted again and this time heard men's voices—but couldn't be sure they were responding to him.

God, help me. The searing pain blurred his vision—and memory filled the space where reason failed. Flashes of his life appeared before his eyes.

Playing with Lorraine under the *vardos* wagon his grand-père owned. His maman in the quilted bed with intricately carved woodwork, bright paint, and gold leaf—the scent of smoke and lavender filling the room as she breathed her last.

Steam clogged his lungs, suffocating him. He held the

compressor closer so the air rushing from the valve pushed away the steam rising into his face. *God, help me.*

Marching down the muddy streets of Paris, praying Amalie and Martin would fare well while he was away.

The roar from the compressed water grew louder as it filled the tunnel and scorched his calves. *God, help me.*

The night in that terrible prison train when he begged Lorraine to point the way to Martin and Amalie—only to learn they'd not survived the Bloody Week.

His legs screamed in pain, scalding water rising to his knees. *God, help me.*

When he delivered the ransom for the Willot babies and had fallen to the foes he betrayed, Beau had lain bleeding in an alley, barely holding on to consciousness. Praying. *God, help me. Help me!* He was sinking, fading into a thick darkness he'd never return from.

"Help me!" Beau managed, his voice muffled beneath the roar of water and the rush of the compressor.

Someone grabbed him firmly, a tight hold that steadied him. A coat was thrown over him. Three men hauled him through the water. They ran, steam blocking the way, but Bear shouted near him.

"Go! Go! We need to get some boots on this boy before his legs are scalded to the bone!" Water splashed up as they ran through the flood.

They reached the cooling room—now flooded—and climbed onto a pile of beams. Alarms rang. Men shouted. Bear, Sanderson, and a miner Beau didn't know shoved his burned feet into heavy gum boots that reached all the way to his hips. He sucked in cool air, his body shaking. With a cry trapped behind his teeth, he gritted them against the pain as he donned the gum coat the men had thrown over him for protection from the hot spring.

The roar of water and wind tore through like a mountain

storm. Bear shouted and gestured toward the tunnel leading out. His words were lost, but Beau understood.

They needed to evacuate the mine—before they were cooked alive.

∼

Clara's pencil hovered above her notebook, half a sentence left undone as the telegraph tapped out news from the East. Mr. Doten had instructed her to pick up the latest from channels across the U.S., and here she was, waiting.

Her pantaloons bunched uncomfortably beneath the men's britches, and her toes were so cold, she'd lost feeling in them hours ago.

A wagoner drove a team of ten mules through town, whipping and swearing at them as he passed. There wasn't much going on in town today. The telegraph office sat near the Wells Fargo building and close to the new *Territorial Enterprise*. She glanced down the street toward the newspaper office's ornate cast-iron pillars—locally forged—and the wooden veranda that stretched across the front.

She sighed. Had she chosen wrong in joining Doten's press? Writing under a pen name?

I want to matter.

The cry came from deep within—then the resounding question. *Why?*

Was it self-centered to want people to read her work and admire her?

But I would help people. Make a difference.

A shriek, sharp and splitting, cut through the morning din.

The warning bell rang once, then again—fast.

Clara stood, her heart jolting. Memories of the fire came flooding back. *No—please, not again.* Her throat tightened with the sharp, metallic taste of fear, and Beau's name rang louder than the bell in her mind. Was that alarm coming from the Consolidated Virginia and California shaft? Beau was working there. And it was his shift!

She stepped out of the telegraph office, the door swinging shut behind her with a hollow thud.

Men's shouts sounded down the street. The telegraph officer followed behind her. "What goes?"

Someone shouted, "Flooding! Below ground! In the Con Virginia!"

Before she realized she had moved, she was already running—arms pumping, heart racing with every frantic step. Muscles unaccustomed to the activity of a reporter screamed for relief, but Clara pushed forward. *Please let him be safe. Let me be wrong.* She sprinted down Taylor Street, where ore dust and coal smoke sharpened the air.

The hoist bell continued its frantic clanging.

She ran past the livery stable, where a mule brayed nervously. Men were turning toward the sound, faces drawn.

She veered downhill toward D, where the Consolidated Virginia and California Shaft loomed, its headframe silhouetted against the sky. Steam hissed from the hoist house, angry and alive.

She didn't stop to think. Beau was down there.

A foreman barked commands in the yard when she came to the hoisting house. "Hey!" He grabbed her arm and hauled her backward. "We don't need no kids down here lookin' for trouble. Now get home."

Clara turned, hardly able to contain her glare, yet possessed enough of her mind to lower her voice. "I'm with the *Gold Hill Daily News.*"

The big foreman glanced around frantically, then glowered.

"I won't get in the way," she promised.

He nodded, motioning for her to go ahead.

Men poured from the hoisting workhouse like floodwaters

breaking free. One plowed into her, nearly knocking her over, but still she fought to reach the door. If Beau was coming up, she'd find him here.

Inside, the air reeked of grease and grit. The cages were rising quickly, overloaded with men—hot, dusty, drenched in sweat.

One young man stumbled forward, helped by another. His skin was peeling from his bare shoulders.

Oh God—don't let that be Beau. Don't let him come up burned, broken. Please...

"We need a doctor!" someone shouted, and somehow his voice carried above the noise.

A group of men rushed off the platform wearing thick gum boots. Beau was among them, moving with visible strain. Most of his long hair had come undone and hung in his face so she could see his nose and part of his chin, which were very red, as was his chest exposed beneath his open coat.

Clara pushed through the crowd as the noise faded to a distant buzz. Someone knocked into her. She shoved forward, ready to embrace Beau—until one of his friends glared at her.

"We don't need the press. We need a doctor."

Right. She was still in men's clothes. But Beau was hurt.

"Move him over here, away from the crowd," she said, doing her best imitation of a man's voice.

It must have worked. Beau didn't react.

The group moved toward the edge of the room and settled him on a stack of timbers.

"You got a flask on you, kid?" The big, bearish man smacked her arm.

"No." She stood there, panting—helpless. She had no medicine. Nothing to dull Beau's pain.

What good is a pen when the people you care about are bleeding in the dirt?

"I'll get a cart. We can haul him to the hospital."

"I can walk," Beau grumbled, his bloodshot eyes searching yet unfocused, then he hung his head as though too weary to hold it upright.

"Sanderson! Bear! Get over here! We need your help," the foreman shouted, waving Beau's friends away.

The two men exchanged a glance, then turned to her.

The bigger one—presumably Bear—handed her a canteen. "Give him some of this and make sure he sees a doctor, will ya?" He stuck out his big paw of a hand.

Clara nodded and gave it a firm, fast shake. That seemed to satisfy him, and he disappeared into the crowd. Dropping to her knees beside Beau, she removed his cap and guided him to drink.

Trembling, he let the water spill over his lips—and drank like a dying man. Who could blame him? His face, neck, and chest were so red. What of his lower half?

When he finished, she set the canteen aside. "You need a doctor."

Beau locked eyes with her, his gaze flashing.

Panic fluttered inside her. She'd forgotten to use her man's voice. Even now, his gaze swept her—eyes, mustache, and the red scarf he'd gifted her, tied around her neck. Then his jaw tightened, and when he spoke, his voice came out raspy and low.

"I don't want to talk to the press." He hobbled forward, grimacing with each step.

A stab of regret hit her in the chest. She'd lied to him. "Now, please, don't be stubborn. You're hurt." She grabbed his arm, but he turned, a groan escaping as he pulled away.

Their eyes met one last time—his with a silent plea, a flicker of pain—and then he shook his head, turned sharply, and vanished into the crowd, leaving her behind with a pounding heart.

Clara followed him outside just in time to see him—along

with a number of other scalded men—climbing into a wagon. He wasn't going to talk to her as long as she was dressed like a man. Especially after she'd promised never to do it again.

Behind her, reporters from the *Territorial Enterprise* and *Chronicle* shouted questions at the injured men. Were there no other representatives from *The Daily News*? The driver set the team in motion, leaving the others behind. They didn't lose heart, though. They pressed on, questioning anyone they could stop.

A tall, slender man with dark hair and a thin mustache stood among them. Theo. What was he doing there? He'd lost his job.

Clara glanced between the rabble and the direction Beau had gone. She was a reporter—wasn't she supposed to stay? Take notes. Speak to the foreman. Get the facts down before they faded.

But the wagon was already rolling up Taylor Street, disappearing among the many business conveyances that constantly navigated the busy thoroughfares. She hesitated, the weight of her notebook tugging at her side.

Words could wait. She shook her head and trailed after the wagon of wounded men.

CHAPTER 17

*L*ungs burning after the trek from the Consolidated Virginia to Mrs. Matthews's—where she hurriedly changed into a modest yet nondescript dress—Clara clutched her side as she strode down R Street. There, St. Mary Louise Hospital perched like a chapel on the bend, smoke curling up from its chimneys. She had to reach Beau, to see that he was taken care of. How bad were his burns? He seemed to struggle to walk and even talk. Was he in great pain? Her hem wet from snowmelt, she hurried toward the long whitewashed steps leading to a porch with columns on either side.

Stepping into the warm lobby, she was greeted by wooden floors and a modest rug near the fireplace, flanked by chairs. Approaching the receiving desk, she cleared her throat. "Hello, Sister." A nun not much older than herself looked up from her papers. "A gentleman named Beau Vulpe was brought here earlier, after being scalded in one of the mines. I wondered if I might see him."

"You are his wife, I presume?" the young nun asked, only to frown when Clara stiffened.

"I am not."

"Well, he is in the men's ward. I'm afraid only staff may enter there. No female visitors are permitted in the ward unless to see a spouse or close relative, as you can imagine."

"But he was hurt." Her voice trembled with immediacy, but even as the words left her mouth, they sounded childish. "Can you tell me how he is doing?"

The nun's features softened. "There have been a few men coming in scalded today. I'm afraid I have no updates I can share, but you can rest assured—we're taking good care of them."

The promise seemed like so little. She stood there, waiting for a different response.

The doors banged open, and two orderlies carried in an unconscious miner, his blistered skin slick and red, the remnants of overalls clinging like a second burn. The nun scurried off to open the door, calling for a stretcher as she did.

Clara wavered a moment in the receiving area. A number of women waited in the lobby, so she made her way to one of the benches there. She took a spot near the cast-iron stove as a piece of the burning wood fell, thumping against the inside. An elderly couple sat leaning together, as though in prayer or in one another's confidence.

A deep longing struck to have Father sitting next to her, his arm around her, telling her all would be well. If he were here, he could go into the back and see Beau, inquire about his condition.

The sunlight crept across the floor and began to fade as the hours passed. Clara couldn't bring herself to leave Beau, but neither could she go to him. So she stayed and prayed.

The double doors opened, and in stalked a man—tall, with a heavy winter overcoat and a bowler hat. Father. He strode right to the desk, the clean scent of cold air trailing behind him. Clara froze, unsure whether to rise or run. Her father's presence made her feel safer—but also smaller, exposed. What would he think when he saw her, obviously not across the country in Baltimore?

"A friend of mine was hurt in a mining accident today. Mr. Beau Vulpe. I would like to see him." His voice was low and steady—the kind of tone that didn't invite contradiction.

The young nun glanced up and quickly nodded her consent.

Clara stood, clasping her hands. "Father?"

He turned slowly, his eyes wide. "Clara?" He crossed the space between them, as though to embrace her, yet he stopped. "Are you here to see Beau?"

"Yes, but I cannot go into the men's ward." Even as she said it, her voice cracked.

Nearby, church bells tolled the seventh hour.

Father turned back around. "I would like my daughter to accompany me to see Mr. Vulpe."

The little nun cast worried glances toward the ward doors. "Well, you see, sir, no ladies are permitted unless they are related."

"She is close to the patient, and I would serve as escort."

Still, the girl shook her head rapidly. "The matron of the ward would not permit it. The moment you stepped through the doors, she would throw you out."

Father's jaw ticked, but Clara placed her hand on his arm. "It is all right, Father. If you could just check on Beau for me…"

His gaze paused on her hand, then he nodded and removed his coat. She took it from him as naturally as anything, and he went into the next room.

Clara sank back onto the bench, exhaling a deep breath. She held his coat in her lap like an anchor—something solid to keep her upright while her thoughts swam. Why wasn't Father surprised to see her? He hadn't even mentioned Baltimore.

When her father returned, his grave expression said more than words. Clara's worries thundered through her. Was Beau scalded beyond recovery? In agony? Had he gone into shock, overheated, and had a heart attack? Unable to move, she watched as Father approached.

He sat beside her on the bench. "I'm afraid he was scalded pretty severely."

Clara's throat closed, and her eyes stung with tears.

"He is resting now, bandaged and settled in for the night. He should sleep."

"Will he recover? Will he walk again?"

"Only God knows. You must pray for him." He placed a hand on Clara's back. "Now, it is dark, and you must be getting home."

She nodded and stood slowly. Part of her wanted to fold into him like a child—but she remained upright, skirts rustling like mourning veils as she followed him toward the door.

Outside, the night was crisp, with hills blanketed with moonlight and the shadow of Mt. Davidson standing tall against the stars. Sure enough, Father had a horse and buggy parked outside. He helped her up into the seat, then went around and climbed in beside her.

"How did you learn about Beau?"

"Mr. MacKay sent word that Beau was hurt just after suppertime." He flicked the reins and sent the buggy into motion.

Clara wavered with the movement yet pressed her feet into the floor. "Beau's been here since early afternoon."

"I imagine there was chaos with the floods." His voice lowered. "Some men didn't make it out."

His logic was hard to argue with. She'd seen the men carried in, scorched and broken. "Did Beau say anything in particular?"

"No. He was in no condition to speak and was sleeping when I arrived."

They rolled up to the higher streets, Mt. Davidson's

precipice towering before them. Unsure of what to say and unwilling to address Father's outburst—when she had nothing to say on that end as well—Clara remained silent, just letting the night settle around them.

A quiet ache bloomed beneath her ribs. *Be with him, God.*

A hymn played through her mind as she faced the mountain, one of Grandmother Alexander's favorites. *Soon as the evening shades prevail, the moon takes up the wondrous tale, and nightly to the listening earth repeats the story of her birth.*

Father softly hummed the tune, as though hearing it too. Clara stared at him, hardly breathing.

The overwhelming feeling of being cared for struck her. By God. By Beau. And now by Father. He didn't even comment when she told him to drop her off at Mrs. Matthews's boardinghouse.

She hadn't leaned on him in years—but tonight, beneath the hush of hymn and moonlight, it felt like she could again.

And maybe that was enough—for now.

~

Where is Clara? The thought thundered louder than the pounding in his skull. He'd just seen her at the hoisting works—a mustache glued to her pretty face, her blue eyes shining out at him like flecks of twilight sky. And now she was gone.

Carbolic acid stung his nose. He breathed deep, trying to work his way up from unconsciousness. His limbs refused to obey, leaden and sluggish under a blanket of pain. Someone brushed his arm. He tried to push them away, to kick off his assailants, but his limbs were pinned, as if shackled by iron.

There was movement down by his legs—and a burning. An agony that wrapped around him like blasting heat in the pit of the mine. Daylight poured through a nearby window. He squinted, trying to make sense of the blurred edges.

"There, laddie. Settle down." Mr. MacKay stood by his bed, a hand on his shoulder. "John and I just wanted to inquire after your health." His Irish brogue curled around every word, giving it a sort of friendliness.

Shadows clouded his vision, and Beau tried to sit up, but straps still held him in place. He lay back, panting. "How bad was it?"

"Oh, you got the worst of it. You don't need to worry, though. I'll cover whatever expenses you have, and if you want to go back into the mines, you'll have a job waiting when you recover."

"*Je vous remercie, monsieur.*"

"You are welcome. We're still unable to work on that level. There's so much water. A few men were trapped down there. Search parties will go down once it's safe."

Beau closed his eyes. "*Mon Dieu*, have mercy." He prayed, shaking his head.

"Mining is a dangerous job." John spoke low, pulling up a chair as he did. "Perhaps this is God's way of steering you down a different path. Many of those men don't have the opportunity you do because of your education." John crossed his arms. "What kind of future is this, Beau, if you ever want to have a wife and family?"

The question hit like a punch to the gut. Exhausted from fitful sleep and fighting pain, Beau just shrugged, replying that he had no good answer—only to realize he spoke French.

"We can talk once you're better." MacKay checked a silver watch, then slipped it back into his pocket. "I'm afraid I have to leave. I want to see you once you've recovered." He gave Beau's shoulder a pat, then shook his hand and left.

All was quiet. Beau drifted to visions of Clara, near but just out of reach—a more preferable option than his dreams of last night that had her falling down mine shafts and drowning in boiling water at the bottom. A flash of horror sent his eyes open.

Clara's father had his arms folded as though in prayer, though he was quiet. He cleared his throat. "You know my sins, so if you say no, it won't offend. But may I pray for you, Beau?"

He nodded and closed his eyes as John started with a quiet, even hesitant prayer, thanking God for Beau's rescue and requesting that the waters recede and the miners lost underground could soon be laid to rest. Then he focused his entire prayer on Beau—asking for God's blessing and guidance. That His unfailing love would shield Beau through his darkest times. That His healing touch would descend upon him and make him well. That God would guide Beau's path to prosperity.

Shamed by the bestowal of such a heartfelt and honest prayer by one whom Beau had hurt, he resisted the urge to shrug away from John's touch.

"And as for Beau's future where my daughter is concerned, we give that over to You, Lord, knowing that You will work Your good and perfect will in both their lives. And that at the end of this life, both will have known the lifelong love of a godly, selfless spouse and a legacy that will carry down generation to generation."

He was quiet for a moment, then he committed the day to God, patted Beau on the shoulder, and left.

Beau lay still, conscience blazing, the prayer echoing louder than the pain. He did not deserve such grace.

CHAPTER 18

Clara swept up the whitewashed stairs of St. Mary Louise Hospital, sunlight striking the red-brick, four-story building. She pressed her gloved hand to the brass doorknob, its chill a cruel contrast to the scalding Beau had suffered two weeks ago. All was quiet in the great building. Stepping into the dim corridor, she made her way to the familiar door, passing a young nun humming a hymn. The woman smiled at Clara.

"I am here to inquire after Monsieur Vulpe," Clara said, as she had since that first day she came to the hospital.

"Yes, Monsieur Vulpe is out back." The nun pointed to a door at the end of a long corridor. "You may see him now."

Clara hurried down the hall and out into the sunlight. A veranda-like porch stretched the length of the building, its pillars—like those out front—supporting the second-story balconies. A green field spilled away below. The view stretched for miles, rolling sagebrush hills fading into violet ridgelines—but all Clara could do was search the space for Beau.

A man in loose clothes sat on the veranda, the wheels of his chair catching the morning light. His muscular build and proud posture tugged at her memory. She saw him clearly—the clean-shaven side of his face and the nose, which might have been regal if not for the slight bend where it had been broken. "Beau?"

His head shifted by a fraction, enough to betray that he knew she was there. "I thought you might stop coming." His voice was healed, sure and deep. Not like the last time she saw him.

"Why would I stop coming?"

His gaze drifted to the yard and fluttering birds in a pinion pine tree.

Why wasn't he answering her? Had the scalding he received in the mine broken his spirit?

"Are you all right?" It seemed a stupid question.

Still, he was quiet.

How could he just sit there like that? Didn't he want to talk to her, after weeks of being apart? She'd not seen him, not spoken with him. Only heard from the sisters that he was fighting an infection. His legs badly scalded. Unable to walk. And that if she did see him, he'd never know because the medicine needed to keep his pain at bay left him in a state of drowsiness.

"Are you still wearing trousers?" he asked, squinting toward the hills.

She'd not lie, even if it cost her. "Yes. I am able to move around town unbothered by men who would otherwise gawk and stare." She settled herself on the banister, the sunlight warming her back. "I didn't know how good you men had it. Being able to see the whole world as it is. Having the right to tell someone to leave your hat alone. To get out of the way, even to simply leave an uncomfortable room. When I wear a dress, I am forced to cater to the men around me. Appear engaged in conversations that do not interest me. Hide in my carriage so dirty miners and drunkards do not lust after me. Walk, talk, and look perfect." She crossed her arms, a flush of unexpected anger blooming in her chest. "I wish I could move freely like you."

"You think I'm free?" His dark eyes flared. "Not all men have those rights, Clara. Or hasn't your time in the world of men taught you that?" He jerked his chin aside, gaze fixed on the horizon beyond her.

A flicker of memory intruded on the sunny day. On that dark Christmas morning, she'd spied the Paiute people who certainly did not have the freedom to move, speak, and live as they liked. But she wasn't wrong. Beau had rights she did not.

"It's hard, is all I am saying. In finishing school, there were so many rules. Ways to walk, talk, dress, even breathe. They seemed so important at the time, and now I see it was all just some silly societal expectation. I want to...to walk on the street unfettered by society's burdens. Hike into those hills and have a picnic or climb to the top of Mount Davidson, but I cannot because I am a woman."

He shook his head. "Mrs. Matthews and some friends of hers climbed Mount Davidson last spring. You can do the things you love, safely."

Of all the impossible conversations to have after his illness and confinement, why this? She'd been hoping to see him. To help him heal. To tell him how much she missed him and prayed for him every single day.

Feeling his gaze on her, Clara looked away.

"Has anyone hurt you?"

She snickered. "No. Who would? I am of no account to anyone here."

"You are L. C. Royall, are you not?"

Unmoving, for she would not lie or admit the truth, Clara held his gaze.

"You wrote about the city not supporting the fire department and insurance charging extra in a time of need. And then there was the article about Peterson's murder going unsolved." Color filled his cheeks, and his jaw ticked. "Do you want to bring danger down on your head?"

She threw her hands out to the side. "I write under a pseudonym. No one knows who I am."

"And no one can follow you? Find where you live? Where you sleep?"

The notion wracked her. Beau was right—she hadn't thought it through. But if she didn't speak up, who would? "It was wrong, what happened to Mr. Peterson. He deserves justice. I am trying to get that for him." Her voice wavered, but she meant it. Some truths demanded light, no matter the cost.

"At the expense of your safety? You are intelligent and resourceful. Surely, you can uphold the same cause without compromising your security."

A wall rose between them—quiet, heavy, and immovable. He broke the silence not with more words, but by grasping the wheels and working them to turn back toward the doors.

Panic prickled her skin. He was shutting her out...again. "Beau, don't leave. I only just arrived. It's been two weeks, for heaven's sake." She touched his shoulder, the firm muscle there giving her pause.

He stopped, glaring at her. "I should have never told you about the salting. It's too dangerous."

"I had a right to know. I wrote the article claiming it was a rich mine."

"You wrote what Theo told you to write, and he put his name at the bottom. I guess his sins found him out."

"He was fired for that false article he wrote about you murdering Mr. Peterson, but Mr. Goodwin also stated, in his retraction, that Theo had written falsely regarding Peterson's mine as well. That was just the day after Sheriff Kelly shared that Peterson suspected his mine was salted and that he was investigating to see if there was any connection between the salting and the murder. I wondered if he would try to blame me, but he didn't. Still, I feel I am partly responsible. As though keeping the truth that I wrote that article hidden makes me a fraud." Shame stirred in her stomach. The truth was, she hadn't told anyone—because she'd wanted the byline more than the backlash.

Beau frowned at her, his black eyebrows drawn low. "Good grief, Clara. You told me yourself that you simply wrote the findings he told you."

"They were my words. And isn't a man's word his bond?"

Beau groaned, massaging the bridge of his nose. "You cannot take everything so literally."

She cocked her head, suddenly wanting to smile. He dragged a hand down his face, exasperated, and she couldn't help it. Poor Beau, he was truly frustrated—but at least he was talking. "Did you know..."

He raised his eyebrows, his hand cupping his face.

"Did you know that in 1801, the London Stock Exchange adopted the Latin phrase *dictum meum pactum*—*my word is my bond*—as its official motto? It stood for integrity as the foundation of British commerce."

"You don't say."

She smiled, though he didn't. He looked at her for a long time. She could almost feel him studying her, the way he might pore over Scripture—searching for truth, for hope.

"I..." Did she dare allow herself to be vulnerable when he was so unsteady? "I missed you. Every day."

Clara gripped the banister to support herself, her gloved fingers digging into the wood as if it might anchor her heart. If Beau rejected her now, she might melt into the porch like ice cream left too long in the Nevada sun. She'd prayed for this moment, replayed it in her mind with a thousand imagined outcomes, but none of them had prepared her for the silence stretching between them like taut thread ready to snap.

He swallowed, the slight knob in his throat moving down toward the collar of the light-blue cotton shirt he wore. "I thought of you every second." His voice faded to a whisper, and he shook his head regretfully. "When I was trapped, I remembered everything I'd done wrong. Everything I lost. Then in the hospital...I kept wishing you would come."

"I did. Sometimes twice a day." Tears burning, she reached for him, and he took her hand in his hard, healed yet rough fingers. "I brought you my Bible to read, the things Mr. Sanderson said you kept in your bag, and some hearty stew from Maudy."

Still, he stared—silent and unreadable.

"Beau, what is wrong? Really? You... Is it because you're hurt? Your legs?" She hadn't even inquired after his health. "I should have asked before. I'm sorry we quarreled."

"My legs are healing. They were burned, but I can walk. They just want me in this chair because moving irritates the burns."

"You can walk?" She was so relieved, she released a breath too quickly and almost laughed. "Oh, I'm so glad." Clara wound her arms around him, hugging him at an odd angle.

Beau clasped her wrist, tugging her down to press his face against the curve of her neck. Her heart thrummed with warmth at the closeness of him. He seemed to rest, quiet, with his eyes closed. Clara caressed his cheek—so smooth—and pressed a kiss to his forehead.

"Ma chérie, you wound me so." His breathing paused, then he looked up, so near she could see the thick, dark lashes, penetrating eyes, and all the fierceness of a man ready to fight. "I can't lie to you anymore. It's not right. Not now—when we've grown so close."

The sweetness in her evaporated, and Clara's stomach churned. She knew he was hiding something and secretly hoped it would resolve on its own—or that he'd make it right

189

before she had to face it. She'd never expected a confession. Remembering Father's confession to Mother, a sick weight dropped into Clara's gut.

"Here. Sit beside me." He gestured to a clean, whitewashed bench propped against the back of the hospital. She did as he requested while Beau wheeled over and stood. He winced when he straightened to his full height, then came to sit near enough that her dress pressed against his leg.

Clara clasped and unclasped her hands, struggling to keep her voice level. "What did you want to tell me?"

"You know that once I lost my wife and son, I sank into a dark time. There was a man in my life who was strong, though—a Frenchman I had served with in the military. He had connections in America, out West. But he was not a law-abiding man. Lorraine—the woman I told you about..."

"The one you rescued from the prison train?"

"Yes. She knew this and refused to move west. She stayed in the East, working at the Sells Brothers' Circus. I stayed, too, but then..." He shook his head. "I was so alone. All the time. I drank and was angry. I scared Lorraine one night when I stumbled in drunk after a fight. I knew I couldn't change, so I went west—to that man I thought was my friend. He went by the name Emil." He watched her as though calculating her reaction.

"And he was an outlaw?"

Beau nodded. "After fighting so long beside Frenchmen, then feeling like there was no room for me in America, stealing from citizens who hated me didn't seem wrong. It felt like I was still at war. I had no one but Emil and the French community. Every now and then, over those four years I was in America, Lorraine would visit or I would see her, and I would do better. But I could never stay on a righteous path." His voice pitched in earnest. "I wanted to do well—but I didn't always know what that was."

She frowned. When she wasn't sure what to do, she turned

to the Bible. There was right and wrong—the black and white of life. How could Beau not find that?

"One day, Emil's brother was sent to prison. He died there. Emil was shattered. He'd already lost his family—like me. When he formed a plan to capture the man responsible for putting his brother in prison, I supported him. We kidnapped him and hauled him down to Utah. But he seemed like a nice kid. I'd feel bad for him, but then I'd remember my people—Emil suffering from the loss."

Clara tugged at the cotton collar of her blouse. "What happened?"

Beau gripped the bench seat and leaned forward, huffing a breath. "Lorraine turned on the gang—on me. She said I was wrong, fighting a war against an innocent man. I had to choose between her and Emil. She said it was a decision between right and wrong, but I didn't see it then. Still, I wasn't willing to let her get hurt. The gang knew she'd turned. So I betrayed them. Turned them in, then left town like a coward."

Clara blinked. "It sounds like you did a good thing, Beau. In the end."

"It doesn't matter. There has to be atonement for sin. I was part of a kidnapping and bank robbery just last year. And here's the worst part." He gripped the bench more tightly, muscular arms drawn taut.

Clara touched his bicep. "I'm sure whatever it is—"

"It was your cousin. Jesse Alexander."

Her breath caught. The wheels in her mind turned. Jesse had been kidnapped—it had been all over the papers. Grandmother had been beside herself, threatening Grandfather Alexander that she'd go to Idaho and find Jesse herself. Then Uncle Titus rescued him, and Jesse fell in love with a female outlaw named...

"Lorraine," Clara whispered, her heart tapping in her chest. She remembered the letters from Aubrey, the articles she'd read. "But all the men responsible for that were caught—some killed, some imprisoned. The last one was arrested..."

Beau raised his brows.

"In August. In Salt Lake City." Her fists clenched. "That was you?"

He didn't move. Didn't breathe.

A chill slid down her center. Clara shot to her feet and paced before him. This couldn't be real. Beau—a man who had shown her nothing but kindness—was the same man who once held her cousin hostage?

But he wasn't cold-blooded. He'd confessed. Sat here, baring his soul. Waiting on her judgment like a man awaiting the noose.

She stepped to the edge of the porch, bathed in sunlight, then turned back to him. "Well, how did you end up in Virginia City?"

"I needed a way to earn money—after I escaped."

"No, no. No, Beau. You're a good man." She stopped in front of him, shaking her head. She'd read enough stories about desperadoes—men who killed without conscience and preyed on the weak. That wasn't Beau. She lowered herself to the bench beside him. "You are..." She gestured toward him, still baffled. "You are the finest man I've ever met. And I don't say that because I love you." She took his hand and squeezed it gently, breathless from her own admission but not really surprised. "From the first moment I met you, you've sacrificed for me. Always. I haven't seen you in two weeks, and the first thing you asked was whether I was wearing pants—your notion of what's dangerous."

"I lied to you. Hid my identity. Fooled you, Clara." He dropped his head. "You mean to tell me you're not angry? Deceived?"

"You told me you were hiding something. And I suppose this is worse than I expected."

"So then..." His arms trembled, as though bearing a weight far heavier than his body could carry. "You forgive me?"

"Yes."

"And you see why I can't court you? Marry you? Love you?"

His words struck her like a blow. Something deep within her shifted, fractured. "Why not?"

It was a foolish question. He was a fugitive. He'd said so himself. Maybe he was preparing her—for a return to prison. For another loss.

"I can't run forever. I tried to leave," he said low, his voice tight. "The day I left you at the house. Then Peterson's mine turned out to be salted. I figured it might reflect poorly on you, and I wanted to protect you from that. I planned to leave the day after Christmas, but then you were gone. I thought..." He closed his eyes, as if to block out the pain. "I thought I'd never see you again. And when you moved in with Mrs. Matthews, I told myself I was staying to watch over you. To keep you safe. But here I've been confined to bed for two weeks while you've been running around Virginia City dressed like a man, writing about things that could get you killed."

A flash of heat on her cheeks, she glanced around to see if anyone might overhear. "I wrote the truth. If no one knows I'm a woman—"

"They will follow you. They will figure it out. Or worse, they will jump you in some dark alley, thinking you're a man. The liberty to speak freely may be an American right, but it is not something to take lightly, Clara. It invites risk."

She drew a deep breath, chest aching. "I won't go back to my father. And if you tell him, I will have to leave for Baltimore. He hurt me, and I cannot live in that miserable house without mourning my mother every day."

"If I do not tell him, you are not safe. What kind of man would I be then?"

How could he threaten her? Take away the one thing in life

she was finally good at? Her freedom—expendable, for safety's sake? "Some things are worth the risk."

"I guess that means you won't listen to reason, then?"

Grinding her teeth, Clara shook her head. "Why won't you *see* reason?"

He sat like a pillar—strong, unmoving—then his shoulders sagged. "How could I risk you—for anything?"

Biting back the angry words, she turned on her heel and walked off the porch steps.

CHAPTER 19

How could Beau be so stubborn? Would he truly turn her over to Father, ending her reporter career? And what of his confession?

She stopped halfway up the snowy steps to Mrs. Matthews's boardinghouse.

Beau was a criminal. He had kidnapped her very own cousin, Jesse. While Aubrey was female, and Clara had been drawn to her older cousin, she and Jesse had played together when they were younger. He wasn't like other boys—being quieter and loving to read. The idea of anyone harming him angered her. Just how far had Beau gone with him? He'd mentioned his violent past. Had he hurt Jesse?

She'd have to get to the bottom of this. Find real evidence. Perhaps she could connect with Jesse by letter, ask about the abduction without raising suspicion. After all, Father seemed to genuinely care for Beau, and she'd hate to ruin their relationship.

She needed a plan.

Clara was still huffing when she opened the front door and

entered the parlor. Maudy and Abe were there before the fireplace, embracing.

"Oh, Clara!" Maudy practically flew at her. "Abe just asked me to marry him."

She nearly fell backward when Maudy came up against her, wrapping her in an embrace.

"Congratulations," she said, even as doubts swirled. Maudy and Abe had only been courting for two months.

Abe grinned wide, shifting his feet a bit. He was tall and lanky, with a thick patch of brown hair and a red mustache. "Th-th-thank you, miss," he managed to say, despite a stutter that often resulted in little speech—though he and Maudy stayed beside the fire talking low for hours on Sundays.

The young couple really were precious, and Abe was not what Clara had expected. He was humble and shy—and very much in love with Maudy. Not a grasping, passionate, bold man. Would his personality make it easier for him to be faithful?

Perhaps they could be happy and Clara was all wrong.

But what of Beau? He was bold—and even passionate about the things he believed in. A deep hurt sank right down the middle of her core. Beau had deceived her, and now, after she'd allowed herself to care for him, they might be separated for good.

"We will have the banns read as soon as possible and marry the next month." Maudy practically sang the words. "That will give me time to tidy up my Sunday dress with some lace and ribbons."

"Oh, Maudy, I have the perfect dress for you. A modest pale blue with black velvet trim. Would you like it?"

"Yes! That's so good of you." Maudy grabbed her in another backbreaking hug, then returned to Abe's side. "That will give us time to alter the dress. Miss Clara is a few inches taller than me." She propped her hands on her hips, smiling wide.

She'd never know that referencing their body types in front of a man was considered vulgar—because Clara would never tell her.

"I have time to collect the gown now." And she would search through her correspondence to find those written by Aubrey regarding the abduction. Clara had also saved newspaper articles on the incident. Maybe the *Daily News* still had a copy tucked away—or the editor remembered the case. She stepped toward the door. "I will be back before dinner."

"I can go with you." Maudy moved to follow her, but Clara waved her off.

"No need. I do so love to walk—and if you stay, you and Abe can sort out your plans. Such as...will you have a honeymoon, and will either of your families be in attendance?"

As though struck mute, Maudy blinked and turned to Abe. She did not look happy, and he took her hands, drawing her closer.

Not wanting to intrude on the private moment, Clara left the way she'd come.

The whole walk down B Street, memories from her conversation with Beau pelted her—his unwillingness to see that she needed to wear men's attire to do the job she loved. That she did forgive him, even as doubt lingered. What if this was how women fell for men who didn't really love them?

The brick home Mother had loved so dearly came into sight. The dormers were still crested with snow, as were some of the windowsills.

She went to the front door yet could not bring herself to knock. What if Tessa saw her and she had to explain what she was doing there? She also risked encountering Daniel if she entered through the main door.

Clara's shoulders sank, a heavy loneliness seeping onto her. Her little brother, whose life she'd already missed too much of, loved her and needed her.

And here you are chasing stories and living in near poverty. All because you are too bitter to live at home.

Biting her lip, she traversed the slippery steps and trudged through the snow to a side door, the argument continuing in her head.

They don't deserve forgiveness!

Against Thee, Thee only, have I sinned, and done this evil in Thy sight. The old King James, as usual, stomped all over her self-righteousness. And she had called Tessa a truly terrible word the night Father lost his temper. It was shameful, yet she could not bring herself to feel sorry. Tessa had been intimate with a married man while his wife lay dying in another room. It was wicked of both of them.

Clara huffed, a plume of white fogging around her face before she pushed open the door to a seldom-used guest room. "You are a fierce taskmaster, Lord." And wasn't that verse taken from David's repentance after committing adultery with Bathsheba?

Of course, the good Lord would bring that scripture to mind.

She imagined God in heaven, looking down with a finger pointed at her. *Now mind your business, daughter.* Didn't that verse apply to all of them—Beau included? If all sin was against God, He alone had the right to withhold forgiveness.

"I hear You, Lord. I am wrong." A flicker of peace settled in her chest, fragile as snow on firewood. But even as she breathed it in, anger bubbled beneath. "You will have to change my heart. I will try to change my thoughts."

A peace stole over her, and she felt lighter. Maybe God was listening to her, after all. She relied more on the Bible than on prayer. But if God heard her—and maybe even answered—she'd try it more often.

Clara cracked a side door and peeked into the sitting room with the bear rug. The fire was crackling its happy song, though the tree was gone. Christmas was over. Her heart sank. She'd forgotten about the celebration, and how special had it been for Daniel on Christmas morning if Father discovered she was gone and left to search for her?

A whine sounded, then the thrumming of little feet with clicking nails. She turned, and Hugo raced up, spinning around her and smacking his front paws against the floor. She shushed him, picked him up and gave him a good rub, and then headed for her bedroom with the fluffy little dog in her arms.

All was peaceful in her room—so wonderfully clean and soft. She set the little Papillon on the bed. Hugo plopped down beside her pillow as though telling her he wasn't leaving. She ran her hand along the bed on her way to her armoire, where she opened the door and drew out the dress that would look so nice on Maudy. Considering how humble the woman was, they might have to remove some of the ruffles and bows.

Digging through the chest she kept at the foot of her bed, Clara gathered the letters from Aubrey written last summer. There were also the newspaper articles, which were easy enough to find. She'd folded them away with the ladies' catalogues and her dictionary. Once she had all the items wrapped in the gown and bundled to her chest, she started toward the door.

"Hugo, come." She patted her leg. He strode across the room as though he hadn't a care in the world. Clara nudged the dog through the door with one foot, then scurried through too. She needed to leave the premises before someone spotted her.

"Clara?" A small voice sounded behind her. She turned to find Daniel, wide-eyed with rosy cheeks. Judging by the condition of his hair, he'd just woken up from a nap.

"What are you doing all alone, sweetheart?" She took his little hand and led him away from the door.

"I had a bad dream. Mama has a headache." He rubbed his rosy cheeks, staring at a wall with a sleepy expression before shifting his attention to her again. "I thought you went back East." The corners of his pouty mouth turned down.

They came to Mother's library and ducked inside. A hint of smoke still tainted the cold air. Black burns marred the bricks where the flames had licked up to the mantel. It was charred and mostly gone. The wooden floor in front of the fire, where the table had fallen, was burned through.

Daniel raised his eyebrows. "What happened to the library?"

"It..." Clara turned, but her brother walked past her to a chest she'd not noticed before.

After he lifted the lid, Daniel tugged out a wooden soldier and stuffed pillow with his initials embroidered on the corner. When had those come to be there? Next, he pulled a book off the shelf, then seated himself on the sofa, looking at her expectantly. "Will you read *The Only True Mother Goose Melodies*?"

"Mother Goose?" She sank down beside him, her dress and papers forsaken at her feet. "Father used to read this to me."

"He's working." Daniel's gaze flicked to the door.

She needed to get back to Maudy—and leave before Tessa discovered her. But Daniel sat waiting, looking around the library, a place he was obviously familiar with, and she hadn't the heart to leave him. Why hadn't she considered that this room was a part of Daniel's home? She'd only seen her own hurt and loss, not even recognizing the new life.

"I would love to read to you, Daniel." Clara leaned back and opened the pages, spotting a well-known rhyme. "Jack and Jill." She smiled, and Daniel laid his head against her chest.

She hugged him close and read or sang her way through the well-loved pages. Eventually, Daniel nodded off to sleep, his hair mussed and cheeks flushed with warmth. He was so beautiful, dark-haired like Father and Uncle Titus. A sadness sank deep inside her as she slipped off the sofa and pushed Daniel back so he would not fall off.

Lingering in the scorched room felt like stepping into the grave of a memory. Another piece of Mother lost, reduced to ash. And yet Daniel lay sleeping there, his arms around his pillow and book. Somehow, her past still lived in his little frame. She would stay at Mrs. Matthews's, but one thing was certain. It was time to stop hiding and be a part of Daniel's life. Even if it cost her pride.

～

The sun had already slipped past the mountain, leaving Virginia City wrapped in the shadow of the cliff. Clara sat on the edge of her bed, shuffling through the papers in her lap—an unfolding tale centered on her cousin Jesse. Kidnapped at Cariboo Mountain and taken all the way to Salt Lake City, Utah, where a final fight erupted—fabulous fodder for an article. Yet there was so little about Beau—just a name. Beau Fox.

She sighed, tracing his name with her finger. He'd given her a false name, though he'd nearly told the truth. After all, *Vulpe* did mean fox. Still, the lie stung.

If only she had more recent articles detailing his arrest in San Francisco. She remembered Father shaking his head and stating how he'd not like to have been on his brother's bad side when the conflict erupted and two babies had been stolen. Had Beau abducted the babies as he had abducted Jesse?

Remembering how peacefully Daniel had slept earlier that day, Clara paused. Beau was repentant, but how could her family ever forgive him? If only there was something she could do to help him.

Maudy's hurried footfalls thundered on the stairs, then she swung in, giggling. "You will never believe it."

Unable to contain a smile, Clara grinned. "What?"

"You have a visitor. A handsome visitor."

That brought a frown. Who would come to see her who could also be counted as handsome? Hopefully, not Theo.

Maudy clicked her tongue, swishing across the room. "A certain French gentleman."

Clara tossed the papers into her bag and started down the stairs in a similar fashion to Maudy, then slowed. After all, running was hardly ladylike, and she had no idea what to expect from Beau after their last conversation.

Past a few boarders and the last of the dinner guests, Clara made her way through the dining room to the front parlor. Several ladies sat sewing, casting furtive glances at Beau's familiar strong back as he faced the window. Feeling as though she were walking through fog, Clara approached him and wrapped her hand around his elbow. "You left the hospital. They dismissed you so soon?"

"I had to see you." He spoke softly, brows low and gaze dark with shadow.

The ladies in rockers had stilled, needles poised over fabric.

"Come into the kitchen with me. We will have some privacy there."

In the kitchen, Mrs. Matthews hefted a large pot of chicken and dumplings from the stove, but her eyebrows shot to her hairline upon seeing them. "What is this, Miss Clara? You will have to see your beau somewhere else. Preferably at a more decent hour."

Cheeks suddenly hot, Clara paused. "Why, Mrs. Matthews. What a thing to say. The sun has barely set, and I merely wanted a word with Mr. Vulpe. He's just come from the hospital."

A softening in the stern woman's face, she relented. "Very well, but I am propping the door open."

"I appreciate that." Clara shook her head as the woman carried dinner into the next room. *My goodness, what did she think Clara intended?*

Beau's arm brushed hers. She'd not meant to stand so close, though she hadn't the inclination to move away. Worry shadowed his countenance, and she sighed. "Ah, Beau. I am sorry we quarreled."

"I kept thinking, what might happen if you went out reporting and got hurt?" He slumped into a chair near the washing sink, and Clara leaned against the counter. A back door led outside, a draft sweeping beneath the jamb.

She hadn't the heart to tell him her stance remained the same. Reporting was important work, and she wasn't ready to give up on her dream.

He sat, his forehead resting in his hands and elbows propped on his knees. "When I was married, Amalie would not argue. She always agreed. As though she didn't care one way or the other."

The criticism stung, though she'd not nibble jealousy's bait. "I could not live that way. Every decision, every remark, every word matters."

"Oui. Your passion for life is *magnifique*."

Clara bit her lips, trying not to smile but failing. Beau studied her, so weary. He was dressed in trousers, a green checked shirt, and a typical overcoat. No scarf. Remembering the night he wrapped it around her neck, and all they faced now weeks later, it was hard to believe he might not be a permanent person in her life.

"I read through letters from my cousin, detailing the kidnapping. There were a few newspaper clippings I had saved as well. Your name is Fox?"

Beau's face darkened. "I didn't come here to talk about that. I need to know—will you keep putting yourself in danger?"

The air between them thickened, as if one wrong word might crack the fragile peace barely formed. She hadn't expected this—another demand to give up her voice. "This is important to me. More important than anything."

His eyes flickered, like a candle disturbed by a draft—shaky, uncertain—then he stood, stepping near her. "Clara..." He took a breath, as though he might say something that could change everything.

Glass shattered and something struck her shoulder.

Beau swept an arm around her, plucking her from her spot. The familiar breath of fire hissed through the air with the telltale scent of kerosene. As she turned, heat flashed across her arm and face. The table was ablaze in the middle of the kitchen.

Clara pulled the back door open and rushed outside. "I will sound the alarm!" She slammed the door behind her, leaving Beau to fight the blaze.

Clara's heart pounded as she whirled, her skirts tangling around her legs. She bolted down the side of the house, each frantic step plunging into ankle-deep snow with a soft crunch. The biting-cold air stung her face. She opened her mouth to shout for help, but the words caught in her throat as a looming figure stepped from the inky shadows.

She collided with a wall of wool and muscle. A sharp pain exploded near her left temple. Time seemed to stand still. Then, as if in slow motion, she fell backward. Arms flailing, she plummeted into the snow, the icy crystals enveloping her like a frigid blanket. A sharp pain at the base of her skull snuffed out her last moment of consciousness.

CHAPTER 20

Blocked from the sink, Beau tore off his heavy coat and used it to beat back the flames feasting on the wooden table where Clara had just been standing.

"Fire!" he shouted, though dinner patrons in the next room were already scrambling to help. One came with a pitcher of water from the meal. Another who could reach the sink grabbed the bucket below and worked the hand pump. The female boarders shrieked.

The fire roared, sustained by the kerosene. Several spots on the floor ignited, but most of the blaze engulfed the table. It jumped to a wall, only to be quickly smothered by a bucket of water. Beau opened the same door he'd sent Clara through and tossed out the chair that had been soaked in kerosene. A large dinner guest lifted the table, and Beau stepped aside so he could heave it outside.

A final bucket of water on the floor ended the blaze, and they stood panting in the smoky kitchen. Beau propped the door open, fanning the air.

"What happened?" Framed in the doorway, Mrs. Matthews stared at the floor, her young son tucked against her side.

Beau knelt beside the damaged area. "Someone threw a kerosene lamp through the window."

"Why?" Mrs. Matthews's eyes filled with tears.

Beau straightened, his shins and feet tender from burns so recently healed. "I cannot say. The chief and an investigator will want to see this. I sent Clara out to sound the alarm. They should be here soon."

The matron nodded, then, with a shaky voice, invited guests to return to the table. Several men ran outside to search for the arsonist, including Beau. What had he been thinking sending Clara out alone? His boots crushed the snow in the backyard, a silent prayer for safety in his mind.

Beau came to the corner of the house. The yard was dark. Clara's footprints were lost among the others that had trodden down the snow that day. She should have reached the church bell pull on the corner by now. An unease shifted in his chest, and he lengthened his stride in that direction. "Clara?"

Maudy tromped up behind him with a lantern. "We should have heard the bells sound already."

"I know." He followed the trail through the snow, his steps becoming faster as worry pitted him. What if the man who set the fire was still out here? What if Clara was—

A dark figure sprawled at the edge of the house.

Beau broke into a run, his heart pounding. He hit the ground on his knees, the jarring impact sending a flare of agony through his legs as his newly healed skin screamed in protest.

Behind him, Maudy hurried over, her lamp spearing light into the darkness. "Oh, no."

The amber hue settled upon Clara, arms askew, blood from a gash on her cheek having dribbled into her light hair.

"Clara? Clara?" Beau hovered above her, relief washing through him when her breath brushed his ear. "She's alive!" But memories of battered, bloodied forms from the war flooded his mind. *God, help me.* The scene before him swayed, and his arms trembled. Beau steadied himself, focusing on her. "Can you hear me?"

"What happened to her?" Maudy raised the lamp, looking for the cause of her friend's pain—as Beau should have.

He scooped her into his arms, the weight of her limp body striking him harder than any fist ever had.

But he didn't move.

If he took her back inside, nothing would change. She'd keep slipping out in trousers, determined to chase truth with ink-stained hands, unprotected and unrepentant.

His jaw clenched. The cold wind tore at his coat, but he barely felt it over the fire flaring in his gut. *I brought this down on her.*

The *clop, clop* of a horse's hooves sounded on the road—like an answer to prayer. Before he could change his mind, Beau strode around the house to hail the passing buggy.

Clara would be furious with him for what he was about to do. But it didn't matter.

Nothing else mattered.

Just Clara.

~

*B*eau paced before the hearth in the Alexanders' front parlor, boots clipping the hardwood like gunfire when he came to the edge of the rug. Each step kept him from launching into ruin. What if Clara never woke up—if the blow to her head had been fatal? His stomach turned, and he paused to breathe deeply, squeezing his eyes closed.

He hadn't reacted so viscerally to blood before Paris, the prison train when he'd learned Amalie and Martin were gone —swept away in the chaos, buried with thousands in mass graves, their cries swallowed by a city in collapse. Amalie hadn't wanted to live in Paris, but he'd insisted she stay. He'd supported Clara living at Mrs. Matthews's—though she'd have been safer on Millionaire Row. If he'd taken her home, supported her in making amends with her father—might she have been spared the attack this very night?

He had failed. Again.

The memories clawed at him, unrelenting. Amalie's hand reaching. Martin's voice, muffled and panicked. The sights, the sounds, the heat—like that day in the mine when the earth tried to swallow him whole. His knees buckled.

"God, please." The trembling of his limbs intensified.

Save me, God.

A hand set on Beau's shoulder, firm and steady.

He breathed deeply, slowly beginning to rise from the mire. When he opened his eyes, it was John—not God—touching him.

Hating to be found in such a state, Beau forced himself to sit on the nearby sofa. "My wife and son perished in Paris. They were massacred."

John closed his eyes momentarily, his voice strong and sure when he opened them. "I am sorry. I imagine seeing Clara hurt brought back the memories." He sat back in a nearby chair, rubbing the bridge of his nose as he often did. "The doctor says she's concussed. Unable to wake up. The blow to the back of her head... She might not see again." His eyes welled with tears.

Beau's body went rigid as John's words sank in. If she couldn't see, she couldn't write. Would Clara fear the dark? Would she never witness the sunset over Mt. Davidson again, or look into the faces of her own children? Was this his fault for sending her out into the yard to get help when it wasn't safe?

John stood, then paced before the fireplace and used the poker to stir the coals in the blazing hearth. "The men who searched for the arsonist who threw the lamp into Mrs. Matthews's kitchen came by. They didn't find the man."

"I told Clara this would happen. That her reporting would get her into trouble."

John put up a staying hand, his eyebrows raised high. "Excuse me? My daughter is reporting again?"

"She's been working for Doten."

"Alf would have told me if she had..." He paused his ministration to the fire. "Don't tell me she's been wandering through town in men's clothes again."

Beau looked down. "She wants to find out who murdered Peterson. She knew a lot about his neighbor leaving town. Sheriff Kelly sat down and gave her a full interview."

John ran a hand through his hair. "She's that new columnist. Royall. Like Ann Newport Royall. Clara met her last summer. That's all she talked about when she came home. So the fire—someone could have followed her from the newspaper. They'd know she is Royall. Aw, Clara." Tipping his head back, John stared at the ceiling. "Sheriff Kelly came by while you were waiting, wanting to know if we knew someone with blond hair, a bowler hat, and a mustache."

Beau stiffened, a vision of that braggart Dodge Peterson marching through his mind.

"I told him no but thought I should pass it on to you since you have spent so much time with Clara of late." John waited, a cat ready to pounce, but Beau had nothing to hide.

"You may tell him that is what Dodge Peterson looks like. Or better yet, I will show him." Beau headed for the door, gripping fists he'd long used to bloody men. Tonight, a coward would pay for his sins. Once and for all. He'd start with Dodge. Next, he'd come for Theo.

"Beau, wait." John strode close behind him from the study to the foyer. "You cannot take vengeance into your own hands and expect that will keep Clara safe from harm."

"You will keep her safe, here in this house."

"If you want to find who hurt her, there are ways. Taking

209

revenge is not one of them. I don't know what you are running from, but you seem to try hard to do the right thing. Do not throw away all your hard-won righteousness for revenge." John gripped his arm, pulling him around.

Beau flinched and jerked free—too sharp, too fast. John's eyes narrowed. Beau closed his fist and lowered it with a tremble. "This is probably connected to the Peterson murder. Clara wouldn't leave it alone. She thought she was helping. I cannot be responsible for the downfall of someone I love again." His voice cracked, but Beau kept his face hard.

John still moved to bar his way. "Going out in the middle of the night will help nothing. Do you really want her to wake up and find you gone? You know she will want to see you, Beau. When you were in the hospital..." He shook his head. "I found her there that day. I don't know how long she'd been waiting in the lobby. I haven't seen her look so lost since I came home from San Francisco when Annalise died."

Clara's tender heart must have been bruised when he was hurt. She was so innocent, and she loved him dearly. Guilt like a yoke around his neck, Beau forced his head up, trying to keep his chin high. "You need to make peace with her. She needs you to listen to her, to show her you love her."

John grabbed him by both shoulders. "This is not the way, Beau. Just think..."

Beau shook his head, meeting John's gaze. "I am a soldier. If it means I can prevent further harm to Clara, perhaps God will forgive me." He stuck out his hand, and John, resignation lining his features, shook it firmly. "You have been a good friend to me. I pray you will forgive me someday."

And with that, he stepped out into the icy wind, his heart heavier than ever. How quickly he had lost the woman he loved and the friend he had respected. Perhaps it was fitting—he was no stranger to conflict. If he could ensure Clara's safety, it might be possible that God would forgive the violence that lived in him. *I only want her safe, Lord.*

The warmth in his veins was a lie—it was vengeance, coursing quick and hot, feeding the thrill of pursuit. Dodge had walked free once, shielded by John's restraint and Beau's mercy. There would be no mercy now. This time, the hunt was personal. And when it ended, those he loved would sleep safer for it.

CHAPTER 21

He sat in the shadows beneath the second story of the saloon, where craps tables served loud men and busty ladies. Beau swished his water, cleaned with cheap spirits, in a cup—a bowl of untouched stew before him. It was a setup, a façade for anyone who might see him. On either side, miners ate hungrily, barely lifting their heads when a lady sashayed onto the stage and belted out a throaty rendition of "The Little Old Log Cabin in the Lane."

The somber lyrics seemed to mock the lively atmosphere in the saloon, though Beau would not let it deepen his angst. He was here to discover who had attacked Clara and why, and he was starting with the blond miner at the bar. Dodge was talking loudly, his mouth flapping as he revealed several missing teeth. He grabbed a girl around the waist, but she pushed him off, slapping his arm.

He shrugged good-naturedly to a buddy, the other obviously joshing him. Then Dodge's attention shifted across the room, and his genial expression dimmed. He met the gaze of a miner in the usual blue overalls and cap—Mr. Perkins, the lift operator at Mr. Peterson's Mine. He'd brought Clara and Beau up from the mine that day she'd collected her blasted ore sample.

Arms crossed, Mr. Perkins stared at Dodge. Slowly, he made his way across the crowded room, passing tables of patrons partaking food and liquor.

Beau kept his hat low, stirring his stew of grouse, carrots, and radishes.

Dodge emptied his glass, then headed to the back of the room, Perkins trailing close behind.

A toothless miner leaned toward Beau, voice gravelly. "Goin' to eat that, sonny?"

Beau kept his expression impassive. "No. You're welcome to it," he replied softly, but inside, every muscle coiled tightly. He needed to reach Dodge before he missed his chance but could not afford to be conspicuous in this crowd.

The fellow thanked him and dropped Beau's bowl on top of his empty plate. "Nothing like heartbreak stew on a cold night like this. I'll pray a blessing for ye."

Nodding, Beau made his way to the bar. He hadn't touched a drop of spirits since Lorraine turned him in to the law. Then he'd drown himself until Nathan arrived, giving him a reason to work again.

"Whiskey." He pounded the bar as the man at his side nervously tapped his shot glass.

"Say, you don't have enough for two, do ya, Frenchy?"

Accustomed to the heckling, Beau ignored him, but when the glass sailed his way down the slick, polished surface of the bar, Beau caught it near the little man's hand, exchanged it for the empty one, and tipped that one back in a quick motion. He grimaced, slapped down a few coins, and dug into his pocket as if searching for cigarette papers. Then he made his way out back, where men often went to talk quietly or to relieve themselves.

The tall brick buildings stood close together, some touching. It was a side door, and the building on the corner had burned. Rubble stacked high, but two shadows drifted between stacks of cleanup. Dodge, thicker than the lift operator, waved his hands wildly as they stood in the dim shadows.

Beau moved closer, shifting onto the balls of his feet to mute the telltale scuff of his boots. A set of stairs led to the next landing. Beau climbed them until he was close enough to hear, though it was still too dark to see.

"No. No more. I don't care what you saw." The back of Beau's neck washed cold at the dangerous lilt in Dodge's whisper, every word laced with threat. "I won't pay you a cent—"

"If you were going to leave Virginia City, you would have before now. Since you're staying, I see no reason we can't be friends." Mr. Perkins's words rounded as though he was missing a few teeth.

Beau squatted near the dark wall.

"I don't want any more of your money, Dodge. I want in on this game of yours." Perkins spoke firmly, then all was quiet.

A light from one of the high windows glowed above Beau. He ducked lower instinctively, remaining hidden. Dodge was in full view now, blowing a plume of smoke before his face, the golden whiskers on his upper lip glinting in the faint light.

"I don't know what you're talking about."

"Sure you do, son. And I'll tell ya this, you need me. Just think what would have happened if any other man had been operating the lift the day the pretty girl in the pants came down."

Beau's muscles constricted at the mention of Clara.

"Did I squeal then? No. And I won't now, if you let me in on the game." The derisive slowness of the man's voice cast a chill down Beau's spine. He'd not heard a man turn words so playfully since working for Emil in Salt Lake. Both had spoken as one might suspect Satan had when offering Eve the forbidden fruit—cunning, inviting, and confident.

"Fine." Dodge stubbed out his pipe, voice low. "Tomorrow, on the Divide—three hours after sunset. You know the spot?"

"I can guess, but what's to keep you from leaving town?"

"I suppose that's a chance you'll have to take. But if you're worried, I work all day tomorrow, then come here. I'll leave through the back door, and you can follow me."

The man must have signaled his reply because all was quiet. Then Dodge turned and walked down the alley. Mr. Perkins went back into the Delta, the raucous sounds of revelry growing and then lessening as he opened and closed the back door. As silence settled over the alley, Beau waited, giving the men plenty of time to move away.

What game did they speak of? He pulled himself up from the shadows. For now, he'd bide his time.

Tomorrow evening, when Dodge exited the Delta to lead his friend to whatever meeting, Beau would be ready.

~

Light was not her friend. It pierced through sleep like a needle to the temple. Clara's stomach roiled, and she rolled onto her side, hanging off the side of the bed. There was the bowl she remembered, and she heaved for a moment, though nothing came up. A cool hand brushed her bangs from her forehead.

Clara pressed herself back into the pillows, resting one arm over her eyes. "The light..." Her voice scraped, hoarse from stomach acid and crying. "It's too bright."

Fabric rustled, and then, blessedly, shadows eased her headache. Clara breathed deeply, the scent of lavender filling her senses and calming her stomach. The left side of her face throbbed. She touched her cheek and eye, only to wince at the pain. What was happening to her?

She squinted at her surroundings. Curtains wavered overhead, hanging from the tall bedframe. She'd loved the embroidered lace fringes as a girl. "Oh, no." She was back in her father's house. Where was Beau? He must have brought her here.

Water trickled, catching her attention and pulling it right. Tessa sat beside her on the bed, wringing a cloth into a basin. She placed it on Clara's head, giving her enough relief so she closed her eyes. And she remembered—Tessa at her side, holding her hair back, emptying the basin, giving her sips of water, reassuring her that all was well.

Why would she be so kind when the last words Clara had spoken to her were so cruel? Why not just have a maid tend her?

"Do you know what happened, Clara?" Tessa asked, water trickling again.

Memory of that night—the fire, then the snowy side of the house, and a man emerging from the shadows—flashed across her mind. "I was going for help, but there was a man. He hit me. Hard."

"When you fell, you hit your head on a rock or something. Can you see?"

Clara eased her eyelids open. Blurry images took shape. Tessa's face was drawn into a frown, faint creases on her smooth forehead. "I can see, yes."

Tessa sagged, touching her hand to her chest. "Thank You, Jesus." Then she met Clara's gaze. "You could not see when you awoke last night. I was so scared you might lose your sight. A blow to the back of the head can permanently blind a person."

Why was she being so kind?

Clara sat up as best she could, leaning back on the headboard. Hopefully, such a position might prevent her from being sick again. "Where's Beau?" she said quietly, her voice trembling slightly. Her stomach twisted with an unspoken question —*Did he leave me?*

Tessa stiffened, though only slightly, then she stood. "It's been all night and part of the morning. Your father will be able to answer your questions. Let me fetch him." She hurried to the door, her bustle swishing like a peacock's tail behind her. The door swung open on silent hinges.

Hugo dashed between Tessa's feet, tripping her. She caught herself on the doorjamb as Hugo sprang onto the bed and sprang to Clara's side. She touched his feathering black-and-white head, and he in turn licked her hand, whining as though he missed her.

Tessa stabilized herself yet faced the hall, not the dog. "Why, Daniel, I nearly stepped on you. What are you doing there?"

"I want to see Clara." Daniel's pouty voice warmed Clara's heart.

"You know she is very sick," Tessa whispered, pulling the door to close it.

"Tessa?" Clara suddenly spoke, intensifying her headache. "I'd like to see Daniel."

Her stepmother shook her head, mouth opening to speak.

Clara's emotions swelled. "Please? He is my brother." She could not keep the indignation from her voice, nor the deep hurt.

"If he jostles you, speaks too loud, or becomes excited, he might hurt you." Tessa wrung her hands, casting a glance between brother and sister.

"I will sit—really quiet. Not even make a peep. I brought my book, in case sitting is hard." He held up the Mother Goose tome. "Please, Mama. I won't hurt Clara." His sweet little way of speaking—rounding each word so it wasn't quite clear—awakened a well of warmth in Clara.

"Oh, all right. It might be better to have someone here. You can fetch me if Clara is sick." Tessa walked Daniel back as though to help him onto the bed, but he ran and pounced on the mattress. "Daniel Kingsley," his mother scolded, and he straightened out his legs and lay face down, as if hoping to disappear into the mattress.

"Sorry, Mama." The pillow muffled his voice. Slowly, he raised his head. "Can I still stay?"

"*May* I *please* stay?" she corrected him, sighing and shaking her head. "Be gentle, like when mama has a headache." Tenderness shone from her face, then she left the room without a backward glance.

My goodness, Tessa seemed surer of her position as Daniel's mother. Had something changed while Clara was gone? Perhaps the family was better off without her.

Daniel turned over, eying Clara as though he suspected her of wrongdoing. "You left me."

She hadn't expected that, but he wasn't wrong. "I'm sorry, sweetheart. You fell asleep, and I didn't want to wake you." She raised her arm, and he nuzzled against her side. "I missed you, Daniel."

He just nodded and was still for a moment. "I can't read, but I can tell you the story that goes with the pictures." He flipped through the pages.

Clara closed her eyes, hurting too much to answer.

Daniel spoke low and soft, telling the stories she'd heard as a child. Father and Tessa must read to him often. Clara cringed at the idea of Tessa touching her beloved storybook—a treasured companion that had soothed countless nightmares and greeted many dawns throughout her childhood.

So often, it felt as though Tessa had stolen something precious from her life. Even four years later, she didn't want the woman to touch a book. She was wrong.

The storybook was Daniel's now. As it should be. Mother was gone. Her throat tightened. Tessa lived here now, and as his mother, shouldn't she read to him? If Father had given Daniel a brand new book—instead of the one that had been Clara's dearest treasure as a little girl—well, she'd not be happier. It was a special thing, and Daniel should have it.

A door whispered open, and Clara opened her eyes. Father approached with a swift gait. "Clara." He sat beside her, taking her hand. "Tessa said you can see?"

"Yes." She squinted at him, clasping his hand back despite a coolness that ran through her blood. Bitterness.

Oh, no, she didn't want that anymore.

"Were you afraid, Father?"

He kissed her hand. "Yes, we both were." He glanced at Tessa, though she waited by the door, nibbling her fingernail. She tucked it behind her back, as though caught sinning.

What had Tessa been like as a girl? Where was her mother? How had she ended up in a mining town with no family?

"Beau brought you here last night," Father said, pushing aside her hair to see the cut at her temple. "He said..." He glanced at Daniel, then to Tessa. "Could you please take Daniel to breakfast?"

She moved forward, but Daniel whimpered.

"There, son. You may return to see Clara after you've eaten. Now I need to talk to her alone."

Daniel pursed his bottom lip, his chin trembling.

Sensing a squall of emotions threatening, Clara covered his hand. "Perhaps you and your mother could pick me up a bit of toast and tea?"

Tessa nodded and took a begrudging Daniel's hand when they walked into the hall.

The door closed, young ears safely on the other side. Clara turned her attention to her father. "Someone hit me outside Mrs. Matthews's boardinghouse. They set a fire too." Remembering brought her tone to a pitch. "Did Beau get it well in hand?"

"He did. The lamp, filled with kerosene, landed on a table. They were able to toss the table into the snow and soak the rest.

Otherwise, this town might have perished. It was a lamp knocked over at Crazy Kate's Boardinghouse that set the blaze in October."

"I remember." Her memories grew more vivid, and Clara sucked in her breath. "Father, that lamp hit me on the arm. Beau moved me away so quickly. If he hadn't..."

A look of true horror filled her father's face. "He saved you again." He mumbled something inaudible.

"Where is he now?"

Father sighed long and held her hand a little more firmly. "Gone."

Her heart thundered at the thought. "Where did he go?"

"I do not know. I tried to convince him to stay—to at least see you—but he was..." He shook his head. "Dark. Quiet. He refused—especially once the doctor said you must be concussed. That you might not regain your sight."

"So he just left?" How could he? She'd gone to the hospital every day when he'd been hurt.

"Now, Clara. You must understand. The harm that came to you might be linked to the trouble Beau was in weeks ago. He feels that leaving is the only way to keep you safe—that, and bringing you here." His cheeks colored, and he looked down. "You have no reason to believe me, but I will keep you safe. I was wrong that night." His voice grew thick with emotion.

Words failing her, Clara looked away. Her head pounded. Her heart ached. Beau was gone. And thinking of what her father had done just drove the hurt deeper.

Footsteps sounded in the hall—quick, light little steps. Hugo raised his head and perked his ears where he lay beside her. Likely, Daniel had not eaten a bite but got her food and would soon race through the doorway.

Father's thoughts must have gone a similar way, for he gently set her hand down. "If you have anything to say about your mother, me, or Tessa, I will listen."

THE CONVICT'S COURTSHIP

Clara's lips parted in surprise. Her father inclined his head, waiting. Not pressing, just open and patient. For a moment, the silence stretched between them, warm and tremulous. Then she gave the smallest nod, not of agreement, but of possibility.

The footfalls paused, then the door opened ever so slowly. Daniel peeked in, his eyebrows raised. "I brought toast."

Clara smiled, not actually sure she could eat. "Thank you, dear."

He set it on the bedside table, and soon Tessa came in with a tray of tea and a telegram. She passed it to Father, then hung back, her hands clasped. Not clinging to him or chattering.

"News, John?" Tessa peered over Father's shoulder at the paper he held.

Why did she ask when she was obviously reading it?

He looked up from the message. "We will have visitors soon."

"Your brother?"

"And the rest of his family." Father grinned. "It's just as I expected—he's come to flaunt his grandchildren." He ruffled Daniel's hair. "You shall have cousins, Daniel."

"Oh, boy. That'll be a hoot. We can sled and build snowmen, and—"

"I'm afraid these are babies—and girls."

Daniel wrinkled his nose, clearly unimpressed.

Hiding a smile, Clara nibbled on her toast. "I will build a snowman with you, Daniel— just as soon as I am well."

His face wrinkled further. "You are a girl."

Clara laughed and winced at the ache in her head. "Girls can have fun too." The thought struck her—Father had never stopped her from playing outside. He had joined her, teaching her to pack the snow and how to throw good and hard. And he'd been so proud when she landed one in the middle of that nasty boy down the street—the one who was always pulling her braids in church. How had she forgotten that?

Father watched her now, far grayer than in those days. His features were weathered, the creases around his eyes deeper, but love still shone bright in them, just as it did for Daniel. Tessa, however, seemed distant. She rubbed her arms, looked toward the fire, and nibbled her already swollen fingers.

Clara's stomach clenched. She had always wished for Father to love Mother, not Tessa. But now, witnessing his adoration for his children while recalling his overly calculated affection for his new wife in the past, Clara's heart ached with sympathy. She had been the outsider for so long. The last thing she wanted was for Tessa to endure such loneliness, yet she could not quite bring herself to extend a welcome now that Daniel and Father were near.

CHAPTER 22

It felt wrong, smiling when Beau was gone, Mr. Peterson's murder was unsolved, and she'd been attacked just yesterday. Yet the soft crackle of the fire in the hearth and the warm morning light pouring through the high parlor windows cast a gentle balm over Clara's weary heart, as did the baby resting in her arms. Her little cousin, Melanie Willot, was the most precious angel Clara had ever seen, with dark hair and thick eyelashes resting over her round, rosy cheeks.

Clara smiled at her cousin, who sat at her side with a blond baby in her arms. "She is darling. They both are."

Aubrey sighed, and her radiant green eyes shimmered with emotion when she looked between the girls. "Thank you, I agree. I do wish the men were here so you could see Jesse and meet Nathan." Her brown curls cascaded over one shoulder as she turned to Lorraine Durand, Jesse's fiancée. "Do you know when they will be back?"

Lorraine, elegant with her dark curls and refined French poise, acknowledged Aubrey's question with a reserved shake of her head, glancing up slightly from the book she shared with

Daniel. "Non, they might be a long while. Jesse was excited to explore the mountain."

She went back to reading with Daniel. Clara had never seen her little brother so at ease with someone he only just met. Lorraine, though, exuded a quiet calm that belied her past as a bandit.

How close had Lorraine and Beau been? He had married Amalie, so not too close. But a part of Clara—too tall, too talkative, too curious for her own good—felt shy in front of the French-Romani woman.

"How is my cousin?" Clara had yet to see Jesse, who went out early shooting with Aubrey's husband, Nathan Reed.

The tenderness emanating from Lorraine's eyes at the mere mention of her fiancé reflected a woman in love. "Jesse is very well. Eager to see you." She paused, her French accent thicker than Beau's. "He says you are close to the same age and had many adventures at Christmastime in your childhood."

Clara beamed and began sharing a tale of when she and Jesse read *The Swiss Family Robinson*, then secretly smuggled presents from under the tree and hid them all over the house. They thought it was great fun to create a map for the family to follow to find their gifts. However, one of Grandfather Alexander's had been lost, and neither Uncle Titus nor Clara's father were pleased with that.

"Did you ever find the present?" Lorraine asked with a slight laugh.

"Grandmother did, a year later. We'd stored it in an old chest in a spare room that was seldom used."

Suddenly, men's voices sounded from the other room, and Jesse walked in, his brown hair windblown and cheeks flushed from the cold. At his side was a tall man with a lankier build and steely blond hair. He surveyed the gathering, his attention landing first on Aubrey and both babies before he seemed to even notice Clara. He nodded politely.

"Clara?" Jesse hurried toward her, pulling her into a firm hug while being careful of the baby she held. The warmth and safety of his embrace reminded her of loss—like pressing on a sore muscle, painful yet offering relief. Tears stung her eyes as she looked up at him. "It's good to see you, Jess."

"It is so great to see you." He squeezed her shoulders in a brotherly way that warmed her heart. "You were still resting when we left. Have you recovered?" His gaze focused on the bruise where she'd been struck.

"Yes. I was just telling Lorraine about when we stole the Christmas presents and hid them around the house."

Lorraine grinned, speaking quickly in French. Clara wasn't as fluent as her cousins, but she caught the tease—*Jesse, after all, the thief*. It was good that they could speak so freely about her past.

Jesse sat beside her, grinning widely. Daniel made a face at him, and he laughed.

"Oh, Clara." Aubrey stood, reaching for her husband. "This is my husband, Nathan Reed." The baby cried, and Nathan handled her with an ease Clara had rarely seen in a man. He still managed to shake her hand, his face easing into a kind smile.

Her mind flicked to the newspaper article she'd read—about Mr. Reed, before marrying Aubrey, having been a private investigator. They must know something of Beau.

"So how did you two meet?" Clara tilted her head, making light of it, though her heart pounded. She wanted to hear their story—anything to learn more about Beau's connections.

"We met in a bank robbery," Aubrey said softly. "Nathan rescued me that day, and providence seemed to place him in my path again and again. Whenever I was in need."

He curled an arm around her.

"I've read about the kidnapped babies." Clara's attempt to politely press for more fumbled when Aubrey's expression darkened. "I'm sorry. That's not a happy subject. I shouldn't have brought it up." She shouldn't be so selfish.

"Don't fret." Aubrey spoke in a soothing tone as she set her hand on Felicity's tummy. "We are blessed. Somehow, God provided for us to be reunited." She then recounted how a bounty hunter, trying to gain guardianship of his niece, had protected her, and how they'd been searching for lost legal documents rumored to save San Francisco from economic ruin.. It was all very fascinating. Nathan chimed in occasionally, though Aubrey was the finer storyteller. "Nathan had a close friend—Monsieur Beau Fox—who also worked for my in-laws." Aubrey glanced at Lorraine, whose brow furrowed, and her gaze darted away. "He carried the ransom for the girls, at his own expense, and they were returned to us."

"Thank goodness. How frightening." Clara played with the collar of her shirtwaist. "What happened to Mr. Fox? I read he was entangled in Jesse's abduction as well."

"He paid for his goodness at great personal expense," Lorraine cut in, her voice growing firmer. "Beau knew that when he met Monsieur Willot, the old man would blame him for his son's imprisonment. But he did the right thing. Beau never should've been thrown in jail."

"Agreed," Nathan answered, and Jesse clasped Lorraine's hand.

"Why do you say that?" Clara asked a little too quickly, trying not to hold her breath.

Lorraine narrowed her eyes at her. "Because Beau worked behind the scenes to rescue Jesse and Aubrey."

"It's true." Aubrey glanced at Clara. "He was kind to me when I was held captive against my will. We did everything we could to try and lessen Mr. Fox's sentence. If it hadn't been for that bank robbery..."

The flicker of hope inside her was snuffed out. "What bank robbery?"

Lorraine hissed through her teeth and shook her head. "Beau followed a foolish man and robbed a bank in Utah. I hoped the judge might be lenient, but the bank owner appeared in court, furious. Beau received a harsher sentence because of it."

"Did you tell the court what he did to redeem himself?"

"Beau asked us not to mention his heroism because doing so would put him in more danger from bad men."

"Oh." Clara's shoulders lowered. What was she to say? Her family talked of forgiveness, of Beau's repentance—yet his flight from prison still gnawed at her. Why had he run, if he had truly changed?

"Was the prison a very bad place?" Clara shifted her gaze to the fire, her fingers tracing the paisley pattern on her shirt.

Nathan met her gaze and held it for a moment—as if he could see her thoughts etched across her brow. Then he shrugged. "All prisons are. They have work crews that go out daily—laboring wherever they are needed. It's hard work, and security isn't very good. Beau stayed for two months, then ran."

Lorraine mumbled something in French.

Nathan inclined his ear. "What was that?"

"What man, when faced with inhumane treatment, would not run? It's animal instinct to survive."

Clara's sigh lingered, heavy with the echo of her own restless nights. "But running seldom brings the peace we hope for."

"True," Aubrey said at last. "All we can do now is pray for Beau. God knows where he is, and He will work in his heart and life, if Beau allows."

Lorraine nodded jerkily, and once the babies started crying, she and Aubrey went to tend them.

Clara ducked her chin. Her worry that her family would condemn Beau had been misplaced. The real issue was his debt to society. Once her father knew, he'd never consider allowing

Beau to court Clara. Even if Beau paid his debt, it would never be enough.

Jesse studied her, tapping his foot, restless as he often was.

"I think I upset your fiancée, Jess."

"Don't feel bad." He shifted back onto the sofa, glancing between her and Nathan. "Lorraine and Beau grew up together. She feels guilty that she was shown grace, while he was condemned."

"Why is she free and not him?"

"The abduction was her first crime, we didn't want to press charges, and she's a woman. No one wants to put a woman in jail."

"And Jesse said he'd marry her to keep her out of jail," Nathan added with a grin. "Apparently, the judge who presided over Lorraine's case made the suggestion. Nothing like marriage to reform an outlaw."

"Indeed. It's just a shame you and Aubrey decided to marry so soon. Now Grandmother Alexander wants us to have a wedding in Baltimore with all the family there."

Clara forced a smile, but her mind raced with darker thoughts. Beau's escape from prison seemed impossible to undo. If caught, his sentence would be harsher—more years added. They might just tack the murder charge on simply because he'd been at Mr. Peterson's house.

She shivered, remembering the feeling of being watched just last week. Was Beau right—someone involved in Mr. Peterson's death had recognized her and followed her home? That old kerosene lamp had hit her, not him.

Clara sighed. If she could just find the truth so blame would not be cast on Beau. She could take it to Sheriff Kelly, and he would arrest the killer. It was just a shame Father would never let her leave alone to investigate. She'd have to don her men's clothes once more. Beau would hate it if he were here, but he'd never know. He'd left her.

The back door to the Delta Saloon hung slightly ajar, a thin wash or lamplight spilling into the cold night. Inside, Dodge drank whiskey, laughed, and played poker, heedless of the cold wind cutting through the silent city. Beau crouched in the shadows across the alley, eyes fixed on the doorway, alert to every shadow. He'd stalked Theo that day and kept an eye on both Peterson's and Tibbons's house with no sign of anything out of the ordinary.

Dodge had been harder to find, but he couldn't stay away from the Delta for long. Once Beau confronted him, he'd get answers about Peterson's murder.

John's words echoed from memory—*Vengeance is not ours to take.* Such as when he first set foot on American ground, believing the only way to survive in this new land was to settle every score with his fists. He'd been wrong, but there had to be a just way to find out who wanted to hurt Clara. His own friend Nathan Reed had gone from breaking and entering to investigating and working with the law just last summer in San Francisco. Surely, Beau could find a way to pursue justice that abided by the laws of God and man.

The back door creaked open, and out stumbled Dodge. He was drunk, staggering slightly, his speech slurred—a vulnerability that might make him more likely to tell Beau what he knew.

Beau hung back in the thick shadows of the alleyway. Where was Perkins? Wasn't he supposed to be with Dodge? Beau followed at a distance, watching for the other man. Clouds partly covered the moon, but as Dodge reached the point where C Street and B Street joined, a dark shadow followed him toward the Divide—Perkins.

Dodge led him to the small stone structure that overlooked

the canyon below. He went not to Mr. Peterson's humble home but to Mr. Tibbons's.

Beau edged closer to the picket fence, mindful of the muddy patches. His boots would leave tracks on the porch, so he sidestepped and instead went around to the back of the house. A faint glow came from the kitchen.

Beau crept up to the window. Inside, an indistinguishable form moved into the hallway. Perkins or Dodge? And why would they go to Mr. Tibbons's house?

The cold, unmistakable cocking of a gun at his back froze Beau near the end of the house.

"Raise your hands." A deep male voice spoke low, its firmness a guarantee that whoever held him at gunpoint would have no problem shooting. "Turn around—slowly."

There was something familiar about that voice. It couldn't be…could it? Beau turned to face the tall, hatted figure of a man in a sheepskin coat near the fence. As the clouds rolled away from the moon, the light lent credibility to Beau's suspicions.

"Nathan Reed?" He spoke, still holding a peaceful stance.

"Beau, it's you." Nathan holstered the gun, a gust of breath blooming white before his face. "What are you doing here? John Alexander said there was a murder. Is that what Clara is doing here?"

Beau's head shifted back, his gut like ice. "Clara is here?" He looked around for the lovely lady he'd last seen unconscious and bleeding.

"Yeah, you were watching her through the window, weren't you?"

"That was Clara?" Beau went to the back door, pushing it open without reserve. How could she do this? Sneak around in the middle of the night. Break into someone's home. The same one just entered by two rough men? If they'd entered by way of the front and her the back, wouldn't they meet?

The back door creaked softly as Beau slipped it open. He

cringed inwardly and sidestepped around a modest kitchen table. Nathan closed the door, placing a chair in front so they would know if someone entered or exited while they were searching the house. Nathan slunk toward the hallway. A floorboard creaked ever so slightly under his weight. Both men stilled. Beau motioned for him to continue. Where were Clara and the men?

A search of the house turned up nothing. When they met in the kitchen again, Nathan shrugged. "No one is here."

Beau rubbed the back of his neck. He had to locate Clara before some harm came to her. "Why are *you* here?" Beau asked Nathan in a hushed voice.

"I heard that Miss Clara got into some trouble recently reporting for a local newspaper. When she was asking questions about you and the kidnapping today, I thought she was just curious. Then she sneaked out of the house this evening, so I followed her in case she ran into trouble."

"She must be trying to find out who attacked her. How could she come here at night, though? It's not safe."

If Dodge had found her and dragged her out the front door while he was in the back yard talking to Nathan... A wave of panic washed over him. Beau bolted for the door, clipping Nathan's shoulder in the process. He'd haul Clara home and this time just lock her in her room. No, there were too many windows she could sneak out of. A cellar might be more practical, though far too inhumane.

Wait—a cellar. Beau froze at the bottom step in the cold night air. Many houses in Virginia City had a lower story wholly or partially underground. Back in the kitchen, ignoring a bewildered Nathan, Beau checked the walls. Sure enough, there was a small door that appeared to be little more than part of the cabinetry. He eased it open. Men's voices sailed up from the space. Faint light revealed a narrow stair leading down, cut into the hillside.

Nathan nudged his shoulder, signaling for him to move forward. He carried his weight on his heels, as the length of the stairs didn't allow space for his entire foot. The earthy smell from below closed around him, reminding him of the mines when one first began to descend. At the bottom of the stairs sat stacks of crates, and the shadow of a man moved back and forth across the room.

"I don't know why you keep saying that. We cannot stay here forever." A young male voice spoke, familiar for its New York accent. Theo Atticus?

"I say we leave the area. There is no sense in remaining in Virginia City when we can move on, set up shop elsewhere. The con is a good one." A man with a British accent responded, a snooty tone to his words.

"Sounds like you fellas stayed in Virginia City too long." Perkins's toothlessness made him unmistakable. "If Dodge's old man hadn't been too smart for his own—"

The unmistakable sound of a fist meeting flesh preceded a yowl of pain. Then a scuffle ensued.

"Do not speak of my pa," Dodge practically roared.

"Men, cease your quarreling." The British man spoke over the fight, irritation and resignation clear in his tone.

"Come on, Dodge, he didn't mean anything." Theo's tone was high, urgent.

Nathan nudged Beau again, signaling he was ready. The men were distracted by the conflict. The time was now.

Beau squatted low when he peered around the corner so Nathan might also have space to survey the room before entering.

Dodge was fighting Perkins, whose overalls were marred with dirt from his fall. Theo paced as though torn between intervening and remaining safe.

A businessman with a cane and black suit inspected his nails. "Are you two nearly finished?"

Tied to a chair was a small man in a nightshirt. No sign of Clara. Hopefully, she'd gone home when she found the house empty.

Perkins knocked Dodge to the floor and stood over him, fists clenched. "You were high and mighty when you were the boss's son, but you're nothing now."

Dodge let out a fierce shout, then he reached for his gun.

"No!" Theo lunged forward, but before he could reach him, a sudden crack echoed through the small space.

Mr. Perkins staggered, then sank to his knees, leaning forward before falling quietly on the floor.

Beau rushed in, pushing Theo off balance.

Dodge lowered his gun, staring blankly at the miner as though not realizing what he'd done. Beau kicked the gun from his hand, and it went flying.

With Dodge in shock, Beau went for the dandy with the cane. His eyes widened beneath wiry red eyebrows, then Beau was on him, shoving him to the ground. Beau hit him once to immobilize.

Meanwhile, Nathan had Theo in a similar hold.

Dodge started for the stairway. Beau darted in front of him, blocking his escape. The man rammed him backward into the stone wall. Beau's head hit hard, black spots flickering in his vision. He broke Dodge's grip by bringing both his arms up, then forcing his elbows down into Dodge's arms.

Nathan knelt beside the prone Mr. Perkins, the blood-saturated patch of earth around him growing larger. "He's dead."

Dodge cursed Beau, calling him a filthy Frenchman, bringing his knee up to unman him. The dirty fighter.

Beau caught Dodge's chin with a sharp punch, staggering him back.

Dodge hit the ground, stunned and gasping.

All was quiet, then movement behind Nathan and close to the stairs caught his eye. A sixth intruder lunged from behind the crates at the base of the stairs and freed the old man tied to the chair. The two bolted toward the steps.

Beau sprinted across the room as Nathan reached for the man's gown. The elderly man cried out as he fell. Nathan was quick to catch him and offer reassurance.

Beau targeted the faster man, pulling him by the coat so he fell backward. Beau wrapped his arms around him, but before he could issue a threat, a high feminine shriek cut through the air, echoing off the walls, freezing everyone in place.

CHAPTER 23

Beau spun her around, his grip firm. Clara's stormy blue eyes flickered wide, catching the lamp's glow and revealing her dirt-smudged cheeks. "Ah, ma chère, what are you doing here?"

"Beau!" She fought her arms free and wrapped them around his neck, squeezing so tight, he could hardly breathe. He held her close, then darted a quick glance around the room. Nathan, gun drawn, had the situation under control, his voice steady as he ordered the men to be still. Clara's breath hitched, then escaped in a shudder as she pressed her face into Beau's shoulder, voice cracking—soft but raw, like shards of glass. "I thought I'd never see you again. Why did you leave?"

"You know why, but I can't do this now." He gently wiped her tears and set her away from himself, in the stairwell a couple of steps up where the men could not gawk at her. "Stay here—promise me. I need you safe."

Already, Dodge's loud complaints and curses filled the cellar.

"I don't want them to see you." He tugged her coat down a little lower over her knees, struck by how slender her legs were.

Her eyes widened at the contact, and Beau withdrew, remembering her innocence when he'd kissed her.

"I don't think it matters. They must know who I am—that I report for Doten—to have attacked me at Mrs. Matthews's house."

"You'll hang for this, Vulpe!" Dodge railed behind him. "Attacking me—your days are numbered, convict!"

That stilled him, though Beau turned slowly, closing his arms. "Murder is a hanging crime, Dodge, or did you forget?"

Nose bleeding and face red, Dodge snorted. "What's the word of a respected mine owner against a man who escaped from the Utah Territorial Penitentiary?"

Beau flexed his jaw, attempting to keep his expression like stone.

Dodge needed no sign of weakness, though. He was a mastiff with his teeth sunk deep, and he'd not let go. "I bet you didn't know that my pa sat on your jury in Salt Lake."

Beau's gut tightened. So Mr. Peterson had been there. Why hadn't he told Beau outright? More, why had he employed him instead of turning him over to the law? Dodge sneered, gaze flicking between Beau and Nathan. "Beau Fox—the kidnapper, the bank robber, the half-breed Gypsy—don't forget who he really is."

He clenched his fists at the coarse term, yet shrugged, refusing to let his past hold him back anymore. "Interesting that your pére knew who I was but did not report me. Instead, he gave me a job."

"Speaks to your character." Nathan answered easily, his relaxed stance imparting a calm Beau wouldn't have thought possible. He already knew Beau's dark past yet still had followed him into the cellar, trusting him completely. Even now, Clara waited behind him, quiet, though no doubt she was bursting to join the conversation.

"Ma foi, I think Mr. Peterson preferred my work to Dodge's."

Beau kicked out a leg, standing in a more relaxed position. "You know, he actually hired me back after Dodge fired me?"

Nathan bunched his chin. "I'm not surprised. This fella doesn't seem too bright."

The redheaded dandy stepped forward. "I don't care what disputes you have with Dodge Peterson. I demand to be released. I've done nothing wrong, and when I leave this place, I'm headed far away. You needn't worry about seeing me again—I give you my word."

"This fella sure thinks highly of himself." Nathan snickered. "What's his name?"

"I don't know. Looks Irish, but sounds like a Brit."

The man in question sputtered, a vein pulsing on his head. It wasn't the first time Beau and Nathan had used a back-and-forth exchange to fluster an opponent.

"Beau?" Clara tugged on the back of his coat.

He turned, finding her sitting with her legs crossed and hands folded, pale wisps of hair showing below her blue knit hat and contrasting his ruby-red scarf. She waved him closer, and he stepped near, blocking the light from the room so she was cast in deeper shadows. The warmth of her collided with his angst and anger, fraying the raw edges of his heart.

"He is Mr. Phineas Malcolm, the geologist you were looking for. I bet Theo paid him to write that false report about Mr. Peterson's mine. And the poor dead man was the lift operator in the mine. They're a team." Her voice raised in excitement. "Theo is here too. Dodge probably hired him. Ask him about it."

He nodded and turned away, but she caught him back by the arm.

"Mr. Tibbons is innocent, though. I think they've been holding him here against his will. He's old and needs to be taken care of. I'd like to take him to the kitchen and tend to him."

He shook his head. "The moment he sees you like this..."—his hand swept toward her trousers—"your reputation will be ruined."

Her mouth pulled into a frown, no small amount of doubt in her eyes. "That's a poor reason not to help. He's in need of care."

"It doesn't matter as long as you are safe."

Clara stood, crossing her arms. "I won't sacrifice what's right for safety. Besides, if I am disgraced, it's my own fault—a consequence of the choices I've made."

But it was his job to protect her from anything and anyone who might do her precious heart harm. Beau ground his teeth, shaking his head.

Clara had been the one to free Mr. Tibbons. She must have been hiding behind the crates in the corner when Beau came down.

"Who are you talking to, Vulpe?" Dodge called from behind. Nathan telling him to hush.

Clara stepped nearer, curling her fingers around Beau's arm. "I've stayed here because you asked, and I've already let you down before—going out dressed like a man after promising not to. But Mr. Tibbons needs help. I will build a fire in the stove and get him something to eat. I can also get some rope so you can tie up these men and call on Sheriff Kelly."

Beau nodded. After all, it was a good plan and she was right—Mr. Tibbons should be tended to. He faced the elderly man. "Mr. Tibbons, what is your part in this?"

White hair messy and hanging into his face, Mr. Tibbons looked at the men in the cellar. They remained silent, but the threat hung in the air, so he lowered his head and shrugged. It was still a risk to let the old man go, but Clara must be right. He wasn't a threat to her.

Beau just had to see one more thing. "Dodge, you

kidnapped the old man before he could tell Sheriff Kelly that you drove the buggy back that night, didn't you?"

Eyes flashing wide, Dodge scoffed. "I don't know what you're talking about. I wasn't even here that night."

Mr. Tibbons stood still, but Theo—a bruise over one eye—nodded ever so slightly when Beau focused on him.

That was enough for Beau. "Mr. Tibbons, would you be so kind as to build a fire upstairs in the kitchen and start some coffee?"

Mr. Tibbons nodded, then hobbled up the stairs with Clara. She might be safe for a moment, but they still needed to get to the bottom of Peterson's murder.

~

Later that night, Beau fixated on the crucifix hanging in Mr. Tibbons's parlor, the weight in his chest as heavy as a stone. The house was warm and inviting, as Mr. Peterson's had been nearly one month ago on Christmas Eve, yet Beau felt cold. By the look of Christ's ribs where he hung on the cross, breath had not been easily gained that day either.

"You have cleared the way, Lord. The cup is before me, but I do not want to drink it." Was it wrong to ask for mercy?

Footsteps sounded behind him. Nerves prickled like needles up his spine, but it was Clara pausing in the doorway, her long braid over one shoulder. "Mr. Tibbons is settled for the night." Despite the loose-fitting men's clothes, her beauty shone like a star in a clear sky.

Beau nodded. "Nathan went to fetch the sheriff." He offered his hand, and she came to him, allowing him to wrap her in his arms. Insides crumbling, he managed to speak over his rampage of thoughts. "It wounds my heart to see you dressed like this."

She drew back. "Why would it hurt you?"

"You are not safe."

"And how does a skirt make a woman safe? Beau, I have fewer men gawking at me in this than in a dress."

"That is because they don't know you are a woman, and it is winter. In the summer..." He shook his head, resisting the urge to glance at the feminine qualities the shirt did little to hide.

"I know this, but I don't plan to wear a disguise forever. I just needed to get started." Pleading shone in her eyes.

Agreeing and simply asking her to change now would be easy, but Clara was too strong-willed to trust such a plan. So he'd bruise her tender heart for truth's sake. "This is no better than the offer Theo made you back in December to write under a pseudonym, then once you are established, to reveal yourself."

Cheeks flushing, she opened her mouth to speak, but Beau cut her off.

"Do you think that Alf Doten will continue taking your work once he realizes you lied to him?"

Tears sparkled for an instant on her eyelashes, then she spoke through stiff lips. "Then what am I to do? Never write? Never even have the chance to do what I love?"

"I am sorry. Sorry that I cannot change the world. That I am the one to, in so many ways, show you life's cruelties. Clara, we live in a fallen world. You can take comfort that if God has called you to write, He will make a way. Will He not?"

She nodded, her shoulders stooped. Then she shook her head. "I don't know why we are talking about my writing when Dodge is going to tell the sheriff who you really are as soon as he can." Clara sniffed, pulling a dainty handkerchief from her pocket to dab her eyes. "You must run, Beau. If they find you here, it's over. I cannot bear to lose another loved one."

He let out a shaky laugh, tempted to accept her challenge and whisk her away with him. "What happened to doing the right thing? I cannot run anymore. Too many people have been harmed, and it's not right that I should go free. Not pay for my sins."

She grasped his arm, beginning to speak, but he couldn't stand to hear her contradictions. It would be too easy for her to drag him from his conviction.

"Your family is in town—Titus, Jesse, Mademoiselle Aubrey. I can make amends once and for all, then repay my debt to society. Something I was too weak to do in the fall. I'll always just be running if I don't settle this now."

"You wish to make amends with my family." Clara still gripped his arm, her words cautious, uncertain.

"I do."

"So then, once you are free, you will come back?" She raised her eyebrows, all youthful hopefulness.

"Back for what?"

She startled as though slapped.

"Forgive me, Clara. I thought you understood." He widened his stance, grounding himself in a desperate attempt to speak a reality he hated. "I cannot marry you, love you."

Eyes welling with tears, her face crumbled for an instant. Then she turned her back to him and crossed her arms.

His regrets crowded in. *I should have taken better care of her heart.* "I need you to give up on the possibility. We have no future." Just saying so felt cruel and unnecessary.

Her shoulders became more rigid, and she covered her mouth with one hand, muffling her words when she said, "Rather hypocritical, don't you think? To seek atonement for sins, yet reject sanctification?"

He searched his mind for those terms, yet together they did not make sense. "I do not understand that."

"What is the use of paying your debt to society and accepting God's forgiveness if you never live your life as a free man afterward?"

"There are consequences. My choices affect others. I am responsible."

She turned now, wiping away tears, though the plume of red in her cheeks signaled anger. "I think you are afraid to love me. Afraid to risk your heart when life is so fragile. When you already lost so much." Her voice softened. "Amalie and Martin. While I understand grief and its ability to cripple the heart and soul, I won't justify cowardice."

His jaw tightened, and Beau jabbed his thumb against his chest. "I am no coward."

She placed a hand on his arm, cooling his ire a degree. "I, of all people, know of your heroism, but that will not set you free. I fear for you, Beau, that even once you are released from prison, you will never be free."

She didn't know how wrong she was, since going back to prison and resisting the criminals there would likely cost his life, as it nearly had last October.

A distant rumble of hooves sounded—a pounding echo that promised no mercy. Not once Sheriff Kelly arrested him. Beau clenched his jaw and tightened his fists as danger drew closer. When Clara stepped away, he braced himself, feeling more exposed than ever. He had to find strength to withstand this, or all the sacrifice, the loss and the hurting, would be for naught.

CHAPTER 24

The icy air bit through Beau's shirt, making him shiver as Sheriff Kelly unlatched his cuffs—a gesture that felt less like mercy and more like the hush before a storm. Could he endure seeing Clara so broken and hurt? His stomach twisted nauseatingly.

I hope this honors You, Lord, because it is killing me.

Sheriff Kelly was kind enough to escort Beau to the Alexanders' residence in the hour preceding dawn the following day, before the morning paper was released. John had made it clear when he agreed that Beau could address the family at his home that he would not allow the chains in case they upset his wife and daughter.

Now, the sheriff stood beside him on the Alexanders' porch, the cold air curling around them in the early dawn. "Are ye sure ye're ready for this, lad?"

"I owe this family an explanation before I go back," Beau said quietly, voice steady despite the ache in his chest. Lord willing, they would hear the truth and not mistake it for excuses.

In the warm parlor, Sheriff Kelly shook John's hand. The

elder Alexander brother wore signs of exhaustion including dark shadows beneath his eyes, but his gaze held steady and sharp.

"Beau," he said, grip firm and steady, acknowledging him as an equal—even if Beau hardly felt it.

Nathan was the first of the family to enter, Jesse at his side.

"Beau, I'm glad you came." Nathan approached, his hand extended. "It's a brave thing you're doing, man." And he shook his hand as if to congratulate him.

A knot twisted in Beau's stomach, sour bile rising, and he barely managed a nod. He faced Jesse Alexander—a man he'd captured, beaten, and wronged badly—and struggled to meet his gaze. Jesse stood firm, anger flaring from his eyes like the heat from the blazing hearth. Sheriff Kelly and John were poised as though expecting an outburst.

Jesse offered his hand. "For my fiancée."

He didn't say the words, *I forgive you*, but they hung in the air. Beau shook Jesse's hand, then a woman's voice suddenly filled the room—a fragile, broken cry. Lorraine threw herself at Beau, and he caught her in his arms. She trembled with sobs, as if grief and loss had filled her to the brim and spilled over. Memories threatened to drown him—the roar of the prison train and the cold stones of Castle Garden. He fought tears himself, the ache rising in his throat.

"It's not your fault," he said in French once her grip loosened.

"I should be right beside you," she whispered, cheeks flushed and eyes bloodshot.

"Non. You chose right—above country, above family. That is good, Lorraine." He softly squeezed her hands. His face burned with embarrassment—such a personal display before so many he had wronged.

Titus had slipped in quietly with Aubrey and Tessa. Clara

lingered near the doorway, eyes downcast. She looked impossibly small—despite being the tallest woman in the room. Unlike her usual bright clothes of red, green, and blue, she wore a simple blouse and gray skirt. Her silence—like an accusation—confirmed that Beau had broken her heart. Did she understand French? Had she misread the exchange between him and Lorraine?

Jesse, who had given Lorraine a handkerchief and gently held her hand, showed no signs of worry or jealousy. That was good.

Titus stepped forward, as though he, not his brother, was the man of the house. "Mr. Fox, when Nathan told us you wanted to speak to us before returning to prison, I was against it. But since my family seems so determined to forgive you, I cannot object further. Make no mistake—justice will be done in the end."

John glared. Lorraine tensed, but Beau simply nodded in compliance.

"Please, sit." John gestured to the furniture around the fire, the ladies selecting places first—except Clara. She stayed near the door, her gaze fixed on the floor. John and Tessa studied her, but no one moved toward her.

Beau sat next, then Jesse and John. Titus, the sheriff, and Nathan remained standing. Beau braced himself, feeling the weight of many eyes fixed on him. He forced himself to speak the confession he'd practiced all last night.

"I have wronged your family to a great degree. I knew it the moment I was arrested in Salt Lake, and I wanted to explain. When I escaped, I thought I was justified. I did not mean to harm anyone, but I did."

"Then why didn't you stay in prison?" Titus asked, his voice cold.

Almost at the same moment, Nathan's tone sharpened with suspicion. "Why did you leave, Beau? They say Utah Penitentiary is the easiest to break out of. You stayed nearly a month before running."

Beau frowned, recognizing Nathan's intent—not to accuse, but to understand, to find some reason that might justify what he'd done. It was a kindness, but Beau hadn't come to the Alexanders seeking absolution. He was here to face the truth, to take responsibility for the pain he'd caused, not to explain it away.

Beau clenched his jaw, the weight of his sins pressing against him. Truth or not, he already knew he might lose everything. He turned to Jesse. "I hurt you, stole your freedom, and you did not deserve that. Neither did your sister." He made eye contact with Aubrey. "I hope you will forgive me."

"Why, Mr. Fox, do not be so modest." Aubrey raised her chin and cast her gaze about the room as if daring anyone to contradict her. "True, Mr. Fox was a part of the gang that kidnapped me, but as I've said before, he was kind to me. He gave me hope that help was coming, and while it was not publicized in the papers, Pa and the police never would have found Jesse in time to save his life if not for Beau."

"If you offer me forgiveness, you should also extend it to Beau." Lorraine looked at her future father-in-law. "I should be in chains beside him."

"That's not so, Lori." Beau raised a hand in a calming gesture. "You didn't help rob the bank in Utah. You stood for what was right, and so you go free. As you should."

"They offer me freedom, not you," Lorraine replied in French, wringing her hands. "It's not fair."

He refused to argue, though John chimed in before anyone else could.

"For my part, Beau, I forgive you. You did what you could to right your wrongs with Titus's family. You saved both his granddaughters, kept my son from harm, and rescued Clara from a mine shaft. I wish you could go free now, because it seems you're a hero. We are too quick to villainize people in our society when what they need is support, forgiveness, and love to move forward and be successful."

Titus Alexander glared at John, pressing his lips together before he said, "He isn't Kingsley."

Everyone fell silent for a moment.

Beau blinked at the mercy he hadn't expected. Clearly, John was remembering his wayward older brother whom no one had given a second chance. If only Beau could be different than Kingsley Alexander, he might help to heal John's old wounds. But it was too late for that now.

Nathan crossed his arms and looked at him, his expression serious. "You seem contrite. But you believed you deserved to go to prison before you were sentenced last fall. So I keep coming back to this question—why did you leave the penitentiary?"

Not wanting to make excuses, Beau shook his head.

"Was your life in danger? Maybe from an old colleague?"

Emil. No, perplexingly, he hadn't encountered that man during his short stay in prison—a fact that still puzzled him.

"You know, I wrote Marshal Morris this Christmas." Jesse glanced at Lorraine, then back. "He mentioned the prison was under investigation. Beau, did something illegal happen there? If so, you have to report it."

"That's right, lad." Sheriff Kelly chimed in. "Prisons are awful places, but all should have humane standards."

A gang that left the prison to rob stage coaches must have influence among the guards and outside help. No one would help for the sake of the prisoners—except the marshal was already investigating, so maybe things would change. If they did, going back to prison might not mean losing his life. And perhaps Clara would understand why he had to say goodbye now.

Her eyes were locked on him, yet darted away when he

looked her way. While fair of complexion, Clara's skin tone this morning was nearing pale, dark circles beneath her eyes adding years to her countenance. Had she slept at all last night? Had she eaten anything that morning? He hadn't. Slowly, she shifted her gaze back to him and raised her eyebrows as if saying—*what could it hurt?*

Beau nodded. "There was a secret group of outlaws in the prison. They would leave when we went outside to work on the stone walls. There's a cave where they keep supplies—at least, that's what I was told. They go to nearby farms and get horses. They rob the stages heading to Salt Lake, Wells Fargo couriers, and regular travelers. They hide the loot and then return to the prison."

The fire crackled in the hearth. Sheriff Kelly's eyebrows raised, his voice calm and measured. "A man with your...*skills* would be a fine addition to the lot. Did they try to bring ye in?"

Beau rolled his shoulders, memories like the crack of an old broken bone surfacing. He forced numbness into his core, exhausted by the pain—both physical and mental. Still, the memories assailed him—being thrown to the stone floor, pinned in the corner of the cell while inmates kicked and punched his ribs, back, and shoulders. He'd woken in the middle of the night to the coppery scent of blood mingled with the stench of urine, hands crusted with wounds he'd gained trying to protect himself. He'd decided then that, rather than die or join another gang of outlaws, he would run. It was the lesser of the three evils, but his sins had caught up with him. "They tried to kill me when I refused, so I ran."

"Beau, you must report them." Clara, ever the voice of truth, stepped away from her place by the door. "Something has to be done to stop those men before they hurt more people. And what kind of justice is this, when a man who is sentenced to repay his debt to society is forced to choose between illegal activity and death? It's not right." She crossed her arms, looking at John and Titus as though urging them to speak up as well.

"Oui, Clara is right." Lorraine grasped Jesse's wrist, though her eyes stayed fixed on Sheriff Kelly. "You are the law. What will you do for justice?"

He raised his eyebrows, blustering for a moment. "Sure, but I'm only a town sheriff. There's not much I can do here in Nevada. I'm just tryin' to hold the town together after the fire."

"Jesse..." Clara stepped forward to take a spot beside her cousin. "You must write Marshal Morris. He is a federal officer. If there is any chance he can help Beau."

Nodding, Jesse looked at Beau. "Would you be willing to talk to Marshal Morris about your experience?"

"Oui, but I will need to see him before I am returned to the prison."

Clara's breath caught. "You cannot return when it's not safe. What if this gang kills you?"

All was quiet in the room. Clara looked from face to face, as if trying to find someone to contradict her.

"If we act quickly, it might not be a problem when Beau returns," Jesse said, though he didn't sound convinced.

Both Lorraine and Clara looked at Beau as though he were already dead.

Beau stood, glancing at Sheriff Kelly. "I have said all I can."

"All right. We'll leave now." The sheriff turned to John, offering him a sturdy handshake. "Thank you for your hospitality, sir. It's a real Christian thing your family has done—forgiving this young man."

Lorraine came forward with Jesse. She embraced Beau and told him she would pray for his safety. Nathan and Aubrey promised the same, and Beau tried to sincerely thank them, but his attention wavered to Clara. She hung back from the group, uncertain—lost. Her focus might stray his way, but she did not raise her eyes to meet his. Aubrey seemed to notice and went toward her, as did Tessa.

As Beau neared the door, Sheriff Kelly gripped his arm, reminding him he was still in custody. Clara was all the way across the room now, her arms crossed, shaking her head at Aubrey. Finally, she turned on her heel and swept away, Tessa —not Aubrey— following her. Why had her stepmother, whom Clara seemed to despise more than anyone, followed her in her time of need instead of her beloved cousin?

Beau glanced at John, who was arguing with Titus, but his mind was elsewhere. Who would be there for Clara if she and her stepmother clashed once more? Would she be sent away to Baltimore, to her grandparents' house? If that happened, he'd never see her again. Maybe—just maybe—that was for the best in the end.

CHAPTER 25

Clara hurried to her mother's library—hoping to find a fragment of peace before her world shattered completely. But she found only hopelessness. Shaking from anger and fatigue, she hugged herself as she paced in the cold room. Repairs had been started on the floor, and the fireplace cleaned, but the room was still abandoned. Cold. Like a tomb. Her heart, encased in stone, refused to thaw. She was alone and always would be.

"Why, Lord? I realize I am not the best of Your children. I don't expect an easy life, but first Mother and now Beau." She faced the foggy window where traces of daylight glowed on the glass. "Why bring him here? I wish I'd never even seen him."

If it had been another miner who found her in that dark tunnel, who'd simply helped her above surface and directed her to get home, Beau would be away, free, and she wouldn't be unraveling inside all over again. The ache in her chest clenched tighter, making her lungs feel too small, too tight to draw breath.

She sank onto the sofa where she'd last read *Mother Goose* to Daniel, but no precious moment was this. She wanted to scream and cry all at once. Rage at God and also beg Him to rescue Beau, but there was no way out. Plunged into the darkness behind her closed eyelids, she tried to breathe. *Think. Think.* There had to be an answer. Some way to help him.

A distant tapping sounded, like the ticking of a clock, part of the room.

I am drowning. I can't keep going.

Everything she'd done since returning to Virginia City meant nothing. Not writing for the paper, spending time with Daniel, or trying to love Father. Least of all, her time knowing Beau—every step of the way, she'd made his life harder. He'd tried to leave Virginia City, but she'd stopped him. If he'd walked away in the beginning, he would be safe. He'd stayed for her and was now going back to prison, possibly to die.

The tapping grew louder.

God knew that Beau was a righteous man who tried to atone for his sins. Why wasn't that enough? God should have just given him a way to be free.

"You didn't answer, so I let myself in." Tessa spoke beside her, her voice quiet, sad yet strong.

Moving her hands away from her face, Clara smirked, a numbness rolling over her. "You might as well. It is your house now." She stood to leave yet stilled at the internal chastening—*what happened to trying to forgive?*

Now God spoke to her, chastising her? Of all days, He condemned her when she needed His help? She could have screamed an objection from Mount Davidson's precipice, risking a lightning strike from heaven, she was so angry.

Tessa stared back at her, not surprised or hurt. She wasn't fighting or running away as she usually did. Just as she hadn't run away when Clara was sick.

"I'm sorry, Tessa, I just..." Clara shook her head, her arms suddenly too tired to remain crossed. "I'm just so angry. First, Mother and now Beau. God could save them both, but He won't. I prayed for Mother to get better for years. And now, if I ask God to save Beau, He'll just do the same thing."

Tessa shivered, hugging herself. When Clara met her gaze, she spoke.

"I'm sorry. I'm not very good with situations like this. God allows people to die. I... my..." She shook her head. "It's hard to understand. But as long as we're alive, we have to look forward to tomorrow. Make the most of today, even when we don't get the life we wanted." She shrugged. "I know—it's not very hopeful. My faith isn't strong, but I know that God is good, and He loves you very much."

"Why?" Clara's voice was small, like a child's, but she so desperately needed to know. "Why would God love me? And if He does, why do these things happen?"

"Why does He love you?" Tessa actually smiled. "Why does a mother love her babe, a painter his work, a writer her articles? It is the nature of creators."

"Oh." Clara sniffed, her breathing leveling out a bit. It did make sense when Tessa put it like that. "But why doesn't He..." It was a childish thing to ask.

"Why does He allow heartbreak?" Tessa offered, and Clara nodded. "I suppose there are many reasons." Tessa sat on the sofa, settling Daniel's pillow on her lap. "We know that nothing in the world works as it should because all of nature is cursed. That's one reason. God also sees our story from beginning to end, so He knows the healing, the new life to come. When we are blind with pain, He guides us because He sees the way."

Clara moved toward the sofa, one step at a time, and finally sank into the cushions. "Tessa, where is your family?" She'd wondered before yet never cared enough to ask.

"Back east. At least, my aunt and her family are. I'm not, uh —that is..." A blush entered her cheeks, and she raised her chin. "I am like Aubrey and Nathan's little girl, Felicity."

A foundling child. Her heart grew a little softer for having heard all about Felicity and Melanie's story from Nathan and Aubrey—who had been open about the girls' parentage the night before.

"I'm sorry for your loss. Is that why you...?" Oh, heavens, she could not ask such a personal question.

"Why I what—ended up in a mining town, poor, and destitute?"

That had not been what Clara was thinking, but it was close enough. "Yes."

"Maybe. Who's to say how our childhood affects us? I think a great deal, which is why John and I work so hard to give Daniel the best we have. Even though we are far from perfect." Tessa played with the tassels on the pillow and bit her lip for a moment. "I grew up in New York. There was a boy who lived down the street, Mark Kilwiene, and we married very young."

Tessa was married before Father? What had happened to the man? Hopefully, she wasn't divorced too.

"Mark was in and out of the workhouse, same as me. Sometimes it seemed as though he was the only light in my life. We decided to go west to find a better life. We hopped trains, stages, worked for food and passage all the way to the West Coast."

"Sounds like an adventure."

Tessa snickered. "Some might say that. San Francisco was a rough town, though. Mark said it was too much like New York, so we came to Virginia City. Mark worked the mines, and I cleaned houses. We were able to scrape together enough for a little shack in Gold Hill. It felt like a mansion after the poorhouse and the rail cars. Mark and I started talking about having a family someday." Her eyes got that far-off look, yet there was the distinct glow of warmth there, then it dimmed.

"One day, I was taking out the milk bottles, my last chore of the day. The table was set for supper. Mark would be home any minute, but his foreman came to see me. He said there'd been an accident. Mark fell. They found him at the bottom of a shaft. Five hundred feet. He'd been dead for hours before they knew. Probably around three o'clock when I was doing the laundry." Tears ran down Tessa's cheeks, though she didn't seem to notice them. She still stared into the distance, as though reliving that day.

"I am so sorry." It seemed so little in light of such a devastating loss.

Tessa sniffed, wiping away tears. "After that, I gave up on life. I started drinking so I wouldn't have to hurt all the time. I stopped going to church. I made decisions, did things, that no proper lady should do." She looked at Clara with meaning. "I was still in a bad place when I discovered I was with child. There is a foundling home in San Francisco. I would have to go there to birth my baby. That is when I realized how selfishly I'd been living. How reckless I'd been, not caring about right or wrong, or the people I hurt along the way."

Her tears returned. "Daniel would be like me. No mama or papa to love him. Unwanted by the world, and it was all my fault. When we got to San Francisco, John checked me into a hotel and left. He said he would go to the homes and find the best one, but then he didn't come back for days. I prayed the whole time that God would have my baby die in birth and just take him to heaven. An unforgivable prayer, but at that point..." She shook her head.

Clara's eyes, burning once again, blurred so her view of her stepmother was obscured. She shed her tears and saw Tessa clearly. "Then Father came and said my mother was dead, that he would marry you and give Daniel a home?"

Tessa nodded, biting her lip when it trembled. "We hardly knew one another, and I still cried for Mark every single night, but there was a baby. I couldn't just stay in the past. I told God, if He would bless my marriage with John and give my baby a good home, that I would never drink, or—or do any of the terrible things I did. That I would trust Him for my happiness, not any one person, whether that be John, Mark, or the baby."

So here was the key to living and loving without losing oneself entirely as Mother had. Trusting God and placing one's whole heart in His hands. *But You are so far away.* It was not as though God would wrap His arms around her when she was scared or lonely.

"These are not very romantic notions, I know." Tessa drew out a hanky and blew her nose with a great, manly blow that reminded Clara so much of Maudy, she almost smiled. "Life is seldom simple or gentle—more like a storm than a fairy tale. We have moments of pure joy though, such as when Daniel wakes up and just wants to be held, or when your father embraces you. Falling in love, though—that is risky business."

How strange that Tessa would make such true statements. That her happiness should never rely on a man. With the prospect of never seeing Beau again, of his life in peril, Clara could hardly keep herself standing. She just wanted to curl up in a ball and hide from the world.

"I know you judge me, and I don't blame you." Tessa shrugged, inspecting her raw cuticles. "Anything you want to say, or ask me, you can."

"I...can't think of anything." Clara hesitated. Tessa had just bared her soul, sharing wounds and secrets when Clara had done nothing to earn such trust. "I have hurled insults at you in the past. That was wrong."

Tessa's eyebrows rose, her eyes wide. "Oh, I didn't blame you for that."

"Still, it was wrong."

Tessa drew a breath, then let it out slowly. "I know this house is special to you, that it is where all your memories are. I don't want to trample on them. I am just trying to give my son a good life." She pressed her fingers to her eyes, as though keeping a headache at bay.

"This house is full of grief. Every room, like revisiting a grave." Clara looked around at Mother's library, her gaze landing on the chest of toys in the corner and the fairy tale tomes nearby. "But you are right—Daniel should have a good life. A good home. I hope this house will be that for him."

"Thank you. He is a sweet boy. And he should be waking any moment." Tessa scooted to the edge of the sofa. "Oh, Clara, Mr. Vulpe does seem like a good man. Perhaps Jesse's plan to contact the US Marshal will save his life in the end. I pray so."

"Me too." Clara offered her stepmother a smile as Tessa left the room. Beau's words returned to her—*I cannot love you*—the memory so crippling that she focused on simply breathing. This was her test, like Mother's when Father was unfaithful and Tessa's when Mark died.

She clenched her fists, determined—she would face whatever lay ahead, trusting in God. "I won't break as I did when Mother died, Lord, because I have You. No matter how hard, or what happens, I don't want to rely on anyone but You." Even if that meant she would never be married to Beau—let alone loved by him. God would be enough.

CHAPTER 26

The sunlight shown over the half-constructed Storey County Courthouse—a red-brick and wood structure with an ornate facade, including double arched windows and a central arched entrance—as Clara approached the building's stone walls and iron-banded doors. Above, the sky's fierce blue promised spring was on its way. But the moment her employer strode up the boardwalk on B Street, her eagerness to be near Beau, to uncover the mystery of Mr. Peterson's murder and interview Sheriff Kelly, faded.

Alf Doten had been at the house earlier that day. Clara had heard his raised voice, along with her father's. Whatever discussion her father and Mr. Doten had, he'd left the house like a storm cloud. Even now, his dark eyebrows hung low over narrowed, piercing eyes.

"Miss Alexander—or should I call you 'Miss Royall'? I can't decide."

Clara's cheeks grew hot. She lifted her chin. "I should not have lied to you. I hope you can find it in your heart to forgive me."

"You think this is just a matter of forgiving?" He tugged a

newspaper from beneath his arm and unfolded it to the front page.

There, in thick black ink, was the headline—*Secret Female Reporter Dresses Like a Man to Get Editor Out of a Bind*. The subheading further mocked her, hinting that Mr. Doten's paper was so desperate, it had to hire debutantes fresh from finishing school, and that the paper's future was now gossip, fashion, and recipes—a ladies' magazine in disguise.

"*The Enterprise* printed this? After you let them use your building when theirs burned down?" Clara's voice came out disbelieving. She was more grateful than ever she'd separated herself from that paper.

"Of course. The editor is a shark—owned by a conniving politician who seeks only to further his own gains. Since I stand with the fire department, he'll attack where he senses weakness." He refolded the paper and slid it back under his arm. "I won't continue with my sentiments. I don't want to see you cry, and your father is a friend of mine. Maybe this is what happens when a woman meddles in a man's world."

Her hands trembling, Clara cleared her throat. "I believe your subscription list went up when I joined your paper and contributed my regular column. It wasn't until a man threw a fit over a talented woman joining your ranks that chaos ensued—like a child hoarding toys and screaming when one is taken away."

She dipped into a quick curtsy, not missing the flash of surprise on Mr. Doten's face. Then, hiking up her skirts—more like Maudy than herself—she rushed into the courthouse. Inside, she closed herself into the coolness and shut her eyes, breathing deeply. What horror—being found out and mocked across town. The ladies' society would host a banquet soon, fundraising for the new Fourth Ward School. Her mother had been part of it, along with many other notable women. Now they wouldn't dare invite her—she'd exposed Virginia City to the indecency of her pants.

Lord, help me bear this.

Her writing career was over, and she would be cast out of polite society. She could still go to church with Maudy, but would that be fair? Maudy already struggled beneath nearly constant condemnation for her past as a lady of the night. How could Clara pile more on her?

A man cleared his throat in the echoing room.

Clara opened her eyes to a large space—a table in the middle, weapon cabinets in the back. Iron-barred doors, each too dark to see through, lined the walls. They must not have windows—probably meant to keep whoever lurked inside hidden. Was Beau housed in there?

A clank of metal drew her attention around. Theo, of all people, sat at the table, wrists clipped with manacles, his gaze fixed on her. Sheriff Kelly towered at his side, both hands on his hips.

"May I help ye, Miss Royall?" Sheriff Kelly grimaced. "I mean, Miss Alexander."

Clara's stomach clenched, her hands tightening around her shawl as she clutched the basket of food she'd brought for Beau. So he had seen the article and knew she'd lied about who she was. No longer could she pass herself off as a member of the press with the privilege of investigating the town's latest news. Her disguise had been unmasked. She was simply Clara Alexander now.

"I..." Her voice wavered. Why did she feel so weak? "I came to bring some food to one of the prisoners."

Theo's eyes lit with hope, and Clara amended, "I mean two of the prisoners."

Sheriff Kelly stepped forward, sniffing. "That's kind of ye, lass. But ye know I've got to search everything brought into the jail for contraband, right?"

Was he teasing? Clara removed the cloth covering the sweet rolls and freshly churned butter. "I brought some extra, if you have a plate."

"Did ye?" His face shifted from a frown to the brightest of beams. "That's grand, then."

One of the heavy doors swung open behind her as Sheriff Kelly said, "Ye was the best reporter at the *Daily News*. The finest I've ever had the pleasure of speakin' with."

"Thank you, sir." Clara glanced back, catching Mr. Doten paused in midstride behind her.

"This is an investigation." Sheriff Kelly frowned at him, voice suddenly gruff. "We don't have time for the press."

Doten's gaze swung to Clara, then, as if a blessing from heaven aimed down on her in the half-built courthouse, he flicked his eyebrows up in question. Clara stared, unblinking, her thoughts racing. Mr. Doten had been so angry outside. Did he really want her to work for him? Was he just using her because Sheriff Kelly liked her? If so, was that necessarily a bad thing?

She turned back around. "We'll be as unobtrusive as possible, Sheriff. I understand you have an investigation to carry out. Mr. Peterson was a good man. I'd never want to interfere. That said, you were so kind to give me an interview two weeks ago. I would be eternally grateful if you allowed me to write a follow-up story."

"All right, all right. Don't go laying on the flattery, lass. I'll let you stay." He shot a glance at Alf Doten, straightening. "Provided you do indeed work for the Gold Hill paper." For all the gentleness he showed Clara, Sheriff Kelly gave Editor Doten a dark scowl. "I heard ye were fired."

Clara turned, trying not to grimace when she made eye contact with Doten. Some color rose to his cheeks.

"More false news spread by my competitors, I assure you, sheriff." Mr. Doten clasped his hands loosely, leaning slightly forward, eager but composed. "If you don't mind, though, I'd like to watch my newest reporter at work."

Sheriff Kelly nodded, and Clara, still a little shaky, set the basket down on the table and began serving the men.

"Now, Mr. Atticus..." Kelly sat down, his hands resting firmly on the table. "You're in real trouble. Murder, imprisonin' an elderly man, and...the attack on Miss Royall—I mean, Miss Alexander here." He nodded toward her as she spread butter on her bread.

Theo looked at Clara, then Doten and Kelly. "I'll tell you everything—a full confession—but Miss Alexander is the only reporter I will speak to. Keep the rest of them away."

"All righty. That's fine by me. Just let me get some paper and a pen." He went to a desk that was pushed up against a wall behind him and withdrew the supplies he needed, while Clara set out their servings of rolls and butter.

Now for the prisoners... The cells loomed on every side. Which one was Beau in? Clara peered around as she approached the first door.

Theo watched her and inclined his head, signaling she was going in the right direction.

"Beau?" she called softly, peering past the crisscrossed bars into the darkened room. There was a shuffle, then the sound of footsteps.

Beau emerged from the darkness, light pouring over his fierce features—no spark of joy, not even a sign of recognition. Clara placed the bread on the small window intended for food. "I brought you some bread," she offered meekly.

He tilted his head. "Have *you* eaten today?"

Her stomach felt as though it touched her backbone, though nothing—no matter how it looked or smelled—awakened her appetite. "I'm not very hungry," she whispered, aware of the men at the table nearby, speaking of foods their mothers made that they loved. Sheriff Kelly handed out mugs and poured coffee—some even for Theo. Despite their conversation, they might overhear her.

"I'm not hungry either." Beau moved as if to slip back into the shadows.

"I added some cinnamon and honey to the butter," Clara offered quickly, trying to sound casual.

Beau rubbed his hands on his pants. "Not really clean in here."

Clara unwrapped the bundle and tore off a piece, offering it to him.

He waved her off. "You first."

Sick to her stomach, Clara took a small bite of the bread. The butter melted and sugar swarmed her tongue, but her jaw felt too tired to chew. She certainly didn't want to swallow.

"Your turn," she said, presenting him a piece. Expecting him to take it, she watched as he leaned down and took a bite from the morsel, his warm breath sweeping her hand.

After finishing the bite, he crossed his thick, muscular arms over his chest, as if to bar himself from her. "So you're still writing for Doten?"

"It would seem so—at least today." She dared to glance at the editor, who actually grinned at the sheriff, bread still in his mouth. "We spoke briefly outside. He wasn't intending to keep me on staff, but I think Sheriff Kelly may have changed his mind."

"How will you proceed from here now that everyone in the county knows you worked in disguise for Doten?"

Cheeks growing hot, Clara kept her chin high. "I am not sure. I plan to consult my father and Mr. Doten on the matter. Reporting on this case is important. If the people of Virginia City and Gold Hill like it, I shall likely stay on. If not, I'll be back where I started. Just a girl with a pencil and a hope of making a difference." She shrugged away the feeling of self-pity, for Beau was facing something far more hopeless than she.

"You had best not spend more time with me, then." His voice hardened, and he stepped back. "Being associated with me could hurt your future."

"Beau, please..." Breathless, she clung to any connection with him, afraid he might slip away. "Please, stay near a moment." It wasn't just about the distance. It felt like everything—her career, her future, her heart—depended on this moment. "If there's ever a time when you're willing to risk your heart again..."

His jaw was tense and his gaze steeled, not at all welcoming.

"I'll wait for you, and you needn't worry about me. I've made peace with Tessa and will live at my father's house. I'll find a way to write that's safe and honest. And if you ever come back..." She raised her eyebrows, heart pounding painfully as he withheld even the slightest sign of softness. But she couldn't judge him for remaining stalwart in the face of what lay ahead. And, as Tessa said, joy shouldn't depend on any one person. She forced a smile and pulled her hand back from the window—when Beau's rough fingers claimed her wrist.

"My surname is Vulpe. I gave the registrar at immigration a false name, Fox, because I was running from myself." He bowed and pressed his lips to the back of her hand, then lingered there, almost as if sealing a final farewell. "If there was ever a time when we could be together, you'd be my *mon seul amour*."

My only love. Holding her breath, Clara turned her hand and pressed her fingertips briefly to his cheek.

Beau closed his eyes for an instant, then when he opened them, he didn't meet her gaze. He took the bread and slipped back into the cell, where she could barely make out his outline as he sat on what looked like a cot.

Theo glanced away as she turned, though she sensed that all the men had been aware of her exchange with Beau. What would they think of her for loving a convict? Would such a connection ruin her future? Regardless of what they thought, she'd rather be Beau's wife than write for the biggest newspaper in the country. And how could she tell him to live a life of courage, of sanctification after atonement, if she wasn't willing to bear that cross with him?

Sheriff Kelly pointed her toward Mr. Malcolm's and then Dodge's cell. Clara saw no sign of either man when she set the bundle of bread within reach. Back at the table, Sheriff Kelly pulled out a chair, and she settled herself beside him. Then she fished her pencil and reporter's pad from her basket and shot the sheriff an expectant look.

He aimed a brow at Theo, who finished his last bite of bread before saying, "In November, someone slid a message under my door about testing a mine's ore sample. But there were stipulations. The report had to say the mineral quality was high, regardless of geological findings. At first, I ignored the message. Then one night, Dodge Peterson appeared with a stack of banknotes. I wanted the money, but I hate the mines. I paid the hoist engineer to let someone go into the mine and collect a sample."

Clara paused her writing, avoiding Theo's gaze. Mr. Doten and Sheriff Kelly might join forces to throw her out of the courthouse once they found out the truth. That she was the person who stole the ore sample.

"I'll need a name, mind ye?" Sheriff Kelly raised his eyebrows.

Theo bit his lip, then sighed. "I told Mr. Perkins who to look for, and he'd escort this person up from the mine. There would be no search because this person was a woman."

Mr. Doten, who had been leaning back in his chair, dropped the front legs to the floor. "Miss Alexander? Don't tell me it was you."

Her cheeks burned hot. Clara cleared her throat. "I was desperate to begin my writing career. I didn't use caution or wisdom. You might as well know because the editor at the

Enterprise knows—and it will likely come out at some point, anyway."

"The mines are deadly." Kelly glowered at her, then at Theo, enunciating each word with a jab of his pen when he said, "You had no right influencing her to go down there. If I had a daughter..." He huffed and folded his arms across his barrel chest.

"I've since seen the errors of my ways. The other night, when I searched Mr. Tibbon's house, I found myself trapped in the cellar with those criminals—Dodge, Theo, and Mr. Perkins. I've never been so scared in my life. I don't know what I would have done if Mr. Reed and Mr. Vulpe hadn't intervened."

Doten nodded slowly. "I am glad to hear that because I'd never allow a reporter of mine to put herself into harm's way. We're newspaper men, not lawmen or...or, or private investigators. Understand?"

"I do," she said, glancing at Sheriff Kelly, who drew in a deep breath.

"Now that we have that settled, Mr. Atticus..." He made a rolling gesture. "Please continue."

Theo took a drink of his coffee. "After that, I paid the geologist, Mr. Malcolm, to reference him in the report published in the *Enterprise*. The mine stock went up, and Dodge wanted to sell. That's when he salted the mine, but Peterson still wouldn't sell."

Dodge grumbled something from his cell, then fell quiet. Mr. Malcolm remained silent as well. He hadn't touched his food.

"Is Mr. Malcolm ill?" Goodness knew he'd had plenty to say in the cellar.

"No." Kelly gave a grumble of a chuckle. "He tried to run earlier and, uh, hit his head. He'll be sleeping for a while."

Clara instinctively touched her temple where she'd been struck that night in the snow. The bruise was still dark, although she'd brushed her hair over it and applied makeup in an attempt to hide the ugly mark.

She focused on her note-taking as Theo rambled on.

"The day after the report printed, your dad found me." Theo addressed Clara, crossing his arms as he scowled. "He said that he had the mine tested before Peterson bought it and knew that the ore value was not as high as the article claimed. I didn't tell Dodge. I just hoped it would all go away. Then Mr. Vulpe started asking questions. Mr. Malcolm got scared and left town. On Christmas Eve, I tried to find that first report in your father's study, but Vulpe drove me off. I went to Dodge then and said I was done. I wanted out. Dodge was visiting some girl at a...uh..."—he hesitated, then seemed to adjust what he'd been about to say—"boardinghouse. Before I could tell him, Mr. Peterson drove up in a buggy shouting. He was livid. Said Dodge salted the mine and that he wasn't getting him out of trouble this time. Dodge cursed him and went to walk away, but the old man was in a temper and shoved him. Dodge pushed him back. The old fellow hit his head when he fell." Theo's eyes watered as he looked back at Dodge's cell. "The truth is, he did all this trying to make him proud. Sell the mine before they went bust."

Of course, if Dodge had hired a proper geologist in the beginning, he wouldn't have gotten into this mess.

"Dodge nearly lost his mind when his father wouldn't wake up. He was staggering drunk as it was. When he passed out, I... ah..." He cleared his throat and shook his head, brows raised as he blew between his lips. "I took them both back to Peterson's house. I only wanted to help. Dodge didn't mean to kill his father."

Sheriff Kelly nodded gravely while Clara kept her eyes on her paper.

What a terrible turn of events. To be responsible for one's

own parent's death. She'd been devastated when Mother died, but to have caused it...

And here she had accused Father of just that. He must be wounded by her belief, even if it was validated. What a burden to bear.

"Everything was bad after that." Theo ran his hand through his dirty hair, making it stand on end. "I thought we'd all be arrested, but then Vulpe was taken into custody. We thought we were in the clear. At the time, it seemed like a godsend. Vulpe was an escaped convict—a real criminal. I found the articles detailing his arrest—half Roma, half French, about thirty, and Vulpe means *fox*. He escaped the penitentiary in Utah just a week before the fire, though, so no one noticed when he came to Virginia City."

"So you were going to let him pay for a crime he didn't commit? You named him a murderer." Clara's tone sharpened despite her effort to stay calm.

He shook his head. "I know. I was a coward. Dodge said if Vulpe was arrested, we would all go free. Dodge didn't know then that Vulpe was actually Beau Fox. He probably killed someone in the past. I told myself this was just his sins finding him out." He faced Clara when Doten and Kelly scowled at him in disgust. "What would you do, Clara? Go in disguise and try to break Vulpe free?"

"Yes! You tried to incriminate an innocent man so the real culprit could go free. That's wrong." Clara sighed, tapping her pencil against the table. She had to keep Theo going, telling the truth so Peterson would finally have justice and Beau's name would be cleared. "I shouldn't raise my voice at you, Theo. It's your story to tell. I won't interrupt again."

Doten rumpled his lip, his thick mustache twitching while Sheriff Kelly, who had let her take over the interview, continued to jot down notes.

Theo slowly nodded. "It doesn't matter, anyway. I'm

doomed, but so's your fella, Clara, and it's not my fault. I didn't tell Dodge who Vulpe is. I'm not all bad."

Sick to her stomach and unable to offer him understanding, Clara asked, "How *did* he find out Beau's true identity?"

Theo rolled his jaw. "It was just the other day. Dodge was drinking, moaning about his father passing. He started going through his things and found a letter from Mr. Peterson to the United States Marshals at the Utah Territorial Penitentiary. Peterson wrote it back in October but never sent it. He hired Vulpe instead. Seems he liked him. Dodge hated him even more. Jealousy is a nasty, humiliating thing to have to live with." He shrugged, shaking his head. "That man was volatile. I never should have worked with him. Anyway, Dodge was breathing down my neck, threatening to pistol whip me if I didn't get the geologist's report that your dad had. I lost my job at the *Enterprise* and was so angry."

"Is that when you told him that I am L. C. Royall?" She'd not believed Theo could hurt her further after the way he'd led her on with the newspaper business, but goodness. Had he really disclosed her identity to a killer?

"I didn't tell him, Clara. He followed you home that night. He overheard you and Vulpe arguing about you wearing pants. He thought he'd take you both out and be done with all the problems, then Malcolm came back with a plan—a con. He suggested we could go to different places, ripping off good people—like the Diamond Hoax of '72. I didn't want any part of it."

"When did ye take Tibbons?" Kelly was writing almost as quickly as Clara.

"I didn't know Dodge had him. I'm just glad he didn't kill the old man. Tibbons tried to get me to help him. Said Dodge kept him tied up every day while he was at work and gallivanting at night. I know I should have helped him, but Dodge was so mean. I was scared." He cupped his face in his hands, breathing hard, his words muffled as he added, "I never should have come to Virginia City."

Clara laid her pencil down. All the pieces of the puzzle had fallen into place, yet a throbbing emptiness filled her. "What about the miner who operated the lift?"

"I didn't know about him until he showed up last night. Dodge and Malcolm were bragging about this game—this con, the idea of tricking investors into buying dry claims, just like with Peterson. The lift operator wanted to be part of that. Everyone's afraid the mines will dry up."

Clara nodded. She'd heard rumors the mines' output was depreciating back in seventy-four. Would God really let them lose everything?

The chains clinked as Theo opened his hands. "Miners keep digging deeper, trying to reach high-grade ore. They're investing in fancy drills and pumps—advanced technology—and racking up expenses. When the Comstock breathes its last, Virginia City will disappear off this mountain, just like so many Paiute villages that stood here before it. I just hope I'm not here to see it."

The skin on her arms tightened at the notion that the wealth of Virginia City would melt away like snow in springtime. If the mines truly dried up soon, what would Beau have left to return to after his time in prison? He might be lost to her —gone for good.

CHAPTER 27

Boots crunching on the icy street in Salt Lake City, Beau stepped from the hack after Jesse with Nathan close behind. Around him, the city bustled with carriages, streetcars, and pedestrians hurrying in every direction. Gray clouds to the west hid the sun.

Over the past few days on the train, they'd pored over what they knew about the gang in the penitentiary. Now, it was time to see if Marshal Morris and his connections would offer Beau a deal to infiltrate and expose the gang.

Beau faced the adobe courthouse, a looming bastion in the Utah wilderness, its high cornices a silent challenge. Doubts nagged at his resolve. Beyond, the rugged Wasatch Range rose sharply from the valley floor—jagged ridges, rocky slopes, and pine forests stretched across the lower elevations, mirroring the barrier he felt within himself. Would the mission succeed, or was it a fool's errand that might cost him everything?

"Let's go." Nathan bumped him forward, and Beau walked —not with chains, though Jesse occasionally looked on him with suspicion—but with unbound hands. He'd never entered a place of civil law so free—at least not in America.

Inside, a great hall opened before them, and their footsteps echoed amid the multitude of others. Men hurried this way and that, dressed well in frockcoats and hats. Thoughts crowded his mind—first Clara, and the faintest hope of returning to her. Her promise to be safe, heed wisdom, and find a way to work within the social confines warmed him through with respect.

The memory of Theo's confession and his tale of Dodge's sad story—which Beau had overheard in the jail—cooled him. To be responsible for his own father's death? No wonder Dodge had been so hostile.

Jesse led them to a large wooden door and studied the metal nameplate there. He glanced back, locking eyes with Beau. "This is it."

He pushed inward, and they stepped into a room that looked like a judge's chambers. Three men sat in comfortable chairs, all wearing suits.

"Gentlemen, good morning." Jesse offered a handshake to an elderly man. Despite his frock coat and neatly combed hair, the man had a weathered, wild look. Jesse addressed him as Marshal Morris when they shook hands. His long gray mustache hung loosely on each side, and wiry eyebrows contrasted thinning hair. "Marshal, this is my brother-in-law, Nathan Reed, and the man I told you about—Beau Vulpe, also known as Beau Fox."

Nathan offered his hand, and so did Beau when the marshal reached for his. Anytime he'd met law enforcement, he was either running or fighting. Would this man really help him?

"I'm glad you've come in, son." The marshal shook his hand firmly. The casual squeeze reminded him of Mr. MacKay's at the Christmas party. Pushing aside the memory of the kindest employer he'd ever known, Beau faced the other men.

One he instantly recognized—Mr. Simmons, the district attorney for the territory, who had been at his hearing last fall when he pleaded guilty to abduction, unlawful confinement, and robbery charges. Simmons had pushed for as harsh a sentence as possible—ten years.

"Mr. Fox, good morning," Simmons said, his greeting curt. Beau managed not to squeeze his hand too tightly when they shook.

"And this is Senator Charles Quin Cannon. Without his devotion and drive to catch the gang, we wouldn't be here." Marshal Morris cupped the senator's shoulder.

The man grasped Beau's hand firmly. "My son was shot when the gang that operates out of the penitentiary held up a stagecoach outside the city." His nasal voice contrasted with his large stature. "I sure hope you are the answer to my prayers." He kept shaking Beau's hand as he spoke, a sharp contrast to the mild-mannered marshal and the slender, nervous attorney.

"I'm sorry about your son. Hopefully, we can stop them once and for all," Beau said as the men took seats around the hearth, Nathan and Jesse pulling up extra chairs.

Mr. Cannon sat on the edge of his chair, clasping his hands together in front of his rotund belly. "When they told me a criminal had come forward, claiming a gang operated out of the penitentiary, it finally made sense. They always seem to know when there's a Wells Fargo courier. But there's no pattern to their strikes. Sometimes three times a week, then not again until three months later. There's nothing particular about their horses, their riding, or the method of their holdups. I've hired private detectives, trackers, and consulted with the best marshals in the country and still haven't been able to catch them." He shook his head, his lips rumpled in a sneer beneath his feathery mustache.

Beau nodded, taking it all in. "Having a good plan will be the most important part of all this." He had initially thought the men offering him a deal would just tell him what to do, but after days of running through scenarios with Nathan and Jesse on the train, and trying to understand the intricacies of such an operation, he realized it would take more than just alerting the authorities during a holdup. If he was to make it out alive and return to Clara, he'd need to disclose hiding places, connections inside and outside the prison, and likely, secret passageways out.

Simmons tried to sit higher in his chair—typical of a man who felt he lacked something. Would his insecurities be a hindrance?

Marshal Morris seemed more than comfortable, with one ankle resting on the opposite knee. "What do you know of their activities?" he asked Beau.

"When I was there last fall, I heard these men have a system in place—a way to leave the penitentiary, hide their gear, get horses. They must have connections on the outside to operate as they do." Beau exhaled a deep breath, looking to the senator. "This may take longer than I thought, sir."

Red flushed the portly politician's face. "My son will never walk again. If you can catch this pack of thieves, no matter how long it takes, I'll give you anything, Fox."

"All I want is to atone for my sins and gain my freedom. Also, my name is Vulpe. Beau Vulpe. My father was Lucien Théodore Vulpe of Lorraine, France, before it was ceded to Germany. Fox is a—how do you say it—alias?"

"Yes." The senator's eyebrows raised, then his eyes narrowed. "You are not what I expected, Mr. Vulpe. Were you a soldier in the latest conflict between Germany and France?"

"Yes, sir, a *capitaine*."

"Well, that's fine." Cannon grinned at the marshal and the attorney as though they, too, should be impressed. Simmons sniffed, and the marshal took in the information with a nod.

Beau's ears burned, and he ground his teeth. Being admired for success in a war that had cost him everything and had been started by his own greedy, grasping government did not sit well, but he would no longer hide from any part of his past. He'd tried and done so many different things—engineer, soldier, father, carpenter, farrier, bounty hunter, scout, and thief. Every experience had contributed to who he was. If he were to right his wrongs and reunite with Clara, he needed to draw upon every skill he had ever acquired.

Nathan shifted in his chair, glancing at Jesse and then the men. "We'd like to get the specifications in writing—what Beau must do, what results you want, and what he gets in return."

"What he gets in return?" The attorney turned up his nose.

"Yes, a full pardon." Jesse spoke up now. "It's Beau's life on the line. The last time he encountered the Sugar House Gang, he refused to join, and they nearly killed him."

Beau had shared that in confidence, but it made Jesse's argument stronger.

"He's the one risking his life, not you." Jesse looked directly at the shifting lawyer, then the senator. "Monsieur Vulpe is the only man who can bring these men to justice."

Simmons piped up. "You talk like an attorney."

Jesse grinned. "I studied law for a year. Decided I wanted a more honest line of work."

So Jesse Alexander, like Beau, had dropped out of school. Beau rolled his shoulders. He wasn't a complete mess. Beau had actually loved engineering. After years of heckling, slurs, and unfair treatment, he'd just wanted to be free of French high society.

Even among the Roma, he'd never quite belonged. The only place he'd ever felt wanted was in Virginia City—with Clara, John, and MacKay. He didn't deserve any of it, but as Clara said, "None of us deserve the good things God gives."

Simmons and Jesse argued over Beau's sentencing and whether it could be commuted.

The senator kept butting in, occasionally reassuring a scowling Nathan that all would be well. He'd gotten men off murder charges before—a notion that turned Beau's stomach. Doubtful they all deserved it. But did he?

"You cannot just come in here making demands, Mr. Alexander." The wiry Simmons sniffed, dabbing his nose with a handkerchief that looked as though it belonged to his grandmother.

"A full pardon," Beau said despite the cold sweat breaking across his neck. "That's what I will accept. I nearly died last time I faced this gang, and now you tell me they're more organized than before."

"You're lucky we don't just throw you back in jail." Simmons narrowed his eyes to slits, the thin lines of his mustache like the whiskers of a mouse.

"You're lucky I turned myself in and returned here willingly—to do the right thing." Beau faced Senator Cannon and they shook hands. "Get me a contract with a full pardon if I deliver information that leads to the capture of the Sugar House Gang. I will sign it."

"And I will have a lawyer look it over," Jesse chimed in.

"I know a judge who can help draw this up." Cannon scooted to the edge of his chair, and removing a fat cigar from his coat pocket, he waved the big, ugly thing at Simmons. "You needn't stay, George. I won't need your help, after all."

The lawyer left in a huff, but the marshal nodded briefly to Beau when they made eye contact. "I can come to the hotel you boys are staying at, and we'll talk out the details. Either way, Mr. Vulpe, you'll need to be in custody, but I don't want to put you in just yet. Not until we've got a plan and all the paperwork ready for you. How does that sound?"

Beau stood, ready to leave before the senator offered him a cigar and tried to befriend him. "Sounds fine, sir." And maybe it would be fine in the end. One thing was certain—it would not be safe or easy.

~

*T*he road to the penitentiary, known as the Sugar House by locals, wound through the outskirts of Salt Lake City. Snow covered the ground so everything looked clean and white, but nothing about where he was going was pure. Inside the swaying prison wagon, Beau sat among other men of a familiar bent—silent, bleak, angry. The unmistakable scent of cold iron and unwashed bodies clung to the air, but at least, with them all crammed into the small space, they were not freezing cold.

Trees rolled by outside the window. A man pressed his face against the bars. "There it is."

Beau didn't bother looking. He remembered too well the castle-like structure—imposing and solid, immovable. The outer wall connected to the main front building, thick stone rising twelve feet high. The adobe beneath was crumbling in places, where the newer stone had not yet replaced it.

A single iron gate stood at the front, flanked by two guards in worn uniforms, rifles slung casually but eyes sharp. The wagon rolled on, its springs crying, the harnesses and tack of the horses creaking. Beyond the gate, the yard stretched wide and bare, trampled dirt bordered by crude wooden structures and the looming cell house.

They drove around to the main block, and the wagon door opened. White light poured in. Squinting, Beau climbed out with the others and went through the too-familiar motions of removing all his belongings, clothes, and boots. Everything he owned was stripped from him and replaced with striped pants and a shirt, the fabric rough and worn. The shoes were little more than leather moccasins.

He was herded with the other men down stone-cold, dark halls. The guard leading the way turned before coming to an iron gate. "My name is Marshal Royce. I am in charge of the work duty—most days."

Beau kept his eyes down, not reacting though his skin prickled. Marshal Morris had told him to relay information about the gang through a guard by the name of Royce. Here was the man, and Beau had to hide that connection for both their sakes.

Marshal Royce led them on to the cell house, added just that year—a squat, two-story building with narrow barred windows. It cast long shadows over the land in the dim morning light. From the dreaded building came the clank of chains and the low murmur of voices—some prayerful, some bitter. The air inside the walls felt heavier—as if the wind refused to cross the threshold. It caught in his chest like mountain air—air you try to breathe, but it's never enough.

Eyes stinging, neck crawling with unease, Beau kept his chin up. It was always like this—the feeling of being suffocated, closed in, as if the walls themselves pressed against him. He just had to get through each day and each night. Keep his head down and work as he'd done before, and keep his eyes open for any signs of the Sugar House Gang.

Inside the big log dining house, the men sat at long tables—more than six hundred of them. Beau carried his plate from the chow line to an empty spot. He hardly looked up as he drank the black coffee and tore a piece off the boiled beef.

When last he'd been here, he'd kept to himself. The gang members would expect the same, but he was also taking stock of every corridor, room, path, wall, and floor. The twelve-foot wall had not been difficult to climb over last year. He could leave anytime he wanted to but was staying of his own free will. He had to remember that, or the caged animal inside him would rebel, and he would be out of control once and for all.

After dinner, he was shown to his cell, which he shared with two others who hardly spoke.

The next morning, a fight broke out on the way to the mess hall. Beau kept back, watching as two desperate, exhausted men fought over a place to sit.

After the meal, the men trudged outside to work. The walls stretched far across a great field, where rows of a garden were barely visible beneath the snowfall. Beau passed the execution yard. A wooden scaffold stood in eerie silence. Many a man had fallen there by firing squad, and for lesser sins than his. He didn't need to be told about the shallow graves outside the wall. He'd helped dig two for condemned men during his short stay here.

He was directed to the partially constructed four-story cell house within the yard where he and others like him participated in back-breaking work. Men labored in their striped uniforms with makeshift jackets of blankets to ward off the cold.

Near the end of his first day, Beau tipped a bucket of water back and gulped thirstily, the cool liquid running down his throat and shocking his empty stomach. A man bumped him from behind, jarring him so he spilled water down his front.

"Watch your step," Beau barked over the pounding of hammers.

The man turned—tall and lean, with muscular arms, white-blond hair, and a familiar grin. "You watch your step, *camarade*."

Beau stood still, relief and dread flooding him at once. Emil Willot was here—alive and well, and likely up to no good, as always. In fact, Marshal Morris's description of the gang's movements and attacks had the precision of a military command. If Emil was leading the Sugar House Gang, that could mean life or death for Beau.

CHAPTER 28

The mess hall buzzed with movement and murmured conversations as Beau moved through the tables. It was Sunday, and everyone had an extra serving of beef and one apple. The sides were bruised, but just seeing the sweet fruit made Beau's mouth water.

He now understood how the groups in the dining hall formed—by age, race, or class. Mostly race. Since he fell somewhere in the middle, he had no place to sit. Today Emil rose from the hunched group of men he'd been sitting with and waved Beau over to his table.

It had been a week, and still no one had contacted him as they did last time. He also hadn't spied anyone from the old gang. Perhaps he was right and Emil was in charge.

"Bonjour," Emil greeted him when he sat down.

Beau replied in kind, then paused to pray over his meal.

"I see you are on a righteous path again." Emil took a bite from his apple, a dull crunch signaling it was overripe.

Not liking to be reminded of his past failed attempts to do right, Beau just shrugged.

Emil chomped on his fruit again, then spoke in French. "My père said you were in San Francisco."

"I was. And in Salt Lake when he had me beaten and turned over to the police for forsaking you."

Emil grimaced, then chuckled. "He is not very forgiving. Was he justified in beating you, though? Hm? How did you get away the night I was arrested?"

Beau took a bite from his own apple before a crazed or desperate inmate could come and try to steal it. He shrugged noncommittally. "Someone followed me to the hideout. I backtracked, trying to find who it was, but I ran into a posse. By then, it was too late. What would you have me do?"

Emil nodded, glancing around at the other prisoners in striped clothes. He pressed his thumb into his fruit, his expression growing serious. "You saw my sister-in-law and niece this last summer?"

His skin prickled, but Beau kept his focus on his food and simply nodded. "Not the heir your père was hoping for."

Emil groaned and shook his head. "An heir. That's a man's greatest hope." His shoulders rose and fell as he looked off into the distance. He seemed steadier than the last time Beau saw him. After Emil learned his younger brother had died here in this very prison, he was neither well nor sane.

"Richard says you were here last fall. I didn't see you."

Beau glanced up to find Richard, a dark-haired man with a patchy beard, meeting his gaze over Emil's shoulder.

A flash of memory struck him—being trapped in the corner of his cell, the men closing in on him...including Richard, one of the gang members.

With a blaze under his skin, Beau slammed his plate into Richard's face, nearly hitting Emil in the process. He dragged the coward to the floor and pummeled him, Emil barely jumping out of the way in time to avoid going down in the fray.

"Look out, Beau. He's got a friend," Emil shouted amid the cheering of fellow inmates.

Sure enough, a second man jabbed his heel into Beau's lower back. Grabbing the attacker's ankle, he wrenched it upward and twisted, sending him sprawling on the floor.

Emil leapt away, laughing and swearing in French while guards fought to pull the men apart.

Beau's punishment was an underground cell, a hole in the ground with bars at the top. The temperatures dropped to freezing. With the moon hanging high in the sky and God seemingly out of reach, Beau suffered through, wondering if this would be his end.

The next day, he was hauled into his cell before the sky had fully darkened.

Lying on his side on a cot, fleas biting him, the dank scent of mildew and urine all around, he tried to remember the warm evenings at Mrs. Matthews's boarding house, reading to Clara before the hearth, but they seemed so far away—like God. He tried to recall Bible verses he'd memorized, repeating them over and over, but darkness hung over him.

Tormented by memories of war and loss, Beau closed his eyes and repeated the only prayer he could remember. "'Yea, though I walk through the valley of the shadow of death, I will fear no evil...'"

Eventually, he drifted off, then woke suddenly to a call nearby.

"Beau?" It was a whispered, heavily French voice—Emil.

Unable to sit up without hitting the bunk of the man above him, Beau raised his head and made out the outline of a man standing in his cell.

"Come, your dreams haunt even me." Emil grasped his arm and gave him a shake.

Hating the statement—nightmares being something they'd shared in the past when camped and the other awakened from terrors of war—Beau slid off his bed. He hit the floor, landing on his feet, then strode through the open door with Emil. Metal hinges whined under the weight when he closed it. The man held a ring of keys, one of which he used to lock Beau's cell. Beau's cellmates raised their heads yet did not move to follow. Odd. Did they know something Beau did not?

Emil led the way down the corridor as though on a stroll to a garden party. There was no guard in sight, and no prisoners seemed to notice them. When Emil pushed a door open to reveal the moonlit yard under a blanket of snow, a frigid wind swirled.

Their steps crunched the snow all the way across the yard and to the kitchen. Stomach tight in his ribs, Beau glanced around expecting a guard, the metal click of a gun being cocked, or the deafening shot of the bullet that would end his life, but they reached the cellar where food was stored unharmed.

Emil had no fear of the underground, though if he'd gone as far down in the mines as Beau, he might have. He employed the ring of keys again and unlocked the cellar door.

"You just have your own set of keys to every door in the prison?" Beau spoke between clenched teeth as he tried to keep the shivering at bay.

Emil only snickered, then down into the darkness they went.

This must be part of the gang's secret lair. Would Emil show him the way out of the prison tonight? Tell him how they moved on the roads unnoticed and uninhibited? Could it really be so easy?

The cellar was so dark, Beau kept his hand on Emil's shoulder when he moved forward as though knowing every step. A door creaked, and light spilled from in front of Emil, filling the cellar. There was another door in the stone wall at the back of the storage room. He grinned over one shoulder, half of his face lit.

For a moment, Beau hesitated, then stepped into the tunnel with Emil. Instead of the sturdy, square beams typical of the Comstock, it was supported by rough pine trunks. They came to a room with a fireplace burning and several men gathered on makeshift chairs. Among them was Richard and his long-haired friend who had kicked Beau in the back.

Beau let out a short, humorless laugh and shrugged, but his shoulders were as tight as cords. "You should not trust that one. He and his miserable friends nearly killed me last time I was here."

Richard rose, noticeably shorter than Beau—likely no taller than Clara. He exhibited no signs of having spent a night in an underground cell as Beau had. "We tried to enlist him, and he refused." Despite a tense tremor in his voice, he crossed his arms.

Beau raised an eyebrow, a faint, skeptical smile curling on his lips. "You think I would follow you, *nabot*?"

Emil settled on a barrel, cracking open a jar of pickled onions. "A nabot no longer runs this gang." He shot Beau a meaningful look.

"I've gone straight. I don't want to rob anymore."

"I knew you'd say that. Come, Beau, why do you torture yourself with righteous notions of being a good man? Good men who refuse to do what is necessary to survive are weak men. Neither of us is weak." He sipped the pungent liquid from the jar. "What has caused your latest bout of guilt?" He grew still, frowning. "It's not Lorraine, is it?"

"No. I just want to be better, stronger. Perhaps if I had been wiser in the past, those I protected would not have been lost."

A shadow crossed Emil's face. "Would you judge me so?"

"No. The war was too great for any one man to defeat. There is nothing you could have done in the end."

"If that is how you feel, you might consider forgiving yourself as well."

The comment—one he could not quite believe—stilled Beau. It was his fault that his wife and son had died. Could Emil be right, though? That he was not to blame? *This is when I need You, God. When I don't know right from wrong.*

For a moment, Emil studied him, then glanced down. "How is Lorraine?"

So Emil regretted how he, in his grief, had turned on his goddaughter? "She is well. Engaged to Jesse Alexander."

Emil's nostrils flared when he drew in a deep breath. "My père said the family was good, wealthy. Perhaps she'll find what she has been looking for."

She had already, but likely, Beau's appearance had unearthed old wounds. A shame, that.

"Richard? Henry?" Emil addressed the two men who still stood near the fire. "I don't want any more trouble between you and Fox. He is a friend of mine. I will see to him, and you will see to yourselves." He gave them a knowing look, and the men nodded, then turned back to the fire, Richard showing a prominent limp he hadn't had the last time Beau was here. He would have to keep an eye on that one.

"Sit, and tell me more of my family." Emil handed Beau the jar of onions, then dug into a crate for pickled cod.

Starved from hardly eating and exhausted from little sleep in the last two weeks and the agony of cold nights, Beau filled his mouth. He didn't want to tell Emil about Mademoiselle Aubrey and her babies, so what could he share?

"Your stepmother and father are dealing with the Germans —trying to hold onto their home." He sipped the vinegar, the harsh liquid hitting his stomach like a splash of spirits on an empty gut. "You should go home. Leave this country. Your father is aging, and there's nothing for you here. In Germany, no one will care that you deserted your battalion to try and save your family in wartime."

"My père will care." Emil shrugged, looking away, then crossing his arms and stretching out his long legs. "How did you get caught this time?"

A memory of Clara flashed through his mind. She'd captured his heart, making it impossible for him to run any longer.

"A woman?" Emil's eyes widened. "Let me guess—her family disapproved and turned you in? No, a jealous suitor discovered your dark past?"

Beau actually grinned at the irony, then spoke between bites of cod. "Something like that."

"Perhaps it is you who should go to Elsaß–Lothringen." Emil used the new German name for the part of Lorraine annexed by Germany.

"Maybe." He paused his eating, the harsh food needing time to settle. Emil rubbed his chin. He was a hound following a scent, and Beau needed to distract him lest he unearth something close to the truth. "I didn't see you when I was here last year."

"I was very sick. The air. It kills me, slowly. If I couldn't come here—leave sometimes—I wouldn't be alive. It was Richard who showed me how to survive."

"How so?"

"Non." Emil stood, arms crossed. "I do not trust you, Rom. Like a fox—you are sly and ready to run away, but you will fight when least expected. You are different now. Why? Is it the girl?"

Rather than allow suspicion of another kind to dawn on his old employer, Beau let himself remember the gentle brush of Clara's hand on his cheek.

"A man who looks like that when thinking of a woman has a good reason to want to leave this place." Emil gestured for Beau to rise, then led him back the way they came. "Would you risk another escape?"

"I have no money. What good is escape when I have no way to survive, let alone reach her again?"

"What if I could find a way to get you all the money you could ever need or want?"

Beau stopped, grasping Emil's arm. "How?"

The older man chuckled. "Not yet, Beau. I want to know I can trust you again. It is just a shame you came at the very worst time."

What an odd thing to say. It did not bode well, as though they were on the precipice of some happening. Whatever it was, Beau had to be ready. This was his very last chance, and he could not fail.

∼

Clara bowed her head and closed her eyes as her maid carefully fastened the hooks at the back of her dress, the fabric as heavy as the weight of the day. Her prayers felt like a fragile thread stretched across the chaos of the past month.

Would this day—without Beau, without any certainty of their future—finally unravel her hopes? To stand witness to the union of Maudy and the man she loved in holy matrimony, while her own heart remained suspended in uncertainty... could she bear it?

"You are getting a mite too thin, miss." Her maid, Katy, fastened the last of her hooks, giving her a disapproving look in the mirror.

Indeed, Clara's plan to trust God had not settled her stomach enough to restore her appetite now that Beau was far away. Sleeplessness also plagued her, as the rings beneath her eyes attested, but she stayed busy so as to at least be useful in the turmoil following her scandal—that of a self-important debutante who fell in love with a convict, further disgracing the Alexander name. Mr. Goodwin had prophesied this, and now he railed against her in his paper, targeting the *Daily News* and its stalwart editor who stood by her side.

A light tap sounded on the door.

"Come." She stood to slip on her gloves.

The door swung open, and Daniel strode inside, wearing a jacket and tie, his socks pulled up to his knees. Tessa wore a green silk gown, its delicate ruffles touching her collarbones, the fabric shimmering in the daylight.

Clara's stepmother went out regularly with her, though the latest remarks of the warring newspapers criticized her extravagant and often ill-suited fashion taste. Tessa simply laughed at these and commented that if the journalists criticizing her had ever lived in New York workhouses, they might indulge in extra ruffles as well. That had also been the day Clara learned her stepmother could not read. Clara had apologized at supper for the newspaper targeting Tessa, and Tessa had admitted her illiteracy due to an eye condition that often caused headaches.

Now she tucked her hand into Daniel's. "We are ready." She smiled brightly, though the pallor of her cheeks indicated she'd likely suffered another headache last night.

When they descended from their carriage in front of the First Presbyterian Church on C Street, a teamster drove twelve mules up the road in an unholy fashion, cursing and cracking his long whip. Tessa shielded Daniel's ears and hurried to the church. Snow still skirted the eaves of the Carpenter Gothic-style building, highlighting the humble architecture and colorful stained-glass windows below the steeple and bell tower.

Inside, light spilled from the eastern window onto the pulpit, illuminating the room with a heavenly hue. Clara settled on one of the pews, the worn wood creaking beneath her as Tessa and Daniel took seats nearby. One row up, Mrs.

Matthews and her young son sat with a few neighbors. Strangers Clara had never seen also dotted the little church. It was a small gathering, but precious—a miracle long in coming.

Abe stood up front near the minister, his eyes riveted on the door as it swung open, letting in a stream of sunlight intensified by the snow. Maudy stepped in on the arm of her stern-looking father, her lovely blue gown like the warmth of springtime. All in attendance stood. As the lady at the piano began a hymn, Maudy walked down the aisle.

The minister began. "Brethren, we gather not for spectacle, but for sacred purpose. This day, Abraham Rankin and Maudy McCready stand before God to enter into a holy covenant."

Clara wound her fingers together, squeezing hard. Would she ever be wed to Beau? Tears blurred the blue and white stripes of her dress.

The minister continued, reading from Ecclesiastes about two being better than one, standing against an adversary or lying down together to stay warm. Such intimate notions warmed her through, yet beneath it all, her heart tightened.

Soon Abe spoke his vows with quiet conviction. "I, Abraham, take thee, M-Maudy, to be my w-w-wedded wife."

Maudy released one of his hands to place hers near his face so he could not see the congregation—only her—and he spoke more clearly.

Once vows were made, the minister prayed over the couple, then turned them to face the congregation. "I present to you Mr. and Mrs. Abraham Rankin."

After a cheer from the crowd died down, the minister announced that a supper would be held at Mrs. Matthews's boardinghouse. When the crowd began to disperse, Clara caught Maudy's attention where she stood with the minister and Abe, ready to sign the record book.

Maudy came forward, leaving a wide-eyed Abe behind, and

embraced Clara. "I am so glad you came." She spun around. "The dress?"

"Lovely, Maudy. You could not look more beautiful."

"Thank you." A shadow crossed Maudy's face despite her radiance. "I'm so sorry for the trouble with the papers and poor Mr. Vulpe. Abe's read every word to me. It seems some reporters manufacture fiction in place of facts. If you send supplies to Mr. Vulpe in the penitentiary, I'd like to include some socks I've knit." Maudy gripped her hands, glancing back at her patient groom and the frowning officiate. "I must be going. I'm praying for you both."

She hugged Clara tightly, so securely that Clara felt her burden lighten for just an instant.

On the way home, Clara turned to her stepmother. "Tessa? Do you think Father would allow me to travel to Salt Lake to give Beau some comforts?" Perhaps she could see him while she was there.

Tessa adjusted the lap blanket over Daniel. "I don't know. Perhaps. He has a soft spot for Monsieur Vulpe, but it may be difficult for him to be away from the business. He would not want you to go alone."

Clara sighed, looking out the small window. The snow had lessened in anticipation of spring. Soon, warmth would descend upon the mountain, thawing the ice of winter. Buds would bloom, leaves would unfurl, and the sandy soil would produce green grass. Spring was her favorite time of year, but truly, how long would it take for her own spring to bloom? How long would Beau be away, and Clara powerless to help?

"I can't just stay here, doing nothing." The carriage bounced on a rut in the road, and Clara met her stepmother's gaze. "I will grow sick."

Tessa sighed, cupping her hand over Clara's arm. "We will speak with John once we're home."

Clara nodded, mind racing. One thing was certain—she could not simply stay still and wait any longer.

CHAPTER 29

Father and Uncle Titus were still at the Washoe Club playing billiards when the sun began to sink behind Mount Davidson—while Clara's thoughts drifted to her plan to leave Virginia City. Though sunlight glowed on the snowy roofs of the houses on the lower streets, their windows all dimmed. She stepped away from her own window and surveyed the parlor. Tessa and Aubrey were talking on the floor, the girls on a blanket before them.

Lorraine kept a silent watch from a different window. Was such quietness part of her nature, or was she worried about Beau also? Clara approached her, noting the piece of wood pinched in Lorraine's hand. A carving?

Lorraine turned her head, meeting Clara's gaze with eyes nearly as dark as obsidian.

"Do you whittle?" Clara asked, hardly able to breathe for how similar Lorraine's eyes were to Beau's.

"No. This is one of the items Beau left behind in San Francisco." She opened her hand to reveal a bear cub. "He whittled it for his son."

"Martin?"

THE CONVICT'S COURTSHIP

Fine black eyebrows rose, and Lorraine nodded. "He told you about his son."

"We were...are close."

"The papers say you are in love with him." The French woman tilted her head, standing very still.

"They are right in that, though in many other things, not so much."

"When did you discover that Beau was Monsieur Beau Fox—the criminal who kidnapped the Alexander heir?" She said it as though repeating the paper, then folded her arms, her expression hardening.

"He told me when he was in the hospital, eight weeks after we met."

Lorraine placed a hand on Clara's arm. "Beau told you who he was? Was he trapped? Was the law after him?"

"No. Then, he was just working for one of the local mines."

She removed her hand from Clara to clasp the elbow of her opposite arm. "I am surprised he stayed in Virginia City after learning some of the Alexander family lived here. Did he stay for you?"

Chest tightening, Clara massaged her collarbone. "Yes. He wanted to leave—he should have—but I kept dragging him back in."

"Into what?"

"Whatever trouble I was in. He stayed at great expense to himself. I can't help but wish he'd left."

"Non. Beau would be running forever if he did. This is his reckoning. If he can be free, he should. He was like a wave washed by the sea—a man without an anchor. And Beau always craved belonging. If he can atone and live a righteous life, he might finally be whole."

"I hope you are right." Clara blinked, her eyes stinging, unwilling to cry before someone so strong. If only Father would return so she could do something to help Beau. She glanced at the front door.

"You are waiting for someone?" Lorraine's gaze strayed out the window as Father and Uncle Titus came up the walk, both taking long strides.

"Yes, my father. I want to put together some things for Beau—socks, a shirt, a blanket—things he can have in prison."

"Aha." With a bitter twist of her mouth, Lorraine shook her head. "He is a criminal. There will be no soft comforts for him. The best you can do is pray." She squeezed Clara's arm, then moved away to greet her future father-in-law.

Clara clenched her fists, anger sparking in her chest like flint against stone. Was she truly meant to wait, suspended in a kind of purgatory, unsure whether the man she loved would walk free or waste the next decade behind bars?

When Father strode through the doorway, grinning at Uncle Titus, Clara stepped in his direction.

"Clara?" His smile faded and he veered toward her. "What is wrong?"

She filled her lungs as if bracing against a winter wind. "I can't abide another day of waiting. I have to do something."

He sighed long and took her shoulders. "There is nothing to do."

"Then I want to go to Salt Lake—to see him. Lorraine said he cannot even have a pair of socks. It's not right. What if being there wears him down?" She lowered her voice. "Beau is so hurt from the war, his many losses. I am afraid."

He wrapped his arms around her, holding her with warmth and security. And though her ache eased, she'd never be completely warm inside until Beau was her husband, holding her.

Lorraine's and Uncle Titus's hushed voices sounded with some urgency, then Uncle turned toward them, hands on his hips. "Well, John, it seems the women have been conspiring."

Father draped an arm around Clara's shoulders, his features stern. "Now is not the time for humor, Titus."

"Agreed. When I leave here, I am taking Lorraine to Salt Lake City. She must see a judge there to ensure she is still leading a good life." He crossed his big, barrel-like arms over the chest of his frock coat. "It was part of the agreement when she went free. We will meet Jesse there. Nathan is already on his way back here. If you do not object to your daughter visiting a criminal in prison, I will take her to the Sugar House."

Clara gasped, but Father scowled. "How generous of you." He gritted the last words between his teeth, though his younger brother seemed unaffected.

"Likely, he is as happy to have his daughter visit a criminal as you are to see your son marry one." Lorraine crossed her arms, her chest rising and falling. "At least in heaven, we shall put these things aside, even if we force generations to come to carry such burdens." She glanced toward the babies, and Aubrey frowned up from the floor.

"I really do think forgiveness should be the legacy of the Alexanders, don't you, Papa?" Only Aubrey could turn chastisement into a plea. Indeed, Uncle Titus's shoulders relaxed, as did that fierce scowl of his.

"Very well, daughter, your rebuke is justified. I just can't see..." He paused when he met Father's gaze.

Neck and face red, Father glared at his brother as though he wanted to fly at him. Clara didn't remember him being violent in her younger years, but then she'd only ever interacted with Father at home with Mother, who rarely opposed him in anything. How would he feel if Clara married Beau? Would he give his blessing? That wasn't like the case of Lorraine, who had only ever committed one crime and was a beautiful, cultured lady.

"Thank you for the offer, Uncle." Clara went to him and kissed his cheek.

He grinned down at her, the rest of his frustration washing away. "My, how you remind me of your mother and aunt."

The smile that came upon her broke through her sadness, if only briefly. "No one has ever paid me such a high compliment."

"It's the eyes." He tapped her chin, then she returned to Father, who still stood with his fists clenched beside the window.

"I have not considered how you might feel about my future with Beau." She spoke low, clasping her hands before her.

He shook his head, the lines around his mouth deepening. "I wrestle with myself and the Lord on the matter. He is a fine man, but you will be forever scorned. Every one of us here in Virginia City is a scandal. I will not lie—I hoped for something more for you, Clara."

"But you seemed to support my interest in him in the past."

"Before I knew he was a criminal. Poor is not the same as criminal. Your children will carry the stain, too, which is why..." His jaw tightened, teeth grinding as though the words themselves pained him.

"Why what?" She held her breath, for her father would certainly not tell her anything good.

"Why you must be at peace with whatever God wills or allows."

The words struck her like a winter gust. She stumbled back a step, her breath catching. "Do you mean to say if Beau dies?" Her voice scraped raw, thinner than she intended.

He reached for her, enclosing her hands in his. "I mean, whatever happens. You have to trust God. For now, I will allow you to go to Salt Lake City with your uncle. That does not mean you will go to the prison."

"What good am—"

"Clara, drawing attention to Beau while he is doing this

might endanger him. Your uncle will speak with the marshals. If that is not enough, you may stay here."

Shoulders sinking, she forced her chin high. "I am grateful, truly. At least then if something goes wrong, I will be near. I will take whatever I can, and I will be safe."

"Well..." Father shifted, grinning sideways at her. "That is a relief."

"I promised Beau I would." Clara stifled a sigh. She would rather don a disguise and storm straight into Salt Lake to rouse the churches about inmate cruelty and launch a crusade for proper socks and blankets. The thought was far more tempting than riding along with her uncle.

CHAPTER 30

*L*ater the same week, Beau marched toward the gatehouse with a work crew to dig a trench that would feed fresh water to the main building. Beau shifted closer to the wall where Marshal Royce stood on guard duty. The scrap of paper weighed heavily in his pocket, hope and dread twisting within him. He was far better at speaking and reading English than actually writing it, but hopefully, if he could pass the note to Royce, the marshal would understand he'd made contact.

All he had was this list of gang members, Emil's access to the keys, and the hidden room in the cellar—proof that he was indeed working to hold up his part of the bargain. It was the beginning of a case to take down the Sugar House Gang once and for all.

But part of Beau hated betraying Emil, who had saved his life in the war.

As he neared the gatehouse, the guard known as Royce met his gaze. Beau stumbled, knocking into the man. Slipping the paper into his pocket was easy enough.

Royce shouted and shoved him backward, pulling a baton in the process. Beau apologized and moved on through.

Up ahead, Richard craned his head back and narrowed his gaze on Beau. He'd noticed the contact, but did he know what it was? Richard was a jealous, insecure, and desperate type, eager to stab one in the back to further his own interests.

Despite the freezing labor, it was good to be out in the dry air and hear the water rushing nearby. Beau went to work with the crew, digging the trench that would be the new streambed. With his knowledge of water resource engineering, he would be of more use working on the system needed to divert the current stream, but he'd not give away more of himself to this place.

Even here, Emil made cold, grueling work tolerable. He spoke to the men as though commanding a troop, driving them forward with praise and working beside them. It was no wonder so many lost men followed him.

Of course, Emil had also bribed Beau as a rascally eight-year-old boy to pick the pocket of a fellow soldier he'd lost a bet with. Emil was selfish, always consumed with his desires first. Beau had to remember that.

Already the days at the prison dragged in such a way that it seemed like Virginia City, Clara, the deal he'd made with the federal marshals, and even his misdeeds against the Alexanders, had happened in a dream. Every night, he covered his ears to keep out the groans of inmates. He repeated the verses he could remember—his only comfort—and sensed a firm hand upon his shoulder, reminding him he was not ever alone. If not for the faith God gifted him, he might have run. His dreams were too dark, his demons too fierce, for him to stay and not lose his mind.

Three days later, the sun had hardly crested the horizon when whistles screeched from the yard. The work crews had just started from the mess hall to their assigned stations, white snow crunching beneath their feet. It glittered in the early-morning sunlight, as did the icicles hanging from the laundry roof. Guards stiffened and drew their clubs, assessing the inmates as though they would attack. More than a few wide-eyed men looked ready to bolt.

More alarms blared—a panicked note that reminded Beau of the day when the fire had raged through Virginia City.

"Go back! Back to the cellblock." A guard wielded his club, hitting prisoners to herd them like animals. They swarmed like panicked cattle, trampling anything that came into their path.

At last, while locked in his second-story cell, the cries of an inmate who had chosen to tangle with a guard filled Beau's ears until his stomach clenched. He stood on his cot to see out of the narrow window between the stone walls. Black smoke billowed from the laundry. Were his cellmates there? Some men worked at the huge water baths over fires. Was that why he was alone in his room?

He said a prayer for safety for all involved, but he hadn't even finished when the door behind him swung open. Richard, of all people, stood before him, a ring of keys in hand. His yellowish eyes, testifying to far too much drinking in his life, held the placidness of a mud puddle.

"He says you should come." There was no small amount of resentment in his tone.

Richard had tried to kill him once. Could he really trust him? A bigger question—was he willing to be left behind? *Lord, preserve me.*

Beau nodded, then followed Richard through the unlocked door, down the stairs to the inmates' cries for freedom. The screams echoed in his mind, dredging up memories of prisoners in France, yet he *could not* afford to lose his focus now. Rather than go to the cellar, as Beau assumed they would, Richard led him to another cell and slammed the door behind him. Emil poked his head out from under a bunk and waved them down. "Bring the keys. No sense in making this easy for them."

Soon they were underground, in a tight tunnel that scraped Beau's shoulders. Emil was nearly as tall as Beau but slimmer. Dirt in his eyes, even in his nose, Beau crawled and squirmed through the cold earth, taking breaths when he could. Every now and then, Richard smacked his feet, and Beau made sure to kick backward at him.

At last, when the dirt became too thick to breathe and Beau thought he'd been led to his death, he pushed through to open air. He rolled down an incline and stopped in cold snow. Water trickled and horses moved nearby. Men's voices murmured. Though he tried to open his eyes, the light was painfully blinding.

He was like a babe newly born, unable to use his God-given senses to detect the world, aside from the sting of cold and the flurry of mixed sounds. Beau sat on his haunches, a near-constant prayer for wisdom and endurance thrumming in his spirit.

When he could bear the light, he made out large, dark beasts of burden, with men as filthy as he mounted on them. The stark, naked trunks of trees rose up around him.

Emil shoved a pair of reins into his hands. "We aren't free yet. This is prison land." He swung into the saddle, and Beau did the same, his body wet with sweat and trembling from cold. Richard, Henry, a younger man, and Beau made them a party of five. When Emil headed into the trees, they all followed in a line.

They rode straight into the snow-crested mountains at a northwest angle. Crossing the country by horseback was wise, no matter how challenging, because everyone would be watching the railroad. The ride was indeed miserable—over hills, through forests, and snowdrifts—for at least five miles until they reached a small cabin.

Inside, they were welcomed by farmers who offered them food and dry clothes, then they were on their way again. The farmers gave no names. Warm, with his belly full, Beau couldn't imagine turning them over to the law, though the supplies and fresh horses had obviously been waiting for the gang.

Bundled in a thick sheepskin coat, new boots, and clothes that actually fit, Beau gained Emil's side once the sun started sinking low in the sky. "Where are we going?"

Emil glanced at him. "East."

A strange statement because they were heading north—in the direction of the nearest major railroad terminal. Was Emil guiding them to Wyoming, where they would board a train and ride the Pacific Railroad to the east, or would they board a train in Ogden? "For what purpose?"

"To camp. Now stop asking questions." He shifted his head back with meaning, though Beau didn't need to be told of the men behind them—hardened by life and crime, glaring daggers at him. "I vouched for you. I cover the cost of your passage, as I did when we left France. Do not make me regret it."

An eeriness crept across his skin. There was too much finality in what Emil said for them just to be out on a run, robbing a stage. He was supposed to collect information. Discover outside connections and the places for hiding loot. Rolling his shoulders in practiced calm, Beau faced a man neither friend nor adversary. "I did not ask to come."

"I cannot help it if you are a fool, but I could not leave you behind, especially after losing Louis and Lorraine."

Beau expected they'd make camp soon, but instead, they arrived at yet another farm nestled in a wild valley laden with snow and trees. Stumps dotted the land where timber had been cleared, except for several fields surrounding the house.

The young man with Emil approached cautiously. An elderly man with a long beard came out on the porch with a shotgun and spoke to them. It was impossible to hear their words across the distance. Emil offered their elderly host money, and the gang turned toward the barn—except for the young man.

He went to the house, and when an old woman appeared on the porch and let out a joyous cry, he embraced her. She must be a relation. What was the kid thinking by involving his family? He brought calamity to their door, to be sure, and now Beau would have to turn them in.

Later that night, high in the loft where the hay was warm and the sounds of the slumbering beasts below settled him with more calm than when he roomed with Sanderson, Beau tried to sleep. But worry kept him awake.

The murmur of men's voices from the floor below crept into the hayloft, intruding on his light slumber. Then Emil's clipped words became clear. "You do not need to trust him. I take responsibility for his being here—and his end if that is needed."

"It's not fair," Richard's unmistakable reply came. "We worked for years, and for what? So that filthy coward could tag along for free."

Emil's thick accent dripped with anger as he snapped, "Yes, you worked for years and saw nothing for it except the occasional romp in town and failed escapes. You would be nothing —probably dead—if I had not come in and organized your ragtag troop."

Beau did not move for fear the mere shifting upon the floor would alert the others to his wakefulness.

One of the others—likely Henry—chimed in. "Fox refused to join last year. If he changed his mind, he could stay with the rest of the gang. Actually do some work. Prove he's worth his salt."

"He signaled that guard, Royce, at the Sugar House, passed him something," Richard added.

Emil's next words hissed as though through teeth. "What did he pass him, Richard? Did you see it?"

Stubborn silence, then Richard's voice, firm and unwavering. "No. But I know a pass-off when I see it."

"I don't know. I was walking by Fox. Looked like he tripped to me." There was the youthful voice of the kid who should be far away, not with a gang of outlaws, putting his family at risk.

The slosh of liquid—probably spirits—signaled that the men were drinking, then Henry said in a hoarse voice, "Won't matter anymore. We did the guard up fine in the laundry fire. That marshal won't be telling anyone anything ever again—except'n St. Pete."

The men snickered, but Beau's blood ran cold. Marshal Royce must have come to a bad end. What a shame. Had it been by flame? *Lord, let him not have suffered terribly.*

"I do not care about the guard, nor about your jealous squabbling." Emil's sharp reply cut the air, followed by the rasp of leather and the unmistakable click of cold steel. The sounds alone stilled Beau's breath in his chest. "If any man wants to object to Monsieur Fox, my friend, accompanying me, say so now—and I will amend your troubles."

All grew quiet. Beau had seen Emil's swiftness with a gun before and imagined the scene below—Emil with a revolver at waist level, finger on the trigger, face as calm as a young woman's at her knitting. It was unnerving to see a man so at ease with killing—especially when he directed his weapon at you. Only now he defended, even protected Beau. How could Beau betray him?

"Your guest, your business, boss," came one of the men's quick answer. The others must have agreed, for a moment of silence passed before Emil spoke again.

"We part ways in Wyoming. If you give me cause to shoot you between now and then, I shall—leaving your carcass for the beasts to devour."

A horse snorted below, and another animal let out a huffing breath. But none of the humans replied.

"We leave at dawn. Now, get some rest." There was that calm strength in Emil's voice, then the general consensus of the group.

Beau tried to rest, but unease gnawed at him. Once the gang split, Beau would be powerless to turn them over. And the more time he spent with Emil, the less he wanted to betray him to the law. Yet the longer he remained with Richard and Henry, the more certain he felt that a bullet would find his back.

~

Clara leaned her cheek against the windowpane, seeking relief from the stifling warmth of the luxury railroad car Uncle Titus and Father had insisted on for the trip. The long journey from Virginia City lay behind yet many miles were still ahead. Would she find what she was searching for in Salt Lake?

"How do you say this word?" Lorraine lounged on a sofa near the opposite window, her nose buried in Jane Austen's *Sense and Sensibility*.

"Can you read me the line?" Clara propped her chin on a hand, and Lorraine read from her novel.

"'It is not time or opportunity that is to determine intimacy—it is disposition alone. Seven years would be insuff...'"

"Insufficient. That is when Marianne tells Elinor seven years is not enough time for some people to fall in love, while seven days is enough for others."

Lorraine smiled but pressed her lips together to hide her

expression. "I knew Jesse only a few weeks when I realized I wanted him in my life permanently. Aubrey says that for her and Nathan, it was just months." She focused on Clara. "How long for you and Beau?"

"I do not know for him. He only told me that if things were different, he would love me."

"Aha, I am sure he wishes to spare you pain."

"Likely. As for me, I cannot say when I realized I wanted to marry him. But when he was burned in the mining accident, I knew I was willing to take a risk."

Uncle Titus's big boots sounded on the metal steps outside. He pushed open the door with a grim face, gaze flicking away as if he carried bad news.

Clara held her breath and sat up straighter. "Uncle, what is wrong?"

He perched on the sofa beside her, taking her hand in his. "I told your papa I would telegraph him to let him know how the trip is going. He sent a wire ahead of us. I just picked it up." He waved a Western Union Telegraph, the paper glowing in the sunlight. "It seems there has been some activity at the prison."

Clara squeezed his hand, holding on as though that might save her weary heart.

"Beau turned over some information—names of the gang, including Emil Willot." He glanced at Lorraine, whose eyes widened. "He, along with Beau and others in the gang, escaped yesterday, heading into the hills on horseback."

The world pinched to a bright dot. Sound muffled, the clack of a passing railcar outside reduced to a slow heartbeat. Head terribly heavy and lungs squeezing, Clara wavered. "How did the men get away? And...horses? In the prison?"

Uncle Titus patted her hand. "No, honey, but that's not the point. Beau is gone, and the marshals are out looking for him."

Lorraine stood, her novel falling to the floor. "If they find him, will they listen to him or shoot?"

He grimaced. "We have no way of knowing."

Clara massaged her temples, squeezing her eyes shut at a vision of Beau falling at the hands of a marshal or Emil. What was Beau doing? Had prison been too much for him to take? Had he squandered his only lasting chance at freedom?

CHAPTER 31

Beau drew on the reins, and his horse slowed to a stop on the outskirts of Ogden. Emil halted just ahead, yet sat a long moment looking down into the valley—the town a scatter of low roofs with smoking chimneys, hemmed in by the white teeth of the Wasatch that held back the low, heavy winter clouds. He breathed in the cold. The steam of his exhale hung between him and the town. He turned back to the three waiting figures—Beau, Henry and Richard. The youngest inmate had been gone that morning when they rose to ride for Ogden.

"Richard, Henry, this is where we part ways," he said flatly.

The two men exchanged a brief, wary look. Richard moved his mount forward, enough to offer his hand, which Emil took with a firm, short shake. Neither man smiled.

Beau kept his mount steady, facing them all. The reins bit into his palm, and he forced his jaw to loosen. He had been blindly following because he had no better option, but now, with Ogden—the terminus for the Utah Central Railroad and the Utah and Northern Railways— before him, he had to act.

He could either reach out to the law empty handed or take on three armed men before they scattered.

"Go east, then circle around and come into town from that direction so we aren't seen together." Emil gestured to the right of Ogden. "You would be wise to separate, get rid of those horses, and leave town as quickly as possible."

"Godspeed, Willot." Henry gave Emil a lazy salute, then turned his horse eastward.

Neither of the men acknowledged Beau before riding into the trees. Likely, they would circle around and head for the railroad. Emil had told Beau the day before that he was also heading east, so why did he sit on his horse as if waiting?

A biting wind carved through the valley, sharp and relentless, as if warning him of the dangers ahead. Beau tipped his hat down to block the force. "What now, Emil?"

"One question keeps coming back to me." The Frenchman sighed, looking out over the valley and back at Beau. "Can I trust you?"

"The fact that you ask me answers the question."

"I know my answer. I want yours."

For what purpose? To gauge his reaction, to read his features, or for the opportunity to twist his words? It was a simple question, though.

"Yes, you can trust me." Though he'd regret it because Beau was determined to redeem himself once and for all. It didn't matter that Emil had once been his friend and given him a purpose after the war. They'd both been wrong, and atonement was near, whether by Beau's hand or God's.

"Swear to me, on Amalie's and Martin's memory, you mean me no harm." Emil pressed, though Beau glowered.

"I would not disrespect my family by taking an oath, and what good would it do if I did? You believe as you will." He looked away sharply, not liking how his insides churned.

"It is your faith that has changed." It was an accusation,

indeed, for Emil looked darker than ever. "You have given in to holy sentiments that will do you no good when it's time to survive. God will not save you from the hand of a man."

"Faith does not make a man weak."

"It does. How many clergy died in violent ways during the Bloody Week in Paris? For what? The praise of men?" Emil studied Beau, his brown leather hat wavering when a strong wind blew. "You were always ready to do whatever was necessary to survive, to win. You have your faith, but you've lost who you are. What else have you given up since I last saw you?"

Shaking his head, Beau looked toward the city. Unfortunately, Emil was behaving in true Willot fashion—a crazed light in his eyes, suspicion likely driving him mad. What a shame Beau couldn't simply tell Emil that trusting God, no matter the cost, was worth it in the end. If he died now, he'd be reunited with Martin and Amalie. But then, he'd leave Clara behind—breaking her fragile heart. He'd also never know what it was like to be her husband, father of her children. He'd never know what it was like to live a good life without shame.

Turning to Emil with a slight shrug, Beau said, "My faith has grown since last we knew each other, but look how often I have been on the run. It's hard not to pray when there's constantly someone on your back."

Emil shifted his head back, his gaze still probing.

Beau raised his hands as though surrendering. "If you do not trust me, let us part ways here. I do not wish to battle you, and I am grateful for the chance at freedom."

Rather than respond, Emil turned his horse and headed west.

Breathing in the cold air for a moment, Beau waited—just in case he turned around—but he didn't. And Beau let him go even though he knew he should go after him. Fight him. Arrest him and take him to the local law enforcement.

The land was so still and quiet, it was hard to believe that below the town, life bustled on. A train chugged across the trestle over Weber River, heading for the depot. If Richard and Henry entered Ogden, especially if they boarded a train, Beau would likely never see them again, and turning over the gang was part of his contract. All he could do was head east and hope to capture them.

He urged his mount forward, deeper into the trees.

~

The forest outside Ogden was a ghostly stretch of sparse pines, barely enough cover for anyone hiding. Beau let his mount pick its way through the trees, a cold wind shifting through the branches to chill his neck. Richard and Henry couldn't have gone far. He'd trailed them for a few minutes now, and it wouldn't take long to reach town. A flicker of movement up ahead made his pulse quicken.

Richard stood near a tree, his horse and Henry's nearby. A stream trickled through the snowbanks, though Henry was not there.

Beau breathed deeply and reined in his horse.

Richard walked away from the tree, several yards ahead of Beau. He was speaking to someone as he knelt by the stream to fill a canteen, a rifle clutched to his chest.

Beau dismounted with swift silence. The snow crunched ever so slightly beneath his boots. Hopefully, it would also muffle any stick he might tread on and break. He crept closer, with still no sign of Henry. Beau picked up a tree limb thick enough to serve as a club. Gunshots would alert anyone within hearing range, including Emil.

Richard sat on a log, coughing and still talking. Where was Henry? There was nowhere for him to hide. Beau glanced around the woods and met the blue gaze of the long-haired man stalking him.

Caught in the moment, neither of them moved.

Then Henry opened his mouth. "He's here!"

Richard swung around and raised his rifle.

Beau ducked instinctively. He was closer to Henry than Richard, but if the fool fired, he might bring anyone within hearing distance crashing down on all of them. This close to town, the law would investigate.

"Don't shoot!" Henry shouted to his friend as he ran straight at Beau, his own rifle in both hands. Bulging eyes, wild and unhinged, and pale gums above bared teeth reflected malnourishment.

As Henry's footsteps pounded past the trees, Beau hurled his club at Richard, striking him midstride and causing him to stumble. He went down with a shout. Charging straight at Henry, Beau grasped the rifle and forced his head into his opponent's. Both of them fell into the snow, struggling for control of the weapon. Henry's grip slipped, and Beau rolled to his feet, jamming the weapon into Henry's head and knocking him unconscious.

Richard stood with his rifle aimed at Beau, determination in his gaze as he stared down the barrel. Beau knelt, swept his knife from his boot, and flung it across the space between them. It sliced through the leather collar of Richard's coat, finding a deadly mark.

Sounds magnified around Beau—the trickle of the stream, the pounding of his heart, the whisper of wind in the trees, Richard's labored breathing, and Henry's, now little more than a snore.

Beau had always hated killing and avoided it whenever he could. Many of his dreams were riddled with memories of men —his foes and friends—breathing their last. It was such a terrible, final thing. Unnatural and ungodly. *Should I have let him shoot me, Lord?*

If he had, Emil would get away. The marshals might never

take down the Sugar House Gang. He would die with everyone, including Clara, believing he was a criminal to the end. Beau raised his head, half expecting the old soldier to be nearby. He was alone, except for Henry. Richard was facing his maker.

Beau stood and collected a length of rope from one of the men's saddlebags. Inside were banknotes—likely stolen—and a newspaper ad for a dance hall in Reno. That was how the men planned to spend their freedom? Squander it on wine and women? He shook his head at such foolishness and tied Henry's wrists and then his feet.

Even from the corner of his eye, he could see the red spot underneath Richard. He tried not to notice, yet his mouth began to water and his head to spin. Beau paused, breathing deeply and trying not to be sick. "Lord, forgive me?"

He didn't get an answer, so he finished securing and gagging Henry. Leaving the horses tied near their masters, Beau mounted his own horse on shaky legs and headed for town.

He had to send a message to Marshal Morris in Salt Lake giving his whereabouts, and contact the local sheriff, offering the locations of two escaped convicts. Then he'd hunt down Emil and secure his future with Clara. Since Emil had given him no directions on how to find him, Beau would start his search at the Union Pacific Railroad Depot.

CHAPTER 32

The train rumbled across the Weber River Trestle, heading straight for the humble two-story wooden Union Pacific Depot. Uncle Titus stood near the rear door, as he had for some time now, contemplating only God knew what. Likely, Lorraine's meeting with the judge in Salt Lake. He thought Beau should pay for his crimes. Clara sighed and focused on the mountains, so majestic and unyielding on the outskirts of the city.

A number of hotels stood near the tracks, offering rest for weary travelers. The city filled this part of the valley, though the depot was not at its center but on the outskirts. Dark tones of gray and black set off the snow, blending with the low-hanging clouds. The steam whistle sounded, and the train began to slow.

Lorraine glanced at her from across the car, her smile soft. "Mr. Alexander will check the telegraph office once we've stopped. Perhaps there will be news."

Clara tried to smile, yet all she managed was a nod.

Once the train screeched to a halt, Clara gathered her skirts and stood. "I would like to walk around the station a bit while you run to the telegraph office."

Her uncle tilted his head, his eyebrows low as he checked his pocket watch. "We haven't much time."

Lorraine rose, reaching for her scarf, which hung by the door. "I will walk with Clara. We will not leave the platform, Mr. Alexander—*s'il vous plaît*?"

Uncle Titus's expression relaxed, and he took Lorraine's hand, kissing it. "You needn't be so formal, Mademoiselle Lorraine. You will soon be my son's wife and my daughter. I only ask that you ladies remain close to the train, and if anyone bothers you, that you board immediately."

"Oui, we will do as you wish," Lorraine replied, curtsying.

"Yes, Uncle." Clara smiled as he took her hand in a gentle squeeze, then kissed it and stepped off the train.

"He is a kind man." Lorraine went to the coat rack by the door and lifted her cape and hat.

"He is. Though the Alexander men can be fierce." Clara wrapped her red scarf around her neck. She paused, breathing in the scent—even though it no longer smelled like Beau after several washes and her wearing of it.

"You act like a woman in love, Clara." Lorraine paused by the door, suddenly gripping her arm. "Beau is wild at heart. He always has been. He cannot help that."

Not liking Lorraine's tone of warning, Clara let go of her hand. "Why are you telling me this?"

Lorraine pressed her lips together. "For years, since we came to America, Beau would leave Emil and come to the Sells Brothers Circus where I worked. He tried to live honestly, then he'd disappear—back to drink and the criminal life. I just don't want to see your heart broken."

"Already, it's cracking." Clara laughed too quickly, the sound sharp and fragile.

"Emil always had a strong influence over Beau. He's the only one from our childhood still around—and he once was a good, kind man. But he's desperate. If Beau is with him, he's unlikely to return to you."

Chest aching as though Lorraine had dropped an anvil on it, Clara turned toward the door. "Beau told me about this struggle. I cannot betray him by doubting him."

Lorraine set a palm over her heart and looked Clara straight in the eye. "I've seen this before. Beau's weak. No anchor in life, and he's never had one. It's not betrayal to heed wise counsel—to guard your heart."

Still, Clara shook her head, her voice growing firmer. "You don't understand. I'm not foolish. Beau has proven himself countless times. Maybe the change you prayed for is already beginning."

Lorraine opened her mouth as though to argue, then shook her head, her lips pulling into what might pass for a smile, and motioned Clara outside. The wind whipped into her face. Clara slipped her scarf over her nose for protection. Passengers mulled around on the platform—men in suits and very few ladies in long dresses. The land around them was bare and desolate. Snow crested a boardwalk leading back into town, about a quarter mile away.

A man on a buff horse rode down the wooden walk, wearing a thick buckskin coat with sheep wool, like those mountain men wore. Beneath his hat, gray and blond strands hung around his ears, in need of trimming. He looked her way, his gaze narrowing beyond her before he dismounted and went to a hitching post.

Lorraine stepped onto the platform, slipping her arm through Clara's. "Goodness, it is cold. I'm starting to wish I had remained aboard." She blinked thick black eyelashes against a breeze.

Not wanting to draw attention, Clara didn't dare look back at the man, though she no longer sensed him out of the corner of her eye. "The man with the buff horse—he's in his forties, handsome. Do you know him?"

"There are many men here." Lorraine gestured around them. "He's by..." She looked back. The horse and rider were gone. Lorraine eased onto her tiptoes. "I see no one familiar. Why? Do you think you saw Beau? Here?"

"No. For a moment, a man seemed to be looking at you." Perhaps he'd looked beyond both of them.

They walked arm in arm, weaving past workers unloading cargo. A second train rolled past, coming from the east. The station was very busy, even though the town itself was not. They strolled the length of the platform, then turned toward their car when the wind, blustering down from the mountain, sent a chill through Clara.

"Care to duck into the ladies' waiting room to warm up?"

Lorraine, still squinting against the cold, nodded.

They hurried toward the depot, passing one of the store buildings, when a man reached out and seized Lorraine's arm. He pulled her into the narrow space, forcing Clara in as well.

Lorraine shouted and slapped at him, but he blocked her and seized both her arms. "*Reste calme,* ma chère." He shook her gently, then grasped Clara's wrist. "Do not cry out." His sharp gaze—cold as ice—stilled her.

He was the man on the buff horse, the one who had looked at Lorraine. He pushed them farther between the buildings. Here, the dimness felt too chilly. With the light shining behind him, he spoke again in French to Lorraine. "Did Beau tell you to meet him? Have you connected with him?" He cast a sideways glance before turning back, sounding upset. "I thought you were marrying the Alexander whelp."

"I..." All of Lorraine's boldness seemed to fade. "I am simply traveling with my friend. Why would you ask me about Beau? He is in prison."

Shoulders rising and falling, he studied Lorraine.

Clara gripped her arm, squeezing. Hopefully, she would remain strong. This man must be Emil Willot. Why else would he be asking about Beau? She glanced backward and forward, searching for escape. The space between the buildings led to the back of the depot, where the ground looked wet and muddy. Trees crowded close, but not enough to hide if they ran that way. Uncle Titus had just left, so he wouldn't miss them for some time. It wasn't likely anyone in the crowd had seen them. There were too many people. They'd have to find a way out of this mess.

"Miss Durand, do you know this man?" Clara asked in English, trying to keep her tone steady so Emil wouldn't suspect their true connection.

"I... Yes. An old family friend." She patted his arm. Emil hadn't hurt her, and newspaper articles claimed he was connected to Lorraine's family in France.

"Wouldn't a café be a better place to reunite? This place is dirty and smells bad." She wrinkled her nose and waved her hand in front of her face.

Emil narrowed his eyes at her. He was nearly as tall as Beau, imposing in his manner—the way he blocked their escape and spoke with finality. He watched Lorraine with uncertainty, his brow softening for a moment when he switched to French. "You look well."

"You do not." Her voice was quiet, sad. "Is there some other time—"

"Why are you here?"

"This is Junction City." Lorraine used the local term for Ogden, gesturing back toward the platform, her movements relaxed. "I told you I am traveling through. What are *you* doing here?"

He sighed, looking left, then right before drawing a gun.

Lorraine startled backward into Clara, nearly knocking her over. "What are you doing?"

"I cannot afford for you to go to the authorities, but I promise, I will not hurt you." He pushed her, driving both her and Clara toward the other side of the building. "And tell your friend not to scream, or I *will* hurt *her*."

Lorraine interpreted, though Clara knew enough to keep her lips closed. Was Emil telling the truth, or was he just moving them to a place where no one could see what he was doing to them? And where was Beau? He was supposed to be with Emil.

Clara reached the trees at the opposite end of the building just in time to see Beau press himself to the side of the wall. He was there, waiting to rescue them. But Emil had a gun. He would shoot Beau. His dark eyes met hers, and Beau reached for her, ready to pull her to safety, no doubt, but where would that leave Lorraine and Emil?

Clara stepped to the side and hooked Lorraine's ankle. She also tried to catch her, but they both landed on the soft ground. Beau seized Emil's gun hand and pulled him into the open. A shot exploded in the treetops, ringing in Clara's ears. Wings beat as birds perched in the branches flew away.

Emil's eyes bulged, his lips peeling back from his dingy teeth as he named Beau *"un renégat."*

Beau blocked the first punch. "And you are *déchu*. Do not blame me for your sins."

The next few blows came so quickly that neither man spoke. There was only the rush of breath from Emil's chest as Beau punched him in the gut, then Beau's shout when he jabbed his boot into Emil's chest, slamming him back into the building. Lorraine raised the gun, pointing it at Emil, though her hand trembled. Beau snatched it away and levered the hammer back.

"You will not escape today. I am sorry. But you have to atone. We all do." His shoulders rose and fell.

Emil glared up from the ground, blood dripping from his nose, his face red and his eyes shining with hatred. "I trusted you. When other men would've stuck you in your sleep, I saved you! Just like when you were a whelp hanging from your mother's skirts. Who brought you food? Who brought your maman's medicines?"

Lorraine covered her mouth against a sob, her eyes filled with tears. "That does not turn your wrongs into rights. You broke the law."

Emil's face contorted, then he lunged at Beau. The gun went off, deafening in the still air, and Emil sagged against Beau's body.

"Non! Emil?" Beau held him upright, peering into his face as the man blinked and looked around. "Lorraine? Go for help!"

She raced through the two buildings, her footfalls fading. Men's shouts echoed from the front of the depot. The pounding of footsteps on the platform signaled that help would soon arrive. Beau's face was white, the front of his coat stained red.

"Non, non. Emil. Open your eyes." He shook Emil, then lowered him to the muddy earth, pressing his hand to the chest wound.

Clara tugged a handkerchief from her sleeve, ripping the long, ruffled cuff in the process. The fabric would have to do. She pulled it off, seams hissing in protest. "Open his coat, Beau." She knelt beside him, working at the top buttons while Beau focused on the bottom ones. Once the thick garment was loosened, Clara folded the sleeve and pressed it into the wound. Emil groaned, breathing through his teeth and trembling.

"There, Emil. Stay calm. Breathe," she said softly. She forced the cloth into the wound, earning more protests, then pressed the thick coat over the makeshift dressing, applying enough pressure to slow the bleeding without blocking his breath.

"Am I going to die?" Emil kicked his feet, his breath coming rapidly in panicked bursts.

"No. No, your breathing is clear. There is no blood in your lungs," she said, locking eyes with him. "My mother had tuberculosis, so I know what bad lungs sound like. Yours are good."

Beau shifted back slightly, and Clara pressed more firmly against him. Hopefully, the contact would bring some comfort, but for now, she focused on Emil. "Breathe with me. In and out."

Crowds gathered around them, inquiring what had happened. Clara dared not break contact with Emil, which left Beau to do the talking.

"This man accosted the ladies. I intervened." His voice was dazed. He shook his head, then looked up at one of the men. "He needs a doctor. If we can move him somewhere warm, then send the doctor there...and...get the sheriff."

Two men took off as though racing to see who would reach the finish line first. Beau stayed at Clara's side as she calmed Emil and tried to keep him awake, but he drifted off before the doctor arrived.

CHAPTER 33

Clara paced the private car at the depot in Ogden, the sounds of the people outside muted by the walls. She paused, the concave ceiling preventing her from seeing the sky above. It had been clear that morning—brilliantly blue and bright—so much so that Lorraine had tipped her head back and sighed contentedly. Even now, she sat by a window with her nose in a book, as though she had no doubt Beau would go free. Clara tried to mirror such faith, but she'd hardly slept all night.

Uncle Titus had updated them the evening before. Emil was alive, being treated in the Ogden Hospital with a flesh wound—a true miracle. He'd stay there until he was healed, then be shipped back to prison. Beau was at the local jail waiting to hear from the marshals. She wanted to be logical and acknowledge that they had to be certain he was uncompromised, but anger burned at the idea of him in such a dank place after his heroism.

She wanted him free, beside her always. Might God look down from heaven and simply answer her prayers of the last month? Footsteps sounded on the stairs outside, then Uncle

Titus pushed through the door, ducking to avoid the doorframe as the man behind him did the same.

Beau! He met her gaze with deep, dark eyes, the intensity there like a flint spark. Fearing the fire of emotions kindling to life at the sight of him, Clara managed a shaky step.

"Beau!" Lorraine ran to him, grasping both of his hands, then kissing his cheek. She spoke in French, firing questions at him in rapid succession, though Beau kept glancing at Clara.

She wrung her hands, frozen in place. If she ran to him, simply grasping his hands would not be enough. She might wrap her arms around him and never let go. So she stood there while another woman greeted the man she loved.

"Goodness, Lorraine, let's not keep the marshal out in the cold." Uncle Titus ushered Lorraine aside so Marshal Morris could enter after Beau.

Chains bound Beau's wrists. Why was he bound when he'd turned the gang over to the law? Before Clara could ask, the marshal was removing the restraints.

"Here you go, sonny." He cranked the key in the first cuff, the metal piece falling off. Beau stood very still. The second cuff followed, and he stared at his wrists, then, massaging them, turned to Clara.

The others spoke general greetings and comments about the expected arrival time in Salt Lake, but their words seemed to blend together as Beau took a step forward.

"Won't you sit down?" she motioned toward the sofa she'd spent much of the trip on.

He was so tall. She'd forgotten until seeing him in the train car, passing the windows. He approached her with a presence that washed over her like a warm wave, and when he stopped, she swayed toward him.

He took her hand, the rough pads of his fingers scraping her skin. "Ladies first."

She smiled, holding her breath, but before Clara could sit,

Lorraine settled herself there instead. "Beau, my goodness, I am so glad you are well. The marshal says you did it. That you will go free."

Beau blinked as though processing his friend's words and actions. He squeezed Clara's hand, though his attention momentarily shifted to her uncle, at which point he released her.

Cheeks hot, Clara pressed her hand to them. How could Lorraine be so thoughtless, just plunking herself down beside Beau when he'd just offered the space to Clara? Clearing her throat, she raised her chin. "He will go free, will he not, Marshal Morris?"

The elderly lawman smoothed his mustache, pressing it down with his thumb and forefinger. "Mr. Vulpe has already shared enough information regarding the escapees and remaining Sugar House Gang to believe he will gain that pardon."

He and Uncle Titus remained standing. They were probably waiting for her to sit, but Lorraine was in her spot. The train moved forward, causing Clara to sway. She settled herself in a fine wingback chair nearby, the men following suit. Heart aching to be near Beau, Clara fought to keep her face calm. Lorraine was his good friend, and she was rightly excited about the inevitable pardon. He deserved that loyalty. It was a gift.

Lorraine looked between Clara and Beau, her eyes growing wide as though realizing what she'd done. Clara offered her a quick smile and listened to the marshal.

"Beau gave us the names of all the men in the gang, and we have them in custody now—except, of course, for the one who went to see the undertaker."

"Are you certain that will be enough?" Lorraine worried a handkerchief that looked nearly shredded.

"Well, I think it should be. Beau also sent a telegraph before his run-in with Emil at the station, alerting the sheriff in Ogden about the whereabouts of a gang member who authorities apprehended at a farm outside Salt Lake." Morris fished in his pocket for his pipe, eyeballed it, then put it back.

Clara clasped her hands tightly, resisting the urge to surge to her feet and pace. How could the marshal behave in such a relaxed manner? This was Beau's life on the line.

He continued, as calm as one might be at a Sunday picnic. "Once we verify the tunnel and the secret room at the penitentiary is indeed there, he will have upheld his part of the bargain."

"So then..." Her voice was too soft. A dizzy spell swept over her, causing the rail car to sway even more. Clara cleared her throat and tried again. "Beau—he'll go free?"

"I don't see why not. There's no telling how many lives he saved—taking down Richard, Henry, and Emil. The gang was bigger than those who escaped, so it's likely Emil left the group active—ready to use the same tactics to carry out robberies. I sent a list of their names last night when this young man gave his statement..."

The marshal's tone continued in a way that seemed to praise Beau, but Clara could only hear the news—Beau would go free. He'd no longer have to run, no longer have to hide. He could live a good, safe life. Eyes stinging, she blinked. He could go to church without fearing the law coming to arrest him. He could go to church with her.

A tear spilled down her cheek. She swiped at it, but more followed. Good gracious, she'd soon have a puddle on the floor if she didn't control herself. "Excuse me."

She stood, walking with trembling knees to the end of the rail car, where a large window displayed the mountains slanting into the valley below. Pressing a hand to her forehead, she closed her eyes and took a breath—yet she held it when she opened them to discover that Beau approached her. With him came the tide of emotion she'd worked so hard to keep at bay for months. She wanted to laugh and cry at the same time. Wishing she could turn into him, rest her head against his collarbone, and breathe in the moment, Clara remained still.

Beau touched her shoulder, then brought her opposite hand up to his lips. "This has been quite an adventure." He was so calm, a spark of playfulness in his eyes.

How could he recall their banter from November, when she'd pretended to be the president's daughter? Maybe, given everything that had happened, this teasing approach was easier.

"You..." She swallowed, scrambling mentally. "You never told me why you went on your adventure. What you were looking for."

His gaze drifted to her eyes, and his head tipped closer, as though he, too, was drawn by the unspoken pull between them. "You know, your eyes are like the cool, peaceful twilight over the Washoe Valley." He hesitated, then added softly, "As for what I was looking for—I was looking to survive. I didn't know that among the riches in the mountain, I'd find the truest treasure in a pair of overalls."

She smiled then, and even chuckled softly. "Imagine when we tell our grandchildren."

He raised an eyebrow.

Clara sucked in a breath. My goodness, had she overstepped?

"I..." His voice rasped, deep and full of emotion. "I think they would not believe that of one so beautiful and proper." He set his hand on her waist.

Clara glanced at her uncle, who, surprisingly, was not glaring in their direction.

Beau drew her closer. "Thank you for helping Emil. When I shot him..." He closed his eyes for a moment.

"You rescued me. Lorraine too. I don't know what Emil was

going to do, but it wasn't good. You would have been justified—"

"I know, but Emil was my friend. You were so brave and calm. There when I needed you."

Truly? She had merely held a bandage in place and told the man to breathe, as she'd done for her mother countless times.

"Clara, once all this is over, I'd like to speak to your father and ask for your hand—properly."

Her smile spilled out, a warm rush in her center threatening to burst her laughter. She placed her hand on his chest, noting his intake of breath. "I hoped you would. I think you will find him receptive."

"I can go back to work for MacKay. There's still a lot left to do in the mine, especially concerning the water pumps. We need to make it safer for the men."

"Does this mean you're going to use your training?"

He swallowed, the knob in his throat moving up and down beneath smooth, olive-toned skin. "I'm going to try."

"That's perfect."

He nodded, his thumb rubbing across her shoulder. "What about your reporting?"

"Mr. Doten has kept me on, but he has strict rules. I can't go into saloons, mines, anywhere unsafe. Some people want to talk to me and others don't, so I'm learning that being a female reporter makes some things easier and some harder. Oh..." She smiled wide, and Beau raised his eyebrows expectantly. "*The Sunday Magazine* wants me to contribute to a regular column."

He cocked his head. "Is that something you want to do?"

"Yes. I used to love writing Bible studies. I, uh, wanted to write them for young ladies before I went to finishing school. It might be a good option if, one day, I need to be at home more and cannot go out reporting."

Beau became very still. "Such as when you're a mother," he

said softly, cupping her jaw with his rough thumb caressing her cheek.

Fighting a smile, Clara shrugged one shoulder. "Reporters work long hours, and my husband might not want me to be away at night."

His eyes lit up, and Clara's cheeks burned. Good heavens, she hadn't meant to insinuate anything.

"I—I mean, it might not be safe," she managed to add, but Beau was drawing closer, stealing her breath and her clear thoughts, which didn't matter when he touched his lips to hers for a brief yet heavenly kiss.

"I missed you, Beau." She leaned her head against his chest, watching the snowy day fly by outside.

"I plan to remedy that. I will not be away from you for a long time—ever, if I can help it." He kissed her brow, and together, they watched the Utah landscape slide past, snow and ice shimmering in the sunlight. A herd of elk picked their way across the ground, munching at patches of grass. Several lifted their heads, the antlers of the males gleaming in the morning sun. Clara sighed. "It looks like spring is nearly here."

Beau tightened his arm around her. "I'm certainly ready for the new season."

Did you enjoy this book? We hope so!
Would you take a quick minute to leave a review where you purchased the book?
It doesn't have to be long. Just a sentence or two telling what you liked about the story!

Love Christian Historical Romance?
Looking for your next favorite book?
Become a Wild Heart Books insider and receive a FREE ebook and get exclusive updates on new releases before anyone else.
Sign up for our newsletter now.
https://wildheartbooks.org/newsletter

ABOUT THE AUTHOR

KyLee Woodley is a cheery romantic who loves to write about bygone days and heartwarming romance with a pinch of adventure. She teaches preschool at a lab school in Texas, where she lives with her husband of nineteen years and their three children. On weekends, KyLee cohosts and produces the **Historical Bookworm Show**—a steadily growing author interview podcast for history lovers and readers of historical fiction.

    Keep up to date with KyLee's news on book releases, signings, and other events at https://kyleewoodley.com

ACKNOWLEDGMENTS

Firstly, and always, I thank God for guiding my life and gifting me with the call to write. For a woman who was practically illiterate at the age of fifteen, this is a testament to His miracle-working greatness. Secondly, thank you to my children and husband who have believed in me and supported me over the years. I do not deserve such confident cheerleaders.

Many writers from American Christian Fiction Writers have supported me and my work for years, but for this book, a special thanks to Christie Kern, Karissa Riffel Fisher, Stephanie Goddard, and Darcy Fornier for your priceless critiques.

To the team at Wild Heart Books, thank you for your dedication to excellence, especially my editor, Denise Farnsworth. Your kind guidance and exceptional editorial skills helped me get through this one.

AUTHOR NOTE

Dear Reader,

I hope you enjoyed Beau and Clara's love story. I knew when I wrote about Beau in book one that he was the kind of bad guy who needed redemption. Then you saw him in book two, trying to redeem himself from the shadows. In book three, he meets Clara, who is broken because of her fractured family—something foreshadowed in my short story, *The Debutante's Revenge*, which features a scorned French woman and the two Alexander brothers. (If you want to read it, just sign up for my newsletter!) I am so glad you stuck around for Beau and Clara's happily-ever-after and the conclusion of The Outlaw Hearts Series.

Finally, I would be ever so grateful if you would post a review of *The Convict's Courtship*.

Praying for blessings and inspiration in your reading-life. ~ KyLee

HISTORICAL NOTE

Virginia City, Nevada, is a storied boomtown nestled on Mount Davidson that was first settled after a silver strike started what was later called the Comstock Lode. After the discovery of rich silver deposits in 1859 by Henry Comstock and his partners, prospectors flooded the area, transforming it from a remote mining camp into one of the most productive silver districts in American history. The wealth generated by the Comstock Lode fueled rapid growth, making Virginia City a bustling center of commerce, politics, and culture during the post-Civil War era. The discovery led to a surge of immigration from across the United States and around the world, with miners, entrepreneurs, and prospectors flocking to the region, eager to capitalize on the lucrative finds. The boom brought not only wealth but also a reputation for lawlessness and rugged individualism, shaping Virginia City into a legendary frontier town that thrived amid its challenges and opportunities.

The appearance of Paiute Native People in Virginia City on Christmas morning is based on a firsthand account by Dan De Quille, a journalist for the *Territorial Enterprise* in the 1870s. Unfortunately, these displaced individuals were treated as

HISTORICAL NOTE

second-class citizens, often making their homes outside the city for many years. Despite their longstanding presence and rich cultural heritage, they faced discrimination and marginalization from the growing mining community. Some worked as laborers, servants, and in other positions of service.

After the devastating fire of 1875, the town quickly rebuilt, featuring well-known establishments such as the Delta Saloon, Bucket of Blood, Washoe Club, Crystal Bar, and the *Territorial Enterprise*; and you can visit all of these places today. Please note—I took creative license with the timeline of these places opening after the fire.

The city's hospital, originally St. Mary Louise, built on land donated by Mary Louise Mackay, now stands as St. Mary's Art Center, symbolizing resilience and history. Nearby Gold Hill offers scenic views, with remnants of the past such as the old fire bell, train depot, and historically significant structures that capture the lively days of the silver rush.

The Consolidated Virginia & California Mine, with its deep shaft and advanced equipment, showcases the technological scale of the mining operations and was the site of Beau's severe accident. The rough and lively Bucket of Blood Saloon and the elegant Washoe Club highlight the contrasting social environments, from crime and violence to elite socializing, forming the vibrant backdrop to Virginia City's complex history.

As for the amazing cast of people in *The Convict's Courtship*, I am pleased to tell you that Virginia City's past was shaped by influential figures whose lives and actions left lasting impacts. Frank McNair served as fire chief, overseeing the vital station that responded to the ongoing hazards and systemic debates about public safety following the Great Fire of 1875. Prominent citizens like Mackay were part of the Millionaires' Club that met in the Washoe Club. A lesser-known character, Mrs. Matthews, surprised me with her appearance. I read her book *Ten Years in Nevada* (1869–1879), which gave me a perspective

HISTORICAL NOTE

from a working-class woman of that day. When Clara left home, it just made sense that she would stay at Mrs. Matthews's, even though I really wanted her to stay at the Tahoe House Hotel. These historical people embody the diverse social fabric and personal stories that contributed to Virginia City's lively history during Nevada's gold and silver rush era.

One last thing: the scene where Beau was scalded in the Consolidated Virginia Mine was based on an article Mary Matthews shared in her book. Historically, the accident took place in the Julia Mine at the 2,000 level when a miner using a Burleigh drill broke an underground hot spring. His releasing the compressed air to keep the steam from killing him and burning his upper body was completely accurate, as was the account that men with gumboots and coats rescued the man trapped by the stream. The article was called "TAPPING HOT WATER. A Singular Occurrence in Julia Mine—Narrow Escape of a Miner." You may read it in *Ten Years in Nevada* (1869~1879) by Mrs. Mary Matilda Matthews (p. 276).

For new releases and special promotions, subscribe to KyLee Woodley's mailing list: https://KyLeeWoodley.com

Want more?

If you love historical romance, check out the other Wild Heart books!

Lassoed by the Lawman by Renae Brumbaugh Green

Juliana Duke's dreams don't include ranching.

But as the only child of Oscar and Maria Duke and heiress of the vast Duke Ranch, her job is to marry a rancher and produce a male heir. When Lt. Cody Steves rides onto the scene, her resolve to place duty over daydreams is shaken. Now that her heart's been lassoed by the handsome lawman, will she be able to love another?

Cody Steves wants marriage and family, but he loves being a Texas Ranger. At any time, he could ride into a job and not come out alive. How could any decent man marry, knowing he could leave a widow and orphans behind? But the beautiful Juliana Duke captures him in a way no other has.

When he learns of a secret plot to take over the Duke Ranch, Cody must risk everything to save Juliana. Little does he know, the outcome will be nothing like he's planned.

Call in the Canyons by Kathleen Denly

The bandits who murdered her father are back, but can she trust the sheriff to protect her home and her heart?

Sheriff Heath Monroe believed the wrong man, and although California's most notorious gang leader was eventually brought to justice, Heath's error shattered the confidence of the people he serves. With reelection looming, Heath is desperate to prove his worth. So when he learns of a new threat to the citizens of California, he doesn't hesitate to take action, even though he knows the job will endanger the lives of those he cares about—something he swore he'd never do again. Haunted by the ghosts of past mistakes and second-guessing every decision, Heath sets out to put an end to California's most dangerous bandit gang, once and for all.

Virginia Baker works hard to keep her desert cattle ranch going, and even harder to keep all men off her land. When the bandits who murdered her father return to her valley, memories of a friendship cut tragically short drive her to work with the all-male posse pursuing the gang in search of justice. Despite her determination to remain guarded, Heath Monroe's steadfast integrity and unexpected humility begin to crack her defenses. But can she rely on the widower leading them, or will his secrets confirm her belief that no man is to be trusted?

Angel from the East

His path to redemption lies in the hands of the citified newcomer who believes the worst of him.

Caleb Morgan has had everything stolen from him—his strength, the job he loved, even his good name. He's determined to even the score with the man responsible, until he meets the captivating new owner of the Double E Ranch.

Though he's drawn to her compassion, he fears she may never see beyond his supposed wrongdoings, unless he can prove his innocence and reclaim his honor.

Eliza Roberts is a teacher, not a rancher. But if she has any hope of selling the ranch she inherited from her grandfather and continuing on to her new life in California, she needs to restore it to some semblance of order. If only the man her grandfather advised her to trust wasn't refusing to help her.

When an offer of courtship arises from the current foreman, Eliza sees the practicality in the offer. So why does her heart keep wandering back to Caleb? And why can't she shake the feeling that something's not right at the Double E Ranch? Will she have the courage to follow the clues behind the strange mishaps at the Double E—and possibly embrace a different life than she imagined?

www.ingramcontent.com/pod-product-compliance
Lightning Source LLC
LaVergne TN
LVHW011928070526
838202LV00054B/4531